The Sakhalin Collection

Robert W. Smith

New Leaf ◗ Illinois

All rights reserved. No part of this book may be reproduced or transmitted in any form whatsoever without expressed written permission from the publisher. For more information contact: WigWam Publishing Co., P.O. Box 6992, Villa Park, IL 60181.

This is a work of fiction. Names, characters, places and incidences are either a product of the author's imagination or used fictitiously. Any similarity to actual organizations and persons, living or deceased, is entirely coincidental.

A New Leaf Book
Published by WigWam Publishing Co.
P.O. Box 6992
Villa Park, IL 60181
http://www.newleafbooks.net

Copyright © 2007 Robert W. Smith

Library of Congress Cataloging-in-Publication Data

Smith, Robert W., 1950-
  The Sakhalin collection / by Robert W. Smith.
     p. cm.
  "A New Leaf book."
  ISBN 978-1-930076-38-9
  1. Koreans—Russia (Federation)—Sakhalin (Sakhalinskaia oblast?)—Fiction. 2. World War, 1939-1945—Prisoners and prisons, Japanese—Fiction. 3. World War, 1939-1945—Conscript labor—Fiction. I. Title.
  PS3619.M59247S36 2007
  813'.6—dc22
                      2007024693

Printed in the U.S.A.

Acknowledgements

Faded memories of distant travels pepper these pages. Two friends helped color them. Linda Gorey was my expert in all things Japan and Japanese, and Nakagawa Yoshihiro my link to a Wakkanai of the past. To both, my thanks.

There is no shame in not knowing; the shame lies in not finding out.
 –Russian Proverb, author unknown

HISTORICAL NOTE

During World War II the Empire of Japan abducted over a million Korean citizens from their homeland and brought them forcibly to the Japanese Islands to staff the war factories. More than sixty thousand of those toiled in the mines and mills of southern Sakhalin Island, then governed by Japan. The Japanese called the place Karafuto.

Near the war's end, hundreds of thousands of Japanese fled the island, leaving some forty-three thousand Korean conscripts to the mercy of Stalin's victorious Red Army. Under Soviet rule, the Koreans continued to work and die in squalor and misery for decades while the world's great democracies all but ignored their plight.

Most are dead now. Several hundred have finally been returned to South Korea to live out their days. A few are still on Sakhalin, the memory of home a long forgotten dream.

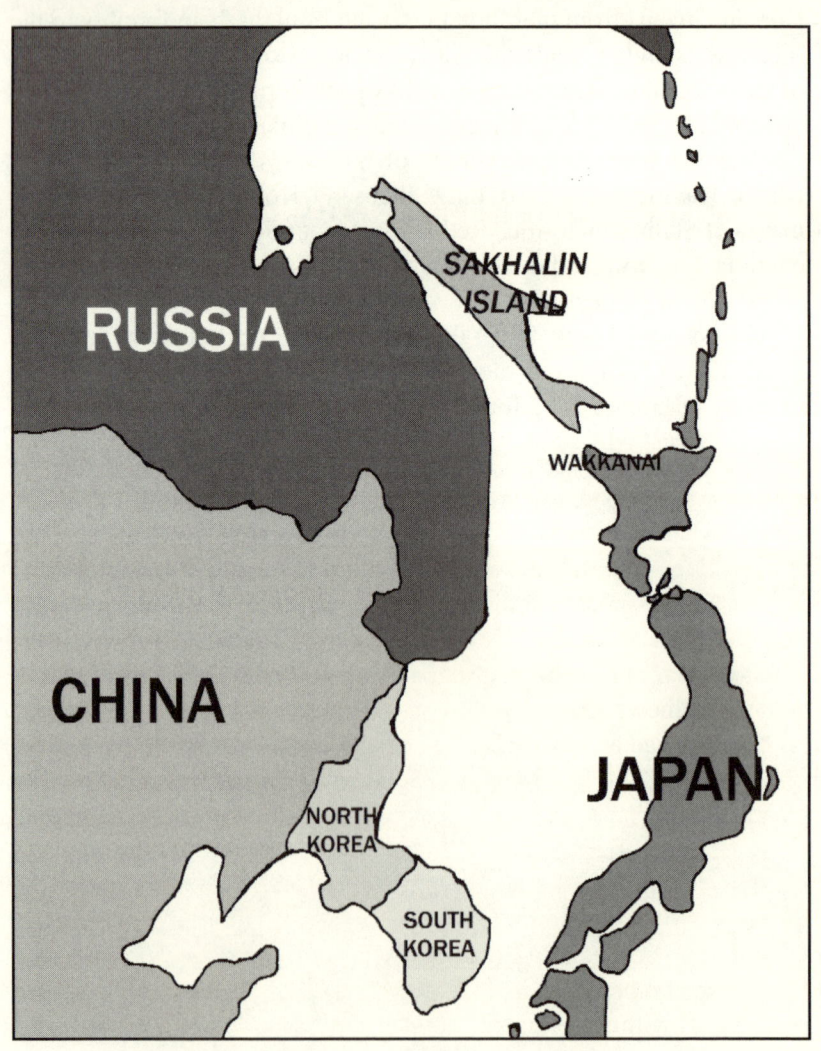

ONE

**I've been to the jungle, and it's not what you think.
At the thought of returning, I'm not tickled pink.**

*Tachikawa Air Force Base,
Honshu, Japan (outside Tokyo)
A Monday morning in late January, 1970*

Dan Matthews stopped on the hilltop to catch a breath and consider the unexpected audience with his commanding officer. A midday summons from the Commanding Officer might once have triggered the fear of incoming mortar rounds, but not today, because today Agent Matthews carried his own cause for anxiety. An unforeseen opportunity had arisen, certain to chart the remaining course of his life one way or the other. The worst this major could do was send him to Vietnam—again.

The headquarters building breached the concrete horizon below, defiantly straddling the shoulder of Taxiway Bravo just beyond. A dozen or so F-4 Phantoms lined the parking areas, menacing warriors, lacking only an enemy to engage in the peaceful Land of the Rising Sun. Dan Matthews headed downhill toward the front stairs and his rendezvous with uncertainty, the ever-present image of white-capped Mount Fuji casting a long shadow across the Nippon landscape.

He stood dutifully outside the major's office, waiting for the command to enter. Just once, he thought, it would be nice to hear the man's voice within some close proximity to the knock on his door. For whatever reason, Major Coughlin liked to make people wait. Still, as commanding officers went, Dan had seen worse and had somehow managed to avoid an encounter with the major's well-documented intolerance of enlisted types.

"Come in," came the familiar voice from behind the flimsy door. Inside the room, Dan found the plus-sized carcass of Major Emil Coughlin sprouting from behind the mahogany desk. The Air Force wouldn't hesitate to spend one thousand bucks on a desk, but not for forty-two-year-old majors. Rumor had it the money had secretly come from the man's own pocket. Worse than that, the entire base knew that Coughlin had been passed over twice for promotion to Lieutenant Colonel. One more snub and he would be plain old "Mister" Coughlin in the blink of an eye. For whatever reason, Coughlin insisted on presenting himself as a man on the move. All these things conspired to lend an air of vulnerability to the fellow that rendered him almost tolerable.

And it was clear that, from the major's twisted perspective, he'd adopted Dan Matthews as a kind of exception to the rule, confirming the special status with a couple of choice temporary duty assignments last year to Hawaii and Bangkok. The former trip had actually spawned Dan's recent turmoil. He wasn't exactly comfortable with the situation and did nothing to encourage it, nothing beyond what the Air Force expected of him every day. But with the war still raging down in Vietnam, Tokyo was good duty, as good as any, and Dan's prospects for a long-term stay had been excellent—until last week anyway.

"Yes, sir," Dan replied, already closing the door. Though still a lowly staff sergeant, he did not snap to attention. The plainclothes-dressed agents in the Air Force Office of Special Investigations, or OSI, did not observe most rank-based, military protocols. "I would have been here sooner, sir, but I was in the middle of an interview when you called. I just got your message."

Coughlin smiled nervously and motioned to one of the chairs opposite his desk. "It's all right, Matthews."

The spartan metal chair contrasted to the opulence of Coughlin's desk, but looked more at home in the room. "Thank you, sir."

Coughlin reached across the desk, offering a pack of Lucky Strikes. "Smoke?"

Dan raised his palm to the offering, giving Coughlin the same answer he always gave, and without a hint of sarcasm. "No thanks, Major. Haven't had one in two years."

The major nodded. "Sure. I just forgot. So what are you working on?"

"Mostly domestics, sir, and a couple of thefts in maintenance. I was just on my way over to get a haircut when I picked up your message."

Coughlin peered up from the lonely, manila folder sitting on his desk. "No time for that, but it's okay. You won't need a haircut where you're going."

The major's last sentence sounded an ominous note. He still had the power to make Dan's life miserable, but for just how long was an open question.

Coughlin leaned back and clasped his baby-smooth hands behind his balding head, exposing a patch of perspiration under each arm. "I'll be frank with you, Matthews. We have an opportunity here to do something important, but the thing is, I'm not at liberty to give you all the background." The two buttons above the major's belt looked as if they would break away and launch across the room at any moment. "I can only give you the assignment and ask you to keep in mind how critical it is."

Here was a perfect example of how Dan had managed to thrive in the military without ever embracing its discipline or strict limitations on personal achievement. He held his tongue and summoned his patience.

The part about "won't need a haircut where you're going" was still ringing in Dan's ear and he was betting Coughlin knew it. The next words Dan expected to hear from the major were "tropical inoculations." That would pretty much seal the deal. Dan Matthews would be on his way home to South Vietnam.

Coughlin leaned forward abruptly and slapped his palm on the desk, as though something had sprung to mind. "By the way, the first sergeant mentioned that your enlistment is up in three weeks. He said your reenlistment papers are still on his desk—unsigned. I assume that was an oversight."

As the lawyers might say, there was no question pending, but a raised eyebrow told him the major didn't see it that way. The ball was squarely in Dan's court now, and anything other than complete disclosure at this point would be deception. Major Coughlin deserved his complete candor, if not his unqualified respect. Dan had learned years ago that straight talk was a valued currency in the U.S. military. And there was no denying the practice had kept him off Coughlin's "latrine patrol" until now. "No sir. It wasn't an oversight. The thing is, I'm not certain I'm going to reenlist."

That was the truth of it, the whole goddamn, complicated, up-in-the-air truth. Dan was nearly thirty, and one more reenlistment would pretty much seal his status as a lifer. But he didn't want to be a lifer, never had. The first two reenlistments just kind of happened. Last week he'd been offered what could prove to be a once-in-a-lifetime opportunity, a high-paying job as a detective in Kailua-Kona, Hawaii. But how many faceless Joes before him had cut the cord, reached for the brass ring and been swallowed up in its empty promise? In three weeks he'd still be an investigator, but for whom was an open question.

Coughlin's wide-eyed stare and open mouth told him the major had taken the disclosure as some sort of personal betrayal. "Why didn't you tell me?"

The truth might work for him as well as against. "Because I have no idea what I'm gonna do, sir. I have an opportunity on the outside and I'm considering it. That's as far as it goes. Besides, this all came up less than a week ago."

The major's shoulders seemed to relax a bit; his tone mellowed. "Well, can you at least tell me about it?"

Dan wanted to say what was on his mind, but this major would just find a way to take it personally. The excitement of working counterespionage is what had drawn him into the OSI, but nearly three years after graduating from the Investigations Academy at Andrews Air Force Base, the closest he'd come to spies was his television set. For Dan Matthews, an endless parade of wife beaters and petty thieves would either end abruptly or become his life's calling. He knew he wouldn't find excitement and intrigue in Hawaii either, and had begun instead to think of other things, like what he really wanted to do with the rest of his life and with whom.

Before Dan could answer, the entire building began to vibrate as a low rumble erupted and gathered momentum in the distance. Coughlin rose from the desk in a well-practiced maneuver and turned toward the window as a mighty Phantom punctuated their conversation with a thunderous roar and a blinding ball of fire. Dan was off the hook for the moment as the major gazed in longing silence, the jet's afterburner igniting a furious thunder and propelling it straight toward the heavens. Might be salt in the wound, Dan thought, and thirty times a day to boot.

Then, without turning around, Coughlin said softly, "I started out in flight school, Matthews. Did you know that?"

An awkward silence settled over the room, but Dan felt obligated to manufacture a reply. "No sir. I didn't," was the best he could muster. Uncomfortable as it was, the not quite surprising confession answered more questions than it raised. Coughlin wasn't an Academy man and the absence of wings on his chest announced he'd never held flight status, a wingless bird nesting on the concrete, forced to endure the taunting ritual of his soaring brothers as they spun their warriors' tales in the Officer's Club each night. Inferiority, Dan knew, had fueled the careers of many a desk-bound fly-boy.

The major was still facing the window, hands clasped behind his back. He seemed transfixed on the jet's fiery trail and lost in thought. As the war bird disappeared into the clouds, the wingless major returned to the familiarity of his mahogany cockpit and shrugged. "Oh, well," then guided the manila folder carefully across the expanse like a pawn to King's four until it lay directly beneath Dan's eyes. "Have a look," he said.

Dan didn't care to look. He already knew very well how to spell South Vietnam, but flipped open the thin folder. He saw the service record of twenty-year-old Airman First Class Reginald Kincaid, several supplemental reports, and an incident report. The words "dead American" caught his eye.

"You're going to Wakkanai again," Coughlin announced matter-of-factly, his moment of weakness having passed.

Wakkanai was a frozen outpost at the northern tip of Japan, colder than a Vietnamese hooker, but at least nobody would be shooting at him. "I don't mind, sir. The only thing I don't like about it is the plane ride. The wind probably blows a hundred miles an hour out there on Cape Soya, near the airport. Even the Air America pilots get jittery about landing there."

"I know," Coughlin said, "I've only been there once, but it was enough. There must have been twelve feet of snow on the ground in March, and it was just getting started." The major stood and began to pace the room awkwardly, like he was about to drop round two. "This airman was stabbed in Wakkanai City. Your assignment is to investigate and report. It won't take you more than a few days, but it's important, believe it or not, and you're the only one I trust to do it right."

The last part was disingenuous and condescending, but Coughlin probably figured Dan was too dumb to see it. Investigate what? Dan thought. "Is he dead, sir?" It was the obvious first question, and would explain why the major considered the assignment so important. Besides, a murder investigation would be just the thing to get his mind off this pipe dream of a civilian life. And if it's so important, why send a sergeant instead of an officer agent?

"Not only is he not dead," Coughlin replied, "but he's here at Tachikawa in the hospital. His stab wound was too extensive to treat at the Wakkanai infirmary, so they medevaced him."

Okay, so dead American wasn't the punch line. "I'll get right over there after I read the file."

Coughlin turned to face him. "Good. You might get some of the heavy lifting done before heading north. Your flight leaves from Yokota at six a.m."

"Is he all right?"

Coughlin shrugged. "I guess it was pretty serious, but he's okay now. He's awake and the doctor said you could talk to him. They'll be sending him back up there in a couple of days. I've arranged for him to see a psychiatrist here before he goes back. See, there are a few things you should know that you won't read in the file."

Here goes. "Like what?"

Coughlin's face seemed to tighten up. Resting his hands on the desk, he leaned forward and hesitated, like he was searching for words. "Kincaid has a Top-Secret Crypto security clearance and the base commander up there thinks he's a risky proposition, kind of a nut case. He's a loner, drinks a lot, might even be a homosexual."

The major had saved his breaking pitch for the last inning, adding the word homosexual almost as an afterthought. "Is that what this is, sir?" It wasn't the OSI's job to do background checks for security clearances. Initiating a criminal investigation for homosexual conduct was a way to get the OSI involved directly in getting rid of an "undesirable." With some evidence this kid had sucked a dick or two in private, everybody'd get what they wanted, except Kincaid, of course. He'd likely get mustered out with a general discharge. What bothered Dan was that the evidence was generally scant and often unreliable.

But sergeants didn't choose their assignments. They just obeyed orders.

Coughlin seemed to sense his disgust. "Look, Dan, there's another reason I'm giving this assignment to you in particular. You know what it is?"

Dan knew he'd have to learn the real answer to that question on his own, but decided to play along. "No, sir. What is it?"

"You're born military, mind your own business and do your work. You may not give it any thought, but most of my agents have an agenda—advancement, promotion, cutting corners, whatever. You've been with me a year and a half and I hardly know you personally, but you're the best I have, and the most reliable. I've recommended your promotion to tech sergeant be fast tracked."

Juvenile psychology. The only thing Coughlin really knew about him, Dan thought, was that he'd never made the major look bad—not yet anyway. Their relationship had never been tested by adversity. Whatever this assignment was, it was not routine. It was one thing to keep your mouth shut, another to walk into an ambush blindfolded. "Why do they keep him up there, sir? Why not just cut orders and reassign him or cut his access to classified material? Why go through all the time and expense of an investigation?"

"It's not that simple. It's a matter of protocol. If they reassigned him it would have to be to another Security Service unit and that would be saving Peter to fuck Paul. If they just pull his access, there needs to be some justification. They want this kid permanently excluded from classified material, but the fact is he's very good at his job."

"That's a lot of work just to fire somebody. What's his job?"

"He's a Russian linguist. With your security clearance, I assume you've been up on the operations center there at the base, right?"

"Yes sir. I've been inside the complex, but I've never had a briefing about the operations."

Coughlin looked away and began to fiddle with a pencil, kneading and spinning it with his fingers. It was a sign to Dan that the major might harbor his own suspicions about the mission, though he would never express them outright. "Use your imagination for now," Coughlin suggested. "They're only a few miles from the Soviet Union up there. The point is this young airman is in a sensitive position. There are high-level security concerns about his mental state and his continued exposure to a top-secret environment."

Pushing it any further, Dan knew, would be counterproductive. Major Coughlin would never openly question the propriety of an assignment, especially to a staff sergeant.

The major pointed at the folder in Dan's hand. "It's all in there. The thing happened off base. He's made up some goofy story about saving a woman from attack in the city, claims there was a dead American airman lying in the snow next to the two Asians attacking the girl. It's pretty clearly a bunch of bullshit."

How would he know that? Dan wondered. "I take it there are no missing airmen at Wakkanai and the Japanese police have no reports of a missing or assaulted woman," he said.

"You take it correctly."

"So what I won't find in the reports is that they believe he stabbed himself," Dan suggested. "Is that about it?"

Coughlin nodded. "That or he tried to suck the wrong cock. It seems pretty cut and dried. From here it looks like they'll just pull his security clearance as a homosexual and give him a general discharge, depending on your report. I doubt he'll even be charged. You know how these things go. I'll make sure you get the psychiatrist's report."

Dan wondered why such a menial investigation would rate such high priority. "Okay, Major," he replied, up and turning for the door. "I'll read the file and get right over there. We'll see what this Kincaid has to say." He had a pressing personal matter to deal with first, but there was no need to make Coughlin his confidant.

"And Matthews," Coughlin added, "keep in mind there's one thing he didn't make up. Somebody drove him back to the base and had dressed his wound. Find out if he knows who and stop back here when you leave the hospital. I want to hear your report right away."

As he neared the door, Coughlin's voice stopped him. "One more thing."

He turned back, one hand on the knob. "Yes sir."

"Was it your visit with that retired colonel last year?"

It was a reference to his TDY, temporary duty, in Hawaii. He'd mentioned his visit with his old squadron commander from Vietnam. The two had been close friends, and Grant Billings retired from the Air Force to accept a civilian position as Chief of Police. "Yes sir. Grant called me out of the blue last week. Believe me, it's not something I've been planning, but I'm giving it some hard thought."

Coughlin managed a forced smile. "Yeah, I've seen the boating magazines all over your desk. But think carefully, Matthews. You'd be leaving a lot on the table. You've built a good career in the Air Force."

"I know, sir. I appreciate your input, and I wasn't trying to hide it from you."

The major nodded, seemingly appeased. "Good luck."

"Thank you sir." As the office door closed behind him, Dan heard the faint, but distinct sound of another door, this one opening from somewhere within Major Coughlin's office. He paused momentarily, his police instincts aroused by the curious development just beyond the paper-thin wall. He thought about reentering abruptly on the pretext of leaving something behind, but dismissed the idea as quickly as it had come. If curiosity killed the cat, Dan thought, consider what it would do to a lowly staff sergeant.

TWO

**Heads you'll sink; tails you'll float,
but with luck you might be cruisin' on a thirty-foot boat.**

"Fifteen thousand is a hell of a salary, Colonel," Dan said over the scratchy connection, "but guys tell me the cost of housing and stuff down there is out of control. I mean I appreciate your going out on a limb for me. I really do. It's just that I'm not sure."

"First of all," came the distant voice of his former commanding officer, "it's Grant now, not Colonel, Dan. But I understand your situation. You've got what? Eight years left to retirement?"

Grant had put his finger on it. Reupping the first time had been the toughest. Dan was maybe twenty-one, twenty-two at most. Only two things on your mind at that age: pussy and booze, both easy to come by and bad for your health in the long run. The second reenlistment was a bit tougher. He'd have been around twenty-six then. Old buddies from the neighborhood were married with good jobs, the ones who weren't in jail anyway. The thought of starting over at that age had just scared the hell out of him. But now, with a solid opportunity in his own field, it could be a different story. Thirty wasn't too late to grow up and live the American dream. So here he was, opportunity at his doorstep and not a fucking clue what to do. "Yeah. Eight years to retirement."

"Easy for me to say. Right, Dan? Being retired already. It's a lot to give up and I won't beat you up about it. But you're a good man, and I need good men. As for the rest of it, all I can say is that there are millions of guys with half your skills and not a trace of your work ethic, and most of 'em doin' very well in the outside world. Just think it over carefully before you say no, son."

Asking Grant's advice was out of the question. Colonel Grant Billings had treated him like a man since the day a skinny, young airman reported to his squadron for duty at Da Nang Air Base; and a man made decisions like this for himself. The lack of a wife and kids, even of a real family back home in Chicago only heightened his dilemma. Responsibility had a way of making decisions for a man. Dan Matthews was perfectly free to fuck up his own life in any way he desired. There was no one to disappoint, no one to cheer or worry. The automated voice interrupted with a request for more quarters and Dan was ready with the needed six. "Thanks, Grant. When do you need to know?"

"I'll give you the whole three weeks, kid. The job is yours if you want it. Just do what you think is right. Aloha."

As Dan passed the information booth in the main lobby, the young, Japanese receptionist smiled. He had avoided going to the hospital for the last eight months until today, and now his face was becoming a fixture. He didn't like the place because it reminded him of the war—and other things. Tachikawa was one of the main evacuation hospitals for serious casualties, and business had been booming lately.

During his thirteen-month tour with the 366th Security Police Squadron up at Da Nang in '66 and '67, the war was still popular back in the world. In those days young marines carried the brunt of the battle against North Vietnamese regulars from forward firebases along the Demilitarized Zone. The endless stream of body bags and limbless, young warriors gave the war a personal face for Dan, and a dim-witted airman had tacked on another passel of bad memories.

It had been just another wet, sweltering night in Nam. As midnight flight leader, one of Dan's routine duties was to keep tabs on the sentries guarding the fighters and the perimeter wire. It was before the '68 Tet Offensive, but during a time when poorly organized and equipped Viet Cong units occasionally mustered enough courage to lob a few shells onto the base from beyond the no man's land separating jungle from concrete runway.

As near as Dan had figured it, much later from his hospital bed, the monsoon rains had masked the noise of the jeep engine as he approached a north-wire sentry post. Headlights were only recommended for those bent on suicide by sniper. As Dan approached the sentry on foot, the sleeping young airman was startled to consciousness and promptly emptied an entire M-16 clip in Dan's direction. Only a single bullet found its mark, and not an entirely bad mark from Dan's hindsight perspective, as the bullet passed cleanly through his thigh, missing his dick by less than an inch.

He remembered the way to Ward Three. As he entered through the swinging door, he saw the two straight rows of hospital beds, all occupied, Purple Heart medals pinned prominently on a dozen or more pillows. Some general or other had obviously been around earlier.

The casualties were mostly army these days, many of them draftees; but the brave, young faces were indistinguishable from those of the marines at Da Nang. Several of the young soldiers appeared ravaged beyond hope, oblivious to the tiny purple shrouds decorating their pillows, each supporting a bronze profile that looked like George Washington. He remembered being in such a ward, on a hospital ship, and vividly recalled the embarrassment of lying among such brave men with his accidental wound.

Dan browsed the charts at the foot of the beds until he found Reginald Kincaid. Except for the missing medal, the boy looked more like a war hero than a self-destructive nut case or flaming homosexual. His huge feet hung over the bottom of the bed in a comical display. "Airman Kincaid?"

"Yes sir," the young man replied, looking up from his book. His face was thin by act of God with sharply defined features and made Dan think of a boyish Abe Lincoln.

"Don't call me sir. I'm Agent Matthews from OSI. What are you reading?"

The kid shrugged. "Oh, just something the nurse brought me. They have a list of books they keep in the hospital. It's kind of like a mini-library and helps pass the time."

Dan made a point of glancing at the cover as the airman closed the thick book and rested it on the bed stand: *The Rise and Fall of the Third Reich* by William L. Shirer. He clearly wasn't the comic book type. "Do you know what the OSI is?"

"Oh, sure. The civvies kind of fooled me, but I should have known. Everybody's heard of you guys, but I don't know anyone who's actually met one of you. That's good, I guess. Up until now anyway." The kid offered a natural, easy smile. "Are you an officer or enlisted?"

Kincaid seemed pretty well informed. Time to assert control. "That's between me and my military records. To you I'm just Agent Matthews."

The terse response seemed to just roll off the boy's back. "I'm not in trouble, am I?"

His question had a ring of naiveté that caught Dan off guard. He reached for the metal chair along the wall and seated himself beside the bed. "I've been assigned to look into your case. That's all." He wasn't about to let the young airman become the interrogator. He had underestimated people before.

"Sure, I understand."

"If you feel up to it, I'd like to ask you some questions about the other night."

Kincaid struggled to prop himself up on the pillow. "I feel pretty good now. I'll tell you everything. I mean I want to tell you everything." He smiled weakly. "I guess I don't have anything else on my schedule."

The young man seemed pleasant enough, and his sense of humor had a disarming quality. Dan said, "Great. I'd like to start with the statement you made to the Security Police at the base infirmary. Do you remember talking to them?"

"Vaguely. They had me pretty drugged up. I don't even remember going to the infirmary, but I remember talking to someone. It was like I woke up and he was there. He was asking me questions while they were prepping me for transport."

"Do you remember what you told him?"

"Not exactly, but I suppose I told him the truth, whatever I remembered of it anyway."

A shrewd answer, Dan thought. "Would you mind telling me what you remember? From the beginning. I'll stop you if I need to ask a question."

If the request aggravated Kincaid, he was hiding it pretty well. "Sure," he replied. "I don't mind at all. I got off the p.m. shift on the hill at midnight. I went back to the barracks and changed clothes, then walked into town."

Dan knew the route well enough. "That's over a mile and a half. Was it snowing?"

This time the smile was more of the teasing variety. "It's always snowing up there, except maybe in July and August."

Dan found his familiarity annoying. This was supposed to be an interrogation. "That's a long way to walk for a beer."

"I like it in town. I don't mind walking in the snow. And there are no buses or shuttles after midnight. So you walk or you call a taxi."

"The NCO Club is open until two in the morning," Dan reminded him. "What is it about the city that makes you want to walk that far in blizzard conditions?"

"I have friends in the city. Besides, I don't care for the NCO Club. Maybe it's the Country-Western music. I just don't go there unless it's to get a hamburger or play the slots for a little while before bed. Look, Agent Matthews, I know you're in charge of this investigation, but could you just tell me if the girl's all right?"

The question took Dan by surprise and he wasn't about to be distracted or played like a fiddle by some twenty-year-old airman. "Listen. You need to understand that I'm investigating a serious crime. I'm not here to hold your hand and comfort you. So how about you just answer my questions for now?"

Kincaid looked genuinely hurt. It didn't appear to be an act, but the service record said he was extremely intelligent. "Fine. Where did I leave off?"

"You were walking into the city."

"Sure. I was just beyond Fish Alley on the outskirts when I heard a scuffle off the main drag."

"What did you hear?"

"I heard a woman scream."

Precisely what the report had said, but there are screams and there are screams. "Was she screaming in Japanese?"

"She wasn't saying anything. She just screamed. That's all I heard."

Dan made a note and said, "I've seen your description of the two Asian men. Do you think you could identify either of them?"

"In a heartbeat."

"Your statement to the Security Police up at Wakkanai ended at the point you were stabbed," Dan said, remembering the conversation with Coughlin. "How did you get back to Wakkanai Air Station?"

His question had been disingenuous by design. The cops at Wakkanai had asked the same question, and Kincaid had claimed he didn't know, that he was unconscious. The guard at the main gate reported hearing a horn from beyond the snow bank on the main coast road. According to his report, someone had propped Kincaid up carefully in the snow, near the gate. Whoever had dropped him off, Dan figured, endured considerable risk to make sure he didn't bleed to death. It was the best place to start.

"I have no idea. To be honest, I thought I was dead; must have passed out right after I was stabbed. I remember getting stabbed, then waking up in the infirmary. That's it."

"What about the girl? Do you have any idea who she was?"

"No, I don't. Say, did I do something wrong?"

This kid was either stupid or brilliant. Maybe even both. "I'm told you'll be returning to Wakkanai in a couple of days. We'll talk more up there. For now, I'd just like to ask you a couple of more questions-about the American in the snow."

On the walk back to HQ, headquarters, Dan couldn't stop thinking about Kincaid's account of the supposed dead American in the snow. He found it more than troubling. If this young airman were so smart, why would he insist the man was American? It was the easiest part of the story to discredit. It would be impossible to cover up even a single missing American airman in the entire Pacific Air Command.

Of course, maybe the man had simply gotten up and walked away from the scene. But in that case, why would he not have reported the incident? By now, every person at Wakkanai Air Station had to know an airman had been stabbed.

No, if Kincaid were lying, he would have been better off simply saying there was a body in the snow. He was too smart to make such a stupid mistake. Then again, if he were really off his rocker, what difference did it make? He might even believe this bullshit story himself.

Dan was less than a hundred yards from headquarters when he heard the bugle begin to sound "Retreat." He watched the last of the sun slip behind Mt. Fuji and turned toward the colors, right hand on his heart.

Kincaid's mental state would be up to the doctors to figure out, Dan thought. His job would be to complete an objective investigation.

He'd go up to Wakkanai and poke around, maybe talk to some people who knew Kincaid. When the kid got back to the base, Dan would have him reenact the entire incident at the scene of the alleged crime.

The last note sounded and Dan resumed his walk. In the end his questions were just idle curiosity. If his job was to serve this kid up on a platter, then so be it. Dan Matthews would never presume to question the motives of the United States Air Force, and the Air Force wasn't in the habit of justifying itself to sergeants.

But why were they in such a hurry to prove Kincaid was a homo and get rid of him? Nothing in the file even suggested homosexual conduct, and Dan found the omission problematic. Could this young airman really be a threat to national security? It was the world's worst kept secret that they spied on the Russians up at Wakkanai. So what? The damn Russians had to know already. What could Airman Reginald Kincaid possibly know that worried the Air Force? Dan told himself he'd be perfectly content taking that unanswered question to his grave.

THREE

**Into the land of eternal ice,
where the wind can freeze you, then kill you twice.**

Tuesday, 8:55 a.m.
Wakkanai, Hokkaido, Japan

Dan felt a sigh of relief as the wheels of the aircraft finally touched the runway—for the second time. Bouncing was acceptable at Wakkanai airport, so long as you came to rest right side up.

The early departure had meant he didn't have to eat breakfast before flying. He hated flying, something he didn't discover until after joining the Air Force. His flight from Chicago to boot camp at Lackland Air Force had been the first of his life and made him deathly ill.

Mercifully, he'd been assigned directly to police training from boot camp. He didn't ask for an assignment to what was then called the Air Police, but was relieved to have avoided an aircrew assignment. Flying only when necessary for transport was bad enough.

Before making his way to the door, he poked his head into the WWII-era cockpit. The two middle-aged pilots were smiling, but still perspiring profusely. "Thanks for the ride, guys," he said.

The civilian captain turned and managed a smile. "All in a day's work." The two pilots then laughed in unison as if at a private joke.

Dan figured they were relieved at not having to ride the ancient C-47 to a bucking bronco landing.

Nearly toppled as he stepped into the brutal wind, Dan scurried down the portable stairway amidst the six or seven other passengers, all uniformed military, three of them officers. He'd come to believe that enlisted types tend not to trust people in civilian clothes, so he'd worn a set of fatigues, complete with staff sergeant stripes, and packed a spare.

The tiny building some fifty yards to the west looked more like a warming house for ice skaters than a terminal. Dan filed in behind the officers along the shoveled path. He was not surprised to see a blue Chevy sedan parked outside the terminal, waiting for the three officers courtesy of the base commander. A small taxi lay tucked in behind it, outside the nearly deserted passenger terminal. The three enlisted people, two with duffle bags, crammed into the backseat behind Dan.

The taxi driver turned back and flashed a warm smile. "*Ohayo gozaimasu.* You aru go base-u?"

On his last trip up north, he'd found the Northern Hokkaido people to be generally warmer and less hurried than their counterparts in metropolitan Tokyo. Dan was about to answer when he heard a voice from behind speaking to no one in particular. "Where the fuck does he think we're going? San Diego?"

Best to ignore him, Dan thought. With no war to fight, these forgotten airmen at the end of the free world had little to occupy their minds. Fistfights were all too common and could erupt over almost anything. "Yes," Dan replied. "We're going to the base." The airman sitting directly behind him smelled like a tub of stale beer and the man's breath was foul enough to wake a sleeping volcano. Dan tried to remember how long the taxi ride was on his last trip. The smell of fish along the way would be a relief.

He found the bachelor officers' quarters unchanged, even palatial when compared to the open bay Quonset hut reserved for visiting enlisted men. His small, private room in the dormitory-like building came equipped with a closet and a chest of drawers. Enlisted agents on TDY were granted this necessary concession to help conceal rank. Dan was grateful for the perk, even if it didn't fool the majors and colonels.

He headed into a steady snow toward the NCO Club to grab a hamburger and beer. On a full stomach he'd craft a plan to get this unpleasant business settled in short order. He wanted to get back to Tachi by the end of the week, where he could devote full attention to his personal dilemma.

Tropical thoughts almost carried him past his destination. He backtracked only to find the door of the white, frame building locked. Dan spotted a small group of civilian dressed airmen walking past on the snow-packed road. "Excuse me," he said. "You guys know why the club is closed?"

He heard a laugh escape from under the tall man's fur hood. "It's Tuesday," the man declared. "Sergeant Gavin runs the place. He has a *josan* in Asahikawa and sometimes he misses the Sunday night train. There isn't another one until Tuesday morning. The staff knows he can't get back today until at least two." The man pulled back a thick sleeve to reveal his watch, then smiled. "They'll be here in a half hour or so."

The three were walking again and Dan followed along. "Great. I don't eat chow hall food. Where can I get a good meal that doesn't include raw fish?"

The man on the left laughed. "Across from the main gate," he answered, "Mama Young's. We're going over there now. You new here?"

"Just TDY for a few days. Thanks, I'll join you for lunch if you don't mind. What do they have that's good over there?"

"Pussy," the tall man replied, "but you won't be seeing it up close."

"Give him a break," Dan's new friend said. "The guy just got here." He turned toward Dan on the move and extended a gloved hand from the long sleeve. "I'm Frank Doherty. The wise guy is Rob Norton and the silent one here is Tony Capello."

Doherty didn't look old enough to shave and none of the three could fool a farsighted bartender. Dan shook Frank's hand and the other two nodded. "Dan Matthews, glad to meet you guys. So what did Rob mean about not seeing it up close?"

"He has the hots for the waitress there," Tony said. "Hell, everybody does. She's built like Angie Dickinson on a smaller scale, with laser-beam, green eyes."

"That's a fact," said Frank. "And as far as anybody on base can tell, the whole package is going to waste."

"Yeah," Rob added, "and they're round eyes too. Well, half-round anyway." For whatever reason, Rob chuckled at his own ignorance as the four men carried their conversation through the gently falling snow and up the road toward the main gate.

"She's half American," Frank explained. "At least that's the story, although I really can't see it myself. Su Li Young is her name. The strange thing is she hates Americans, all Americans. They say her father was some guy stationed here with the occupation forces. He banged up the mother and rotated back to the world without marrying her. She and the mother are double-dog shit as far as the local Japanese are concerned."

Dan figured as long as the food was good, he didn't care if the girl was a Soviet spy. "Thanks, I'll tag along," he said, as the group filed past the guard shack toward the main road.

They entered the weathered, nondescript building through a low-hanging door. A few airmen in fatigues lined the bar and a couple of big guys in civvies filled a booth against the wall. Dan's eyes couldn't find any young women, never mind one resembling a brick shithouse. "Is she off on Tuesdays?"

"I'm shocked," said Tony. "She's always here. It's like she doesn't have a life."

The men made their way, as if by habit, to a table in the corner and began to shake the fresh snow from their parkas. "You mean outside of busting our balls," Rob corrected.

"Lighten up," Frank said. "I've never seen her be rude to anybody and I couldn't even count all the drunks who slobber over her every day."

Dan hung his coat on a hook beside the others and took the open chair. "Su Li Young isn't even a Japanese name," he pointed out. "If I'm not mistaken, it's Korean. How did the old woman and her daughter end up over here?" It had nothing to do with his mission, but Dan was intensely curious and surprised to find Koreans living amongst the homogeneous population, especially way up here in the rural north. Besides, it was common knowledge there was no love lost between the Japanese and the Koreans.

"Who gives a fuck?" Rob said, looking around for a waitress. "They all look the same to me."

"Mama," Tony called to the woman behind the bar, "where is Su Li today?"

"Why you care?" the woman said.

Dan could see she wasn't nearly as old as she'd looked at first glance. Her back was bowed, probably from hard work and her skin was a shade darker than that of the general population. It was taut, even around the eyes and more cracked than wrinkled. He would almost describe her as handsome, with an air of dignity about her. The woman had likely spent most of her life outside and in extremely harsh conditions.

"Su Li no like GI anyway," she said good-naturedly. "Specially not ugly ones like you. You boys wanna eat or you just pull Mama's chain?"

"You like pork cutlet, Dan?" Frank asked. "It's kind of her specialty. It's pretty good and it's also probably the only thing you could eat."

"Keep telling yourself it's pork, if it makes you feel better, Doherty," Rob said. "We all know it was somebody's kitty cat a few days ago."

Frank looked directly at Dan and smiled. "Don't worry," he said. "If he really thought that he wouldn't order it five or six times a week."

"I'll give it a shot. I'm not a raw fish guy," Dan said.

"Four *poku-katsu*, Mama," Frank shouted across the room, "and four Sapporo."

"Okay," said Mama Young. "You come get beer at bar. I not waitress. Su Li sick today."

The pork cutlet with rice was as good as Dan had ever eaten, and it made the three beers go down smoothly, too smoothly. He knew he should have stopped at two. He was perfectly at ease around the three young airmen, even Rob, and might have killed a few more hours with these guys. He'd known many Rob Nortons in his Asian tours. They were people who needed to exploit the differences among cultures and races, not the similarities. Maybe it made them feel better about being so far away from home. They were boring, but never far away. He liked the other two and could tune Norton out at will.

Finally, Tony looked at Dan and said, "So what's your job anyway? Why did they send you up to the end of the world?"

Well, the lunch hour was over, Dan thought. There was no point in lying to them. He was there to complete a mission, unpleasant as it was. Maybe they'd open up a little after seeing him in such an unguarded mode. More likely the answer would just put a chill in the air. They'd see him as a phony, trying to get them to rat by sucking up. He should have remained aloof. Just sit in an office and call them in one by one for interrogation. People are most likely to talk when they're intimidated. But what did it matter? He'd enjoyed the lunch and what were the chances one of these three would have relevant information anyway? "I'm with OSI," he answered. "I'm here from Tachi on an investigation. How about you guys?"

The collective silence confirmed his social relationship with the men had just ended abruptly. After a few seconds Tony Capello said, "You know how it is with security regs. We can only say so much. I'm a Morse operator. Frank there is a Russian Linguist."

Capello laughed nervously and spoke again. "And Rob here doesn't need to worry about security. He a dumb-ass truck driver."

Doherty looked him squarely in the eye. It was no longer a friendly face. "Why the sergeant stripes? Are you working undercover?"

The sarcasm wasn't lost on Dan and maybe he even had it coming. "No, I really am enlisted, but don't spread it around. You won't see the uniform again."

"It's getting late," Frank said. "I've got to get some sleep before my shift." He rose and began the process of battening down his parka. The others quickly followed suit.

Dan figured he had nothing to lose by asking a few quick questions. "Do you guys know Reggie Kincaid? I think he does the same job you do, Frank."

"Yeah," Frank replied. "I know him to talk to him. He's an okay guy. Too bad, what happened to him. Will he be all right?"

"I spoke with him yesterday. He'll be fine."

"He comes in here all right, but I don't know him very well," Rob added. "I don't usually hang out with the geniuses. These two fucks just happen to live in the next room over, so I have a drink with them now and then."

Dan didn't know if he was kidding. "Does he come in here often?" he asked, looking directly at Capello.

"Yeah," the young man replied. "He likes the food here, but he mostly stays to himself."

He might need to talk to Doherty and Capello again, so he thought it best not to push the issue for now. Maybe Mama Young would be more forthcoming. "Well, it was good to meet you guys," he said, shaking each right hand in turn. "Thanks for the helping hand. I think I'll stick around for a cup of coffee." His conversation with the young airmen hadn't been a total washout. He'd learned Kincaid frequented

Mama Young's, so a chat with the proprietress seemed his next logical step.

He was the only customer at the bar and Mama Young didn't keep him waiting. "Another beer?"

"Do you have coffee?"

She smiled broadly, exposing an impressive array of strong, if yellowing teeth. "Sure," she said. "Got fresh coffee. Just a minute," and disappeared into the back of the building. She came back from behind the curtained doorway a few seconds later carrying a small cup and saucer. "You like it. Very hot."

"Thank you, Mama. May I ask you a few questions?"

"Why not? Got no customers now." She had not stopped to face him, but continued about her various tasks behind the counter, waiting for this new American to amuse her, no doubt.

"Do you know Reggie Kincaid? Does he come in here?"

She was chopping some kind of vegetable and didn't look up. He figured the old girl might be hard of hearing and raised his voice a bit. "Mama, do you know Reggie Kincaid?"

Still, she ignored him, so he left his seat and moved down the counter until the two were nearly face-to-face. "I'm sorry, Mama. You must not have heard me. I'm trying to find out about an American. His name is Reggie Kincaid. Does he come in here?"

The woman had apparently tuned him out. But why? Dan was completely mystified. He decided to wait her out rather than risk giving offense. He'd come to believe patience is a forgotten virtue in American culture.

He returned to his coffee to let the scenario play out. When the small batch of yellow vegetables had disappeared into a single pyramid of tiny bits, Mama Young walked over to him, still brandishing the gleaming vegetable knife in her left hand. There was no trace of playfulness in her eyes. "He in trouble?" Before he could answer she compounded her question. "Who are you and why you asking about that boy?"

That boy? The woman's offensive posture intrigued and baffled him. "I'm an investigator," he explained. "Airman Kincaid was injured a few nights ago and the Air Force has assigned me to look into it. That's all."

She pointed to his stripes and said, "You not investigator. You goddamn sergeant. Goddamn sergeant not investigator."

She had a point, he thought. Wearing the uniform had been a bad idea all around. How could he explain the nuances of command structure to someone who only spoke GI English? He reached for his wallet and promptly produced his OSI identification card. If she wanted official, he thought, that should do the trick. "Here's my identification. I'm an investigator here from Tachikawa to look into the incident the other night."

Ignoring his overture, the woman returned to her vegetables and began packing them into a metal container. "He all right?" she asked, her tone returning to earth.

"I'm sorry. What did you say?"

"Reggie, he gonna be better?"

It was beginning to make sense. Her use of Kincaid's first name and her concern for his health told Dan his official status was irrelevant to this woman. Kincaid was apparently a friend, and she viewed Dan as some kind of threat to the young man. Hell, she was probably right on the money. "He'll be fine, Mama. In fact, he'll be back up here in a couple of days, good as new. Is he a friend of yours?"

It was as if his last question had reignited the woman's anger. "Why you investigate? What Reggie did wrong? He good boy, always respectful to Mama and Su Li."

She wasn't about to answer his one little question until he'd answered her two. If he wanted any information from this crafty old woman, he'd have to trade for it. Maybe give her just enough to keep her talking. "It's routine in cases like this," he explained. "I need to check out his story and make a report. He doesn't know who hurt him. I'll try to find out. Do you understand?"

"You some kind of FBI?"

Mama Young would be a tough nut to crack. "Just an investigator. Can you tell me what you know about Reggie?"

"Reggie tell you about himself. Why you not ask him?"

Since the pot was already stirring, why turn up the flame and see what boiled over? "Does he sometimes drink too much, Mama?"

Her eyes narrowed and she resumed her attack dog posture. "Why? You try to blame this on him?"

There was no telling what this woman knew, and no way to get to it either, not now anyway. "No. I just want to learn what happened and why. That's all." Exasperated, he said, "Please, just tell me what you know about all this."

She flashed him a scornful look. "I tell you everything I know. Don't know any more. No charge for the coffee."

Dan reached for the big parka, feeling like he'd just been fleeced by a wolf in sheep's clothing. This old woman was clearly beyond intimidation, but it would be pointless for Dan to lose his patience now. He reminded himself her attitude wasn't a reaction against him so much as an expression of her concern for Reggie Kincaid. Why? Somehow, he suspected the answer to that question would go a long way toward completing his investigation. He decided not to antagonize her further and reached for the doorknob. "Thanks for the coffee, Mama. I'm sorry if I offended you."

Su Li could barely restrain herself from bursting through the curtain and breaking a sake bottle over the American policeman's head. She'd carefully listened in on his conversation with her mother, Yoon Hae Young, from their small, but comfortably furnished living space just beyond the curtain. She was relieved to hear that Reggie was going to live.

Despite the tsunami that was her life, Su Li couldn't get Reggie out of her mind. He might easily have died saving her. Had he recognized her? She'd agonized over that question since the other night. If he had, then the entire plan might collapse. It was still impossible to know.

Contrary to the rumors perpetuated by the loud-mouthed drunks from the base, she didn't hate them all. She didn't hate any of them really, but had no intention of ending up like her poor mother, a spouseless outcast in a cruel, foreign land. She could have predicted young Reggie would be the one to save her life at the risk of his own. Well, if the Americans were going to turn on Reggie, they would get no help from Su Li and her mother.

When she heard the door close behind the American policeman, Su Li pulled back the curtain. "Mother," she said in Korean, "why did you even speak with him?" Actually, Su Li had never been to Korea and was more comfortable speaking Japanese, except when she was angry. The two women had always played out their frequent arguments in the Korean tongue, even when Su Li was a little girl. They had always made up in Korean as well. Besides, her mother hated to speak Japanese.

"What did I say? Nothing. I only tried to find out how much he already knows. That's all. I gave him no information."

"It's too dangerous now," Su Li said. "I don't pretend to understand any of it, but Reggie saved my life, and nearly lost his own in the process. Those men would have killed him had we not driven up on them in the truck. They'll go to any length to stop us."

Su Li walked back into the living space and settled into a kitchen chair. Her mother followed. "We still don't know if Reggie recognized you, Su Li," Yoon Hae cautioned.

It was true enough, she knew, but Reggie was still the key to their survival. "We know that if he did," Su Li reasoned, "he didn't let on. Otherwise, the police and heaven knows who else would have come for me by now."

"I think it will be all right," her mother said, placing a hand gently over her daughter's. "But you must not be seen for a few days or so until the bruises on your face heal. You're fortunate the injury was not more serious. Now you must leave this business to others, stronger and more experienced. You have done enough, Su Li."

But the entire business had taken on a life of its own and Yoon Hae did not fully appreciate the complexity of Su Li's role. "I will do what I must, Mother. I have no wish to harm innocents like young Reggie. By now he's told his story about rescuing a woman from attack and being stabbed by the attackers. But who will believe him? There was no body found in the snow. More to the point, no woman came forward to confirm his story and express her gratitude. They'll think he's lying."

"Yes, it appears that way," Yoon Hae conceded.

Reggie Kincaid was only one person. What was the life and welfare of one soul worth when compared to the importance of her mission? And yet Su Li could not abandon her thoughts of the brave American. "What more can they do to him? He nearly bled to death."

"That's what worries me, Su Li. They can do whatever they wish."

Su Li understood only too well her mother's fear. "Yes. What if the Americans are involved in this as well?"

Yoon Hae's expression turned grim. "It's possible. And in that case, God help us all."

"Especially young Reggie," Su Li added.

FOUR

**He's a wily old goat with a temper to boot,
and I don't think you'd ever describe him as cute.**

Tuesday, 9:00 p.m.

Su Li Young and her friend, Ishikawa Yoshihiro, known to his mates as Hiro, moved quickly and quietly through the dark, icy streets of the waterfront. Su Li knew all too well the Port of Wakkanai district was no place for a young woman at night, but the irony amused her. These days it didn't much matter where she was. Trouble seemed to follow her like an old dog; and yet she looked forward to her clandestine meetings with old Captain Nikolai Subarov.

Although Su Li had never been onboard a fishing trawler, her imagination painted a clear picture of the most unhygienic and inhospitable living conditions imaginable. Yet, somehow, Captain Subarov always managed to look clean and distinguished for their infrequent meetings, resplendent in a remarkably unsoiled, gray wool, naval coat with bronze buttons. Su Li guessed his distorted, weather-beaten cap had once sported a matching patent leather bill.

They rounded the darkened corner onto a narrow lane of neon-lit bars. The night was warm for these parts and a cold fog had rolled in from the water, swallowing the snow-covered street in a soupy haze.

Traces of neon on either side marked their path to the O Bar. The drunken chatter of foreigners pierced the fog ahead—Russians, by the sound of them and heading their way. Su Li and Hiro hugged the building and quickened their pace, giving the two unruly Soviets easy passage. The burly fishermen, covered in wool and whiskers, passed slowly but not without comment. Insults were recognizable in any language, Su Li thought. "You need not have come with me, Hiro-san," she whispered, pulling the fur-lined hood back from her head. "The danger is past."

Hiro scoffed. "You have no idea when the danger begins and when it ends, Su Li. I am beginning to think this entire plan will fail and we will all end up in prison—or worse."

She struggled to suppress a flash of anger and stopped to face her friend directly in front of the O Bar. "If we fail, I'll happily go to prison. After all, what is this place to me but a prison?"

Su Li did not need to see Hiro's expression to know she'd hurt him. She felt deeply ashamed, for her young Japanese friend shared in every risk. She touched his sleeve and said, "I'm sorry. I didn't mean to hurt you like that."

Hiro flashed an understanding smile and reached for the door. "I know. Perhaps I, too, am Korean, unknowingly, and my genes are driving me to this madness. Now let's meet your mysterious captain."

As they entered the O Bar, Su Li spotted her captain through the darkness and smoke, entertaining two hostesses in a corner booth. He shoed them away quickly as Su Li and Hiro approached. "It's been too long, Su Li," Subarov said in Japanese, enfolding her in a gentle bear hug. The captain then lifted her chin gently with the palm of his hand and turned it slightly into the dim light. "What happened to your cheek?"

She loved to hear the captain speak. He was the only Russian she had ever known. They had met seven times over the last eighteen months; yet his fluency in Japanese never failed to amuse her. His husky, baritone voice had perfected the improper dialect of the Northern Hokkaido people. Even Su Li herself hadn't done that. If she closed her eyes and just listened, she could easily envision some gregarious Sumo wrestler gorging himself at the evening meal with ritual delight.

"They are only bruises, Captain-san," she replied, "hardly worth mentioning." His enormous hands were rough and callused but gentle, with massive knuckles and joints protruding from under a course, leathery hide. Salty and weathered as he was, the old captain made her feel at ease and as near to safe as she could imagine in these dark days.

Su Li knew the old man had carefully choreographed his appearance to soften it, maybe for her benefit and maybe for his. Probably though, it was a little of both. Choreographed or not, his attention flattered her in a way that made her feel unique and worthwhile, although her instincts warned her of a darker side to this old pirate.

Su Li and Hiro eased into the booth. His presence seemed to draw the smile on her face. "It's good to see you again" she said, "although I thought of you only last week while watching John Wayne in a late night movie. He played a sea captain and each time he opened his mouth to speak in badly dubbed Japanese I couldn't help but laugh."

The captain flashed a quorum of yellow teeth, showcasing his freshly trimmed beard and penetrating, blue eyes. "She mocks me, Boris," he said, "and compares me to some womanly American film star." Boris was the old man's playful, Russian code name for Hiro and the young man obviously delighted in it. "Tell me, Boris, have you managed to steal a kiss from her since my last visit?"

Hiro only blushed. Su Li knew the old man's teasing was good-natured and harmless, but he was undeniably perceptive. Hiro had been in love with her since their school days together. They were life-long friends and Su Li had never given him reason to expect more. A part of her even wished she could return his affection. Still, she had surely taken advantage of his friendship by involving him in such dangerous business.

The captain took a long draw from his beer and the conversation settled to a whisper as smoke swirled around them in the dim light. "Your face tells me all is not well, Su Li-san."

"Not well at all," she admitted. "We were nearly captured. It's very fortunate you didn't send your cargo ashore."

"I couldn't have. The wind shifted a few hours earlier and brought the floating ice and rough seas from the northeast. A landing in those conditions would have spelled disaster."

"It's lucky for all of us," Hiro added. "But where is your cargo?"

Just then the burly bartender appeared at the booth. "All right," he said, "you can't just sit here and gab. What are you drinking?"

"Bring them a beer," the captain replied, "and me as well while you're at it. This one will be gone flat by the time you get back." The bartender sneered and went on his way.

Hiro touched the captain's arm impatiently and said, "Captain-san, where is your cargo?"

The old man grinned again, a mischievous grin this time, but did not answer. His face told Su Li all she needed to know and more than she wanted. It meant the captain had sailed right into a Japanese port with his illicit cargo on board. "You are truly insane," she whispered. "John Wayne would never do such a foolish thing."

"Maybe not so foolish," Hiro said. "Maritime law gives any fishing vessel access to this port for emergency repairs, supplies, and a dozen other reasons, and I can tell you the authorities of the municipality, even the defense forces would never be so bold as to search a Soviet vessel without hard evidence."

"I've told you before, Boris," the old man said playfully, "I'm not a Soviet. I am a Russian." His mood became somber as he returned to the subject at hand. "But we have more important things to discuss."

Su Li decided to raise the unsettling question and leaned forward across the table so as not to be overheard. "How did they know when and where you were arriving?"

"Before the how comes the who," the old captain replied. "The who is Song Hee Choi."

"Who is Song Hee Choi?" Hiro asked.

The bartender's annoying voice interrupted him again. "Hey, you with the beard," he shouted above the music, "I'm not a fucking waitress. Come get your drinks."

Captain Subarov turned to Su Li and handed her a five-thousand yen note. "Would you be so kind as to relieve that loud-mouthed fool of our drinks?"

Su Li was up and back at once, lest she miss the captain's reply. She placed the beers together on the table and whispered, "Then who is Song Hee Choi?"

"He is, or was my first mate and a Sakhalin Korean. He was also a trusted friend and confidant. Fortunately, a little voice told me not to trust him completely. He doesn't know any of you on this side. Song signed on to an oil tanker just before we shipped out from Sakhalin; said he needed the money. It's a sure bet I'll never lay eyes on him again. He sold us out. I should have suspected."

"But others must have known those details," Su Li suggested.

The captain shrugged. "Not a living soul on the Sakhalin side.

Rumors of our activity abound on Sakhalin among the Korean population and travel with the speed and ferocity of a tsunami. Hope cannot be contained in a bottle, Su Li, but very few know or even suspect my involvement. Song and I were the only ones on the Sakhalin side who knew the exact landing place and time. Even the rest of my crew didn't know."

Su Li asked, "Then who is trying to foil our plan?"

The captain hesitated, taking a long, deliberate drink from his fresh beer. When he had drained the glass he flashed a wry smile, his eyes settling on Su Li's untouched brew. "Will you be needing that?"

She pushed the glass across the table and said, "So who is it, Captain-san?"

His mood seemed to darken noticeably. Su Li had never known the captain to worry, but the sight of his furrowed brow unsettled her, for she had no experience in such clandestine matters. She pressed. "Who were the ones who attacked us?"

"There's no way to know," he admitted, "and the thought troubles me. The Japanese? The Russians? It could be either or both."

In her haste, she had forgotten to tell the captain her most disturbing discovery. "Or even the Americans," she declared, suddenly remembering the man lying in the snow.

"What do you mean 'Americans'?"

"Only two of the men who attacked us were Asian," she explained. "One was American. I'm certain of it."

The old captain appeared ready to shake the answer from her mouth. "How do you know? Did you hear him speak?"

"I didn't need to hear him speak. I know Americans, the way they walk, dress, and even fight. He was American."

He seemed to reflect a moment; then his mood lightened. "So we shall add the Americans to our list of possible enemies. One more or less won't deter us." She was pleased to see the captain regain his old swagger. "We'll just proceed with our plan. In the end it won't matter who lines up to stop us. It will be all right. After all, the minnow swims unmolested among the sharks."

Hiro said, "If the Japanese government is involved, why didn't they board and search your vessel?"

Su Li's friend had put words to her own thoughts. The captain said, "They may not know what boat was involved. On the other hand, maybe they're just waiting to ensnare the entire school of fish together."

"That means you might have been followed," Su Li whispered. She felt a fleeting rush of nausea and discreetly scanned the small, smoke-filled establishment, looking for what? A suspicious character? Take your pick, she thought. Almost everyone in this place was hiding from one police agency or another.

"Yes, it does," Captain Subarov said, "and that would put you in grave danger, Su Li."

A part of her knew the gravest risks still lay ahead for all of them, but the immediacy of his observation seemed to bring the danger close enough to touch.

Captain Subarov removed a small hand-drawn map from his inside breast pocket and unfolded it carefully on the table. "Here," he said, pointing to the X. "This is where I'll drop our cargo on Sunday night at the same time. It's exactly sixty-eight kilometers heading west and then south from Cape Noshappu on the main road. This time no one will know but the three of us. This landing point is well onto the western side of Hokkaido where the warmer water of the Sea of Japan will make the landing easier. There will be no floating ice. I'll drop our cargo and return home."

"Be careful, Captain-san," Su Li whispered. "It will be dangerous returning to Sakhalin."

The old man smiled warmly and patted her arm in a comforting gesture. He said, "I'll be all right. An old eel is just as slippery as a young one, only wiser."

Su Li found no comfort in his witticisms and thought briefly about telling him so. She wanted the captain to speak honestly with her, as an equal, but that would never happen. He was a Russian. Still, she could feel his affection to her core, even in this crowded room. It bolstered her and gave her strength. She smiled. "You're a conceited braggart," she said, and braced for the belly laugh that followed.

The captain's voice returned to a sober whisper. "After Sunday night we'll have only one trip left, the most important one. Then we'll be ready to launch the final phase of our plan."

"Captain-san," Su Li said, "we've all placed great faith in you, and I think we've earned your trust in return. Tell us of your final cargo. What is it you have that's so powerful as to alter the fate of so many lives?"

"Soon, Su Li. You will know very soon."

His words had barely registered when Su Li heard the fierce wind announce the arrival of a new patron in the bar. Her eyes followed the short, stocky figure in the doorway as he unbuttoned his coat and shook the snow from his boots. Su Li recognized him even before she saw his face. "Captain-san," she whispered, "it's one of the men who attacked us. He must have followed you here. He's walking toward the bar, just over your right shoulder." In that instant, the man's eyes locked onto Su Li's and she turned away. "He knows I've recognized him. We must get away from here now."

The captain made no attempt to look, but reached over the table and placed his hand gently over Su Li's. His voice was low and rhythmic, clearly intended to have a calming effect. "Listen carefully. You'll be fine. Two of my crewmen are at the bar. In a minute there will be a commotion. The moment it begins, you and Boris will leave quickly and quietly through the backdoor and slip away. We'll proceed with our plan as agreed. Do you understand me?"

Su Li's lips could barely defy the paralyzing fear. "Yes. We understand," she managed to say, her young friend now white with terror. Su Li watched the black-eyed man from the corner of her eye. He propped himself onto a stool with an unobstructed view of their table. The captain had still not turned to see him.

"He's probably alone for the moment," the captain said, "my tail for the evening, but we must assume he's called for backup. There's no time to delay. With luck, we may even discover the identity of those who hunt us."

The captain turned slightly and tipped his glass to a gruff, dark-skinned fisherman at the near end of the long bar. Su Li guessed him to be a Nivkhi, one of the indigenous peoples of Sakhalin and the Kuril Islands. The man watched stoically as the captain rolled his eyes just over his right shoulder. He nodded and whispered something to his friend on the next stool.

"Be ready, now," the captain said, "and godspeed."

Su Li watched as the dark-skinned man walked directly to where the new arrival was seated, waiting for his beer. "You, fuck face," said the Nivkhi in heavily accented Japanese.

The black-eyed man on the barstool gave no indication of hearing the insult.

"You," the Nivkhi repeated, "I'm talking to you, bitch. You stole five thousand yen from me last night, took it right off the bar when I went to take a piss. I want it back."

The man turned to face his accuser. "I'm sorry," he replied. "You're mistaken, but I already have enough enemies." With that, he peeled five bills from a roll and offered them to the Nivkhi. "Take the money." The Nivkhi did not move.

The man on the stool seemed almost to read the mind of his accuser, deciding a fight was unavoidable and determined to strike the first blow. In a lightning move that looked almost choreographed, he spun the barstool violently to the left, planting a wicked kick into the Nivkhi's knee with his right heel. In a flash, he was upon his staggering victim, unleashing a flurry of short, powerful blows.

"Quickly," said the captain, "go."

As Su Li hurried toward the rear exit with Hiro she heard the crash of shattering glass, but did not dare turn to look. She imagined the Nivkhi's companion or her captain had used a beer bottle in an attempt to turn the tide. In a moment, she and Hiro were away and into the freezing darkness of the city.

FIVE

**The forest is in the trees,
but find it on your own if you please.**

Wednesday, 8:00 a.m.

"Wait here, Agent Matthews," said the lanky airman at the Operations Center security post. "Your clearance is approved and I've called for your escort. He should be up in a few minutes."

"Thank you," Dan replied. The Top-Secret Cryptographic security clearance, he had been told, is the highest clearance granted by the Air Force. Dan had never actually read that in any official document, but it was generally accepted as fact throughout the ranks. He suspected that was not the case. When you have real secrets to keep, he reasoned, it makes no sense to publish the names of the people with access to them. He was sure there were higher clearances around, but they didn't talk about them openly and had no use for them at Wakkanai Air Station.

After years of exposure to this Cold War culture of intelligence activity and secret operations, Dan had concluded that nobody's job was as important as the government made it out to be. Of course there were real secrets out there, thousands of them. National Security even demanded some secrets be protected at all cost.

Part of the military's strategy for protecting them was to make every single person involved in intelligence gathering and counterintelligence believe his or her little secret could sink the whole ship if the enemy learned of it. It wasn't true, of course, but Dan had no quarrel with the soundness of the theory. It seemed to have worked well enough over the years.

After only a few minutes at the inside security checkpoint in the shadow of the giant, golf ball-like antenna, a young staff sergeant in starched fatigues appeared from inside the bowels of the complex to greet him. "Good morning," said the affable, young black man. "I'm Elton Bosworth. You must be Agent Matthews."

"My pleasure," Dan replied, already hoping the man would release the vicelike grip on his right hand. Bosworth wasn't a big man, but notable on first impression. He was neat, clean, and snappy, probably no older than twenty-six. It told Dan immediately he was dealing with a man who embraced the military lifestyle and was probably organized and efficient as hell.

"My orders are to accommodate you in any way I can, Agent Matthews," said Bosworth. "Why don't you just call the tune and I'll do my best to make it play."

Dan added discipline to Bosworth's growing list of credits. Somebody told him to meet an OSI agent, show him around and answer his questions. Yet, Bosworth didn't betray a hint of curiosity. "You can call me Dan if you like. May I call you Elton?"

"Sure, Dan, but make it Ellie. What the hell are we anyway but a couple of lifers? My bet is you're a noncom yourself, or else you wouldn't be throwing around your first name."

Dan smiled and resisted the impulse to reply as he hurried to keep up with Ellie's long stride down the funnel-shaped corridor. Lifer? Elton Bosworth seemed a decent enough character, and how would Dan reply anyway? Maybe the man was right and Dan's agony over the question was just a pointless exercise in swimming up stream. "You're right. I'm a staff sergeant, just like you. I have no problem telling you why I'm here, Ellie. I'm investigating the incident the other night involving Reginald Kincaid. I understand he works for you."

"That's right," Ellie said without slowing his pace. "Dog Flight, Russian Language Section. The door to the operations area is just ahead. I'll show you if you like."

"Sure. I guess we can talk while you give me the tour."

Ellie stopped at the large metal doors and turned to Dan. "Well, it won't be a tour, not exactly. There are no limits on access once you're in here, but as a rule we don't wander around areas outside our own workspace. Now if there is something you need to see, my orders are to show you. Come on."

They passed through the doors into what looked like a huge warehouse. Dan had never gotten this far inside the operations building before. He felt like an ant hopelessly lost inside a television set, a very big set. There were wires and machines everywhere, even the bare skeleton of a ceiling was papered with bundles of wiring. They seemed to be walking toward the center of the building. Dan saw a series of gaps in the machinery, geometrically perfect walkways, like spokes on a wheel, leading to the center of the building. There were people all around, most of them enlisted men in fatigues, many seated on sliding chairs wearing headsets with microphones. They were all fiddling with machinery or radios of some kind. Row after row of five-foot, metal racks filled the aisles on both sides, each crammed with electronic equipment or devices. At the far end of each aisle, Dan could see a plain, metal desk, each occupied by an NCO, noncommissioned officer. They were probably the flight leaders.

As they moved closer to the center, he noticed several aisles lined with reel-to-reel tape players, installed at eye level over a long, counterlike desktop. Typewriters lined the counter, one directly under every playback device. Curious, Dan stopped to watch the men at work.

"Russian linguists," Ellie said. "After they get something on tape over at the recording stations, they bring the tape over here and transcribe it onto paper."

"You mean those are Russian language typewriters?"

"Most of them. We call them Cyrillic."

It really shouldn't have surprised him. "Can you tell me what they're listening to?"

"Sure. There are no restrictions on your clearance. They monitor all kinds of enemy communications: Bear bomber exercises, MIG-19s, even the new MIG-21s. They track other things too, like cosmonauts, when they're up, and naval communications."

"So this is what Kincaid does?"

"And does it very well, I might add," Ellie answered. "Dog Flight's station is back there a few aisles, just beyond the Morse operators. Come on. I'll show you."

Ellie was off again with Dan in tow. "So do you speak Russian too?"

"We don't really speak it as much as understand it. And I'd say nobody understands it as well as Airman Kincaid. He's kind of our resident genius." Ellie stopped and turned toward the aisle on his left, providing Dan with a chance to catch his breath. "This is it. You heard about the two Soviet cosmonauts killed in reentry a couple of months ago?"

"Who didn't?"

"Well, thanks to Kincaid, we knew about it forty minutes before the Soviets did."

Dan found himself keenly interested in Bosworth's last revelation. "How did that happen?"

"We monitor the communications as the orbiting craft passes into our range. Part of the time we're hearing it while the Soviets can't. When they were getting ready for reentry, one of our operators heard a series of panicky transmissions. They were impossible to understand. Well, we thought so anyway."

Dan, like everyone else with half a brain, had figured out that the massive antenna was used to eavesdrop on air traffic. The disclosure regarding the Soviet cosmonauts was a complete surprise. "And what did Kincaid have to do with that?"

"The flight leader on duty sent someone over to the barracks to wake him up. He was stone drunk. They poured a pot of coffee down his gullet and slapped the headset on him. He translated the whole thing perfectly in fifteen minutes. It was an actual recording of the cosmonauts struggling to seal the hatch, a recording of their deaths you might say. It was a sad thing. That was the only 'Critic' message we've ever sent since I've been here. And young Airman Kincaid won himself a medal."

"What's 'Critic?'"

"It means we sent a direct message via the National Security Agency to the President."

That was impressive. "Of the United States?"

"Richard M. Nixon himself. I assume they had to wake him up. It was pretty early in the morning back in the world."

Dan was pleased. He had pretty much sized up this Kincaid to a tee during the brief interview at the hospital. He said, "Kincaid's a pretty bright kid, I guess."

"He's a good man, but we have others too. Come on."

At the end of the aisle they emerged into an enormous, circular space, set up as a kind of command and control center. It was filled with wall-size plotting boards and tables, obviously the place where raw intelligence was coordinated to plot the position of Soviet air, land, and naval forces in the area at any given moment. "This is where we put some of it together and make sense out of it," Ellie said. "There's a little snack bar over there if you want a drink or something." He was already moving.

Dan smiled. "Sure, and I'm buying. So, aside from the fact that he's good at his job, what kind of airman is Kincaid?"

Ellie hesitated. He appeared to reflect on the question for a moment. "That's a more difficult question."

"How?"

"I guess you could say he's a loner. I'm not a drinker or nightlife guy myself, but I make it my business to know my men. Kincaid doesn't have any close friends in operations. Oh, don't get me wrong; he's not antisocial or an asshole or anything. He's friendly enough if you talk to him and always willing to help out. It's just that he's, well, I don't know, kind of distant." Ellie turned into a little cubicle housing a few tables and some candy and soda machines along the walls.

Dan dropped his first quarter into the soda machine. "What's your poison, Ellie?"

"You choose, but nothing with strawberry. Thanks."

After getting one for himself, he handed Ellie the soda bottle and said, "That's interesting, about him being distant I mean. But have you ever seem him behave oddly, you know, bizarre or off the wall?"

"You mean whacko, don't you?"

Ellie didn't quite get the drift, not yet. "I suppose I do, in a way. I know where you're going with that, although I don't know why. The answer, in all honesty, is I don't know. He's strange, for sure, but in the end I'd say I like the kid and I trust him."

Dan pointed to a table. "Can you sit for a minute?"

Ellie shrugged. "It's your dime."

Grateful to be off his feet, Dan took a long swig of soda and said, "So what do you mean by strange?"

"I don't see him as a nut job who would hurt himself. That's why you're here, isn't it?"

This was the part he'd dreaded most. "I'm just investigating, Ellie. That's all. I don't have an agenda." He wanted to be honest with Bosworth, and the fact that he couldn't made him feel unclean.

Ellie seemed to be satisfied. "Look, Kincaid's not military, not like you and me, but I get the sense he really likes this place, Wakkanai I mean. Maybe like is the wrong word. Could be he's just comfortable here. It's like he'd be happy just to blend in here and fade away. It's very unusual because it's such a harsh and foreign place to Americans."

It sounded like Kincaid at least had a clear sense of where he belonged. It was enviable in a way. Ellie wasn't taking the hint, so Dan would have to be more direct. "I know this may be uncomfortable, Ellie, but I need to know about his personal habits. Can you shed any light at all on his lifestyle?" He'd used the most inoffensive language he could find, but still felt soiled because there was no way to camouflage the message.

The affability drained from Bosworth's face, and Dan was now facing the dedicated young protector of even younger men, his men. He rose slowly from the chair and said, "So all this was just to get me to tell you he's a cocksucker? Is that what's going on here? You're looking to put this thing on him? Is that it?"

That's exactly what he was looking to do. Ain't I a peach of a guy? He wanted to say. "That's not what's going on here, but it's a base I have to cover."

"Well, let me tell you something, Agent Matthews," Bosworth said, "I run Dog Flight. I can tell dog shit when I see it and bullshit when I hear it. I think I've already said more than I should have. As far as I'm concerned, I've followed my orders to the letter and they don't include helping you or anyone else railroad my man. So, if you have any other official requests of me, make them now. If not, get the fuck out of my face and leave your pass at the gate."

Hawaii was looking better and better by the minute. Maybe he'd have better luck with the Security Police.

Dan managed to track down Airman First Class Buford Rockwell in the mess hall as the man was downing an early lunch. Not wanting to startle the youngster, he went through the chow line, scooping up a ready-made ham sandwich and a big glass of cold milk. When he couldn't produce a meal card at the checkout, Dan was forced to fork over eighty-five cents for the lunch. Rockwell was still sitting alone as Dan approached and said, "Mind if I join you for lunch?"

"I've got plenty of friends," the man replied, "but suit yourself."

"Actually, I tracked you down here. I'm Agent Matthews from OSI and I'd like to ask you a few questions about the incident at the main gate a few nights ago."

"Yeah, somebody said you was lookin' for me," the airman replied. "Do I need me a lawyer?"

The question surprised Dan. "Why would you need a lawyer?"

"My CO was hotter 'n a grease fire; said I'm under investigation for dereliction of duty. I guess they think I messed up with them folks in the truck and such."

"What does your CO think you should have done?"

Rockwell shrugged his shoulders. "I guess ol' Cap'n Weber thinks I shoulda scooped those boys up, if they was boys."

"Don't worry about that now. That's not why I'm here, and I won't hurt you over that. Captain won't either, for that matter."

"Then what are you here for?"

Dan tried to ignore the mayonnaise oozing from the corner of the man's mouth. "I've read your report. It says you weren't able to identify the truck that dropped Kincaid off. It only says it was a small truck. It doesn't even say color. There's nothing in there about that. Can you remember anything else about the truck?"

Rockwell laughed, loud enough to attract attention from neighboring tables. "I'm from Texas, Agent Matthews. To me all these trucks and cars is small. I couldn't tell the color. The snow kind of plays tricks on your eyes at night. Hey, can you hand me the fucking salt there?"

Dan handed over the plastic container. "Did you actually see it stop?"

"No. I was in the shack. The snow is piled so high out there I didn't even see the truck pull up. The guy must have had his headlights off. I noticed the light over the embankment when the headlights went back on."

"So then what?"

"Well, sir, then I ran out an' I seen Kincaid propped up nice'n neat against the snow bank. There was a man with his back to me headin' back to the truck. He was wearin' a hood."

"What about Kincaid's wound?" Dan asked. "I understand it was bandaged."

"I wouldn't say bandaged, more like wrapped, I guess. Oh, there was blood on his shirt all right, but somebody had wrapped the wound tight and left the shirt unbuttoned."

The latter revelation had been left out of the report, but Dan found it significant. It was one thing to drop the wounded man back at the base. Someone might do that simply to avoid a murder charge. But carefully dressing the wound? That represented a higher, more personal level of assistance, like someone that night actually knew or cared about our Airman Kincaid. He said, "How was the wound dressed?"

"Almost looked like real bandages to me. There was a strip of white cloth wrapped tight all around his belly. Hey, I gotta' go and get me some more milk. Can this wait a minute?"

Dan held up his palm. "I'll be out of your hair in a second, just a couple more questions. What happened to the wrappings? Did you inventory them according to the protocol?"

"Sure did."

Physical evidence never lied, Dan knew, but it didn't always talk. "When you're finished eating, would you mind meeting me over at headquarters so we can take a look at the physical evidence?"

Rockwell nodded. "Sure. It's just the bandages, his parka, and some clothes. But I'll meet you over there."

"Thanks. Tell me, was he unconscious when you found him?" The report had been silent on that question.

"Pretty much."

It sounded a lot like no. "What does that mean?"

"Well, for the most part he was out. But it's funny; it looked like he was smiling. He was kind of moaning a little every now and then while we was waiting for transport."

Funny? "And what was funny?"

"Well, sir, not funny ha-ha like, just a little strange. I think he called me Chuckie while I was a settin' there with him."

This was a great example of why you couldn't trust military reports, Dan thought. He knew from the protocol that this lowly airman didn't prepare the incident report on the Kincaid stabbing. He simply told his story to a superior with administrative responsibility.

This was business as usual to Dan and a prime reason why he never formed opinions until he personally interviewed the witnesses. He said, "Chuckie? He called you Chuckie?"

"Yep, it was Chuckie. No doubt about it."

Dan figured the reference to "Chuckie" had been omitted from the report out of sheer laziness. It seemed to fit well with the command predisposition that Kincaid was a homosexual. It might even prove to be Dan's first clue that Coughlin was right. "Tell me," he said, "just out of curiosity. What did your CO expect you to do to the guy in the hood, shoot him?"

Rockwell forced the last of the sandwich down his gullet and wiped his mouth with a sleeve. "I guess I don't rightly know. He didn't tell me that. He just told me I should be ready to accept an Article Fifteen punishment for my actions. It'll probably cost me a stripe and a month's pay."

And it probably would have. "Trust me. It won't happen. Your actions in this matter were appropriate and professional and my report will reflect that. Once your CO sees it, you'll never hear about this again."

"Damn," said the young man. "You're a good ol' boy, Agent Matthews."

"Don't think nothin' of it, partner."

SIX

**The smooth talkers tried every trick they could muster,
but the skinny, young kid her defenses did fluster.**

Thursday evening

Reggie did not seem impressed by Cape Soya, Su Li thought, as the two stood defiantly on the point, the frozen wind howling unmolested down from the Sea of Okhotsk. After all, there were hundreds of similar coastal peninsulas all over the island. The difference was this one marked the northern most point in Japan. From in front of the massive, stone monument, they stared out into the blackness of the Soya Strait, punctuated only by a ragged string of tiny lights in the distance. Reggie's focused silence told her he understood the importance of what was to come. He seemed to have a sense for the unspoken word, unusual in an American.

At twenty-five, Su Li had long since mastered the art of dealing with the never-ending waves of American airmen that supported the family's meager existence and howled through their lives like the Cape Soya wind. She understood only too well her skills had been acquired at the expense of bitter tears and wrenching heartbreak.

Su Li had more reason than most to resent these obscenely wealthy, foreign invaders who, night after night, groped her for amusement, insulted her in drunken tirade, and spread vile lies impugning her virtue and character.

At seventeen, in defiance of her mother's warnings, she had fallen desperately in love with a dashing, young, American sergeant from Brooklyn in the U.S.A. She gave Paul Greenberg her virginity, willingly and without reservation with all the passion in her soul. Such was the depth of her commitment that she never questioned his promise to send for her upon his return to Brooklyn. For over a year her letters were returned unopened. Still, she kept them in her tiny box of treasures, every one a tribute to the treachery of the human heart.

Despite these things, Su Li could not deny that her life and that of her mother were inextricably bound to these men, by blood and by necessity. In the end, were the Americans not their only protection from the subtle tyranny of their jailers, the Japanese? But unlike the Americans, whose exile to the shores of this unforgiving place was measured in months, Su Li's exile might well be eternal. Reggie was one of them, certainly; yet there was something about him that seemed almost…well, Korean.

Su Li had nearly died laughing the first time she saw him last year, although good manners had concealed her laughter from all but herself. It had been a particularly miserable night and Su Li was surprised that anyone would venture from the base on such a night. But in he walked, a brand new face beneath an old parka, and cracked his head on the top of the doorframe. He fell backward into the deep snow, out cold. Her mother revived him there in the snow and tended to the cut on his forehead. Recovered, he rose to his feet, forcing a pathetic smile, and promptly reenacted his painful folly.

In the intervening year, Reggie had wandered into the restaurant regularly in the wee hours for a meal, loaded to the gills on the way home from his nightly excursion to the bar district. He always tipped Su Li appropriately when he had money and had even brought them both little gifts from time to time.

Su Li thought him a gentle soul, incapable of raising his voice, a rare mixture in an American. For whatever dark reason, Reggie did not treat himself with the same respect. It had been difficult not to show affection for such a person, but Su Li's ordered life depended upon strict conformance to her self-imposed rules.

Reggie's welcomed appearance at the restaurant earlier that evening had given birth to an idea. Su Li had never been one to act impulsively, but felt a strong bond with this quiet stranger who had risked his own life to save her. The hell with the rules tonight, she'd thought. She had never seen Reggie with a woman, but in some things Su Li was wise beyond her years. She knew he would not require coaxing.

"Reggie-san," she'd said playfully, "you've been here more than a year, yet you have only seen bars."

"How do you know what I've seen? I get around this town, you know."

The false bravado had only made him more attractive to her. In that moment he had been to Su Li honesty and innocence themselves. For an instant she'd wanted to be seventeen again and to be naïve. She could never again be those things, but could surely cherish them in others. He might have died for her that night. Worse, he might have died for someone else, and his act of bravery would then have died with him. Tonight he would receive his just reward, she'd decided.

Su Li might easily have told Reggie to meet her down the road while she slipped out the back door, but his reputation was in need of rebuilding. She'd come out into the restaurant from the living quarters wearing her parka, and in full view of her American customers, had taken Reggie's hand and led him to the front door, every eye in the small restaurant and bar in tow.

Now, standing near the edge of a rocky cliff, Su Li turned back from the distant lights and broke their long silence. "That's Sakhalin Island out there. We don't often see the lights."

Reggie answered without turning his eyes from the horizon. "I know. We get a good view from the hill at the base. I wonder how something so foreign and dangerous can be that close. It looks like just another island out there, but I know it's the enemy, the Soviet Union. There are military bases over there with planes and troops just waiting for the chance to go to war with us. Most of the time it all just seems like a game, except when I look out on the island like this. Seeing it makes the terrible possibilities more real."

She took his arm in hers. This was as good a time as any. "I must tell you something, Reggie-san."

He turned to face her and shrugged. "I already know. You were the woman in the alley that night, but it's all right."

It was the last thing Su Li expected to hear and it rocked her. "How did you know? How long have you known?"

"A while, I guess."

"Come. Let's sit," she said, leading him around the triangular, Soya Point monument, to where they would be protected from the fierce wind. They sat on a step, backs to the stone pillar. "Tell me how you knew."

"Well, I started thinking about it in the hospital. I kept reliving it over and over and each time I saw the woman's face clearer. But I wasn't sure until I saw the bruises on your cheek tonight. I wouldn't have noticed them if I hadn't been looking."

Su Li was barely listening to the last part. She was thinking of the important question. Somehow she knew the answer and needed to confront the guilt it would bring. "If you knew I was the one to confirm your story, why didn't you tell the authorities? Why don't you run to tell them now? Why would you be with such a person of your own free will?" She turned back toward the dark sea and fought to hold back tears.

Reggie shrugged. "I figured you had a good reason. You also saved my life and I think that counts for something."

His answer only made her feel worse, like she had selfishly taken a part of him and used it for her own purpose. She sprang to her feet, stepped out into the wind and it nearly toppled her. Reggie locked onto her arm and began to lead her back toward the waiting taxi. "You don't understand," she said. "I can never admit to being there."

"I don't recall asking you to."

Su Li smiled. This man was both young and inexperienced, but she sensed a maturity beyond his years, or something else. "You are a very unusual man, Reggie-san. I think you have been fooling everyone. You are not American at all. Maybe you are the incarnation of a samurai warrior, pure and noble." The smile faded as the grim reality of her situation took hold. "The Japanese would have done well not to abandon the samurai code in favor of Tojo and his predecessors."

A look of bewilderment flashed in Reggie's eyes as he opened the taxi door and said, "Why do you dislike the Japanese so?"

Su Li did not know where to begin. "I don't dislike them at all. This is the only land I've ever known and I've met many good Japanese people here." She wondered how to make an American understand. The beginning seemed the only place to start. "Did you know I was born here in Japan?"

"No."

Su Li leaned forward and said to the taxi driver in Japanese, "All right, thank you for staying with us. You may drop us at our destination now."

The man bowed but did not turn back. "Yes, of course, I understand."

She turned back to her young American and took his hand. He was so foreign to everything she knew, to everything she believed in. An explanation would be very difficult. "I was born right here in Wakkanai; yet I am not a citizen of Japan and cannot become one."

"Why?"

She sighed. "You are a good person and very bright, Reggie-san, but there is so much you don't understand. The Japanese despise things that are different. They want everything and everyone to be the same."

"What does that mean?"

Even she did not understand, not fully. "They would like my mother and me to change our names to Japanese names and blend into this beehive of a society. We will always be aliens in this country, and we can't leave because we have nowhere to go. We are citizens of nowhere." Hearing herself say what she knew so well made Su Li want to cry, and she was determined this would not be a night for tears.

"I'm sorry. I didn't know any of that." He began to look out the windows, left and right. "Where are we going? The air base is the other way."

Su Li smiled a mischievous smile. "Aren't you tired of the base? You spend most of your time there. Anyway, I have one more thing to show you and it's not even midnight."

Su Li expected him to shrug once again and was amused when he obliged. Reggie was so predictable in some ways. "Why not? I'm up for a little adventure. Go head. Finish your story. I'd like to know why you can't be a citizen if you were born here."

"This is not America, Reggie-san, where oppressed peoples flock to escape their oppressors and find a better life. My mother didn't come here of her own accord. She was kidnapped from her village in Korea by Japanese soldiers in 1938 and brought forcibly to work in their war factories on Karafuto. She was twenty-one the day she was taken and has never seen her family since."

"What is Karafuto?"

Su Li pointed out the window to her left, onto the black water, toward the specks of light, disappearing again in deteriorating weather. "Over the water there. It's the very place you fear. Karafuto was the Japanese name for the south half of Sakhalin Island before 1945. The place was a Japanese territory for over three decades before the end of the war. The Japanese and Russians have slaughtered each other for generations over control of that wretched piece of frozen rock. It has changed masters many times."

"What's going on, Su Li? Whatever it is, you can tell me."

She wondered if it were so. "In order to understand what is happening now, you must understand what happened long ago. It's difficult to say how many of my people were taken to Karafuto in those years, perhaps as many as seventy-five thousand."

"What do you mean, taken?"

Like most of the world, this well-intentioned American had no clue. "There were over a million in all abducted from their homes in Korea by the Japanese conquerors and employed as forced laborers all over Japan."

"I've never heard of that," he declared. "What happened to them?"

"We know for certain that many thousands died before the end of the war as a result of the most inhumane living conditions imaginable. Many more thousands have died on Sakhalin since the Soviets came in 1945."

Reggie wrapped his long arm around her shoulder and pulled her close as the buildings along the road and up the hills became fewer and fewer. "What happened after the war?"

That was the saddest part of all. "In the closing days of the war, there was a great battle for control of the island. Before they were defeated by the Soviets, the Japanese brought several thousand of the forced-laborers, including my mother, here to Hokkaido to work in the factories. The rest they left to the mercy of Stalin. Many are still here on Hokkaido with their children because they can't obtain visas from the government of South Korea."

"And what about the others? What happened to them?"

She turned her eyes out to sea again in the direction of the Sakhalin coast. If only she knew, really knew. "Most are buried over there. The rest, as many as ten or twenty thousand are still there, along with their children, still prisoners, though their jailers now speak Russian."

"I don't understand. You mean the Japanese just left them there and the Soviets didn't send them back?"

"Yes. When the Soviets occupied the southern part of the island in 1945, many of the Japanese had already fled to Hokkaido. There was a shortage of workers to run the coal mines and timber mills. The Soviets simply put the Koreans to work. They've been over there working and dying in squalid conditions ever since."

"Well, if the American government knew—"

"They do know," Su Li countered. "All the world's major governments know. The Red Cross has tried for years to bring their plight to the world stage, but the governments have their own agendas."

"It's almost beyond belief, Su Li."

"It's true," she assured him. "The Soviets won't send them back because they would have to admit twenty-five years of abuse. The Americans don't want them returned because they won't embarrass the Soviets and jeopardize the chance of improving relations. The Japanese are just waiting patiently for the whole story to die along with the survivors."

"What about the South Koreans?"

That had been the bitterest pill for her to swallow. "You've touched upon the greatest tragedy, Reggie-san, and I'm not sure I have an answer. Park Jung Hee is a paranoid dictator, obsessed with anticommunism. He fears he would be repatriating thousands of potential enemy agents. I can't think of any other reason for him not to help. And so my people sit and suffer and die on Sakhalin."

Reggie seemed not to notice the taxi slowing as it approached a one-story, frame building thirty yards or so off the road, on a gentle upslope. Were it not for the lights from inside, Su Li herself would have passed it unnoticed in the virgin snow. "Why are you telling me this, Su Li?" he asked softly.

It was the question she had repeatedly asked herself. Su Li had taken a risk in telling all this to Reggie. She must have done it purely from a sense of obligation and gratitude, for it made no sense. She expected nothing from this man but that he understand the value of his single act of courage. If she misjudged him, the entire plan, years of preparation, might all be in jeopardy. If she stopped now, she could contain the damage. Instead, she decided to follow her heart as she had not for so many years. "Because, Reggie-san, my friends and I are going to send them home to South Korea."

Her young man appeared confused. "All of them?"

"All who want to leave, and those stranded in this Japanese purgatory as well. Our plan is to embarrass the world's major governments into taking action by mobilizing the world press to our cause. The South Korean government wouldn't dare reject us in the face of international pressure. After all, they are Korean."

She handed the driver a handful of hundred-yen notes and said, "Thank you. You don't need to wait."

As they stepped from the taxi, Reggie seemed still not to care where they were going. "And just how do you propose to bring home thousands of Korean captives?" he asked.

"With luck, timing, and careful planning. At the appropriate time several hundred Koreans will converge on the United States Consulate in Sapporo under the eye of the world press. One of our group works for a newspaper. He will help." They were alone on the icy road with only the lights of the building to guide them. "There, just ahead," she said, "steps cut into the ice."

Reggie followed her lead up the icy path. "But why the cloak and dagger? Why is that necessary if we're talking about a simple demonstration?"

She knew this was the point of no return. "Because some of the Koreans will be from Sakhalin Island."

"I see. Well, that explains the ruckus on the waterfront. But I don't see how a demonstration with a group of refuges will generate the splash you're looking for. There are hundreds of demonstrations all across Sapporo every week. Why would this one spark any particular attention?"

She stopped on the last step, just in front of the snow-blanketed building. His barrage of focused questions made her regret the decision to confide in him. But it was too late to stop, although his impartial, honest assessment did little to quiet her anxiety. "We will have more than the people. We'll have something with enough power to embarrass the great nations of the world to action."

He turned to face her. "What?"

The conversation had been steering toward this moment from the first; still, a wave of panic seized her. She knew their plan was only as good as Nikolai Subarov's word. Su Li had wagered everything on the old Russian pirate, even the lives of her friends, and without any knowledge of the carefully crafted plan, Reggie had skillfully targeted her greatest fear. "I don't know," she admitted.

Reggie said nothing. She could see his brown eyes narrow with worry and locked on the now invisible outline of the Soviet coast beyond, still forty-three kilometers from Cape Soya, but somehow closer and more menacing than ever. He turned back to her as if awakening from a dream. "Say, where are we anyway? We're pretty far out of the city. What is this place?"

She smiled, took his arm and squeezed, leading him toward the doorway of the nearly buried building. "You will soon see," she replied, certain he could not detect her smile through the parka. "Thank you for saving me."

Even in the blowing snow she could feel him flinch. "Believe me, if you saw what I did, it wouldn't have impressed you. I just got their attention and made them chase me. That's all." Then he said in a barely audible voice, "Running is what I do best."

Yes, Reggie Kincaid was truly a soul in need of repair. "Come," she said, "I will change your mind."

Her young GI blushed with embarrassment as he whisked passed the hostess at the hotel reception desk ahead of Su Li. He had to stop because he didn't know which of the two hallways to enter. Su Li covered her mouth to conceal her amusement as the hostess counted out the three thousand yen and directed her to the room. There were only four or five in the entire place and the lovers appeared to be the only guests this night.

The tiny room was almost completely empty, save a small, lighted lamp-table and a futon. Reggie shed his parka and reached for the light, but Su Li touched his arm gently. "No, Reggie-san," she whispered in his ear. "Please, leave the light on."

Reggie began to speak, but she placed her finger gently over his lips. "Shhh."

Slowly, she began to unbutton his flannel shirt. It floated to the floor behind her. Su Li could hear his labored breathing as she began to undue his trousers, her soft, brown hair nuzzling the muscles of his abdomen and thighs. He was hard now and it pleased and excited her.

She wanted him to see her naked flesh, to feel and to remember. Su Li stood unashamedly before her hungry man-child and slowly removed her blouse and skirt, letting them fall to the floor. If he lived to be one hundred, this brave, young soul, he would remember her always. He must. She reached for Reggie's large, soft hand and placed it on her firm, rounded breast. She did not speak, for what could she say? His hand quivered and it told her all she needed to know. What would they speak of anyway but tomorrow, and for Su Li tomorrow did not exist. Surely this was a mistake, all of it, but she did not hesitate or waiver. It was right and it was good tonight.

SEVEN

**There once was a tail, and people say he wagged the pup;
but when he tried it with a tiger, it was clear the jig was up.**

Sunday, 5:30 p.m.

Agent Chung Hok Kim of the South Korean CIA waited for Lance Foster in a rented sedan parked just outside the terminal building at Wakkanai Municipal Airport. Even though they had only met once, Chung easily identified the less-than-rugged figure of his middle-aged NSA contact among the dozen or so arriving passengers. The sling supporting Foster's left arm confirmed the identification and Chung pulled the car up to meet him.

"Nice to see you again, Chung," Foster said, pulling back his hood as he crammed into the small car.

"Good day, Mr. Foster," Chung replied. He wondered why Americans always felt the need to be polite. He preferred the chilling sincerity of the North Koreans. In truth, he just didn't like Americans, although his previous experience was limited to a couple of small, joint operations with his American counterparts from the CIA. He'd found them to be undisciplined and generally more concerned with guidelines and protocol than results. Chung swung the car from its parking space and headed back toward the city, a gently blowing snow clearing his way.

Americans, he thought. More than once he had been dispatched to South Vietnam to perform some simple, if unpleasant mission or other for them. It had generally involved the interrogation of sensitive prisoners when the CIA felt the need to withhold information from their South Vietnamese allies. The Americans routinely employed torture as a tool of interrogation, but lacked the courage to dirty their own hands at the task.

This time it would be different, he thought. His mission was strictly a Korean operation and his orders specified the Americans were involved only in an advisory capacity. Chung relished the opportunity to show this paunchy, double-chinned liaison officer from the National Security Agency how to execute an efficient intelligence operation.

"How the fuck can people live here?" Foster asked. "Does it always snow like this?"

Foster amused him. This assignment might bring some personal satisfaction as a bonus. "The locals consider this a clear, mild day. I imagine you'll be here long enough to learn."

Foster huffed. "I sincerely hope not."

As far as Chung was concerned, they could complete any mission successfully without American help, but his superiors disagreed. He was forced to concede they could be right because America's intelligence assets were formidable. And this time it might even be fun because Chung was the agent in charge. "How is the arm?" It was a pity this fool only broke his arm and not his neck. He should leave the real work to professionals.

"It's better. It wasn't broken, but it will take some time to heal. How goes it with you, Chung?"

It annoyed Chung that this arrogant American, nearly a total stranger, would presume to use his first name. "Very well, thank you."

The route into the city took them directly past Soya Point and Chung saw the opportunity to educate the American agent. "Do you see the monument over there? That marks the end of the free world."

Foster shook his head. "I could care less about geography. I just want to wrap this assignment up and get the fuck out of here."

"We've been very busy here since you left for Tokyo," said Chung. "Subarov actually made port in Wakkanai two nights ago."

"What? Then you have him? You have all of them?"

They would have, were it not for Foster's own bumbling incompetence that night in the alley. "Not quite, but soon, very soon."

Foster pressed. "Well, what happened then?"

Chung slowed the sedan to a crawl near Wakkanai Port so as not to miss his turn in the snow. "One of my men was watching the docks when Subarov's boat came in. He followed the old Russian to a sleazy bar in the port district. It appeared he was alone. After a while a young woman and a Japanese man met with him at the bar."

"Was it the woman who escaped us?"

Dealing with this fool on a daily basis might prove the ultimate test of patience. "The very same. Unfortunately, they recognized my agent and the woman escaped with the help of Subarov and his crew. They sailed out of port three hours later."

"I thought you said he was alone," Foster prompted.

Americans only wanted to talk, not listen. Chung followed the left fork toward the business district. "I said he appeared to be alone. Subarov may not be a professional, but he's very clever. They staged a brawl and my man was fortunate to escape before the police arrived. Had they discovered his identity, or lack of one, it would have spelled big trouble."

"Sounds like Subarov would have liked to get his hands on your man."

Chung nodded. "No doubt, but he couldn't afford to wait for the police either."

"Then it was just another dead end," Foster declared. "So what's your plan now?"

"We're working on a few leads," Chung replied, forcing restraint, "trying to identify the players."

"I think it would be best to focus on learning the identity of the woman," Foster said, sounding more like a schoolmaster than a colleague. Chung held his temper in check.

As the small car drew nearer the city, fishing shacks and drying houses gave way to snow-covered houses and small shops on both sides of the road. Foster said, "Jesus Christ, do people actually live in those igloos?"

Chung had come to know many Christians in the service of his country, mostly Americans, but had never been able to understand why they so frequently invoked the name of their great prophet in anger or sarcasm. "Yes," he said. "Fishermen mostly. Without fishing, this place would be a frozen wasteland."

Foster chuckled. "Oh, really? And what is it now?"

Disrespect seemed to be a cultural trait among Americans, Chung had long ago concluded. "I'm not here to make judgments about Japan or its people. I'm here to complete a mission."

Chung could feel the glare of the American's eyes in the passenger seat beside him. The man was considering how to deal with the bold rebuke. "Right," Foster said in a capitulating tone. "I think we should start by identifying the woman. Don't you agree?"

Chung savored the rush of satisfaction. "We shall see." Just like an American, he thought, trying to pull the strings of his little Asian buddy. The Americans could hijack his operation at any time, and Chung knew it. He also knew if the CIA were caught running a covert op on Japanese soil, the damage to U.S.-Japanese relations could be catastrophic and might even jeopardize the U.S. bases in Japan.

Letting the Koreans handle it was the safest way for the Americans. Foster was running a bluff in suggesting operational plans, Chung figured. The American would only go so far as Chung allowed, and he intended to hold a tight rein on this potbellied cowboy. This time he would show the Americans what it takes to win a war.

Still, there was no point in completely alienating Foster at this juncture. The Americans might yet prove useful. Chung decided to temper his approach. "We'll track them down, Mr. Foster, all of them. You may assure your people of that." Chung knew full well that all the determination in the world would be useless energy unless he could outwit the annoying Russian captain.

"I'm sure you will," said Foster.

They were in the heart of the city now, and Chung turned left at the train station onto a narrow lane, toward Foster's hotel. The International was the only Western style hotel in the city, and Chung regretted booking Foster into it; a tactical mistake, he concluded. It would have driven this American crazy to sleep on the floor and wait in line to shit in a hole, rather than have a comfortable American toilet in his room.

"Would you like to come along again and assist us in the field work, Mr. Foster?" Next time this fool might break his neck. Sarcasm was an American weapon, but Chung had long prided himself on his ability to adapt.

"No, thanks. You just get the information however you see fit. I've had my fill of operational work for a while. Besides, NSA doesn't want me to take any chance that might expose their involvement. What more do you have on Subarov?"

"There is nothing more from our people on Sakhalin. Nikolai Subarov is operating within a very tight circle. As you know, our most highly placed agent was forced to withdraw. We have others trying to learn the woman's identity, but so far without success. We must find her. She is the key."

"Well, they sent an OSI agent up here a few days ago to investigate the kid who interfered that night. He's an enlisted man, not an officer."

"Does that make a difference?" Chung asked.

Foster laughed, his mouth wide open, exposing a pair of unsightly tonsils to the world. "Of course. They did that intentionally because enlisted personnel are generally not very bright and never engage in independent thought; you know, easy to control. I'm sure he'll do as he was told."

"In the South Korean Army everyone does as he is told."

Chung stopped the car in front of a nondescript, three-story building in faded, white stucco. "What the fuck is this?" Foster bellowed.

Now Chung really regretted his mistake in trying to accommodate this self-indulgent fool. "This is your hotel, the finest Western hotel this side of Sapporo I am told." He pointed to the gold lettering on the door reading, International Hotel.

"Told by who? Russian agents?"

Foster got out of the car and stood in front of the building, as if waiting for Chung to remove his bag from the back. Chung leaned toward the passenger window and smiled. "I'll park the car and join you in your room. I have a few questions myself."

The American's frown announced his displeasure as he retrieved the bag and disappeared into the hotel without reply.

Chung had not yet knocked when the door to room 206 opened. "Can you believe this?" Foster said, neglecting to even invite Chung inside. He inferred an invitation and stepped into the comfortably appointed room. "I have a fucking closet bigger than this." Then Foster opened the door to the bathroom and said, "Look at this. I'll get claustrophobic taking a shit in here, never mind a shower."

Chung wondered how much room a person needed to take a shit, and sitting down no less. "Terrible," he replied. "But I'm interested in this American agent you mentioned. Why are you so sure he won't find out anything?"

"I just mean he won't ask any questions. For now, he claims Kincaid has no idea who helped him back to the base that night."

"Who is Kincaid?"

"He's the American kid you stabbed," Foster replied coldly. "This agent, Matthews is his name, is moving a little slowly and may require some prodding. But I'll take care of that."

"Please see that you do." He had chosen his words carefully to reinforce his position of authority in this operation and establish the ground rules for future dealings with the American. "He can identify me, one of my agents, and maybe even you, Mr. Foster. The young man might do a great deal of damage."

Foster flashed him a cold stare, but did not reply.

Chung reached over and pulled the toilet chain, watching the swirling water disappear into the bowl. "I became very amused by this luxury when I was in your country. Many Americans even read the newspaper sitting on these things." Then he turned to face Foster, matching his stare. "But I believe shit should be dealt with quickly and decisively."

"I said I would see to it," Foster snapped. The man's pouting pleased Chung to no end. The American had passed on an opportunity to challenge Chung's authority and, in so doing, had assumed the role of inferior.

"What does this agent know?" Chung asked.

"Nothing. Even his commanding officer is completely in the dark. He knows only what we require of him. You'll be free to complete your mission without interference. We don't need any more alarms going off."

"Thank you, Mr. Foster."

"And Chung, I'm instructed to advise you my government wants no more injuries to American personnel. I explained that the last one was unavoidable, but that's it."

Chung struggled silently to conceal his anger. Even his own superiors would not address him in such a manner. "Of course," he forced himself to say. "That was an unfortunate development. You may assure your government all effort will be made to protect American personnel."

"Good."

"May we assume your government has agreed not to advise the Japanese authorities of our problem?" Chung asked. It was critical to his mission that the Japanese not learn of the refugees' plan or the joint Korean-American operation to stop them.

"Yes. It would be against our interests if the Soviets or the Japanese learned of our problem. That's the way my government sees it."

"It would be a disaster if the Soviets found out," Chung added for emphasis.

Foster moved back into room and settled into the upholstered armchair. He pointed to the bed. "Sit down."

"No, thank you."

Foster lifted his legs and rested them on the lamp table, showing Chung the soles of his shoes. Chung could have easily split the bridge of the American's nose with a bullet and not batted an eye. "Suit yourself, Chung, but actually alerting the Soviets would be a double disaster; a disaster for you because they would soon figure out our intelligence comes from South Korean agents living among the Sakhalin Koreans, and for us because your agents would all be dead in twenty-four hours."

The unexpected admission swept Chung right off his feet; he seated himself on the bed in a formal gesture of acknowledgement. "I'm pleased you appreciate the contribution of our agents on the ground. Technology is a good thing, but there's no substitute for human intelligence."

"I can't argue with you there."

This relatively minor accolade from the American triggered a rush of pride. He said, "Together, we will bring this operation to a successful and speedy conclusion. I'm certain of it."

Foster raised his arm, palm forward. "Whoa, let's not go calling this a joint operation. This thing falls on you, pal. Our position is, you found out about it, you fix it. Besides, the last thing the United States needs is to be perceived as having embarrassed the Russians at such a critical time."

That was more like the Americans Chung knew and loathed. Foster was telling him the American government needed complete deniability in the event the operation turned sour, as if he didn't know. "But we may need to call upon your technical capabilities."

"No problem. NSA has assets in the Navy as well as the Air Force. That's another reason you're dealing with NSA and not CIA. As you may know, there are a number of small electronic surveillance vessels, trawlers, regularly patrolling in international waters off the coasts of China, North Korea, and the Soviet Far East."

Chung liked the sound of that. The Russian captain was a slippery character. "These will all be available to us?" he asked.

"Immediately. NSA will shift some of those assets to patrol the Soya Strait. They won't be boarding any Soviet or Japanese ships, but they can find Subarov's boat easy enough and track it. The boats are out there anyway. A subtle course change here and there will go unnoticed."

"He is very clever," Chung pointed out. "He might use a different boat."

"We're aware of that. They'll track every suspicious vessel that comes within reach of the Hokkaido coast. Our intercept station here at Wakkanai can overhear literally every voice transmission within our area of interest. Let's just pray we don't hit another dead end."

Chung thought Foster's pessimistic comment defeatist and wondered if the American was even competent to act as liaison officer. He leaned forward and spoke slowly. "Our success will not require prayer, Mr. Foster. It will depend on absolute commitment to the mission and a determination to succeed. And I wouldn't call it a dead end just yet. Subarov is lurking out there, somewhere on the Sea of Japan, waiting to make his delivery."

Foster stood and moved to the door. "He's already done it. I'd bet on it. Think about it, Chung. Is he crazy enough to enter Wakkanai Port if he hadn't?"

Chung was on his feet, annoyed that the American would show him his ample backside. "He's a dangerous man. Do not underestimate him."

"If he hasn't made shore yet," Foster said, opening the door, "they'll make contact and arrange another rendezvous. I suppose the safest thing is to assume we can still stop the landing."

"I agree, but even if we're too late this time, our intelligence confirms there will be another—the last one. In light of recent developments, Subarov will need to act quickly. As you know, he's holding something that might cause real embarrassment to a number of governments."

Foster closed the door and turned to face Chung, twin eyebrows digging furrows into the bridge of his nose. "Yes. I almost forget that.

My briefing didn't specify exactly what that might be, and you didn't mention it the other night. Can you enlighten me?"

Chung saw no need to be too specific. He'd play it close to the vest and tell the NSA only enough to keep them on board. "Documents, Mr. Foster, a collection of documents."

"What kind of documents?" Foster pressed.

"We can only speculate that it's some explosive combination or other. Who knows? Whatever is in his collection, it's important enough for Subarov to risk his life over. I intend to be ready when he next returns from Sakhalin."

"I'm sure we won't have another problem," Foster said. "Let's remember, we're dealing with fishermen here, not professional intelligence operatives."

The last remark Chung found personally insulting. He actually regretted Foster's abrupt retirement from field work. Who knows? In such a dangerous business, fatalities in the line of duty are not uncommon. "Thank you for this valuable information, Mr. Foster."

Foster flashed a condescending smile. "Sarcasm, eh? It doesn't become you. Still, you would have had them last time, but for a round of old-fashioned bad luck. I doubt they match up well with us."

Chung had absorbed his fill of Americans for this night and reached for the doorknob. "Good night, Mr. Foster."

"Good night," replied the American. Then, as Chung turned to leave, he said, "Look, this is none of my business, but I can't help wonder why your government doesn't just make some quiet settlement with the Russians and take these people back home. You could sort them out there. They're all Koreans, aren't they?"

The question startled Chung as being both unexpected and extremely unprofessional. It was bad form to take the conversation beyond the point of operational necessity, and absolutely insane to discuss policy questions with agents of foreign governments. Foster understood the rules and should never question their wisdom. Chung said, "Nothing is ever as simple as it appears, Mr. Foster, especially not in politics, and I don't trouble myself with such matters. Good night."

It was only a short drive through narrow, downtown streets to the storefront, Chinese restaurant. Finding a parking place along the snow-buried street proved a bigger challenge. Chung found his young apprentice, Fu Lee Cho, already waiting at the counter. "How did the meeting go, sir?" Fu asked.

The young man's punctuality pleased the hungry agent, but Fu's troublesome curiosity had quickly evened the score. "It went well, Fu. I'm tired. Let's just leave it at that for now and order. I think I'll just have a bite of sushi and get some rest. What about you?"

"The same."

"So tell me, did you manage to turn up anything at all that might give us a place to start?"

"I believe I might have, sir. I tracked down the bartender from that place where the girl gave us the slip. I had to pay two thousand yen just to get his home address."

Gave *you* the slip, Chung wanted to say. "Get on with it, Fu. Do you think our government is going to fuck you out of a lousy two thousand yen for information?"

"Actually, sir, the bartender cost me eight thousand, so the total is ten."

That was all Chung could take. "I can count. Now tell me what you have."

"Well, I don't think he's a very reliable character. It appears he's on the run himself because his identification papers looked like cheap forgeries, but the man claims he recognized the Japanese boy, the one who was with the girl."

"It would be a big break if we could get our hands on that boy," Chung said. "He could lead us to the girl and who knows what else? He might even know the details of their plan."

"Well, he thinks the boy works somewhere down the road from the bar, at the Municipal Port, or maybe the newspaper."

"How does he know that?"

"Because he sees the kid pass by in the evenings, on his way home from work. He looks clean cut and out of place in that district, so our guy just figures he works nearby."

It sounded promising. "Exactly what time does the boy pass by in the evening?"

Fu withdrew a small notebook from his breast pocket and leafed through wrinkled pages. "Maybe seven-thirty or eight o'clock. The witness isn't sure, but he thinks it's early, early for a bartender I mean."

Chung checked his watch and said, "It's after seven now. Let's not take any chances. We might get lucky. Eat quickly, Fu, and let's get over there."

"Of course, sir, but we may not see him tonight. The bartender couldn't say what days of the week the man passes by."

"Maybe he works on Sundays," Chung countered. "We'll just have to go and see. Do you think the port shuts down just because it's the weekend?"

"I agree with you, sir. I'm just pointing out that we may have to keep going back every night for a while."

Fu had an irritating habit of emphasizing the obvious. "Will you be able to recognize him?"

"Of course, but I may need to get under his parka hood and take a look."

Chung smiled, then lied. "Good. You have your quirks, but you might make a very good agent one day."

EIGHT

**I'll throw one back at the end of the day,
while the other guys plot their third down play.**

Sunday, 7:00 p.m.

The snow was blinding, but the twang of steel guitars in the night marked the way. His investigation in tatters, Dan was in the mood for some friendly company. The concept of a "weekend," he knew, was irrelevant at the NCO Club, any NCO Club. Whether it was in San Antonio, Texas or Osan, South Korea, the drill was pretty much the same, as was the decor.

On a military base, somebody was always going off duty in the mood to drink or gamble and suffer scratchy George Jones records on the jukebox. Dan was no Country music fan, but all things considered, it was comforting to have something he could count on.

He'd come to prefer the familiar camaraderie of the enlisted men to the swankier digs up the road. The brass considered his access to the Officers' Club a sweet "bennie," but Dan would rather have had an extra fifty bucks a month. He peeled back the heavy door under the simple sign and shook the snow from his clothes and boots. The revelry was in full gear as he claimed a seat along the bar in the darkened, cavernous room. "What I get you, handsome?" asked the attractive oriental woman behind the bar. A few days ago he'd have assumed her to be Japanese. But now who knew?

"Beer, American," he replied. "Thanks."

"Not see you in here before," the woman said, smiling. "You new?"

"TDY," he said, and she seemed to lose interest, resting his beer on the bar without so much as a nod.

He tried to let go of the case for a while, sipping his beer amidst the relaxing sounds of slot machines, animated blackjack players and the tormented wailing of Tammy Wynette. What was the difference between thirty and thirty-eight anyway? Maybe a couple of inches around the waist or an extra chin or two. With his full twenty-year retirement, he'd still be a month short of thirty-nine. He could get any number of menial jobs, and with the pension, never have to worry about his next meal or putting a roof over his head. Sure, the Air Force might not be the American dream in its full glory, but it had given him a decent life and he'd be hard pressed to throw it away in favor of the unknown at thirty years old, however attractive the alternative.

As he slid his dead soldier high on the bar to signal for a refill, a violent jolt to the back sent the last swallow on a seldom-traveled path up his sinuses and out his nostrils. Dan was not amused at the indignity, but held his temper when he saw Rob Norton settle onto the neighboring stool with a shit-eating grin. "Agent Matthews," he said, "what the hell are you doing over here, especially on a Sunday night?"

So much for Dan's break. He guessed right off that Norton had something to sell. A part of him wanted to drop the loud-mouthed prick with a right cross and be done with him. But there was a case to solve and Norton obviously knew something important enough to offer him protection from an old-fashioned ass whipping. It would give him an inflated sense of importance—for a night at least.

Fighting his instincts, Dan decided to play along. "Rob, I thought you guys didn't talk to OSI agents. I'm flattered. Can I buy you a beer?" Afterward he might smash the empty bottle over Norton's vile and repugnant excuse for a brain.

"Why, I'd just love a drink, Agent Matthews," Norton replied, "but I have a taste for old Johnny Walker tonight. Will your expense account cover that?"

"Red or Black?" Dan forced himself to ask.

Norton flashed that grin for the second time. One more would be a painful mistake. "Black, of course," Norton answered, then hollered to the bartender, "Hey, Sumiko, Johnny Walker Black, double, *kudasai*."

Dan hoped his information was worth the price, in time, not money. He said, "So what have you been up to, Rob?"

Norton downed half the two-dollar drink in one swallow and wiped his mouth with the back of his hand. "Me? Shit, I don't do anything but work and drink beer. I'm just counting down to my out date. I'm one twenty-four and back to the world. I get my thrills vicariously, as those geniuses would say."

"I don't follow," Dan said. He feigned his best smile.

Norton laughed. "I can barely keep up with the sexual exploits of your boy, Reggie Kincaid."

It took a second or two for the startling declaration to travel from his ears to his brain. "Really! What's he been up to, or maybe I should say into?" The last part made Dan feel like a real lowlife, even as he forced himself to say it.

Norton wasn't going to be merciful by answering the question directly. "You know, I've always considered myself a pretty good judge of women, but I have to admit I misjudged that one."

Dan thought it best to play along. "Which one?"

"You mean you haven't heard?" Norton asked.

Norton's Scotch had disappeared. Dan said, "Not a word." This was an interrogation now, although Rob Norton hadn't a clue. "How about another, Rob?"

"Sure," Norton replied raising his hand, but his empty was already sitting in the refill spot.

"So don't keep me in suspense. Who's the girl? If it is a girl." His own scripted remark gave Dan a fleeting sense of how it must feel to be a sleazeball like Norton.

Norton's laugh might have been predictable. "I know what you mean, Dan. I guess you could say it was a double surprise then. I thought Kincaid might be a fag, but I was almost sure that Korean chick was a lesbian. I was off base both times."

"You mean he's involved with Su Li Young?" Dan asked. He'd been taken off guard or would have asked the question in Norton's vile dialect.

"Banging the shit out of her," Norton replied.

"How do you know for sure?"

"More like how do you not know? Every GI on the base knows."

Dan thought two drinks was a pretty cheap price for the information if it were reliable. "So what exactly do you know?"

Norton called to the bartender. "Sumiko," pointing to the empty glass. She poured. "Kincaid was in the restaurant a couple of nights ago, early. The place was pretty crowded at the time, so you have a few dozen witnesses, if you like. The way I heard it, Su Li just walked over to the booth where Kincaid was and snuggled up."

"Maybe she was just joking," Dan suggested.

"Some joke. After a few minutes, they were going at it right there in the booth. She was giving him a hand job through his pants. They finished a drink, then strolled out of Mama Young's like Siamese twins." Norton downed the drink in one gulp, slamming the empty on the bar. "Kincaid walked out with a raging hard-on, right hand on Su Li's ass, and his tongue down her throat."

God knows how big the story had been blown out of proportion. Whatever Norton had heard, he'd no doubt added a few juicy details of his own. Experience had taught Dan that such incredible tales often contain an element of truth. In this case, even a little truth would be a big break. He decided to squeeze every detail out of his offensive companion. But Norton had freeloaded his last drink. "Wow, that's a shocker. I interviewed Mama Young and a shitload of guys who go in there. None of them gave me any reason to link Su Li and Reggie, but it doesn't make sense. My bet is it's been going on for a while."

Norton was having none of it. "I'm telling you, the only thing she ever served him up to that night was beer. Believe me, I'd have known it if Kincaid or anyone else was into that."

"What makes you say that?"

"Shit, Kincaid's been here over a year. He's been going over there since day one. She never gave him more than a *konnichi-wa*. People would have noticed something if he was banging her. No sir, this was right out of the blue. Hell, maybe I wasn't wrong about him. I'll bet he just paid her to do a show for the customers. He probably is a fag. But I was sure wrong about Su Li."

"How's that?"

Norton wiped his mouth with a sleeve. "Say, that Johnny is going down real easy tonight; still got a powerful thirst."

Dan smiled. "Oh, we'll have time for that. First tell me about Su Li."

He might have predicted Norton's greasy smile. "There was no faking her performance," the man said with feigned conviction, even though repeating third-hand hearsay. "It might have been staged, but she was really into it, from what I heard. In fact, I'm gonna go over and check that shit out myself."

"You do that, Rob," Dan suggested. It was a well spent four bucks, but he couldn't get away from Norton fast enough. He rose from the stool, collecting his change from the bar, all but the fifty cent tip. "I've got to run, Rob. It was nice talking to you."

Norton looked hurt. "Hey, what about my drink?"

For a second Dan considered unloading on Norton, but he might need him again and just pretended not to hear. Rob Norton was out of Dan's thoughts by the time he'd reached the door and gotten into his parka. What if just enough of the man's story was true to conclude that Reggie and Su Li had a romantic relationship? If they did, Dan reasoned, it had to have started very recently. But why now? Why after a whole year of knowing each other? Something must have triggered it.

He fought a head wind on the trip back to the BOQ, bachelor officer quarters, a steady snow forcing the hood low over his face. Painstakingly negotiating the road like a blind man, it occurred to him this was all headed in one inescapable direction. Su Li Young must be the girl Reggie saved in the alley. The farther he followed this logic, the more disturbing it became. If Reggie knew Su Li was the girl, why didn't he say so right away? Or even now? Better yet, why didn't Su Li herself step up and say so?

The facts were piling up quickly in his head now, and maybe even based on a faulty assumption. Yet, his mind had already settled on its own proposition. Reggie was protecting her. But from what and why?

Other things corroborated the theory as well; maybe not hard facts yet, but conclusions drawn from Dan's own observations and interviews. Like Mama Young protecting Kincaid and her hostility toward Dan during their recent encounter.

Inside the barracks, he stumbled on a small group of civilian contractors playing poker in the dayroom. "Hey fella," said a burly, ironworker type from the table, "wanna try your luck?"

Dan looked at the pot and found it ample enough to warrant attention. These private contractors were known to make tons of money too. He figured it might be time to make a little dough, instead of giving it away. "I think I will. Thanks. Just let me get out of these wet clothes."

As he reached into his duffel for a dry pair of pants, it occurred to him his mission might be drawing to a conclusion. Reggie Kincaid was apparently not a homo, although Major Coughlin would likely take no comfort in that. Still, nobody would expect him to falsify a report. They'd just have to find another way to bury this Kincaid.

He wondered what was really going on here. Why would they go to all the trouble of sending him up here just to prove one insignificant airman is queer? Why was this case so important to the major's career? And why was there such an interest at command level to discredit and discharge Reginald Kincaid? Dan couldn't help but think back to that day in Coughlin's office. Who was the person hiding on the other side of the door? The answer to that question would go a long way to answering the rest.

He pulled up a chair and dropped five twenties onto the table. "Start me out with a hundred in chips," he said to the iron worker. "What's the game?"

The round-faced fellow with thick, matching glasses chuckled while his ample titties bounced beneath the Italian knit, button-down shirt. "Five card stud at the moment, squire," he said in a thick Irish brogue. "'Tis dealer's choice; ten dollar openers, jacks or better with twenty, forty and sixty dollar limits."

As the Irishman shuffled, Dan's thoughts returned to his assignment. He could wrap it up now, write his final report and head back to Tachi tomorrow. If this Kincaid harbored a secret yearning for boys, he'd done a pretty good job of pretending to be a cunt hound, just like all the other idiots running around this base. Coughlin would get over it in a couple of days.

Still, a voice inside told Dan he couldn't walk away, not yet. The unanswered questions gnawed at him like an old dog on a fresh bone. Maybe Kincaid was growing on him; maybe it was just the detective in him, but he had to have the answers and still had a couple of weeks to get them, if only for himself. He could handle Coughlin.

He picked up the hand and carefully cupped the cards for viewing. Four cards to an inside straight, with a lonely ace of hearts at the top. The irony made him smile. Only a fool would draw to an inside straight and dump the ace.

"Hey, fella," the dealer said. "It's over to you. Can you open?"

"No," said Dan and the bald man to his right grinned and dropped the first twenty into the pot. The key was Su Li Young, he thought. He'd start with her. His watch told him it was still not eight p.m.—

plenty of time to kill. He could borrow a car from the duty officer later and try his luck on a little Sunday night stakeout.

He counted out the chips and smiled. "I'll take one card please."

7:50 p.m.

The bar was crowded with the usual, assorted port scum, so Chung sent his junior partner for the drinks while he secured a small table along the front window. It gave them a commanding view over the expanse of road between the municipal bus stop and the port complex.

The boy would have to pass directly into view in order to get home. Chung figured there was a five-out-of-seven chance he would pass by tonight. Sunday night was the perfect time for this operation. He hoped for a lucky break.

It was dark outside, but Fu might at least tentatively identify the kid if he appeared. They could check out a likely suspect or two easily enough in the deserted streets of the district once he turned the corner.

Fu returned with two bottles of Sapporo, and Chung directed him to the seat with the clearest view. The young agent began to drink his beer, prompting a smoldering reaction from Chung. "Leave the fucking beer, will you? We're here to do a job. Just keep your eyes on the street. If you see anyone who even looks like him, we'll check it out."

"Right, sir," Fu replied, but Chung could see the younger man had already downed a good portion of the bottle. He wondered if Fu might be mocking him. It wouldn't be the first time either.

Chung barely had time to regain his composure when Fu said, "There, turn around slowly, sir. Look across the street. He just came around the corner."

Chung spoke even before he could see the man. "Is it he, Fu?"

The young agent did not hesitate. "Yes, sir. I'm certain of it. I remember the nylon coat. It was black, the very same style. That's him all right."

Chung couldn't believe his luck. The boy might know everything. At the very least, he'd lead them to the girl. The rest would be easy. "All right, let's follow the plan. You get the car. I'll follow him. Are you clear on the route he'll take?"

"Of course. He'll turn away from the water at Tora-nishi and then right at the next street. It has to be there because the bus stop is two blocks down. I'll pull the car up just as he makes the turn."

"Good. He's only a puny kid. He won't be problem. I'll grab him up when you stop and throw him in the backseat. Let's go."

Chung gave the boy plenty of room. After all, he knew exactly where the kid was going. Why take the chance of spooking him where someone might notice? He'd selected the pickup spot without time for the proper planning, but it seemed remote and deserted this time of night, a perfect location for such an operation.

The boy was moving quickly as Chung scurried silently into position, well out of his victim's line of sight. Chung had considered simply taking another route in order to beat him to the pickup point. It would be less risky if he were prepositioned for an ambush. But what if the kid decided to change course for some reason? He was simply too valuable at this point. Chung had to stay with him and make do.

As the young man turned up Tora-nishi, Chung began to close the gap. The fish market area, bustling during the weekdays, was nearly clear of snow, but his mind struggled to block out the overpowering stench. Moving at a quick trot, he hugged the old, wooden buildings along the way, mostly small, fish packing operations and marine outfitters. As expected, the area was completely deserted, but only one block long. They had to grab the kid just as he made the turn, before he could get close to the bus depot and more populated area just beyond.

Although Chung had identified some serious deficiencies in his young apprentice, Fu had always proven competent and steady in operational situations. Chung was confident the plan would proceed without a hitch.

As the young Japanese man neared the corner, he looked back unexpectedly while Chung was moving over an exposed area between buildings. Chung's prey was now alerted and exploded forward like a gazelle.

The boy's speed paled in comparison to the fleet-footed American airman's. Still, in a flat out run Chung might not catch him before the kid reached the safety of the bus depot or one of the bars nearby. It was a stupid mistake that might cost Chung days, even weeks in lost opportunity. If he escaped now, all of Subarov's people would be alerted and the mission itself might even be in jeopardy.

Chung accelerated into an all out sprint, but his prey had already widened the distance and was turning the last corner. He'd missed his chance and fucked up the entire mission with no help from Fu. He figured his only chance now was to find Fu and chase the kid down quickly with the car. Failing that, they would simply have to follow the bus and hope an opportunity presented itself. At least they might learn where he lived.

Chung reached the corner, already struggling for breath in the frigid air. Where was Fu? This kid probably wouldn't go near the bus depot now. If he were smart, Chung thought, he'd duck off into some dark alley and get lost in the snow. They might have lost him for good.

As he made the turn, Fu and the car were nowhere to be seen. He could blame the entire fiasco on his young partner, but the thought did little to ease his anxiety. Chung slowed to a walk and turned back toward the O Bar in defeat when he heard a faint moaning from somewhere on his left.

Cautiously, he followed the sound into a narrow walk between two decrepit buildings. There, in the dark amidst a throng of foul-smelling, cardboard boxes, he saw his young protégé securing the hands of the Japanese kid with what appeared to be a shoelace. There was a wool glove stuffed into the young man's mouth.

As Chung approached, Fu collapsed back against the wall of the building, utterly exhausted. After a few labored breaths he turned to Chung and said, "He's not much of a fighter, sir, but he was very determined to make it home."

Chung saw no reason to hide his glee. "Excellent work, Fu. I never doubted you would adjust to the situation. Tell me what happened."

Fu was on his feet, and no doubt buoyed by the praise. "I could see the intersection clearly from where I was parked, sir. When he spotted you I just knew I had to get between him and the bus depot. I got well past him and parked the car. Then I just waited behind a building. He walked right into my arms before he decided he had somewhere else to go."

"Well, let's get him out of here. We've made enough of a racket already. Are you sure the place is ready?"

"Of course, sir. It's not much for comfort, but I got the old stove fired up. It should keep the place warm enough for you to work, although we'll need to rely on a couple of battery lights. I don't think you'll want to stay longer than you need to."

"The faster the better, Fu. The faster the better."

NINE

**This damn car's colder than a well digger's ass,
but if I hurry I can still cut 'em off at the pass.**

Sunday, 11:05 p.m.

Dan sat frozen to the bone in his borrowed car a few doors down from Mama Young's on the dark, narrow road. He hadn't bothered to ask the young first lieutenant if the heater worked, an oversight he might pay for with frostbite—or worse. The three hundred or so extra bucks in his pocket did little to warm him.

Thoughts of palm trees and warm, sun-baked beaches tormented his numbing brain, like a desert mirage to a thirsty traveler. Transfer and reassignment were an accepted fact of life among military personnel, but Major Grant Billing's unexpected retirement from the Air Force had shocked him. After Grant accepted the offer to become Chief of Police in Kailua-Kona, the two men kept in touch regularly by letter. Dan always looked forward to the letters, each describing some new, incredibly beautiful scene from the Big Island. He still found it difficult to believe, for example, the island claimed the country's largest, working, cattle ranch. Despite, or maybe because of his growing affection for the place, Dan was embarrassed to admit he had only been there on one TDY assignment, and then only for two days.

He watched as a couple of drunken GIs staggered into Mama Young's, but nobody came out. Grant's phone call that day had come right out of the blue. One of his four detectives unexpectedly resigned and would Dan be interested in the position? Before that phone call Dan had grudgingly begun to accept lifer status. That seemed like a hundred years ago. Now he just needed to finish this assignment and drive thoughts of Hawaii from his head. Breaking the news to Grant would be hard, but Dan was sure he'd understand. If only this had all come four years earlier.

Coughlin had told him straight out what needed to be done here. Nobody would question his conclusions if he just closed the book on this goddamn Kincaid right now. Someone very high up wanted him out of the way. But why? The question dogged him and had even begun to rob him of sleep. He told himself it really didn't matter why because they weren't trying to put the kid in prison or anything like that. They only wanted him gone. All the rationalizing in the world wouldn't justify scurrilous, unsupported allegations in an official report. No, if they wanted Kincaid that badly, they'd either have to wait until Dan turned up more evidence or find another way to get rid of him. Hints were one thing, but nobody in the chain of command would expect him to lie. He could take the heat of Coughlin's disappointment.

Without warning, Su Li Young emerged from around the corner inside a blue parka. She was heading straight for him. He struggled to crouch low in the front seat, banging his knee hard on the dash in the process as she passed through the narrow walkway, only a few feet from his vehicle. His eyes followed the girl in the rear-view mirror as she darted up the dark street and around the corner.

Keeping the headlights dim, Dan reversed direction at the corner and drove quickly toward the spot where Su Li had disappeared. The glow of headlights suddenly appeared from the darkness and Dan pulled to a stop. He watched as the small truck turned west, passing only inches from his passenger door. Su Li was sitting beside the male driver. He waited to establish a safe distance, then swung into the icy track behind the truck.

With almost no traffic on the snow-covered, coast road, Dan maintained just enough distance to keep the truck's taillights in view. He struggled to keep the small car moving over the treacherous ice and freshly fallen snow. In Hawaii, he knew, such coastal roads were often hundreds of feet above sea level with hairpin turns and sharp cliffs. Fuck Hawaii. At sea level, at least, the only threat to his life, aside from freezing, would be a passing car or truck. After fifteen kilometers or so the road began to turn south and became easier to negotiate.

Losing sight of the truck briefly around a bend, he pressed the accelerator well beyond comfort level until the familiar taillights reappeared. At about one in the morning the truck turned slowly toward the sleepy, gray Sea of Japan onto a small, peninsula road. The cold was bone chilling and Dan had lost the feeling in his fingers many kilometers back. Convinced he would freeze to death within minutes, he pulled his car to the edge of the snow bank and set the blinkers to flash, a danger signal to any passing vehicle. He covered the quarter mile or so in the dark on stiff, lifeless legs and moved slowly toward the tip of the peninsula, where he saw the truck parked facing the water, headlights flashing in some obviously prearranged signal.

On the water he saw only a deep, grayish-black emptiness at first, and then what he expected: a single, powerful beam of light, flashing the return signal in a series of long and short bursts. In the next thirty minutes, Dan seriously considered that he might never again be warm. He was beyond cold, into some kind of neutral state where real danger resides. It had been very poor planning. He might have anticipated something like this and dressed warmer.

Then he saw the two small dinghies emerge from the blackness and three people running to the rocky shore. Su Li and the others were helping a group of elderly people from the tiny boats and into the back of the truck.

Dan knew he had to leave. Following the truck simply wasn't an option. Who could tell how far they'd travel? There was a small village a few miles back. It would have a hotel. He needed to warm his body if he were to survive the night. Besides, if he didn't leave now, they might turn in the direction of his car and find him. What then? He had learned something important tonight, and tomorrow would begin the process of sorting it out and uncovering the link to Reggie Kincaid. Whatever else was going on, it was becoming clear that Kincaid was telling the truth, but likely not the whole truth. This business might be a lot more serious than cock sucking. He would phone Major Coughlin with the unhappy news tomorrow—maybe.

* * *

Monday, 12:15 a.m.

Chung had considered leaving his captive blindfolded, but the two powerful flashlights seemed to compliment the filthy, windowless shack and provide a perfect setting for a high intensity interrogation. He faced one light to the ceiling. It cast his towering, superhuman image across the wall of the tiny shack, a subtle instrument of terror against an already frightened boy.

Chung positioned his victim's chair to face the gigantic shadow and bent low to his ear from behind. The boy was gagged, his hands bound around the chair back. His brown eyes bulged in the wake of Chung's shadow. "Are you frightened, Ishikawa-san?" he asked in Japanese, warm breath on the boy's neck.

The young man, eyes closed and face soaked with tears, replied in a shaky voice, "What are you going to do to me?"

At that moment, Chung didn't know the answer; well, not exactly. Normally, he enjoyed this part of the job and performed it with ritualistic patience, but he needed the information quickly and figured he'd end up with pneumonia if he spent more than an hour or two in this cold, damp shack Fu had selected.

The old, deserted fishing shack was ten kilometers or so north of the city on a small inlet. Its proximity to the water prevented it from being completely buried in snow. The dilapidated wood-burning stove was barely enough to suppress the temperature.

Not that he was criticizing Fu, not this time anyway. In truth, his young protégé had done him a valuable service. Upon their arrival in Wakkanai some weeks ago, Fu had scouted potential hiding places on the outskirts of the city. It was standard tradecraft and one of Fu's great strengths. Such plans would often become paramount in the event they needed to lie low while waiting for a pickup or hide something like a young, Japanese man.

Even the most carefully planned operations could go bad, and this one was no exception, Chung thought. They could hardly have marched their Japanese captive into their hotel to torture him. This was turning out to be a most improvisational assignment.

In general, Chung preferred the more straightforward assignments like body snatches or assassinations. You get in, do the job and leave. With such a clearly defined mission, planning could be more precise and fewer things were likely to go wrong.

The Subarov affair, on the other hand, was a different deal entirely, the kind you can never fully plan for. You can't foil the other guy's operation until you learn what it is. It was shooting from the hip, as the Americans liked to say, more reaction than action. These missions were both difficult and dangerous, and survival often depended more on instinct than planning. But with his own instinct and Fu's planning, Chung believed this operation had an excellent chance of complete success.

Chung smiled down on his hapless victim. "I think you know why you're here." He wanted to get a feeling for the subject before deciding on a course of action. His words hadn't formed a question, but more an opportunity to let Ishikawa talk a bit. With luck, this frightened weakling might just give it all up voluntarily.

The boy continued crying, but did not reply. Chung decided to turn the screw, ever so gently. "I'll be honest with you. We need all the information you have about Subarov and the Koreans. We want the name of the girl. Eventually, you'll tell us everything, so why not spare yourself the pain?"

The crying intensified, but still no reply. "Do I look like someone to trifle with?" Chung shouted. He grabbed the kid's chin and lowered his own head until the two were face-to-face, barely a centimeter apart. Chung lowered his voice to a whisper. "I will hurt you, boy, until you beg to die, and you'll tell me anyway. Is it worth the pain?" Still no reply. Interrogating this Ishikawa might prove a delicate matter, Chung concluded, should the young man find some reservoir of courage in his final hours.

Consistent with his preference for straightforward assignments, Chung preferred purely informational interrogation. Get the information at all cost. His instinctive abilities to intimidate and inflict pain had been largely responsible for his legendary success as an agent. But in a convoluted, politically sensitive mess like this there were often overriding considerations limiting his effectiveness.

This was a covert operation in the strictest sense. Chung's orders were to leave no trace of his presence or mission. Interrogating this Ishikawa with customary methods of persuasion would necessarily leave evidence of physical torture.

The idea came upon him slowly at first. Over the years Chung had trained himself to explore every cloud for a silver lining, to turn every defeat into victory. It was more attitude than design, but had turned the tide in his favor on many a desperate occasion.

Still behind Ishikawa's line of sight, he took Fu's arm and led his partner to the other side of the room. He spoke quietly in Korean. "Fu, you know our orders on this mission with respect to interrogation."

"Yes, sir, no evidence of torture. Our presence and mission are to remain secret."

"Exactly, so think about it. We have the boy and he has information we need. We can't mark him up. We can't even use electric shock because that might be detected in an autopsy or even leave burns visible to the lay observer."

"Maybe we should use the Sodium Pentothal, sir." Fu suggested. "I know it's not really a truth serum, but used properly, it can produce excellent results."

That was precisely where the conversation had been heading, but Chung was less than thrilled. He said, "Of course I'm talking about drugs, Fu, but I don't like leaving the outcome of an interrogation up to chance. Sometimes the drug works and sometimes it doesn't. As you say, it's not a truth serum at all."

"I'm aware of that, sir. It deadens the nervous system, but it can reduce inhibitions considerably and some of our agents have used it quite successfully."

Options were in short supply under the circumstances. "I don't see that we have a choice. Sodium Pentothal is the preferable tool in this case, although I don't like working with those drugs myself. I'm thinking more about after the interrogation. Hopefully, we'll have our information in a couple of hours, but we'll also still have this Ishikawa, alive and essentially uninjured. How can we use that to our advantage?"

"I don't know, sir," Fu answered, "but the drug could be detected in an autopsy, either in an expanded tox screen or a careful examination of the body for punctures."

The answer settled upon Chung all at once, like a warm blanket. "That's the key. They could detect the drug, but they'd only look if they suspected murder. Right?"

"I suppose so. In a standard autopsy they'd only look for opiates, barbiturates, amphetamines, and maybe one or two other categories. Sodium Pentothal is an anesthesia."

Chung felt a rush of satisfaction and smiled. "What if they had no reason to think his death was murder?" He didn't wait for an answer. "Get the bag from the car."

The ten-minute waiting period seemed more like a couple of hours, but Chung gave the drug another five minutes to take effect, just to be sure. When he was finally ready to begin, Ishikawa looked unconscious, or maybe even dead, his head slumped forward in the chair. Chung checked his pulse and breathing. His heart rate had slowed some, but that was a normal reaction to the drug.

"Ishikawa-san," Chung began in a friendly voice. No reply. "Ishikawa-san, can you hear me?"

"Yes." Chung was only centimeters from his face. He could hear the words clearly enough, but the boy's head remained slumped.

"What do your friends call you?"

A few seconds passed. "Hiro."

"And where do you work, Hiro-san?"

"At the newspaper. I'm a reporter."

So far so good. "Do you like working there?"

"I like the work, I suppose."

It was time to get down to business. "Do you have a girlfriend?" The boy smiled playfully, although his eyes were still half closed. Then he giggled. "Hiro-san, do you have a girlfriend?"

Ishikawa answered in a kind of melodic tone. "I wish I had a girlfriend."

"I see. Well, maybe she doesn't know she is your girlfriend. Is that it?"

A broad smile, eyes closed. "Oh, yes. That's exactly it. She doesn't know she's my girlfriend."

"Is she beautiful, this girl?"

"Very beautiful."

Chung had seen the drug used on several occasions, only once successfully. On that occasion the interrogator engaged the subject in a long conversation on a subject of interest to him. Chung seemed to have found his mark. With luck, his diversion and his goal might be one in the same. "And what is the name of this beautiful girl, the one you would like to be your girlfriend?"

"Su Li."

"That's a nice name, Hiro-san. Tell me, have you ever been out for a drink with Su Li?"

"Many times."

Chung inched closer until his lips were almost touching the boy's ear, then whispered. "What's her full name?"

"Su Li Young."

It was time to see if this Su Li Young was the same bitch helping Subarov. "Hiro-san, do you know a place called the O Bar?" No reply. "Hiro-san, did you hear me? Have you ever been to a place called the O Bar?"

"The O Bar, yes, I know it."

Chung resumed a conversational tone. "You were there the other night with your friend, Su Li Young. Do you remember?"

"Yes, I remember."

The agent had what he wanted most. He was beside himself with pride and turned to Fu with a satisfied wink. "And where does Su Li Young live?"

"Mama Young's."

"Of course she lives with her mother, but where does her mother live?"

"Mama Young's," once again was the boy's reply.

Chung moved to face his victim, lifted his chin, and promptly slapped him across the face. "I asked you where Mama Young lives, boy," he shouted.

"Sir," Fu said, placing his hand on Chung's shoulder, "remember our instructions. We know the girl's name. We can figure out the rest. Shouldn't we determine what else he knows?"

Fu was right, he knew. Chung calmed himself and prepared to continue when Fu said, "Sir, maybe you should ask him if Mama Young's is a business of some kind."

It was worth a try. "Hiro-san, is Mama Young's a restaurant?"

"Yes."

Chung turned to his protégé, ready to bask in Fu's admiration, the teacher having just provided a classic lesson by example. Fu was smiling, but it was a mocking smile, no doubt this time. Fu was patronizing him. This youngster believed he had orchestrated the use of the drug and guided Chung through the questioning process. He was sending Chung a message of superiority.

The rage began to build in Chung, but a confrontation with Fu now would be counterproductive. When the mission was over, he'd see to his young friend's future. Now he needed to focus on the mission. "Fu, when we leave here this morning you'll need to pay a visit to Mama Young's. It must be here in Wakkanai City somewhere. Just get the lay of the land and make sure the girl is there."

"But she may recognize me, sir," Fu protested.

"I don't think she got a good look at you. It was my fist she tasted. Still, you best be careful. If you see her leave, follow. If she's not there, pick up what information you can."

"Right, sir. We'll find her."

There was not much doubt of it now. "I think we're over the hill. We'll make our preparations today, then come back here tonight and pick up the boy. Now let's just see what else he knows before we wrap it up."

TEN

**He lied, and that fact is just hard to erase;
but the girl has her own set of troubles to face.**

Monday, 8:00 a.m.

"Get up, Kincaid," Dan hollered through the door. "I don't have all day."

He could hear the kid fumbling around in the room. Dan's visit had obviously caught him asleep and unawares. The delay didn't help Dan's mood.

As Kincaid opened the door, Dan's right hand lashed out, snatched him from the doorway, and pinned his neck against the wall. "All right, airman, I slept a grand total of three hours last night—on the floor in some two-bit flophouse and drove four hours on ice this morning just to get here. I'm through fucking around. I need to know what kind of nasty business you're involved with and I'll give you exactly one minute to tell me."

Kincaid remained mute. His bulging eyes told Dan the young man was duly terrified, but he was nowhere near bubbling with answers. "You can beat me all you like," he said in a stoic voice. "I won't tell you a thing."

Kincaid's insolence served only to stir Dan's rage. "You ignorant, insignificant fuck, you have no idea what you're up against. Do you?"

The kid's sad eyes turned to Dan and pleaded. "Look, Agent Matthews, I never lied to you. Everything I told you happened exactly like I said."

The airman's reminder did not appease him. "You're a very clever young man," Dan whispered, only inches from Kincaid's ear. "We both know you haven't told me what you know. You saved a girl's life that night all right. Her name was Su Li Young. She thanked you by fucking your brains out. Now I need to know what she's up to and how you're involved."

The ruckus began to raise attention and heads appeared, one by one, from the other doors on the second floor. Dan released his grip and pointed into Kincaid's room. "We'll talk in there," he said, and closed the door behind them. "Sit down, Airman Kincaid."

Kincaid chose the crisply made bed, Dan the chair. "I'm serious," said Kincaid. "I have nothing to say." Then he simply closed his eyes, as if preparing to absorb a lethal blow.

Dan had to find a way through that thick skull. "Do you know what they're going to do to you, Kincaid? Is your head that far up your ass? They're going to railroad you out of the service on a Section Eight. Do you know what that is?"

"Sure I do. It means I'm crazy."

"That's right, kid, certifiably out of your fucking mind. Are you?"

"No. Of course I'm not, and I haven't done anything wrong either. If I thought I'd done something wrong, I'd tell you."

The voice had waivered. The youngster was unsettled, off balance and Dan sensed an opportunity. "Who is Chuckie?"

Kincaid's eyes couldn't conceal the shock. "I don't know any Chuckie."

He made a mental note to come back to that subject. "You know what Su Li Young is up to, don't you?"

"Su Li wasn't the woman I helped that night," Kincaid declared. "You're mistaken. If you turn her in, you'll be hurting an innocent person."

"Are you lecturing me?" Dan shouted. "Hell, I'll play. What would I turn her in for? Tell me because I'm curious."

Kincaid flashed him a puzzled look and said, "Do you expect me to believe you don't know?"

The question caught Dan off guard. Did this kid really think he had the answers? Why? What would cause him to jump to that conclusion? "You're playing a dangerous game," he warned. "That girl is involved in something you don't want to be a part of. Listen, Reggie, you're ten thousand miles from home. You wouldn't be the first kid to get suckered by a pretty smile and a good set of tits."

"She's not like that. I haven't done anything wrong and Su Li hasn't either."

"You just don't get it, kid. Somebody high up in the United States government wants you out of the way. I don't know why, but I promise you don't have a prayer. If I don't serve you up, someone else will."

"Doesn't it count for anything that I was telling the truth?"

He had to force the issue, now. "The truth? You just told me Su Li isn't the girl you saved. You lied through your teeth. Don't talk to me about the truth until you're ready to give it to me—all of it."

He wanted to talk. Dan could see the confused torment in his eyes, but he said, "I just can't tell you. Too many people would be hurt, even if that's not your intention."

Dan was exasperated. "Well, Reggie, you're the one who'll be hurt if you don't tell me."

"I can deal with it. But tell me; do you believe I was telling the truth about everything that happened that night? The American? All of it?"

At that moment Dan wanted to be back at Tachikawa interviewing battered wives and reading deep-sea fishing magazines. Nobody had ever called him stupid. He was a detective by job description only. Coughlin had given him a mission, and his job was to carry it out. That conclusion hadn't arrived through an epiphany. He'd always known it.

Dan Matthews knew how the military worked. The enlistment contract didn't mean shit. It was unilateral by definition. Uncle Sam could break the contract and kick your ass out on a whim. The loopholes were anything but reciprocal. The real contract, the unwritten one, went something like this: You do exactly what we tell you, when we tell you and how we tell you. No excuses and no bullshit. If you do, then we'll let you be a part of something, something that will give you an identity and a feeling that your life has a point. We'll feed you, clothe you, house you and give you enough money to get by. But most importantly, young man, we'll give you a place where you are wanted and where you belong.

As Dan considered Reggie's question, it occurred to him that, despite his aversion to military discipline and the gnawing idea that he might have done more with his life, might still, the Air Force had never reneged on that unspoken contract. He took no pleasure in delivering Reggie's answer, but there it was. "Sorry, Reggie, but it's not my job to believe you."

"This isn't exactly a difficult assignment, Matthews," Coughlin's voice howled through the receiver. It was the first time Coughlin had taken that tone. "What's the big problem up there? All you need to do is punch this kid's ticket and get back here. There's no James Bond stuff involved. You were supposed to report twenty-four hours ago."

"You asked me to check out his story. That's what I'm doing, sir."

"Did you read the psychiatrist's report I sent you?"

In fact, he'd just finished reading it for the third time, and it was still lying on the desk in front of him at Security Police Headquarters. "Yes sir. It says the kid suffers from depression, but lots of people are depressed. It's not like he's psychotic or anything. I'm sending you a status report tomorrow. It details my interviews and findings to this point, but the fact is this Kincaid seems pretty well adjusted and his direct superiors don't see him as a security risk. I haven't found anything yet that indicates he's a homosexual. If the base commander has concerns, I'm unable to determine where they came from."

The last remark was imprudent, but he wanted to give Major Coughlin a message. He'd pursued the mission to the best of his ability, and couldn't imagine Coughlin would outright ask him to lie or fake evidence. It wasn't in the contract. But Coughlin had misled him about the base commander's concerns, and Dan wanted the major to know he knew. As an NCO agent, Dan didn't have enough rank to interview a full-bird colonel effectively.

That explained the specific lie, but not the general one: There are legitimate, high-level security concerns regarding Reginald Kincaid. That was bullshit and the base commander story was Coughlin's way of telling Dan the fix was in on this one. The higher-ups wanted to dig up some dirt on this kid—or plant it—and Dan was the guy with the shovel. This was a done deal. It had to be. If the Air Force had any idea Kincaid might be involved in something treasonous or criminal, there'd have been no need for the made-up homo scenario or for sending a sergeant to do an officer's job. No, there never was supposed to be an investigation. Dan felt he had just a little more rope left and decided to use it. "I don't think he stabbed himself, Major, and there's no indication of a deviant lifestyle."

"Oh, no?" Coughlin shouted. "Then who's Chuckie? I've read your daily memos, sparse as they are. Do you think Chuckie is a girl? Goddamnit, Matthews, you're walking a fine line here. Everybody is accountable. I could have sent any number of agents on this mission, but I sent you because I trusted you to carry out the assignment and not to go turning over rocks looking for trouble."

Dan thought the remark revealing. Coughlin seemed almost afraid. "I don't know who Chuckie is, sir. He claims he doesn't know a Chuckie, and the gate guard must have misunderstood. I'm working this as quickly as I can."

The long silence told him Coughlin was about to make a point. "Dan," he began in a fatherly tone, "think about this carefully. You're a staff sergeant. Hell, I'm only a major. There are all kinds of policy considerations and national security issues we know nothing about. You and I take orders. That's who we are and what we do. We're not supposed to question things we don't understand. Now I know you won't go off half-cocked here, because if you do, both of our careers will be in the toilet. Tell me you understand."

He was painting Dan into a corner. Still, there was a lot of sense to the major's logic, sort of a practical application of my country right or wrong. It sickened him, but there was no alternative. Coughlin wasn't telling him to lie, just to write a report that would lend itself to a wide range of inferences. "All right, sir. I understand, but please, just give me another day or two to find out who Chuckie is."

He could almost hear Coughlin's sigh of relief. "Twenty-four hours, Matthews. Twenty-four hours. Now what else have you found out in your little investigation that I don't know yet?"

Dan remembered that sound of a door opening as he left Coughlin's office that day at Tachikawa. A little voice inside told him not to mention Su Li Young—not just yet. "That's about it for now, sir."

9:20 a.m.
Asahikawa, Hokkaido, Japan
Su Li awoke inside a small apartment directly over the Chinese restaurant. She counted fourteen other bodies out cold on the matted floor in

the two small, sparsely furnished rooms. The place was warm, but she found the odor of Chinese food and human bodies nauseating and struggled to open the small window. The rush of freezing wind burned her cheeks.

What snow there was on the ground churned over and over in the steady breeze and thickened the morning air. Although only a few hours drive south of Wakkanai, Asahikawa was widely believed to enjoy a slightly more moderate climate. Its inland location protected it from the fierce Soya wind of the northern coast. Su Li had visited the place often as a child and had fond memories of Mei Ling and her family's small, country house.

Finding her companions, the Pachinko brothers, in this tangle of bodies was no problem. Their real name was Yoshima, but people called them the Pachinkos because their family ran a small Pachinko parlor in downtown Wakkanai. The brothers, like Su Li, were descendants of Sakhalin Koreans, although their parents had adopted a Japanese surname to make life a bit easier for the brothers.

The Pachinkos would not have been Su Li's choice for this mission, but the captain had insisted she take the brothers along on all operations. He felt they were her best security. They were committed to the cause, young, and possessed of great physical strength all right, but she had concluded long ago that, together, they did not house one complete brain. Still, Su Li did not consider defying the captain's will.

Other than herself, the brothers were the only ones in the apartment under fifty-five years of age. Of course, Su Li had no way of knowing the ages of these poor, helpless souls, but simple mathematics and a knowledge of their history gave her the range. One thing for sure, not a single one of them was as old as he looked.

She found the older Yoshima twin first and roused him gently. "Taro-san, wake up your brother and meet me downstairs. We need to talk."

Su Li made her way downstairs and found the Korean owner of the establishment, Mei Ling Ho, making tea in the small, private kitchen in the rear of the restaurant. Mei Ling had proven a reliable and efficient organizer over the last year, arranging temporary housing for many of the aging Korean refugees. Mei Ling herself had not been taken as a forced laborer, but emmigrated to Japan for employment in the early 1930s.

Thousands of Koreans had arrived in Japan this way, yet they had fared no better than the slave laborers in the long run. To earn a living, they did laundry, ran restaurants or operated Pachinko parlors, like the family of young Taro and Jiro.

Mei Ling was devoted to their cause and had recruited more than a dozen families around Northern Hokkaido to feed and house one or two refugees while awaiting the final act in Captain Subarov's play. Her two grandsons operated the clandestine auto ferry service that linked the network of secret hideaways and would deliver the refugees to Sapporo for the climactic event.

"Good morning, Mei Ling," said Su Li in Korean. "I'm afraid we have brought an unusually large number of guests for breakfast, twelve in all, fourteen if you include the Pachinkos. And this bunch is not in good shape; they've been a long time at sea."

"It is good to see you, Su Li," said Mei Ling as the two women embraced warmly. "I'm happy this will be the last group. With nearly two hundred scattered across the countryside, I've run out of places to hide them."

It occurred to Su Li that they were running out of time as well. "It won't be long now. We're nearly ready."

Mei Ling smiled warmly. "You're welcome here. Come. You can help me start breakfast for our guests. But we'd better make two extra portions since those young Pachinkos eat like Sumo wrestlers. We'll make egg pancakes with *kimchi*. Tell me, Su Li, how is your dear mother?"

"Cranky, as always," Su Li said, but Mei Ling was her mother's old friend and deserved an honest answer. "I'm afraid she's very worried about our future, well, my future really."

Before Mei Ling could reply the phone rang. She answered on the second ring. Within a few seconds Su Li knew her mother was on the other end of the line. The two women were speaking Korean so fast Su Li could barely understand. They were talking about the young people putting themselves in great danger. Then Mei Ling held out the receiver to her. "It's your mother. She just wants to know you're all right."

"Hello, Mother. It's probably not a good idea for you to call me here, but everything is fine."

"Everything is not fine," Yoon Hae said.

"What do you mean?"

"Su Li," she whispered, as if whispering would reduce the chance of eavesdropping, "Hiro's mother just phoned me. He didn't come home from work last night. He's always home before midnight."

Su Li gasped, but it was important that Yoon Hae and the others not panic. "Don't jump to conclusions," she cautioned. "He's a grown man. Maybe he spent the night with a friend. I hope it was a woman friend."

"You don't understand. His mother phoned a friend at the newspaper where Hiro works. He told her Hiro was going straight home when they finished work last night. Some of his mates were going out for a drink, but Hiro said he was tired."

Su Li tried to keep calm. Fear could easily infect her little group and then where would they be? These were not hardened secret agents, but simple merchants, fishermen, and waitresses. If only she could reach the captain. "Listen to me carefully, Mother. You must not say anything about this to the others. Do you understand me?"

"But you're all in danger."

"I'll give everyone a proper warning, but I won't start making panicky phone calls until I've considered the implications carefully. You must trust me."

"I do trust you, Su Li. We all do, but what do you think they will do to Hiro?"

Why did everyone expect her to have all the answers? "I don't think the Americans and our Japanese hosts will start murdering us in our beds," she said, even if she didn't believe it herself. "For now, just keep your eyes open and don't leave the house or the restaurant."

In the beginning the thought of being caught hardly gave her pause. What could they do anyway? Throw them all in prison for a year or two at worst? Who really cared enough about the Sakhalin Koreans to make a fuss? Now the situation had changed dramatically. They were playing for life and death stakes.

The group was not dealing with simple, unarmed Japanese policemen. These people might easily have killed Reggie, and probably had every intention to do just that. The world's most powerful governments were determined to stop them at any price. Success in exchange for the quiet deaths of seven or eight ethnic Koreans and a young Japanese idealist would be a bargain to such adversaries.

Su Li tried to think like the captain. She would have to analyze the situation in the cold light of day, without regard to the fate of her dear friend, Hiro. She knew the KGB employed torture as an indispensable tool of the trade. Why would the CIA be any different?

Poor Hiro had gotten in over his head. Sooner or later, he would tell them everything he knew. She hoped it would be sooner, before the pain became too intense. She and the others would just have to deal with it.

Then she thought of Mei Ling. "Mother, you musn't call here again, under any circumstances. Hiro doesn't know of this place or these people. We must never lead them here."

"I understand. Just be careful, Su Li, and don't come back to this place until you know it is safe."

Su Li knew it could be a long wait. "I'll be very careful. I love you. Good-bye."

She turned to Mei Ling, who had obviously gotten the gist of the conversation listening to one side. "My heart is heavy for that poor boy," Mei Ling said. "I pray they don't harm him. Do you know who's taken him?"

"I have an idea, but I can't be certain. As I told my mother, Ishikawa Yoshihiro knows nothing of you, or of our fisherman friend. You and your family will be safe if you use caution."

Su Li needed to talk to someone and the captain wasn't an option. She wouldn't burden her mother with this now and the Pachinko twins were well meaning and lovable, but borderline idiots. She decided to talk to Reggie. He was the brightest person she knew, aside from the captain. He would help her figure out what to do. There was no time to lose. By tomorrow, the entire group could be exposed. Reggie would not be difficult to find tonight, she thought, emerging from the curtain into Mei Ling's restaurant.

Mei Ling followed immediately behind. "But you're in grave danger, Su Li. This thing we've tried to do has become bigger than all of us. I think your mother sees that in a way the younger generation cannot. I, too, fear for your safety. It was never intended that you should lead this little revolt anyway."

"That's what my mother tells me. I think she'd like me to disappear for a while, but I cannot."

"Of course, you can not," Mei Ling said. "I see that just as your mother does. You are a leader, Su Li. It is who you are, and we are all grateful it is so. But take great care from now on."

Just then a woman crept quietly into the kitchen from upstairs, head held low. Su Li turned to greet her but felt paralyzed by the powerful aura of her presence. Su Li could not speak. This was the third time she had come along on one of the rescue missions, and it suddenly occurred to her that, in all those trips, this was her first encounter with one of the Sakhalin Koreans face-to-face. She felt uncomfortable, strangely uneasy, in the woman's presence, and knew her avoidance of the old ones to this point had been no accident.

Since Su Li's first memories, Yoon Hae and the other Korean women had told endless stories of the Sakhalin Koreans, torn from their families and dropped for eternity on an unforgiving enemy island. The stories told of hardships and deprivation almost beyond description, spawning more than a few childhood nightmares for Yoon Hae's only child.

Su Li recognized she could not face these old ones because, in doing so, she would have to face her own weakness. These were people who understood the true meaning of suffering, untainted by the self-pity and indignation upon which Su Li relied so heavily. Helping them from afar was one thing, but real communication with them was something Su Li could not yet bear.

The woman looked seventy, but was probably closer to Yoon Hae's age. Such had been the severity of her life. She was gaunt and frail with an old, long-ago faded scarf around her head. Su Li guessed the scarf had once been new and cherished, sporting bright, happy colors, much like the woman herself.

"My sister is not well," said the woman in Korean, making no attempt to raise her eyes. "Can you help her?"

Still, Su Li could not speak. Thankfully, she heard Mei Ling's voice from behind. "Of course we will help her. I will see to her myself right now. What is her name?"

"Song Yen," the woman replied. "Is this Kyongsang-do? We would like to see our mother."

Her mother? It was not supposed to be like this. It should be hugs and kisses and thank yous; names of long-lost cousins and mutual friends; tears of gratitude and joy. This unpleasant, terrible confrontation held her mute.

She remembered the stories of Kyongsang-do Province from her mother. Near the end of the war, that poor region alone lost thousands of people to Japanese captivity. In the last, frantic wave of conscription, Japanese troops even abandoned all pretext of legality and simply roamed the streets of the villages in trucks looking for able-bodied people to abduct.

Mei Ling led the woman to the small table in the corner of the room. "I will see to your sister," she said, motioning for Su Li to pour the old woman a cup of tea and sit with her.

When Mei Ling left, Su Li felt desperately alone. She poured tea and willed herself to sit, but was unable to touch the woman with words. Watching her was torture enough, but speaking with her would bring the two together in a way Su Li could not endure. She did not even want to know the woman's name. Maybe later, when she had time to prepare and consider these things. Yes, later for sure.

The woman looked up at Su Li and smiled. The old one didn't speak, though she had not hesitated to speak to Mei Ling. It was as if she could sense Su Li's apprehension, her fear. Was she making some gesture of understanding? Compassion?

The woman reached out slowly and placed her hand gently on the back of Su Li's. She wanted to pull the hand back and run, but fear and shame held her frozen in place. The thought of this was too much to bear. This poor, godforsaken woman was trying to comfort her. Was she so shallow and uncaring? Maybe Su Li Young served only herself and not the greater cause of this wretched slice of humanity. In the end she might be no more than a thrill-seeking malcontent.

Mei Ling walked slowly back into the kitchen, and settled onto the mat to complete the trio. She looked calmly at Su Li and then the woman. "I am sorry," she said softly. "Your beloved sister is dead."

It was as if Mei Ling had plunged a dagger into Su Li's own heart. She rose and ran from the room in her tabi socks, then from the restaurant into the icy street, then finally from herself, leaving in her wake a river of tears.

ELEVEN

**There's no place to hide 'til the game is done;
so just dig in and have some fun.**

*Monday, 9:15 p.m.
Wakkanai*

During the course of the long, nighttime drive from Asahikawa, Su Li could not get her good friend, Hiro, out of her mind. She needed to talk to Reggie, but that could wait until tomorrow. She knew his work schedule, his routine, and nearly every place he liked to drink.

As their truck reached the outskirts of Wakkanai City, Su Li decide to make an unscheduled stop against her better judgment. "Jiro-san," she said, "I've decided to stop by the Ishikawa house before we go to Kim Tae Woo's."

"Is that wise, Su Li-san?" Taro said, from the passenger seat beside her. He might not be a rocket scientist, she thought, but in this case his instincts were well grounded in reality. The people who took Hiro were undoubtedly looking for her, and his family's home was an ideal place to wait for her.

"It's probably not a good idea, Su Li-san," Jiro added, glancing over from behind the wheel.

Su Li balanced the risk of her capture against her obligation to the Ishikawa family and knew she had no choice. "I know there's a risk," she said, "but I can't avoid Hiro's mother and father in this time of anxiety. Let's go there now. Besides, if someone is after me, I'd just as soon they find me with you two kung fu killers on my arm."

"But Su Li," Taro protested, "we don't practice the kung fu style. We are masters of jujitsu and the Korean style of karate."

"It's all the same to me, boys," she said. "Just kick up a storm if we find unwanted company tonight."

"We'll protect you, Su Li-san," Jiro said. "You need not worry."

But she was worried, about the lives of all the good people involved in her quest, for it did not take a martial arts philosopher to recognize that loud screams and fancy kicks would provide little protection against a bullet.

The pagoda-style roof, finished in blue, clay tiles was widely admired in the community, but was completely covered in snow this night. Surprisingly, Su Li did not feel reluctant or in any way intimidated at the prospect of this visit, as the truck stopped in front of the two-story, white, stucco home. That changed only when she noticed the police car in the drive.

Su Li paused outside the house to gather herself and to briefly accommodate the flood of memories. The place was well known by the general population of Wakkanai and occupied a prominent location near the town center, within easy distance of the train station. Ishikawa Hitaka, Hiro's father, was a wealthy and well-respected banker in the city. In all the years she had known Hiro, Su Li had only met the father once, and even now, she recoiled at the memory.

It was at least ten years ago, she recalled, but the incident had left a lasting impression on a fourteen-year-old girl. Hiro was walking her home from school one afternoon. He had forgotten that his father was supposed to pick him up, as the family was leaving on a trip to Sapporo.

The older Ishikawa came upon the two school children in his car, only a short distance from Su Li's home. He was furious with young Yoshihiro and severely chastised him in Su Li's presence. She sensed Hiro's humiliation and never mentioned the incident again.

But it was the end of the encounter that had caused her pain. In the midst of his father's ranting, Hiro had tried to introduce his friend, Su Li Young. The father simply ignored Su Li, speaking directly to his son. "You shame me. We don't associate with the likes of these people." Su Li was old enough to understand the remark, but to this day did not know if the older Ishikawa was referring to Koreans or Americans.

She decided to go in alone, lest they think she hired bodyguards for the occasion. Besides, she would rather not have the Pachinkos talking to the police.

Hiro's mother answered the door, a kindly woman of about fifty. She had once taken Su Li home from school to play with Hiro when the father was away on business. "Su Li-san," she said, bowing. The woman wrapped two thick arms around her like Su Li herself were some long-lost relative. "Have you come to give us good news of our son?"

"No, Ishikawa-san," Su Li replied. "I came hoping to hear some."

"Come in," she said. "The policeman is here now. He says it is too early to worry. Yoshihiro may call us by tomorrow and explain his absence in some very simple way." Su Li knew better, but sharing her knowledge would neither help this frightened family nor ease Hiro's suffering.

Hitaka was sitting on the tatami mat in the traditional style when Su Li entered the large room. The tall man beside him at the table could only be the policeman, she thought. Not knowing immediately who she was, the policeman peered at her as an unwelcome intrusion. The elder Hitaka pointed to the mat and Su Li took a place on the floor, well back from the men. He whispered something to the policeman who promptly turned to Su Li. "I am Inspector Tanaka," he said.

On cue, Su Li replied, "I am Su Li Young, a close friend of Ishikawa Yoshihiro." The last part, she figured, might save him the trouble of asking, but would probably just raise more questions.

The inspector, still not having risen, smiled. It looked practiced and fake, but not necessarily hostile. "Oh, I see," he said. Su Li decided he was killing time. She had usurped his first question and he was trying to think of another. She thought she might have the ability to play this game quite effectively. "Then you and Ishikawa were, well, might we say, special friends?"

She wondered if he would take such care not to offend if the two were alone. "No," she replied, so as to leave no room for doubt.

"You are Korean," he said, apparently broadcasting his prowess as a detective.

You are an idiot, she wanted to say. "Only the half that is not American," she replied instead, saving him another rude question. Curiously, it was the first time she had ever embraced the Western side of her heritage—for any reason. Was it possible she had inherited some of those obnoxious American traits after all?

"And when did you see him last?" Tanaka asked.

"Probably a week ago. We had coffee together on his day off, I think."

"How did he seem to you?" The detective glanced down at the father to be sure he was not offended. "You know, how did he seem emotionally?" This time the father looked up at Tanaka and scowled.

"He seemed fine." The truth worked very well. Su Li would have liked to tell this policeman everything, and she would have if there were even a remote chance it would help Hiro. Telling everything would humiliate him in the eyes of his father, incriminate most of her friends, and destroy any chance of the captain's plan succeeding. But it would not help her old friend.

"Was he worried about anything in particular? Or depressed?" The last part drew another hostile stare from the father.

"Nothing like that, Inspector," she answered. "He was happy and looking forward to the next day. I honestly don't know anything that might help." It was true. But what if she did know who had taken Hiro? Would she tell all to this man to save Hiro's life, and in so doing betray her friends? Mercifully, fate had spared her the impossible choice.

Maybe this policeman really could help, and she did not wish to encroach on valuable time. "I really must go," she said, looking at Hiro's mother. "I wanted you to know how much I feel your pain. We all hope for the best." Su Li was careful not to express false hope when real hope was in such short supply.

But the policeman was not finished with her yet. "Are you a relation to the woman who runs Mama Young's out near the base?" It was a question she was not expecting.

"Yes. Why?" If the next question were, Do you know an American airman named Reginald Kincaid? Su Li would be in deep, deep trouble.

"I ate lunch in her restaurant once," he answered innocently enough. "I enjoyed the food. The name is obviously not common in Wakkanai. I just thought you might be related."

Relief. "Her name is Yoon Hae. She's my mother, and I'll pass on your compliment. She will be very pleased."

Su Li turned to go, but he was still not finished. "May I please see your registration card?"

That was the purpose of the hated registration cards; so the government can track the aliens with Japanese faces. "Yes," she answered, already removing the card from her wallet. He wrote down the information and handed the card back, a polite bow for good measure.

On the way back to the truck and her waiting companions, Su Li thought it best not to push her luck. She would have the Pachinkos drop her directly at Kim Tae Woo's house and make do with what things she had in her small bag. Her presence at home now, even for a brief stop, would only further endanger Yoon Hae. She needed to see her mother, but the time would be of her own choosing. Su Li decided to use the address the captain had given her.

She had never met Kim Tae Woo, but the captain had assured her of his unswerving dedication to their cause. His endorsement of Kim's trustworthiness was more than enough to allay her reservations. She thought it best to drop in unannounced.

Upon reaching the southern outskirts of Wakkanai at around ten o'clock, the final few meters of the trip was uphill. Su Li knew the residential area well enough from visiting the home of a schoolmate years ago. It was an area of modest homes along the southern slope of a high, gently cresting hill. The hill overlooked Wakkanai Park to the north, the down slope to the park being far too steep to support construction.

"This is the right street, Jiro-san," she said, "Kinko-cho. The number is one-two-four."

"It must be very near the top of the hill, Su Li," Jiro replied. "Should we go inside with you to be safe?"

"No," Su Li said, "not a living soul knows about Kim other than the captain, me, and now the two of you. It will be safe enough. You might just wait outside in the car to be sure I get inside."

No sooner had she finished than the truck stopped near a small, traditional style house, perched alone, squarely atop the expansive hill. There were perhaps twenty or thirty wooden steps up to the house, cleared of snow with considerable effort. She could see the faint glow of the deeply buried step lights through the snow as she climbed. The house itself was almost completely encased in beautiful, virgin snowdrifts, each rounded and flowing so as to look almost designed.

She could see the glow of lights inside as she pulled the chime chord beside the glass-paneled door. In short order, a middle-aged, gray-haired man appeared from behind the door. His skin was reddened, with a rough hew, and he was sporting a stubby growth of facial hair, the look of a fisherman. "Kim-san?" she asked in Japanese.

The man smiled a perfunctory smile and bowed. "Yes."

Su Li decided on a bold approach. "I'm Su Li Young," she announced in Korean. "Our mutual friend, the captain, told me I might seek shelter here in a storm."

Kim's smile broadened and warmed considerably. "You are welcome, Su Li," he said in Korean. "Please, come into my home."

Su Li turned and signaled to the brothers below, entered, and removed her boots and coat. She followed Kim up the single step and through another sliding door, into an expansive, sparsely furnished sitting room. From the rolled-up futons, it was apparent the space doubled as a bedroom. She could see an old family photograph, mother, father, and three young girls, displayed prominently on a lamp table in the far corner. The children would be grown now, she thought.

Then she saw the small, baseball glove and ball lying carelessly on the tatami mat, as if it had been in recent use. She decided to withhold speculation. Kim and his wife would offer whatever explanation they felt necessary.

A handsome, round-figured woman of similar age joined them from what could only be the kitchen, dressed casually in Western attire. "This is my wife," Kim announced, "Son Yee."

The woman bowed formally toward Su Li. "Welcome to our home."

Su Li bowed and answered at once. "I'm grateful for your hospitality."

Son Yee smiled and disappeared back into the kitchen. "Please, sit," said Kim. "My wife will bring tea and food."

Su Li took a place on the mat beside the small table. "Thank you. I hate to bring trouble to your door, but I need a place to stay for a few days, just to be safe. Can you help me?"

Kim grinned broadly. "Of course. Our home will be your home so long as you need it. But tell me, Su Li, what's the trouble you speak of?"

"I'm not certain yet, but a friend of mine—of ours—has gone missing. He's Japanese, but a trusted member of our group."

"Yes." Kim said, shaking his head. "I've heard the news. It might be very dangerous for you to go home now. Do you know who may have taken him?"

"I have ideas, but I really don't know."

Kim sighed. "I pray they don't harm the young man, whoever they might be."

"I wish I could talk to the captain now," said Su Li. "There are so many things I don't understand. Events are happening quickly, and I'm afraid I'll do the wrong thing."

"Perhaps I can help you there as well," Kim suggested. "My boat will be leaving port Wednesday morning. I'm to rendezvous with our captain in the Sea of Japan a few days from now. He's preparing for his final delivery of goods."

It might be a way to communicate with him, she thought. "Thank you, Kim-san. I'll send a note explaining all that has taken place. Captain Subarov will know what I should do."

Just then Son Yee entered with a tray. She poured tea for them and placed a plate of sandwiches on the table. Son Yee poured a cup for herself and sat beside her husband. "I'm surprised we haven't met," she said to Su Li, "although there must be hundreds of Koreans in this city."

It was a subject Su Li had often considered. "Yes. With such a common bond among us, it's a great pity we haven't sought one another out before this. May I ask how you both ended up in Wakkanai?"

Son Yee lost her smile. Her eyes deflected the question immediately to her husband. He said, "I and my two brothers were taken from our home in Chungchong-do in 1943. All three of us were brought to Karafuto to work in the mines. My oldest brother died of exposure in the first month. We were living outside in the bitter cold and snow while they constructed some crude shacks for us to inhabit."

"I'm sorry," said Su Li, now certain she had been cursed with a regrettable penchant for asking too many personal questions.

"It's all right. I don't mind talking about it. Near the end of the war, the fleeing Japanese took along several thousand of us Koreans to work on Honshu. I ended up in a munitions factory outside Tokyo."

"And the third brother?" The words had escaped her lips before her brain could corral them.

This time Kim did look sad. "I still don't know. Sometimes I find myself hoping to find him among your two hundred, but I know that's unrealistic."

"We're very fortunate to have you with us." It was all Su Li could think to say. At once she remembered the old woman at Mei Ling's. This fear of hers was, of course, a great weakness in her character and she could not understand it, however hard she tried.

"It is I who am fortunate, Su Li. I am neither a brave man nor a wise one, but I yearn for justice for our people. I'm only too happy to follow those, like you and Captain Subarov, who would bring hope to our forgotten ones."

Su Li had many more questions. But as her mother had often said, all questions are answered in time.

10:35 p.m.
Chung could hear Fu's pacing from outside the hotel room door. The young man's lack of patience was just another nail in his professional coffin. He slid the door open and Fu was upon him. "I was worried, sir. I thought something might have gone wrong."

And what would Fu have done if it had? "No. It took me quite a while, but I found the right hotel. It's a one-story building and has an accessible rear door. The best thing is that the clerk on duty is a dimwit. I had to wake her up just to rent the room. It's perfect."

Fu walked immediately to the space heater in the middle of the room and began to remove his coat.

Chung reached for his own coat, lying folded on the mat. "Don't bother getting warm. We'll pick him up now and sedate him. Tell me what happened at the restaurant tonight. Any luck?"

Fu shrugged and began to rebutton his coat. "None at all, sir. I stayed an hour tonight hoping she'd show up. It's not easy. Everyone in the place is American. I listened as carefully as I could, but you know my English is bad. I heard her name spoken many times, but I think it was just talk about her not being there."

Chung believed in brief, succinct reports. Fu was of a different school and it drove him nuts. "What about the old lady? Did she say anything?"

"Yes, I was getting to that, sir. Tonight she told a particularly obnoxious group of Americans that the girl is on holiday in Tokyo. I'm sure of it. It's a bunch of shit, of course, but it tells us we won't find the girl at Mama Young's."

That much was obvious. "And it also tells us she knows we're closing in on her."

"Do you think she knows who we are, sir?" Fu asked.

Chung slid back the flimsy sliding door. "Subarov doesn't know who we are, Fu. How could she? She probably thinks it's the CIA."

Following down the dim hallway, Fu continued his report. "That's not all, sir. The old lady noticed I was there twice in one day, even though I've never set foot in the place before today. She got suspicious and wanted to know what I was doing there. She's smart and sneaky too, acted like she was just being friendly."

"That's not good. If you talked to her, she must have noticed your accent."

"It shouldn't be a problem, sir. I said I was a civilian employee for the U.S. Air Force here on temporary assignment from Osan Air Force Base to install some electronic equipment. She bought it, no doubt at all."

"Good thinking." The young man was smart, ruthless, and ambitious, exactly the kind of young cowboy who would stab Chung in the back at the first opportunity. But, of course, the opportunity would never come. Chung would see to that.

TWELVE

**I'll huff and I'll puff,
but he'll probably blow my brains out anyway.**

Tuesday, 8:15 a.m.

Kim Tae Woo drove slowly, but not too slowly up the coast road, past Mama Young's Restaurant opposite the American base. Su Li's eyes carefully scanned every conceivable hiding place for any trace of surveillance. The street was void of pedestrians and Su Li could spot no suspicious vehicles lurking in the area. She felt she was adapting adequately to this spy craft, but took no solace in the thought. A second pass netted the same results, and she felt safe enough exiting the car a short way up the road.

"Wait for me here," she instructed. "Honk the horn if you see something suspicious. I won't be long."

"Right," Kim replied.

All was quiet along the coast road as she made the short walk. It was a risk, she knew, coming to see Yoon Hae at their home, a far greater risk than going to the Ishikawa house. In all likelihood, whoever was after them would have been at the restaurant yesterday looking for her. Yoon Hae might know. Beyond that, Su Li had to know her mother was safe, and you just can't see through a telephone line.

Anyone might be holding a gun to her head while she pretended there was nothing wrong.

Su Li found herself hoping Hiro had broken down immediately and told everything. After all, he probably didn't know enough to scuttle their mission entirely, and what he did know Su Li could deal with. She told herself they would not harm him if he cooperated fully, at least the Americans wouldn't. By this point, Su Li prayed it was the Americans who had taken Hiro. Any other possibility was simply too terrifying.

The street was still deserted as she neared the restaurant. The businesses didn't open until at least nine o'clock, and then only to serve a few beers to some thirsty stragglers off the midnight shift while they worked up a hunger for lunch. She could be in and out within a few minutes, a tiny, field mouse quietly about its cheese gathering, then back into shadows.

She rapped gently on the back door and Yoon Hae pulled back the curtain. "Su Li," she whispered, opening the door, "you shouldn't have come here."

"It's all right. I'm getting rather proficient at this."

"Not as proficient as you might think," Yoon Hae scolded.

Su Li saw two cups of tea on the table and gasped. Before she could speak she saw a hand move back the floor-length curtain from in the restaurant and through the doorway stepped the American policeman.

"Wait," Yoon Hae pleaded. "Don't be frightened. I think you should talk to him."

"Mother, have you lost your mind?" Su Li shouted. She locked her eyes on the American, lest he reach for a weapon. She had to get word to Kim.

Had Su Li been holding a knife at that moment, she might have plunged it into his throat. Pure arrogance must have brought him here, if not thoughts of murder. What was her mother thinking? What was his name? Matthews, yes, that was it, Dan Matthews. She would never forget it again.

Anger turned to fear, then fear to confusion. Was he here to confront her? To kill her? She might buckle to a bullet or a knife, but not intimidation. She walked straight for him. "I have help outside," she said in English. "You'd best leave now, while you are able."

"Your help," he said, "has a little trouble of his own by now. Let's look out the front window, shall we?"

Su Li made a point of walking behind him, into the restaurant, and up to the front window. The American peeled back the curtain and gazed up the road. "There he is. Take a look yourself."

She did. There was an American car, a big, blue car parked directly behind Kim. He was out of the car talking to an American policeman. Her heart sank. "Now what?"

"Nothing bad will happen," said the American. "The policeman will just talk to your friend until you and me are finished."

She didn't like the sound of it. "Finished what? What do you want?"

"You know who I am?"

She was in no mood to be interrogated. "I know who you say you are. Save your charm."

He moved closer. "Then I'll come right to the point. Reggie Kincaid is in a lot of trouble over you. He could be kicked out of the service because you won't come forward and back up his story. He could be in a lot more trouble over your little game, whatever it is."

This American was very clever. "I ask you again, what do you want?"

"I want to know what you're up to. I want to know what you've got Kincaid involved in."

"I have nothing to say to you," she pronounced. "Do whatever it is your masters instruct. I am not difficult to find. I do the marketing in the morning and generally go to the bank in the afternoon." With that she turned and marched back into the kitchen.

The American followed, undeterred. "I'm not sure what it is you think I'm going to do, but I wouldn't worry about it. I'm an investigator for the Air Force. They give me a case and I investigate it. That's all."

She was immune to his lies and whirled to face him again. "You will never stop us," she whispered. "I want you to hear that from my lips. You will never stop us. Kill us and there will be others."

"Kill you? That's not in my job description, but I might like to stop you as soon as I figure out why you're smuggling people into Japan and who they are."

Nothing she could say would help Hiro or save the cause, so she only turned and walked away. A rush of cold air marked his departure out the front door.

Su Li felt her mother's hand on her shoulder. "I want to speak with you," said Yoon Hae. She knew better than to give Yoon Hae any lip in response to the formal request. "What haven't you told me, my daughter? I tell myself I must live with this growing danger to your life, and I try. Don't be disrespectful to me by concealing the facts."

"I'm not concealing the facts, Mother, only attempting to discover their meaning. I've already decided you need to know everything, if only for your own safety. It appears someone or some group has abducted Hiro. The police are already involved in the case, but they know nothing of our operation." Su Li walked through the curtain and over to the front door; she turned the lock. Easing back the door just a crack, she spotted the big, blue car stopped down the road, waiting for Matthews. "They're gone," she declared.

Yoon Hae, standing directly behind her, asked, "Will they harm him?" as though Su Li had the power to ease her fear upon request.

"I don't know any more about that than you, Mother. I can't think of a reason why they would. It may have been the Americans, and they are practical, if nothing else. Surely they won't start murdering people over the fate of a few thousand Koreans. I can't imagine it. It's not as if their nuclear secrets were at stake."

"They tried to kill Reggie," Yoon Hae reminded her. "Can you reach your captain for advice?"

Su Li shook her head emphatically. "Impossible. He'll rendezvous with Kim Tae Woo at sea later in the week. Kim's boat leaves port Wednesday morning. I'll make sure he tells the captain. It won't be in time to help us, but the captain must know the situation before he risks another landing. He'll give Kim the details. I'm the only one who knows of Kim's involvement—and now you. If something happens to me, Kim will find you."

She could see the terror in her mother's eyes. "Don't even speak such words, Su Li. I never envisioned this would become such a nightmare. It all began as simply a way to bring some attention to the plight of our poor people."

Yoon Hae was right. Had Su Li forseen the dangers she might never have become involved. "What's done is done, Mother. I'm certain things will be happening very soon now. The longer we wait, the greater the risk."

Yoon Hae seemed to collapse slowly into the kitchen chair. "Nikolai Subarov has placed you in grave danger, Su Li. He's stirred up a hornet's nest and now he's off sailing the seas somewhere, fishing."

Su Li was not about to blame these troubles on her noble captain. "It was never his intention. Captain Subarov is a passionate man. He's not perfect, I know, but he'd gladly die for our cause."

Yoon Hae's shoulders slumped in defeat. "Yes, my daughter, I'm certain he is passionate, but he's not here."

It was difficult for Yoon Hae to understand a man like Captain Subarov, Su Li thought. Her mother had spent an entire lifetime in subjugation of one form or another, with survival her only goal. Life's horizon ended at the front door for Yoon Hae Young and who could blame her? The captain was a man of action and vision and Yoon Hae's life had been tattered and stomped by men of action and vision. The sum of Yoon Hae's experience was a breeding ground for skepticism. Su Li sat beside her mother, placing her hand gently on Yoon Hae's back. "Please have faith in him. I do."

Yoon Hae bristled. "He's a White Russian. What can you possibly know about him?"

Had Yoon Hae been harboring her own secrets? "What do you mean a White Russian?"

Yoon Hae nodded and took a moment to gather her thoughts. "There were many like him on Sakhalin during the war. The memories are only too vivid for me."

Her mother seemed to consider the question, as if wondering where to begin. "During the Russion Revolution in 1917 a large group of Russians remained loyal to the czar and formed an army to fight the Bolsheviks. They called themselves White Russians. As the Bolsheviks took power, remnants of the White Russian army fled to Karafuto; we call it Sakhalin now. There they lived out their lives in misery under Japanese rule. Your captain was born on Karafuto. There were many like him. His father was no doubt a White Russian soldier. That's why he speaks perfect Japanese."

Su Li tried to analyze this information even as her brain struggled to process it. "And that's why he hates the Soviet Union?"

"I think it goes deeper than that," her mother replied. "When the Soviets overran Karafuto in 1945, Stalin locked all the Russians up in the gulags for a time, the ones he didn't kill. The story is he didn't kill them all because he needed workers to run the factories, the mines and the fisheries. There weren't enough captive Koreans left alive to do the job."

Su Li felt only a stiffening sense of resolve. "This is no reason to deny him your faith, Mother. His cause is our cause."

"I place my faith in you, Su Li," Yoon Hae replied, touching her gently on the cheek. "I only hope you are right about your captain. Young Ishikawa's life may depend on your judgment. Don't forget; someone tried very hard to kill Reggie."

"Yes, that too troubles me. The Americans would never kill one of their own without good reason and a calculated decision, but that wasn't the case."

"What are you getting at?" her mother asked.

"Think about this. An American agent would not have tried to kill another American who simply stumbled into his operation. There would be no need for it. That means it was someone else who stabbed Reggie."

At that moment a group of boisterous GIs burst through the front door of the restaurant, shaking mountains of snow onto the clean floor. "Morning, Mama," one of them called through the curtain. "We're thirsty as hell. Can we get you to open up a little early?"

Passing into the restaurant, Su Li did her best imitation of a polite smile. "Please, come in. We'll be out in just a minute. Take a seat and warm yourselves." She returned to her mother, still sitting at the table, head in hand. "Did you understand what I just said?" Su Li asked.

"Of course," Yoon Hae said. "I think I understand, but the Japanese don't have the stomach for such business. Their policemen are more referees than officers and they don't even have an intelligence service to speak of."

"Exactly. I can't help but think some other power is somehow involved in this with the Americans."

"It might be the Yakuza," Yoon Hae suggested. "Everyone knows they're mixed up with the Japanese government, and they are certainly not above murder."

The thought made Su Li shutter. "I hope you're wrong. There are no rules where the Yakuza is concerned, and they would do anything for the right price."

"Hey, Su Li," came the obnoxious American voice. "We're dying of thirst."

"Just a second," she yelled.

"One thing I know," Yoon Hae said. "Whoever took Ishikawa is looking for you. Your life is in danger. You have to get away from here now."

Su Li nodded. "I'll stay with Kim and his family, but I won't hide. If they have my name, they can find me anywhere. I think the American investigator was just in here to remind me of that. He's no doubt CIA."

"You don't believe that," Yoon Hae said. "I don't think he's involved. I think he's exactly what he claims to be. He only has bits and pieces of the puzzle. That is my reading."

"Hey, Su Li," came the thundering voice of another American, "you want us to go down the street to Club Seven?"

Yoon Hae poked her head through the curtain and snapped, "You don't be patient and wait, you wear beer bottle over head." With that she plucked three bottles of beer from the cooler and plopped them onto bar, adding an opener for good measure. "Here, this keep you busy for a while."

As she reentered the kitchen Su Li said, "He knows we were bringing in people on boats. He probably knows everything and is only pretending. You could still be right about him though. Maybe he's not involved. Maybe he's just what he says he is. Have you had any other suspicious visitors since yesterday?"

Yoon Hae thought a minute. "Well, there was an Asian in here yesterday."

Su Li nearly let the comment pass. "I know we serve mostly Americans, but it's hardly suspicious when a Japanese man comes in here."

"I understand, Su Li, but this one wasn't Japanese. He was Korean, and he was in here twice, once at lunch and once later for a beer."

It was a bit odd, Su Li thought. "Had you seen him before?"

"Never."

"Korean," Su Li repeated. "It doesn't make any sense. Did you speak with him?"

"Yes, the second time. He told me he works for the American Air Force. He's here from Osan, Korea on an assignment to install some equipment at the base."

"Well," Su Li said, "that makes perfect sense. We've had other Koreans like that over the years."

"I thought so too," Yoon Hae added.

"Anyone else?"

"No."

It seemed to make sense. "All right, I'm going to talk to Reggie about this whole business. He has a very good mind and I trust him completely."

Yoon Hae frowned. "You surprise me. I agree Reggie is a good boy, but he is still in the American Air Force."

Yoon Hae's remark surprised Su Li. "If I am to be betrayed, Mother, it should be by the one who saved me, but it won't come to that. You know these Americans. They're not like the Japanese. They cherish their insolence and call it independence. Reggie is a trusting person, but he's a person of conviction and follows his heart. Reggie is American, but that's exactly why he will not betray us."

"Still," Yoon Hae said, "you mustn't stay here. You must leave now."

"As you wish. Kim is waiting for me outside. In case you need to reach me his address is—"

"No, Su Li. I know the address. I only wish I could forget it, and don't call me from there. Now get your things and go."

"I appreciate your help, Lieutenant," Dan said, reaching for the door handle of the blue Chevy.

"Forget the lieutenant bullshit," the man replied. "Call me Mike. And don't give it another thought. We have standing orders to provide assistance to the OSI whenever possible."

Mike Yamada, the Security Police shift commander, was a handy guy to know in a country where you don't speak the lingo, Dan thought, as the blue Chevy lumbered back toward the main gate. "How did you learn the language, Mike?"

Mike smiled. "I'll give you three guesses, but no prize. It's about how you'd figure it. Born in California to immigrant parents. They find us fair-skinned Americans useful over here in the Land of the Rising Sun."

"I know I do," said Dan. "So what did you find out?"

"The guy was no fool. I asked him why he was hanging around the base. He reminded me very politely that I had no jurisdiction off base and refused to give me identification."

Dan considered the information for a moment. "Well, we have the car registration number. I'll send it off to my HQ. They should come up with a name, but it will take some time."

"There's one more thing," Mike said.

"What's that?"

"I think the guy is a foreigner. I mean he looks Japanese enough, but I detected an accent, and I'm not talking about the local twang either. I mean a real accent."

"Maybe Korean?" Dan suggested.

"Yeah, maybe Korean."

There was a pattern developing, no doubt about it. Whatever was going on had something to do with Koreans specifically. Dan was deeply troubled by his conversation with Su Li Young. He never expected the girl to confess her sins and surrender, but her reaction to his onslaught was contrary to the book on criminals. She had displayed entirely too much defiance and too little fear. He had carefully directed the conversation according to a reliable investigative technique he learned at the Academy. Engage the unwitting suspect in conversation, then shock him by letting him know you're onto his game, even if you're not.

Body language sometimes speaks louder than words. It wasn't scientific like a polygraph, and it wasn't evidence, but it could confirm or reject a suspicion reliably in a second. When confronted with the sudden possibility of discovery and capture, a suspect will invariably flash unmistakable physiological signs of guilt: the twitch of an eye, the licking of the lips or nervous laughter. The signs were varied, but always identifiable.

Su Li didn't so much as flinch or bat an eye when he unloaded the smuggling allegation on her. It just didn't make sense. The fact that he knew should have shocked her into tremors, but it didn't. It was almost like she knew he knew. In fact, the entire conversation, from her perspective, assumed he had read her entire playbook. Why would she make that assumption? Who did she think he was? That was the key. She thought he was someone else. What was it she'd said? I know who you say you are. Dan had more questions now than ever, but one thing for sure, he figured: Su Li didn't fit the profile of a criminal.

As the Chevy pulled up to the bachelor officers' quarters, Mike said, "How about some breakfast? I was just going over to the O Bar and get some ham and eggs. I'll buy."

"Beats chow hall food," Dan replied. "So long as we can leave right after we eat."

"What?"

"Never mind. I accept your offer, but I'm buying today. Let's go."

If the girl wasn't engaged in some criminal enterprise, it just might have something to do with espionage, he thought. A distinctly unpleasant possibility. That could be the reason Coughlin, or whoever's pulling his strings, is so desperate to yank Kincaid's security clearance. Maybe they suspect him of treason. A woman like that might easily get a kid like Reggie to fuck up his life by helping her commit espionage. She was beautiful all right, and probably seductive beyond description.

But if the intelligence types suspected treason or espionage, why keep Dan in the dark? No reason for it. If national security were really at risk, they'd just pull the kid's access to classified information and ask questions later, but that's not what's happening. There's got to be a hidden agenda somewhere.

It seemed a little farfetched, but maybe Kincaid stumbled onto some illegal, covert operation and they just want him out of the way so he doesn't expose it. Dan wasn't naive. He knew the U.S. government was involved in all sorts of activities that would undermine its credibility. Some of them had to be kept secret from even the highest-ranking government officials.

He knew, for example, that the United States Navy routinely carried nuclear weapons into the port of Yokohama in violation of the treaty establishing military bases in Japan. He knew the NSA surveillance aircraft and ground stations operating from Japan routinely spied on Japanese government communications in violation of the same treaty.

These were illegal activities and their disclosure could seriously undermine national security. Maybe Kincaid unknowingly stumbled into something like that. It would explain the American in the snow.

Dan was about to set foot in dangerous water, and if he waded in too far, the tide just might pull him under for good. He heard a voice, a sensual Polynesian voice, telling him, *Do your job. Kincaid is nothing to you.* It was a cinch this Su Li Young was involved in some kind of hanky-panky. This was the woman Reggie had saved in the alley, and now they were doing the horizontal Tango. On paper, Reggie was involved up to his ears and shouldn't have a top-secret clearance anyway. The sensible thing would be to put the hammer down on him now; then go back to Tachi and sign the reenlistment papers—or not.

"Dan, Dan," came the strange voice beside him. "Are you there?"

"Oh, sorry, Mike."

"Man, it was like you were lost in a trance or something. We're here."

He was dead tired, but the cold wind shocked him wide-awake as he opened the door. But what if the girl was right? Or even half right? What if someone else knew what they were up to on the peninsula that night? What if Dan's own government knew? They wouldn't be happy to see him writing about it in unclassified status reports and naming names. If it were a case of espionage or counterintelligence, Dan Matthews wasn't supposed to know about it.

He had to admit it was also remotely possible that both Kincaid and Su Li Young were on the level. Of all the possibilities, that one terrified him the most because it would surely put him on a dead collision course with Major Coughlin. He'd had enough problems with superior officers over the years. The last thing he needed was a confrontation he couldn't win. If it came to that, Reginald Kincaid would have to live with his General Discharge.

But what legitimate reason could Su Li have for smuggling people into Japan from boats in the middle of the night? He'd seen it with his own eyes. As he flashed his identification and walked into the Officers' Club, Dan still had no idea what his final report would say.

THIRTEEN

**Beyond the point of no return,
I kissed him once, then watched him burn.**

Tuesday, 7:30 p.m.

As a rule, Chung liked to drive his own car because it gave him a sense of control, but he was feeling particularly important this evening and decided to ride in the backseat. Fu was behind the wheel as the car pulled up to Foster's hotel. The American was waiting outside. "Good evening, Mr. Foster," Chung said, as the portly NSA man crammed into the seat beside him. "Did you sleep well last night?"

"You know very well I didn't," Foster replied, ignoring Chung's junior partner at the wheel. "This is supposed to be a Western-style hotel, the only one in town with doors and actual beds, I'm told. Somebody needs to tell them how to make a fucking mattress. It's like sleeping on plywood. The room is smaller than a jail cell at Alcatraz and I'm getting sick and tired of not having a shower. The whole damn place reminds me of a pair of Jockey shorts."

For a moment Chung thought he misunderstood the words. "I'm sorry?"

"Jockey shorts and a small hotel," Foster said, smiling. "They're both too small for any ballroom. You get it?"

Chung didn't get it and Foster's loud and unruly display of laughter offended him. He had no wish to see inside the pig's mouth or feel the spray of his bacteria-ridden saliva. "Subarov knows it is only a matter of time. He'll move quickly now to reach his objective."

Foster was looking at his watch, appearing disinterested as the car turned inland, toward the hills. "Is there something wrong, Mr. Foster?" Chung asked.

"In America we eat dinner at dinnertime. If we wait any longer I'll have to order breakfast. Where the hell is this restaurant anyway?"

Rudeness, Chung had learned during his first visit to the United States, had risen to the level of a cultural trait among Americans. He was certain it had some connection to their overindulgence. "We will be there shortly."

Foster sighed. "All right."

"Have your superiors established a plan?" Chung asked, wondering how anyone, even an American, could think of food at such a time.

"Yes. That's what I'm to speak to you about. The NSA has arranged for four trawlers to conduct a coordinated patrol in and around the strait. Three of them have already arrived, although probably too late to stop the delivery you nearly intercepted."

It was more than Chung could have hoped for. "That's not a problem. The next shipment is the last and most important one."

The American squirmed in the seat, searching for legroom. "They will be looking specifically for Subarov's boat, the *Irina*," he explained, "but will identify and track all suspicious vessels. Our ground station here in Wakkanai will monitor all shipping frequencies for voice communications as well. We'll know the position, course, and speed of every vessel operating in and around the Soya Strait. If they try to send anything ashore, we'll know where and when."

Chung was beside himself. "Excellent, but won't you simply be broadcasting NSA's involvement in our operation?"

"Not a chance. Anything and everything that happens within the four walls of that operations center or onboard one of NSA's ships is classified top-secret crypto. Believe me, it will stay within NSA."

Chung tried to conceal his glee. Foster's NSA assets gave him a foolproof way to trump Nikolai Subarov once and for all. The old man and his troublesome cargo would never make shore in Japan. Those were his operational orders and anything less would constitute failure. "Very good. And is that meddling, young airman out of the way yet?"

"No. I'm afraid not."

Chung wanted to tell this overstuffed, American, pencil pusher that he had already seen to it. But he needed to stick to the script. "What seems to be the problem there?"

"The OSI agent they assigned is still dragging his feet. It's very touchy business and my superiors are not happy. We've made our position clear, but even the slight risk this fool presents is enough to preclude our direct involvement in the protocol."

"I'm afraid I don't understand," Chung said. "Why doesn't NSA simply cancel his security clearance and send him away?" Chung was making small talk and part of him wanted to tell Foster they already had the woman's name, just out of spite.

"There's a fear the incident he describes could find its way into the public arena," Foster said. "Believe me; there are troublemakers everywhere lying in wait for just such a leak. Before you know it, we could have some commie-loving senator on the Intelligence Committee up here snooping around. The unanticipated coincidence is our worst enemy in this business, Chung."

Americans. The comment sounded patronizing to Chung. His plan for the American airman was not only brilliant, but now absolutely necessary. "The risk is small, but I do agree it exists." …For the moment.

"By the way," Foster added, "the English language newspaper ran an article today on a missing Japanese man, Ishitara something or other. It's not something that happens every day in this frozen shithole. Would you happen to know anything about that?"

"Nothing."

"If this goes wrong, Chung, it must never come back to NSA or my government. We'll just have to hope this agent gets the job done and work around the problem if necessary. Say, what do you know about this restaurant? I told you, I'm not eating squid or raw fish."

It was just the kind of spineless decision Chung expected from the Americans. "I thought you might appreciate a good steak, Mr. Foster. This place has the best steaks in the city."

Foster huffed. "A good steak in Wakkanai? Everything is relative, but let's give it a shot anyway."

* * *

9:00 p.m.

Reggie would not be difficult to find, Su Li thought, as she boarded the municipal bus for the city. This was his scheduled day off duty and Su Li knew his list of regular hangouts from their late-night conversations. It would be better to find him before ten o'clock. After that, he'd likely be too stinko to focus on serious conversation.

She had been so busy holding back the dam these past two weeks that Reggie had barely crossed her mind. Oddly, he hadn't called or stopped by the restaurant once in that time. Reggie was not difficult to read, and she knew their night of lovemaking had pleased him.

Was it possible that, in giving of herself so unreservedly and honestly, she had merely caused him more pain? In truth, Su Li had given herself to Reggie because her body was all she had to give, all she was capable of giving. She was not in love with him. She did not long for his gentle touch or soft caress, though both had given her great comfort in a moment of mutual need.

She hoped that, somehow, Reggie knew these things and, in allowing her space and time, he had again come to her rescue. More than anything at that moment, she wanted real happiness for Reggie, partly because he so deserved it, and partly because her conscience demanded it.

The bus stopped in the bar district, and the driver, an occasional customer of the restaurant, left her with a warning. "Whatever your business is down here, Su Li, be careful. This area is nearly as bad as the port district."

She smiled, hopefully enough of a smile to compensate for forgetting the man's name. "You are very kind, but I won't be long. It will be all right." She headed up the street for the Club Seven, one of Reggie's regular stops, and found him sitting quietly alone at the bar. She settled onto the neighboring stool. "Hey, GI," she whispered in English, "you likey date?"

The corner of his mouth turned up into the right half of that shy smile Su Li had come to cherish, but his head did not turn. "Actually, I'm waiting for someone. She has long, brown hair and green eyes that could melt steel." He turned to face her. "It's good to see you, Su Li."

She squeezed his arm. "I think if I did not come out to find you, I might not have seen you again."

"Oh, you know better than that. You can't get rid of me that easily. Beer?" he asked, already signaling for the bartender.

"Of course," she replied, thinking she might never find a way to begin this conversation.

"I heard you had another talk with my friend, Agent Matthews."

This business was becoming more complicated every day. "How did you know that? Did he come to you afterward?"

"No, he came to me before, but I didn't tell him anything."

It didn't make sense. "Then how did you know?"

Reggie shrugged. "He's just a very determined fellow. I figured he'd find you. He's not buying that stuff about you being on a holiday."

"Yes, he's clever enough," Su Li admitted, "but if I hadn't made a display of leaving on your arm that night, Matthews might never have linked us. I'm sure he heard about it on the base grapevine. It was a foolish mistake."

"Not such a foolish mistake, maybe," Reggie said, blushing. "It certainly elevated my status in the eyes of my peers. Anyway, Matthews doesn't know anything."

"You're wrong, Reggie-san. He knows far too much. Last Sunday night our seagoing friend brought ashore a group of a dozen old, Sakhalin Koreans. I was there myself to meet them at a remote spot on the western side of the island."

"Did it go badly?"

She was still trying to answer that question for herself. "It went as planned, but that's not the point. The point is this Matthews knows all about it."

Reggie winced. "How is that possible?"

"I believe he may have been the American who fell from the roof the night you saved me."

"But that man was wearing a parka with a hood," Reggie countered. "How can you know that?"

She considered for a moment that Reggie Kincaid might be incapable of seeing bad in anyone. If that were the case, Su Li had made a huge mistake by confiding in him. "I didn't see his face," she admitted, "but everything points to Matthews' involvement, even if he wasn't the man in the snow."

"Then you believe Matthews is really after you and your friends?" he suggested.

"Yes. I'm convinced your government is trying to stop us, and the situation has become more desperate than when we last met."

"It doesn't make any sense at all, Su Li. Matthews undoubtedly knows you were the girl in the alley that night. He told me as much when he came to see me. But why hasn't he reported it?"

"How do you know he hasn't?"

"Because if he had, the Air Force would have pulled my security clearance ten seconds later. At best I'd be on my way to Vietnam. They wouldn't let me within a mile of classified information if they had any inkling I was mixed up with you and your Sakhalin Koreans."

Su Li was relieved to learn Reggie's allegiance to this Matthews was based on sound logic, and not simply a character flaw. She had not misjudged him at all. "So what does it all mean?"

He looked at her glass on the bar. "You haven't touched your beer."

"Beer is not what I need right now," she said. "A clear head will be more help."

"I know what you mean," he said, rising from the stool. "Let's walk awhile."

Outside, Su Li noticed the night was unusually clear and calm, with not a trace of snow in the air. "This is the night we should have gone to Cape Soya Point," she said.

Reggie laughed. "Believe me, I wouldn't change anything about that night—never."

Su Li smiled. "I am happy for that, Reggie-san. Now tell me, what is all this business with Matthews? What does it mean?"

"I think you're right about my government, but wrong about Matthews," he declared. "My government is somehow trying to sabotage your mission all right, but Matthews isn't involved. My bet is someone or some agency in the government is keeping Matthews in the dark and using him to do their bidding."

That was too much for Su Li to buy into. "Well," she reasoned, "even if you're right, Matthews is working for them."

"That's a good point. He's a lifer, after all, and he's only a sergeant, like me. But still, I get the feeling he wouldn't be a willing part in all of this if he'd gotten wind of what's going on."

Su Li would not have been quite so generous in her assessment. "That only means he'll feel some convenient remorse if we're all murdered in our beds."

Reggie laughed. "You're pretty tough for a girl. Agent Matthews is just an honest schmuck trying to do an honest job. He is what he is…but I guess you never know."

"What do you mean?"

He turned to her and smiled. "I mean, I'm helping you, aren't I?"

Su Li punched him playfully on the arm. "You are not really American. We've decided that already."

"Here comes the bus," Reggie said. "Come on. I'll see you home."

They boarded the old city bus and found themselves the only passengers, taking a seat together in the back. "He wants to know what you're up to," Reggie said. "He's convinced I'm telling the truth about what happened that night and wants to know why there was an American involved. I'm sure he's curious about you unloading old people from small boats. I'd say he's pretty confused about now, but if we take a chance he just might help us."

"You mean tell him everything?" Su Li could see the tone of her voice had attracted the attention of the driver and lowered it to a whisper. "Are you insane, Reggie-san?"

"Think about it carefully," he cautioned. "If we don't, he'll conclude you're involved in some illegal activity or espionage and report us both. He'll have no choice. I think you have to gamble. Go to him and tell him everything. At least that way we have a chance."

Su Li had come to Reggie for advice, but not the kind she had just heard. Reggie might be right, but there must be a better way.

"There's more, Su Li."

"What more?"

Reggie wrapped his long fingers around her shoulders and looked her squarely in the eyes. "Is your seagoing friend master of a Soviet fishing trawler called *Irina*?"

Su Li had never been at sea, but suddenly felt as if she were run aground, alone on a tiny, doomed vessel at night, a tsunami bearing down around her head while the deck disintegrated, board by board under her feet. "Yes."

"It will be very difficult for him to reach Japan again undetected," Reggie said. "The NSA has sent four electronic surveillance vessels to find and track him, whether he sails on the *Irina* or another vessel."

She could feel her heart sink. "Then it's hopeless," she said, and for the first time in eighteen months was on the verge of admitting defeat.

"It's not hopeless."

Now she was truly puzzled. "What are you telling me?"

"You know what I do at the base?"

She tried her best to force a smile. "Everyone knows your big,

American secret, Reggie-san. You are a den of spies."

"In a way, I guess we are," he conceded. "The other night, when all this fuss started over the *Irina* and the plotting board told me they were moving surveillance ships in, I realized my government was involved in something I was ashamed of. Those people deserve to go home and no government in the world has a right to say different."

She stood and said, "This is our stop."

With that, Reggie reached into his inside pocket and removed a few folded sheets of paper. "Do you have a way to reach your captain?"

"Yes, we have a Korean friend. He's master of a Japanese fishing trawler. His boat leaves port in the morning and will rendezvous with the captain soon."

Reggie handed her the documents. "Give these to him," he instructed. "He must bring them to your captain. They are the search grids and patterns for each of the four NSA ships. With this information he can plot a course around the electronic surveillance. Tell him to communicate only when necessary. Use code words and rotate frequencies often. I've included a list of the least-used maritime frequencies. If they follow these instructions, their voice communications may not even be detected at all. You're not beaten yet."

Su Li held the precious documents to her chest and tried to collect her thoughts. Reggie was right. Their cause was not hopeless, not yet. Kim Tae Woo was a good and brave man, but the fate of their entire plan might now rest on a single conversation with the captain at sea.

Captain Subarov must be made to understand the significance of the dangers awaiting him. She, in turn, needed his counsel before the situation on land spun hopelessly out of control. Su Li could not entrust such a grave mission to another. She and the captain needed to meet in person, regardless of the risks involved. She would sail with Kim Tae Woo.

"Reggie-san," she said, "you must find a way to stall Matthews until I return. Don't tell him the truth, but keep him from reporting what he knows. Promise me."

The bus stopped and the door opened. He helped Su Li down onto the icy road. "That's a tall order. How the hell would I do that?"

"You'll find a way. You must."

"Well," he replied, "at least tell me where you're going and when you'll be back."

"Let's just say I'm going fishing," she said, "But I should be back within a few days."

"I'll do what I can. Be careful, Su Li."

It suddenly occurred to her that, in turning over this information, Reggie had crossed into a place from which he could never return. She knew the success of her mission must now come at the cost of Reggie's future, and she felt deeply conflicted, even ashamed.

In a single, unselfish act of untainted bravery, Reggie Kincaid had set off a chain of events that might now result in her success and his destruction. She stopped in the icy track and turned to face him. "Reggie-san," she said, "they'll call you a traitor. You'll be imprisoned if they learn of your actions."

"Yes, I've thought about that and I won't say I'm not scared. Part of me wishes I didn't have the ability to help, but I do. Believe me, Su Li, I'm quite capable of taking back those papers and stepping out of this whole mess, so you'd better stop talking and go right now."

Su Li wanted to cry. "You must forgive yourself for what happened in the past. You were a child then and not responsible. You are the bravest man I have ever known."

She heard his sigh before she saw the single tear fighting to escape from his eye into the cold air. "Go now, Su Li. I'll think of something to tell Matthews. Have your mother get word to me at the base when you return."

She grabbed hold of his arm and swallowed hard. Reggie Kincaid had earned nothing less than complete honesty from her, however painful the truth might be. "No, Reggie-san," she whispered, "I am not finished hurting you. There is something else you must understand."

"I understand more than you know," he replied softly, "but thank you." He kissed her lightly on the forehead and slipped away into the night.

FOURTEEN

**Better to remain silent and be thought a fool
than to open your mouth and remove all doubt.**

Wednesday, 4:20 a.m.

Startled by the incessant rapping on his door, Dan flipped on the desk lamp and looked at his watch. The mess hall wouldn't even open for another two hours.

"Agent Matthews," came the voice from the other side, "you have a phone call at the Security Police office. The duty officer sent me over here to get you."

"For Christ's sake, let me get my pants on. I'll be right there." It was a perfect example of why he'd had enough of military life as an OSI agent. He did exactly the same job as the officer agents, but for less than half the pay. Now the duty officer had sent this poor airman to risk a beating, rousting him from his bed like an airman basic on his first morning of boot camp. In truth, he'd been expecting it.

Dan spied the duty officer reading a comic book as he peeled back the door against the biting wind. The man barely acknowledged his presence, pointing toward the phone receiver on the desk. Dan had already picked it up. "Agent Matthews here," he said.

"Matthews," came the voice of Major Coughlin, "you're in a world of shit, and you've put me right in it with you."

Dan tried to rub the sleep from his eyes. "What is it, sir?"

"I just got a phone call from the base commander up there at Wakkanai. It seems the local police found the body of a young, Japanese man at the Yokuska Hotel a few hours ago, and you'll never guess what else they found."

"What's that, sir?"

"They found a note of unrequited love to his fucking boyfriend," Coughlin explained. "Do I need to tell you who his boyfriend was?"

Even a staff sergeant could figure that one out. If the raging wind had failed to clear the cobwebs from Dan's head, the major's startling revelation had just finished the job. "I suspect you're going to tell me it was Airman Kincaid."

"That's right. It was our Airman Kincaid. The same Airman Kincaid whose homosexuality I suggested to you over a week ago. I'm very unhappy with your performance on this assignment, Matthews. I made a bad choice and it may well have ended my career."

"Sir, I haven't disobeyed any direct orders."

"Which is the only reason you're not up on charges," Coughlin snapped. "I tried to tell you this had to be done quickly and quietly, but you turned out to be a hotshot. I'm reassigning you back here while I try and salvage this. But you're the only one I have up there now, so you have to deal with the Japanese police on this—until the next plane back to Yokota."

"I understand, sir. I'm sorry."

"Too late for sorry, Matthews. I still have a chance to save my career—maybe, but you may as well take that job in Hawaii."

"Sir, can you tell me anything about the dead man? Was he murdered or was it a suicide?"

"Apparently, it was either a suicide or a murder made to look like one, and I only have that on third-hand hearsay."

"What about cause of death?"

"You'll get your ass over there and find out. Inspector Tanaka is in charge. He's waiting for you as a courtesy to us. They haven't even moved the body yet."

It was an opportunity Dan would not squander. "I have experience with the Prefectural Police, Major. It's more likely he wants me over there because he needs information, but I'll leave immediately."

"Well, whatever he wants, within reason, you give it to him. Do you understand?"

Dan didn't like the sound of that. "Sir, does that include Airman Kincaid?"

Just an extra meter of silence. "It means anything, including Kincaid."

The order sounded a bit open-ended. "Sir, what if he wants to interrogate Kincaid?"

"His access to Kincaid has already been granted by Pacific Air Command. I don't want you to question him, Matthews. Do you hear me?"

So much for, leave no wounded behind, Dan thought. This was a particularly nasty development. Under the treaty, U.S. personnel could be subject to Japanese criminal law for offenses occurring off base. But there were always things the military could do to see that the GI got a fair trial.

For example, if Dan questioned a suspect prior to the local police, he'd have to give the kid his Article Thirty-One rights off the bat, even though he wasn't in custody. This would at least give the suspect a heads up that he better get himself a lawyer before opening his mouth. On the other hand, if the Japanese questioned him first, he wasn't entitled to hear his rights read. Dan wasn't even sure what his rights were under Japanese law. It was pretty clear Airman Kincaid was dead meat just waiting to be gutted. In effect, the U.S. Air Force had hung him out to dry. "Why not, sir?" he asked.

"You let me down, Matthews. You have no idea the trouble you've caused. Well, let me give you the official answer. This is a civilian police investigation. We're required by treaty to cooperate. If they want to arrest him for murder, good riddance. Am I clear?"

Something else bothered Dan and he might never get another chance to explore it. "Yes, sir," he said, "but how did you get authority from PACAF so quickly? The body is still at the scene."

"It seems Pacific Air Command has its own interest. Their office called me, not the other way around."

This was an ominous development indeed, Dan thought. "What could their interest possibly be, sir? The problem with Kincaid is at the operational level as a possible security risk. Why would PACAF get directly involved on its own?"

Coughlin was silent. Dan guessed the major had said more than he was supposed to. It was also clear he didn't know the answer either. "How the fuck would I know? Are you going to investigate PACAF now? Just get over there and do your fucking job."

"Yes, sir."

But the major wasn't finished. "What you can do when you get back, Matthews, unless you have an objection, is sit down and write a report recommending charges against Kincaid. I'll expect it in the morning, but as of now his access to classified material is terminated and he is under house arrest. Do you understand?"

Arguing with him was pointless. "Yes, sir."

Dan knew two more things for certain: Reggie Kincaid was fucked, and someone or some agency had been using Dan as a stooge all along. At this point it was impossible to tell the good guys from the bad, but murder had raised the stakes and there was no telling how high. It was someone else's problem now.

"And Matthews," Coughlin added, "if you don't finish this and get back here tomorrow, I'll be forced to recommend charges against you."

Coughlin was threatening him. You can't leave active duty status with charges pending. They had to be resolved first, if it took five months or five years. The threat was empty for now, and would remain so if Dan just wrapped this up and headed back to Tachi. One door closes, another opens. It occurred to him that Major Coughlin had just tipped the balance of factors in favor of going to Hawaii. He should have felt lousy at that moment, but didn't; it was more like relief. Dan Matthews was going to be a detective in Kailua-Kona, Hawaii. He'd do what he could for Kincaid, but this business of the dead Japanese guy and the love letter would be enough to finish him off on their own. Poor Reggie was a sitting duck either way. There wasn't a goddamn thing Dan could do to help the kid.

He dressed as quickly as he could. This time there was a car with a driver waiting for him. The PACAF information gnawed at him and he tried to look at it analytically. The Japanese police must have called the base commander, he thought. That's the protocol in such situations. The base commander would then make the OSI notification.

But in this case somebody notified PACAF directly, in addition to calling in OSI. He concluded it could only have been the base commander. Why would he violate the protocol? Dan could think of only one possible reason: the base commander was aware of a standing alert from PACAF for any information concerning Airman Reginald Kincaid.

But why? What interest could the top brass at Pacific Air Command have in one little airman at some obsolete intelligence station? It was a leap, to be sure, but maybe some other agency, one of the clandestine services, had their own interest in Kincaid, having nothing to do with his security clearance or sucking dick.

The Yokuska Hotel looked more like a low-end bed and breakfast. It was a single-story structure of some kind, completely buried. The snow had been carved out around the windows and the front door was only accessible through a kind of porthole, or tunnel through the icy, white shell. The chimney smoke looked like it was coming straight out of the snow. Several police cars were parked outside, along with the coroner's ambulance.

Dan entered the small, front lobby and found eight or ten people milling around, disheveled and smoking. Most were paired off in easily identifiable couples, primarily old men with attractive young women. The men looked nervous as hell.

With windows buried in snow, the only light eminated from a single lamp on the desk and a few low-watt fixtures along the walls. Smoke moved eerily around the bulbs, searching in vain for a means of escape. Dan made his way down the narrow hallway unescorted, to an unnumbered room on the left where the door was slid open and the wheels of Japanese justice were busily at work. There were perhaps six people in the tiny, sparsely furnished room. Each one looked fully occupied on his own specific task, as if the investigation would grind to a halt without him.

The body was lying in the center of the room, naked, and more or less on the futon. The skin was almost white and the body looked to be as cold as the temperature outside. The left arm was extended from the futon, toward the door, beneath it a sea of blood that had turned the tan-colored tatami mat deep red clear to the doorway. Dan could see the gash in the boy's left wrist. Exsanguination seemed a good bet for cause of death.

The medical examiner was leaning over the body, carefully avoiding the massive blood spill while performing a series of measurements on the corpse. The tall man standing behind him was eagerly following the process. Not just tall, more like the Wilt Chamberlain of his race. He'd never known a Japanese man to reach such lofty heights. The man was easily six three. He wore a gray fedora and traditional, Western, wool overcoat, unusual for a Japanese man, and not practical in the harsh climate of the Northern Hokkaido coast. It all told him this was a man to whom image was important. It could only be Tanaka.

He had spotted Dan and was negotiating a safe trail around the blood to the door. The big man smiled, extending his hand, "Ah, you must be Sergeant Matthews. I am Inspector Tanaka," Sergeant Matthews? Dan made a mental note of Tanaka's gaff for future consideration. There were all kinds of extraneous conversations taking place in this investigation. Tanaka had obviously been talking to someone with serious access. He decided to let it go. Maybe jaw flapping was the inspector's habit, and he'd learn more just by listening.

"Right," Dan replied. The man had a firm grip, he noted. If Tanaka considered him a houseboy, it might be in Dan's interest to play along. "I was ordered to report here and assist you in any way possible, sir."

"Good, Sergeant. This very ugly business." His English wasn't good, but better than Dan's Japanese. "What do you know about this?" Tanaka was also direct, Dan concluded. It pleased him to find that one person in this mess could get right to the point.

"Nothing, absolutely nothing."

Tanaka shrugged in disappointment. "The victim is Japanese, a local boy. He worked at the newspaper. On the surface it looks like a suicide."

"On the surface?"

"Yes. We do not make conclusions until all evidence have been examined." He was growing on Dan already. "According to the night clerk, he checked in last night alone. One of the guests came back early this morning when the bars closed and saw the blood seeping under the door into the hallway."

"I see. And how can I be of service to your investigation?"

Tanaka removed a small, plastic evidence bag from his overcoat pocket and handed it to Dan. "Here," he said, "look at this, please. We found it on the night stand."

It was a plain, imitation, gold watch of the garden variety, your every day twenty-dollar watch back in the world. Dan turned the bag over and noticed the inscription on the back: "Run, Reggie, run."

Coughlin had told him about a note, but nothing about this. He thought it best to play dumb. "Interesting. Do you know who this Reggie is?"

Tanaka gave him a funny look, definitely not funny ha-ha. "I thought you might help me with that."

That damn Coughlin had intentionally sent him in here unprepared to make a fool of himself. Tanaka probably knew more about Kincaid than Dan did. Best to just grind it out as best he could. "Well, there is a Reginald Kincaid involved in one of my investigations. He's stationed at the base here. That's the only Reggie I can think of right now."

"Is he same person who was before stabbed in Wakkanai?"

"Yes, he was."

"Do you find this odd coincidence?" Tanaka asked.

"I don't really know." Dan had the feeling he was the subject of an interrogation. Pointedly, Tanaka had made no reference to the note. Dan said, "Do you suspect murder, Inspector?"

Tanaka ignored the question, a clear breach of etiquette. "Tell me, do you have evidence this Kincaid is homosexual?"

Even a houseboy could get his feathers up. Dan said, "I'm told there was also a note, Inspector. May I see it?" There would be no way for Tanaka to avoid that question.

After a five-second stare-off, Tanaka again reached into his pocket. "Of course," he said, in an apparent shift of tactics. He handed Dan another clear evidence bag, this one containing a short, handwritten note on a four-inch square piece of white paper, probably torn from some kind of envelope. The writing was Japanese. "Do you read Japanese, Sergeant Matthews?"

"No. Could you give me the general idea?"

"It is very personal. I am fear it will be humiliation to this boy's father. It seems Mr. Reginald Kincaid ended this relationship, causing the young man great distress, perhaps enough to kill his own life."

"May I ask if you lifted any prints from it, Inspector?"

"Two," he replied, "only two."

Tanaka wasn't giving him much. "You say perhaps this boy committed suicide," Dan pointed out. "Do you have an alternative theory? One that includes murder maybe?"

"As I say, we have not ruled it out. For this reason I am pleased to speak with Mr. Kincaid today. Will you be kind enough to arrange this?" Tanaka handed him a business card.

He seemed to know Dan had no choice. "Of course, but may I ask one question, Inspector?" If Tanaka wanted the interview right away, maybe Dan could trade for it. Tanaka knew he couldn't refuse, but Dan could do plenty to delay.

"Of course."

"May I examine the instrument used to make that wound?"

Tanaka frowned. "That is not possible, I am afraid. It was a fishing knife, very sharp. We lifted one complete thumbprint. Unfortunately for you, the evidence envelope has already been sealed."

"Any partial prints on it, Inspector?"

"No, only one print."

"That's odd. Let me show you what I mean." Dan removed the small utility knife from his pocket and opened the blade, placing the handle firmly in his left palm. "Look, this is how you'd have to hold a knife in order to cut your own wrist." He closed his fingers around the knife and moved the knife until the blade rested across his right wrist.

"Go on," said Tanaka.

"Well, look at my thumb, Inspector. It's touching my index finger, not the knife. You shouldn't have a full thumb print on that knife."

Tanaka frown deepened into a scowl. "This print might have been made when Ishikawa picked up the knife."

"That's certainly possible, but there should be other partial prints on this knife in either case. Why is there just one full print?"

"I understand your point," Tanaka said. "Thank you. I will make note of this fact."

If Tanaka had intended sarcasm, the sincerity in his voice betrayed him. "Thank you, Inspector. Now if you don't need me for anything else, I'll head back to the base and arrange your interview." Dan headed down the dimly lit hallway and heard footsteps not far behind.

"Excuse me, Sergeant Matthews," said Tanaka, "but there is one matter still to be discussed. Do you have evidence Mr. Kincaid is a homosexual?" He was obviously not a man to be sidetracked.

"I really don't," Dan replied.

"Yet one thing troubles me. You were sent here from Tachikawa to conduct an investigation. Is that correct?"

"Absolutely correct, Inspector." The less said the better.

"But what were you sent to investigate? The incident involving Kincaid was a Japanese police matter. They would not send you to investigate such a matter. This I know from experience. What then was your assignment?"

Either this guy was really smart or he'd been tipped off in advance. With Dan's luck, it was probably a combination of both. *You will give him your full cooperation, Sergeant Matthews...anything he wants, Sergeant Matthews.* There was no way around it now because his next request would be to see the reports. Dan said, "He has access to classified information. There was a concern that he might be a security risk."

"A security risk?" Tanaka asked.

"I was to determine if Kincaid had engaged in homosexual conduct." He wanted to help Reggie, but it was out of his hands now.

"Then may I ask you again what evidence you have regarding this?"

"Only what you found in this room, Inspector, nothing else."

"It seems very odd you would receive such an assignment without some evidence or some indication of this deviant activity."

Dan, of course, wanted the answer to the same question, but he'd never sell that to Tanaka. He opted for the standard military cop out. "I just do what I'm told, Inspector. I will make my reports available to you, of course."

"Thank you. That will be very helpful."

"Tell me, Inspector, is it your plan to take Kincaid into custody for any offense?"

"It is too early for such a determination, Sergeant Matthews," he answered. "I must continue to gather and evaluate evidence, then speak to the public prosecutor about this. I do require that he remain on the base until my inquiry is completed."

"Yes, that will be taken care of. I'm authorized to tell you Kincaid will be on house arrest at your disposal until your investigation is complete."

"Very good," said Tanaka

"I'll make the interview arrangements this morning and call you within an hour or so. Tell me, will there be an autopsy?"

"Of course."

"And what about a handwriting analysis? I assume you'll want to determine this young man actually wrote the letter."

The inspector's subtle smirk told Dan it had been a stupid question. "Are you familiar with Japanese writing?"

"No."

"There are three distinct forms of writing, each with its own characteristics. All three do not lend themselves to handwriting analysis because the characters may be easily printed in common form."

"I see."

"Do you?" Tanaka asked. "We do not all carry pistols in the street as in America, but we have investigated many death cases over the years, both suicide and murder. We are quite capable, I assure you."

Despite the inspector's ruffled feathers, Dan had no reason to believe Tanaka harbored a hidden agenda. He seemed competent enough and might end up being the only straight arrow in the whole fucking quiver. There was nothing to be gained by making an enemy of him. "I'm sorry, Inspector," he said. "It wasn't my intention to insult you. There's a lot going on here that I don't understand."

"Are you pleased to explain that remark in detail, Sergeant Matthews?"

Dan could think of at least ten reasons to come clean with Tanaka, and twenty reasons not to. Tanaka had all the forensic resources: pathology, fingerprints, handwriting. He had access to the witnesses and the power to compel cooperation. Tanaka's would be a valuable friendship to acquire, and Dan was holding enough information of his own to pay the price. Aside from that, Dan had decided he liked the guy. Together they could get lucky and figure this whole mess out.

But what then? Dan's own government was probably involved and Tanaka's might well be. What could two cops do against two-thirds of the free world? No, the downside of including Tanaka was unthinkable. He might even be involved himself. That would explain why he was holding his information so close to the vest. Like it or not, Dan was a Maverick on this one, sink or swim.

It occurred to him that Coughlin had done him a favor by keeping him busy all this time with petty crimes. This spy shit was enough to drive you crazy. Stolen beach chairs and hotel thefts were sounding better all the time.

FIFTEEN

**Shit only rolls downhill on an incline.
When the ground is flat it just sits there.**

Wednesday, 7:45 a.m.

"Get up and get some pants on, Reggie," Dan said, banging on his barracks door. "We need to talk."

The door opened slowly and Reggie appeared, still half asleep and standing in his skivvies. The young man's room smelled like a brewery. By the look of him, Dan guessed, he hadn't been asleep more than an hour. "As of this moment you're under house arrest," he said.

Reggie was still fumbling with his trousers and seemed not to understand. "Reggie," Dan said, "did you hear me?"

"Just a minute," the kid answered. "I'll get these buttons. I don't know why they couldn't make these goddamn fatigues with zippers."

This was a cruel way to do it, Dan thought. He said, "Take your time and get cleaned up, kid. I'll run over to the mess hall and get us some coffee. Then we need to talk. All right?"

"Sure. Thanks. I'll be fine in ten or fifteen minutes."

Waiting in line for the coffee, Dan pondered his next move. He tried to do what he always did first in an investigation: break the case down to the most fundamental question. It might be too late to save

Reggie from the vultures, but he'd do what he could until tomorrow's flight back to Yokota. He simply needed to know if Reggie had a sexual relationship with the dead man. That was the key.

If Reggie was indeed the man's lover, then the boy's death was suicide. Reggie wouldn't be stupid enough to leave his watch in the dead man's room. If the two were not lovers, on the other hand, the conclusion was nothing less than terrifying. It had to be a premeditated murder designed to frame Reggie Kincaid as the fall guy, if not the killer. In that case Dan's suspect list would be confined to half a dozen or so of the world's most powerful intelligence agencies.

He paid the thirty cents and headed back across the road to the barracks. Reggie's door was wide open and the young man was sitting at the small desk. "What are you doing there, Reggie?" he asked, resting a cup of hot java on the desk.

"Oh, thanks. I'm just finishing a letter home. I haven't written to my family very often since I've been in service. I figured it was time. Maybe I was right."

"I suppose you were," Dan admitted, taking a seat on the bed. "I'll mail the letter for you when I leave." He thought it best to be straightforward with the kid. "Last night the local police found a body in a downtown hotel room. There was a suicide note near the body. Addressed to you."

Reggie sprang to his feet and cried out. "No, it can't be. Su Li would never harm herself."

Kincaid was either the world's greatest con man or exactly what Dan suspected him to be—one of the gentlest people he'd ever met. "It wasn't Su Li," Dan assured him. "In fact, Reggie, it wasn't a woman. It was the body of a young Japanese man. The note indicates the two of you were lovers and he killed himself when you rejected him."

Reggie slouched and sank slowly back into the wooden chair, his blank stare targeting only the wall. "What?" he whispered. "You think I'm homosexual?"

"I don't know what to think, honestly," Dan confessed, "but they found your wristwatch in the dead guy's room. At least I think it was yours. It had an inscription: 'Run Reggie, run'."

Reggie seemed suddenly to recover his posture and the focus returned to his eyes. He turned to face Dan. "It was mine, all right, a gift from my parents for high school graduation. Running was the only thing I was ever good at in high school. And I think I know the name of the dead man. Was it Ishikawa Yoshihiro?"

"Yes." Whatever else, this Ishikawa had at least known Reggie and probably Su Li as well. "Now keep talking."

"It all makes sense now," Reggie said. "I lost my watch that night when I got stabbed on Fish Alley. They found it and planted it on that kid to get me out of the way. I guess you didn't get your job done quick enough."

"Who is Ishikawa Yoshihiro?"

Reggie's body language told Dan he had triggered some kind of shutdown. "I'm sorry. I can't tell you that; in fact, I wish you'd forget I said the name. Believe me, he wasn't my lover and I'm not a homosexual. But if the dead man is Ishikawa, it's just the beginning."

Dan was no mood for a shutdown. "The beginning of what? You have to tell me everything you know. There's a Japanese policeman coming over here this morning to interview you. You're in a world of shit, Reggie. They might even arrest you for murder. You have to trust me. It has something to do with Su Li Young, doesn't it?"

Nothing.

"Just tell me who killed this guy and planted the watch."

"I don't know the answer to that question, and neither does Su Li. I don't know why they're dumping all this on me. I'm not paranoid. All I did was help someone who was in trouble."

"I know, Reggie. You walked into something that had a life of its own, and shit rolls downhill."

"Not always," Reggie countered. "This time it just kind of landed on both of us I think, and stayed put."

It was a strange thing for the kid to say. He was complicated, to say the least. Just when you were finally ready to throw him to the wolves he'd show you something worth saving. Dan had never once whined to the kid about his own troubles, but he just seemed to know. In his own way, he was asking Dan to believe in him. "Maybe so, Reggie, but it's more complicated than that now. You're involved in something, and I need to know what it is."

Although Reggie remained mute, Dan could see the wheels turning. Threats were meaningless at this point. Reason was his only option. "You know I could have turned you and Su Li in long before this, don't you?"

"Yes."

"Well, doesn't that say anything to you?"

"Of course it does. I told Su Li you could have turned us in. I told her we could trust you, but I made her a promise."

It was a start. "What's she up to, Reggie? If I'm gonna help you I have to know."

"I can't tell you until she comes back," he answered. "She'll be back in a couple of days."

"You don't have a couple of days. She doesn't have a couple of days either. Unless you convince me she's on some noble crusade, I'll have to turn her in—today. Do you understand me?"

That was it. He couldn't do anything else for the boy unless he decided to help himself. Dan didn't have long to wait. Reggie lowered his head in surrender and said, "Ishikawa Yoshihiro was working for Su Li's cause. He was kidnapped the other night on his way home from work. I'm sure he was murdered."

Don't let up now. "Why?"

This time the kid didn't hesitate. "I suppose because some government, maybe even ours, wants to find out Su Li's identity so they can stop her."

In that moment so many things started to make sense. "Stop her from what?" He was ready to leap from the bed and shake the answers from the young man's mouth into one big heap.

"From bringing her people home," Reggie said.

It was a much larger answer than Dan had expected. He looked at his watch and saw he had over three hours before Tanaka would arrive. "Okay," he said. "Let's go have some breakfast at the chow hall and you can tell me all about it."

"Sure."

"And Reggie," Dan added, "you and I are going to take a ride into the city after breakfast."

"I thought I was confined to base."

"You are, but you'll be in my custody. I need you as a translator. There's something that's bothering the hell out of me."

There was only a single police car left when Dan and Reggie pulled up to the Yokuska Hotel in the blue Chevy. Not surprisingly, the place appeared otherwise deserted. The previous night's activities had sent the adulterers scurrying for cover. Tired as he was, Dan couldn't stop thinking about Tanaka's representation that, "According to the night clerk, he checked in alone last night." Tanaka wouldn't have said that unless the clerk had identified the body. That didn't add up. If he checked in alone he couldn't possibly have been kidnapped. And if he wasn't kidnapped, he wasn't murdered.

"All right," he said to Reggie, "let's go shake the tree," and the two men headed for the front entrance. Dan figured Tanaka might be holding back, but maybe it just hadn't occurred to him yet. In either case, Dan would have to find out for himself. The answers were out there somewhere and the clerk was the best place to start.

Reggie was smart and had a mind of his own, so Dan figured he'd better lay down the law before they went in. As they reached the front door, he said, "Reggie, don't say anything I don't tell you to say and translate precisely what you hear. Are you clear on that?"

"Sure. I've got it."

They entered through the ice porthole, bending low and this time the door chime announced their entry. A young man appeared from the open doorway behind the desk. "Good morning," he said in English. "May I help you?"

Flashing his ID card, Dan said, "Good morning. My name is Matthews. This is my partner, Agent Franks. We're with the Office of Special Investigations, the U.S. government agency investigating the death here last night. We'd like to ask you a few questions."

The man bowed and said, "My name is Sakamoto Oshima. I speak Engrish very weru, but I have very few words. I do not understand your question. Wiru you wait one moment? My daughter studies Engrish at schooru."

Reggie interrupted in Japanese without prompting. It was clear enough he was telling the guy to let his daughter be, that Reggie spoke well enough to ask the questions in Japanese.

The man said something to Reggie directly in a friendly tone and waited for a reply.

Dan said, "Ask him if he owns the place."

Following a longer than expected exchange, Reggie turned to Dan and said, "He's the owner all right, he and his wife. The clerk last night was their employee, Watanabe Mitsuko. She lives alone."

"That's more than I asked you to say," Dan said, but Reggie had done okay. "Now, see if you can get him to give you her address."

"That won't be necessary. She lives in a room in the hotel. It's part of her employment arrangement."

"Excellent. Ask him if the hotel keeps a register. I'd like to see the entries for last night."

The next exchange in Japanese didn't sound promising. The man raised his voice several times and repeatedly shook his head back and forth. Reggie said, "He's telling me they don't have a guest register."

Dan aimed his most intimidating stare in the balding man's direction. "That's bullshit. Every hotel has one. That's how they track down guests who damage the property or run out on the bill. Ask him again, Reggie, and be a little creative."

"But you said—"

"I know what I said. Just do it."

The conversation that followed sounded increasingly tense, almost hostile. Dan decided to intervene before he closed a very important door. "Stop, Reggie. Let it go." Keeping this guy friendly was now Dan's top priority. Reluctantly, he removed a ten-dollar bill from his wallet and handed it to Reggie. "I don't think we need to worry about his ethics. Give this to him and tell him we appreciate the time he's giving us."

"But I think he's lying," Reggie said.

"He may be, but he's not going to show us the register. I think I know why."

"Can you share it?"

It was bizarre sharing information with the subject of your investigation, but what the hell. "This hotel is kind of a seedy place. I think that reputation is what keeps his business hopping. My bet is the register wouldn't be worth shit anyway, a bunch of John Smiths or whatever the local equivalent is. Besides, if the cheating businessmen find out he's been giving out their addresses, he'd be looking for a bartending job."

Reggie said, "So should I ask him about the cars?"

"What cars?" Dan asked, and then it hit him. Reggie was giving him a gentle nudge. The register wasn't the only way to keep track of your guests. It wasn't even the most reliable. Good innkeepers kept a list of automobile registration numbers, just in case. Before Reggie could follow up, Dan said, "Sure, ask him about the cars, but very gently."

He hadn't thought to take down the registration numbers of the cars last night. It was a rookie mistake. He'd been so focused on the big picture and his goddamn orders that he'd neglected to work the crime scene. Sure, he thought, it wasn't his job to run the death investigation, but the thought brought no absolution. And Reggie had thought of it right off the bat.

The walls in that place were paper-thin. On second thought, they were fucking paper. One of those philanderers or his girlfriend must surely have heard something coming from that room. Now they might never know. He'd just have to hope the night clerk could give them some answers.

The head shaking told Dan, Reggie had run up against another brick wall. Sakamoto either had the car registrations or, better yet, knew some of his patrons by name. He wasn't about to hand over that kind of information for a sawbuck. But what the hell; you get what you pay for. He'd just see how far his ten bucks would carry him. "Ask him if he would be so kind as to wake up the night clerk for a chat."

This time Sakamoto shook his head vertically, triggering Dan's sigh of relief. He would get his opportunity to question the clerk. Dan followed the proprietor down the dim, narrow hallway. The man stopped at the first door and a conversation with the occupant ensued through the door. When Sakamoto entered the room, Reggie whispered, "Well, you can be sure he's in there telling her what to say and not to say."

"We'll just have to do the best we can. She may still help." He decided to get a good look at the place and kept moving slowly down the long hall, Reggie on his tail.

The hallway ended with a solid wall, but the last door on the left side didn't lead to a hotel room. It was an exterior door. He checked it. Unlocked and operable from both inside and outside. It didn't prove anything, but he noted it with interest. He could see words forming on Reggie's lips and quickly lifted his index finger to his own, "Shhh."

They had to do the interview standing in the cold lobby. Dan used the front desk to take notes. The lamp provided barely enough light for the task. He said, "All right, Reggie, tell Mr. Sakamoto he can wait in the other room. Say we're required to do interviews in private. Say anything, just try to get him out of here for a few minutes."

As Reggie gave Sakamoto his walking papers, the man started yapping like they'd just emptied his till. He wasn't going anywhere, so Dan would have to let the guest register alone. He'd been hoping this

Watanabe might know the names of one or two of the guests as well, but Sakamoto had no doubt covered that angle while he was inside her room.

Dan decided to get right to it. "Okay, Reggie, I understand. Forget it. Tell her who I am and that I'd like to ask her a few questions about last night."

She seemed cooperative enough. Reggie was obviously initiating some small talk first, to calm the woman and establish a rapport. His initiative had already proven invaluable and Dan decided to give him some rope.

Reggie translated her response. "She'll answer whatever questions she can, but—"

"But what? Another sawbuck?"

"I think it would put you over the top," Reggie answered.

"And into the poor house," Dan said, reaching for his wallet.

The middle-aged woman grinned, exposing a wide gap where her left eyetooth had once resided. "Reggie, I want to know if she was working yesterday when Ishikawa checked in. Find out what time he checked in and whether he was alone. That's very important. Find out if he was alone. Okay?"

"I understand."

After about three minutes, Dan had the feeling Reggie was running the show. The kid was reveling in it. What could possibly have happened, Dan wondered, that had robbed such a promising young life of achieving its natural potential? Whatever had derailed this kid's life was a problem for another day. "That's enough already. Would you like to let me in on your conversation?"

Reggie turned and said, "Sorry, she was here all right. The boy checked in around eight o'clock in the evening, and he was definitely alone."

"Well, ask her if she saw his face."

"I already did. She saw his face when he checked in and twice more after he was dead."

"Twice?"

"She went into the room when a guest saw the blood and started screaming, then saw him again when the police took her into the room."

"And she's sure it was the same guy?"

Reggie struck up another conversation. After a few seconds, his voice became excited. Dan said, "What? What the hell is it?"

"Very interesting. She's sure because the guy who checked in was wearing the same black, nylon parka and red stocking cap the police found in the room."

"Okay, but what about the face? Was it the same face?"

Reggie smiled. "I asked her that. She said she was pretty sure, but part of his face was covered by a mask?"

"What? A mask? What do you mean a mask? She would have told Tanaka if the guy was wearing a mask."

"Not necessarily," Reggie said, "not this mask. It was a medical mask. You know, one of those white, surgical masks. In Japan, half the people on the street wear them in the winter. It's supposed to be a hygiene thing. They wear them when they have a cold, or even when they don't want to get one."

A light bulb flashed in Dan's head. "Sure, I know what you mean. On the Tokyo commuter train everybody wears them. She probably wears one herself. She wouldn't have thought it unusual. Ask her if she told the police."

A couple of one-line exchanges, then Reggie said, "They didn't ask."

"It makes perfect sense. Like you say, half the people on the street are wearing them. If they didn't ask, why would she bring it up? I buy it."

"Can I let her go?"

"Yeah. Tell her thank you." So Tanaka made his own little boo-boo in this investigation, Dan thought.

On their way back to the car Dan said, "You did a good job, Reggie."

"Thanks. I was glad to help. It gave me something to do besides sit around and feel sorry for myself. So now we know how they killed him, eh?"

"Not quite, but we're getting there. We know somebody passed himself off as Ishikawa and checked into the hotel. We know they brought the real Ishikawa in through the back door. We don't know who killed him, how or why."

Reggie gave him a boyish look. "But we're getting closer, right?"

The two of them were in shit up to their ears, but Dan couldn't resist a chuckle. "Yes, partner, we're getting closer, but the answers may kill us both."

SIXTEEN

**So I'll catch more flies with gallons of honey,
but why should I have to use my own money?**

Wednesday, 12:00 noon

Dan was waiting for Inspector Tanaka at the main gate when he arrived promptly at noon. "Good afternoon, Inspector," he said, opening the passenger door. "I've arranged for you to use an office over at the Security Police building. It's not far, but we can drive your car down if you like."

He noticed Tanaka did not bow in the customary manner, but offered his hand from the driver's seat. Dan thought it more a stylistic signal of Tanaka's worldliness than an intentional slight. If this detective wanted to play Mike Hammer, Dan could adjust.

"Thank you," said Tanaka, releasing his Herculean grip, "but I prefer to walk. I will take the opportunity to see the base a bit."

"Sure. You can park the car right behind the security post."

They passed the base theater on foot. The small marquee read, "John Wayne in *True Grit*." Tanaka was trying very hard not to look impressed. When they passed the NCO Club, the detective stopped at the small door marked, "Liquor To Go." He said, "You may buy Johnny Walker Red in this place with no tax I am told."

He might have guessed. "Sure, might even find a bottle of O.G.-san." For whatever reason, the Japanese had acquired a taste for Old Grand Dad.

"In Japanese store this whiskey cost more than fifty American dollar—much too expensive for Japanese people."

Dan could take a hint as well as the next guy. He was already out twenty bucks for the day, but this was a deal he couldn't refuse. He still had four coveted liquor rations left for the month. In a couple of weeks he'd either be a civilian or in prison, and the liquor rations would go to waste either way. He just wished he could have pushed them onto Sakamoto and what's her name. "Inspector, I have a couple of rations left on my card. If you like, I'd be happy to get you two bottles of Johnny Walker Red. I think the bottles cost about five dollars each."

The inspector already had his wallet in hand, counting out the equivalent in yen, which Dan figured to be about three and a half thousand. That's exactly what Tanaka handed him. "You are very much a gentleman," he said.

Within five minutes Tanaka had his Johnny Walker stashed safely in the trunk of the police car and the two were making straight for the Security Police headquarters building.

Dan had arranged to have Reggie in the interview room, waiting. It would likely please Tanaka and might generate some further good will. He would rather have taken an hour alone with Reggie first and prepared him for Tanaka's barrage of questions. But Reginald Kincaid was beyond preparation. He had a mind of his own and was determined to handle the interview himself. Dan had no idea what might come out of his mouth in the next few minutes.

What would Dan tell him to say anyway? So far as he could tell, the truth was the only thing that could help Reggie, and the kid had no intention of giving up Su Li and their Captain Subarov to save his own skin.

The story of Su Li, Subarov, and the Sakhalin Koreans was the most amazing narrative Dan had ever heard. It gave him enough ammunition this instant to save Reggie from a murder charge. If Dan came clean with Tanaka now, Reggie's troubles with the locals would be over. That only left the ones with the Air Force and the ones in his own head. But it wasn't Dan's choice to make. Reggie obviously believed this cause was worth his life, and that was enough to keep

Dan's mouth shut. He might be leaving on the next plane, but he wouldn't go out of his way to hurt the kid.

Dan pointed to the Quonset hut on a small hill behind the NCO Club. "That's the building, over there on the left, Inspector."

They entered the white, tin hut and the duty officer greeted them. "Good afternoon Agent Matthews. I'm Lt. Parsons. I've been instructed to assist you in any way possible."

"Thanks," Dan replied. "May I introduce Inspector Tanaka from the Prefectural Police Headquarters?"

Tanaka removed the trademark fedora. "How do you do," he said, again dispensing with the customary bow in favor of the extended right hand. Dan wanted to warn the young lieutenant, but it was out of his hands.

When Parsons had recovered from the handshake, he showed them to a small, partitioned office space in the corner, completely empty save a desk and three metal chairs. Reggie was already seated in one of the chairs. He didn't look up. Tanaka ignored him and Dan thought it best to do likewise.

"You gentlemen can just make yourselves at home," Parsons told them. "You can use the space all afternoon, if you like. Let me know if you need anything."

Dan asked, "What about coffee?"

"Sure, right over there against the wall," the officer said, pointing. Coffee boy apparently wasn't included in Parsons' job description. Maybe he knew Dan was only a sergeant. Everybody else seemed to.

Tanaka took his place behind the desk and began to organize his materials. He arranged his pad, pen, and handwritten notes carefully on the desk. Dan took the chair beside Reggie. He decided to wait and let Tanaka speak first.

There was no introduction or greeting between Tanaka and his subject. The inspector looked up sternly at Reggie and started talking—in Japanese. Dan was completely dismayed, and prayed Reggie had enough savvy to recognize the game. The inspector would rather do the interrogation in his native tongue. It would give him more control and make Reggie more vulnerable.

Tanaka had obviously done his homework. No Japanese person would automatically assume an American GI spoke his language. American airmen were not highly regarded in Japanese society, and were generally considered incapable of mastering the complex nuances of the Japanese language. Dan was betting Tanaka had been around town asking questions about Reggie's language skills—and maybe other things.

He was terrified over how Reggie might react. The kid could easily handle a friendly conversation in Japanese, but a criminal interrogation was another ballgame. Beyond that, Dan may as well be over at the NCO Club having a beer. He wouldn't have a clue what was being said, and Reggie would be out on a limb alone. He had to do something. But Reggie did it for him.

"Inspector," the kid said in English, "I understand the part about your name and that you're going to ask me some questions. But I have to tell you that I don't understand or speak Japanese well enough to be confident in my answers. If you want to speak Japanese, I would like an interpreter present."

A wave of relief swept over Dan. It could prove short-lived, but the kid had passed the first test. Before Dan could enjoy the feeling, Reggie galloped ahead. "If we use a police interpreter, I'd like to have the entire interview tape-recorded."

The youngster was playing with his interrogator. Dan hadn't expected anything like this. There was no trace of nerves or apprehension in his demeanor. Reggie appeared to be savoring the unpleasant encounter and making a game of it. The spectacle was more frightening than amusing.

Reggie's attitude defied logic and presented a portrait of a young man who'd either lost touch with the reality of his situation or had no interest in its outcome. Dan couldn't decide which one scared him more. If this were the Kentucky Derby, the horse named Tanaka had just stumbled badly out of the gate. He'd have to make up ground quickly or wait another year to smell the roses.

Instead of firing back, Tanaka coughed to gain time. Dan knew it and he was sure Reggie knew it as well. "Very well," the inspector finally said, still not fully recovered, "we will speak in English."

Reggie said, "I appreciate that very much, sir." There was no smile, no hint of cockiness and definitely no gloating. The boy's an enigma, Dan thought. Of Reggie's integrity, he still had no doubt, but there was a coldness to the kid, a distance Dan had just seen for the first time, and he wondered if anyone really knew Reginald Kincaid.

"Are you homosexual?" Tanaka asked, opting for the shock approach, although his intended victim had shown no inclination to shudder.

"No, sir," replied Reggie.

"Do you own a watch, Mr. Kincaid?" Tanaka asked.

"I did own a watch. I lost it a while back, in the scuffle on the night I was stabbed."

"Was the watch engraved?"

"Yes, it said, 'Run, Reggie run' on the back."

"On the night you were stabbed, you came to the rescue of a woman. Is this correct?"

"Correct."

Tanaka made a brief entry on his note pad, then looked. "What is the name of this woman?"

"I don't know her name, Inspector. I told the police that. I told the Air Force that. I didn't know her name then and I don't know it now."

Strange that Tanaka would be so quick to take the investigation in that direction. So far as Dan knew, the inspector had nothing to connect the two incidents other than what Reggie had just told him about the watch.

At that moment Parsons appeared with a pitcher of water and some paper cups. "Just in case you fellas need to wet your lips," he said, placing it on the desk.

"Thanks," Dan said. "You read my mind." He poured and drank a full cup before the man even left the cubicle. He'd hung a bad rap on Parsons and regretted it.

"Did you know a Japanese man named Ishikawa Yoshihiro?" Tanaka asked.

"I never met a man by that name." This time, Dan figured, Reggie was on the safe side of perjury, but only barely.

"Have you ever been to the Yokuska Hotel, Mr. Kincaid?"

Reggie still appeared the picture of calm. "I have never been to that hotel."

Tanaka leaned back in the chair and folded his arms, attempting to regain control with his best imitation of Elliott Ness. He said, "By now you must be aware this Ishikawa Yoshihiro was found dead in a hotel room. Is that correct?"

"Yes, I've heard that."

"He was found with your watch. Does this fact surprise you?"

"Yes and no."

"Explain please," Tanaka instructed.

"Well, I lost it in the presence of some very bad guys. I assume they took it for some purpose. But I think anyone would be surprised if his watch were found near a dead body."

It was a good answer; too good maybe.

Tanaka turned a nasty frown. "I have reviewed the report of your injury, Mr. Kincaid. You were given an opportunity to tell the officers what happened. Is this correct?"

"Sure, I told them, a few days later."

"But, curiously, you never mentioned losing your watch. Is this also correct?"

Dan thought Tanaka might be warming up. "That's right," Reggie admitted. "I didn't mention it. I didn't think it was stolen, just lost in the snow. It wasn't worth mentioning. I thought I might even go back and find it when the snow melted a bit."

"Would it surprise you to know a note was also found, a completely dishonorable note describing your depraved conduct with Mr. Ishikawa Yoshihiro? Shall I read you parts of this disgusting letter?"

Tanaka had finally gotten Reggie's goat. The kid looked like he was boiling water inside his head. He said, "No, thank you. I'd rather not hear what's in the fucking letter. I don't know the man. I am not homosexual, and I have no idea how or why the letter got there."

"Well," Tanaka said, pressing his advantage, "that brings us to the most interesting question. Why would someone go to all the trouble of putting your watch in the room and writing such a terrible letter?"

"I don't know. That's your job."

"Think about this," Tanaka said. "Sexual activity with two men is not criminal in Japan, although it is certainly frowned upon. If you admit to a sexual relationship with this Ishikawa, then you will not be charged with his murder. It is not a crime for you if Ishikawa takes his own life because you have rejected him."

Reggie did not reply. This, of course, was the dilemma he faced, Dan knew. The farther Tanaka pressed his investigation of Ishikawa's death, the greater the chance Su Li's little crusade would be exposed.

Tanaka decided to try a different approach. "Is your mother alive?" he asked.

"Yes."

"And your father?"

"He's alive."

"You have dishonored your mother and father in this affair,"

Tanaka said. "Is their shame not important to you?"

Reggie flashed him a blank stare. "I don't mean any disrespect, Inspector. I just don't know how to answer that question. Living here, I've learned that being a respected member of the group is important to the Japanese. You see shame and disgrace as punishment in themselves." The corner of Reggie's mouth curled into a kind of sardonic smile. "You're smart people, I guess. But my own parents? Hell, Inspector, that's a bridge I burned years ago."

From the looks of him, Tanaka hadn't a clue what the kid was talking about. He wasn't alone. "Let me ask you, please," Tanaka said, "do you agree that, if Ishikawa was not your lover, someone has placed you in the frame?"

Under other circumstances, Dan might have thought the misstatement humorous, but not today. Even Reggie declined the opportunity to poke fun. "I suppose that's the logical conclusion, but let me save you some time, if you don't mind."

"Please, proceed."

"I suspect Ishikawa, whoever he was, was murdered. That's what you need to focus on. Somebody went out of his way to make it look like we were lovers. I don't know who or why. I don't know if it had anything to do with my stabbing. But you know as well as I do, I didn't kill him."

"And exactly how do I know you did not kill this man?" Tanaka asked with a scowl.

"Simple. That note you're talking about, whether it's legitimate or not, is the best evidence of my innocence."

Tanaka looked intrigued. "Perhaps you are correct in this. May you please explain it to me?"

"Sure. If he was my lover and he wrote the note, then it's a clear case of suicide. You clear your case and I leave the service in disgrace. On the other hand, if the note's a fake or if somebody forced him to write it, I'm still innocent."

Tanaka seemed to be caught up in Reggie's game and unaware that he no longer controlled his interrogation. Dan poured another cup of water and one for Reggie. The inspector said, "I do not see it that way, Mr. Kincaid."

"Think about it," Reggie said. "There's only one possible motive for me killing my lover. That's to keep the Air Force from finding out I'm homosexual. So why would I leave a note like that? It all adds up to my innocence, any way you cut it. Look, Inspector, I want you to find out who killed that boy. I really do. You're just looking in the wrong place."

"Where do you believe I should look?" he asked.

"I don't know, but I know you're hoping the note was legitimate and that I'm a big, tall queen bee."

"Why is that?" Tanaka asked.

"Because the alternative scares the hell out of you. That's Pandora's Box to you. You're afraid when you open it, something big will jump out and bite you. You have a lot of work to do here, Inspector, but I just can't help you any further."

Reggie's whole schpiel hadn't offered Tanaka a scintilla of new information, Dan observed, but it had pretty well summed up the inspector's problem. Unless Reggie's prints turned up inside that hotel room, Tanaka would be starting from square one. He waited for the inspector to begin his journey into the unknown.

He would have to wait a little longer. Tanaka said, "I must ask you to remain available for more questioning. Thank you." He rose from the chair and turned to Dan. "That concludes my questions for today. May I speak with you privately?"

He ignored Reggie completely. So far as Tanaka was concerned, Reggie was persona non grata: either a cold-blooded murderer or a sexual deviant. In Tanaka's world, Dan suspected, the two things were different, but without distinction. Tanaka had proven this American was a morally bankrupt person and resented having to choose among his vices.

"Of course, Inspector," Dan replied, already standing. "Airman Kincaid, please return to your barracks, and you are still under house arrest and confined to base."

"Yes, Agent Matthews," Reggie replied, and walked quietly from the cubicle.

Tanaka held up his arm for Reggie to stop. "I have one more request. I would like to send a technician over here later to get fingerprints. Will this be a problem?"

"Absolutely not," Dan said.

When Reggie had cleared the building, Tanaka asked, "I am told this Kincaid speaks Russian. Is this correct?"

The question caught Dan completely off guard. "I'm sorry, Inspector, that is classified information. You need to submit that question to PACAF in writing."

"Of course. My apology."

Somebody with serious access had been throwing this guy bones. "May I ask why that fact would be of interest to you?"

Tanaka seemed to relax, and Dan caught a brief glimpse of the man behind the façade. Dan thought it might have been the Scotch. The inspector scratched his head, his left hand toying with the fedora in his right. "Ahhh," he said, "this is a very difficult case, Sergeant Matthews. Here is many questions without answers. I have much hope the autopsy and forensic reports will help, but I think we will not find this Kincaid's fingerprints in the room."

"I agree."

"Please, my name is Tanaka Fukio. My friends call me Fuki."

It wasn't exactly the shining emerald of nicknames. "Thank you, Inspector. You are very kind, but I am a sergeant. Your rank requires me to address you as an officer, but I insist you call me Dan."

If his face was any indication, Dan's reply made Tanaka as happy as a whore on payday. "Very well, Dan-san. What is your opinion of this business?"

"Inspector, I'm as confused as you. My gut feeling is Kincaid is telling the truth, although even that wouldn't go very far toward solving your case."

"Yes. This is the problem. Whatever the involvement of Kincaid, there is another part to this, something under the surface."

Considering he had almost no information, Tanaka's analysis was remarkable in its accuracy. Dan had all kinds of information now, but he still had no idea what was happening. "I agree with you, Inspector," he said. "There is something else happening here."

"Dan-san, you asked why I wanted to know about Kincaid's Russian language ability. I propose to you, what if this case is somehow involving espionage? It has happened before, you know. Wakkanai is fertile ground for such things, with Russian and North Korean fishing boats having access to our port."

Tanaka's words triggered a wave of nausea in Dan's stomach. A Russian boat captain, a beautiful woman and smuggled refugees from the Soviet Union. Very dangerous business he was involved in. It wasn't beyond the realm of possibility that Reggie had been taken in by a KGB operation. Su Li herself might even be a covert operative for the KGB. Hell, he thought, worrying about that now was pointless. If they were Soviet spies, he'd already committed enough crimes by omission to earn a lifetime cell at Fort Leavenworth. "I hope you're wrong," was all he could muster.

He had a reservation on the six a.m. flight down to Yokota, but some demon in his gut just wouldn't let this go. He'd have a talk with Major Coughlin and plead for another twenty-four hour extension. He was so close to the answers now he could smell the conspiracy. It was high time he got to the bottom of it, and this incredible tale of abducted Koreans on Sakhalin seemed a good place to start. A long-distance phone call topped his agenda as he ushered the Japanese inspector to the door.

SEVENTEEN

Who the hell said you can't choose your relatives?

Thursday, 5:00 a.m.
Somewhere on the Sea of Japan

"Su Li, you must wake up now," came the familiar voice invading her dream. "Su Li, we are about to come alongside the *Irina*."

"Where are we?" Su Li whispered, still lacking the strength to rise. "What happened?"

"We are well south into the Sea of Japan, near the three-mile limit off the shore of Vladivostok," Kim said. "We hit some bad weather last night and you became ill." He held up a cup of tea and smiled. "You must drink some hot tea and have something to eat. You should regain your strength before you meet with the captain. He wants you to come aboard. It will be all right. It is cold, of course, but the sea is gentle today."

Su Li felt as though she had come back from the dead. The painful misery of the previous night had left no holdover effect, save the ravenous cry of her empty stomach and a serious thirst. "May I have some water, Kim?" she asked, already downing the first slice of sugared bread.

"Of course," he replied. "I'll get it, but be careful with the tea. It's very hot. Don't eat too quickly or your stomach will still be queasy."

Captain Subarov himself climbed down the rope netting at the stern and helped her from the small dinghy. "No need to wait," he said to the young crewman at the oars. The powerful arm around her waist hauled her effortlessly up to the rail.

The captain brought her directly to his small cabin, his arm still locked around her waist. He pulled back her fur-lined hood and eased her onto his bunk. "Su Li," he said, "It distresses me to see you placing yourself in danger."

"In a moment you'll understand why it was necessary, Captain-san," she said in Japanese. "Someone has kidnapped Hiro. He's been gone for days without a word."

The captain sat down beside her on the bunk and slowly removed his hat. "Then your little voyage to sea is even more dangerous than I imagined. Poor Boris. You must prepare yourself for the worst. I was afraid of something like this. They'll be emboldened now. Tell me what you know."

"The police questioned me, and I lied to them. I pretended to know nothing, even though my information may have helped find him."

The captain sighed. "It was all you could do. Even I don't know who is behind this. And you know the police can't help poor Boris now. This is terrible news, Su Li, but it can't possibly be the reason you came out to sea."

"No," she said. "It wasn't. I came because you're in danger. The Americans are involved for certain. They have spy ships on the Soya Strait and in the Sea of Japan looking for you. They're even using specially equipped airplanes. They intend to stop you."

His tired face grimaced. "How do you know this?"

"Reggie, the young American who saved me, brought me the information. He learned of it in the secret part of the base where he works. They spy on the Russians from there."

"He's a good friend, this Reggie," said the captain. "What else did he say?"

"He said the Americans are monitoring all standard marine frequencies. They can hear everything. He gave me some papers showing where they will search." She removed the papers from her pocket and handed them to the captain. "I'm not a seaman, but I think these will help."

He spread the papers on his bunk and seemed to understand their significance immediately. The captain quickly moved over to the small desk and retrieved a rolled-up chart from a bin. He spread the chart out on the desk and began to work with a pencil and a navigational instrument unknown to her. "What are you doing, Captain-san?" she asked.

His eyes did not rise from the chart. "Plotting a course."

Su Li peered over his shoulder as he measured, drew lines, and wrote little numbers on the chart. The land masses on the chart were clearly marked and readily identifiable. A sense of terror overtook her as she followed the newly drawn line around the southern tip of Sakhalin and up toward the Kuril Islands. "Captain-san, what are you doing? You can't approach the Hokkaido coast from the Kurils."

He put the pencil down and turned to her. "Yes. It's the obvious choice. We'll make shore right here," he said, pointing to the map, "at Abashiri."

Su Li was aghast. "It's madness. Your boat will be directly exposed to the floating ice and heavy seas from the Sea of Okhotsk. A landing on the northeast shore of Hokkaido is insane."

A calm look of resignation settled upon his weathered face. "Not insane, but necessary and unexpected. That stretch of sea is nearly void of ships in the dead of winter. Even the American surveillance vessels wouldn't dare go there. Most of the ice breaks up before nearing the coast. If I stay just outside territorial waters, I can navigate the passage safely."

Su Li was having none of it. "You're only saying that for my benefit. The ice will most likely crush you. Then your precious cargo will be lost forever."

The captain picked up a voice tube from its place on the desk and unleashed a short burst of Russian words. He turned toward Su Li and smiled. "My mate will bring us some tea. Now relax and rest assured, Su Li-san, I will not die, not yet, and nothing will be lost."

"When can we expect you to arrive at Abashiri then?"

The captain stroked his short beard. "Hmm…If we depart now and set the fastest course, I'd say two days, three at the outside. We can't afford to wait. With each day our chance of success diminishes. The American investigator may be reporting you even as we speak."

"If he hasn't, then what shall I do about him?"

"Your judgment has been proven wise, my dear," he replied. "Mine is no better and I don't know these men myself. Do what you believe is best, but don't come to Abashiri."

"Why not?"

"Because you'll attract unwanted attention," he explained. "I'll hire a car and bring the cargo to Wakkanai myself. We'll meet up there."

"But how can you go now? What of your cargo?"

With that the captain walked over to the bunk and pulled out an old trunk from underneath. "I have some things you should see," he said, lifting the top. "Come over here and sit."

The trunk was filled with small brown bags and tied bundles. There was writing on each one. It looked like the Cyrillic letters of the Russian alphabet. "Choose one," he said.

She chose a neatly tied bundle near the top and handed it to him. He removed its contents, a pile of carefully folded papers held together with a single length of string. He handed her the top sheet. "Read it," he said. "It's in Korean and the writer wouldn't mind. After all these years I still don't read Korean myself. Read it out loud."

Su Li carefully unfolded the faded white paper and began to read:

"My Dear Brother,

I hope this finds you alive and well. I'm sorry I always begin like that. I am sustained by the hope I might someday sit and visit with you in our father's house. Our parents must be gone by now. It has been so many years. I hope you have a good wife and many children, although your ornery disposition would surely test them all to the limit. You always frustrated our mother with your tantrums. I never told you how it amused me.

I long to see Chungchong-do again. I am accustomed to this place, I suppose, but there is no green grass and I cannot see mountains in the distance. I still work every day at the coal mine, but thankfully not down in the holes. Life is not easy but I am still alive. In past years, I knew many people here from our beloved village. Most are gone now. I think the Japanese soldiers will not let you write to me. I will write again. I think of you and our parents every day.

Your loving sister,

Kim Sohn Ha, a winter day, 1963"

"They are almost all like that," the captain said, "each with one or two small details. It might be the name of a factory, a mill, maybe the names of a few friends from neighboring villages in Korea. Together, along with the photographs, they tell the story of the Sakhalin Koreans in human terms. It's a permanent record of their suffering, revealed even in the letters such as this, when the writer tries to conceal the extent of her suffering for the benefit of loved ones back home."

"Those look like photographs," Su Li said, pointing to a small bundle on the top.

"Oh, yes. There are perhaps three hundred in all. The most revealing ones date back to the end of the war, when they suffered most." He handed her the bundle. "Look through some of them at your leisure. You'll see for yourself how they lived, what they looked like, even what they look like now."

She carefully untied the bundle and took the top photo from the pile. It was an old black and white shot of a gaunt, young, Korean man standing in front of a cave of some sort. On the back was written in Korean "Jo Fung Lee in front of the Takobeya, 1945."

"Takobeya means octopus house," Su Li said. "What does this mean?"

"The octopus lives in cracks in the rock," the captain explained. "It's what many of them called their houses. The Japanese didn't understand."

The significance of this entire revelation suddenly dawned on her. "Then this is your precious cargo."

The captain put his arm around her shoulders. "Yes. I'm sorry I couldn't tell you."

Su Li was puzzled. "Why not?"

"We have many enemies, my dear. I was afraid one or more of you might have been captured. Sadly, I was correct. One cannot reveal what one does not know."

Despite his passion, there seemed a coldness to the man Su Li did not care to explore. "But how did you acquire these things?" In her mind she likened the collection to a great archeological find, a window into a long, lost civilization.

The captain dug to the very bottom of the trunk and his hand came out with a small, white envelope. It held only a small stack of photographs. He removed one picture carefully and handed it to Su Li. "She gave the things to me," he said, "most of them."

It was a black and white picture, a full-body snapshot of a young, oriental woman holding a bundle of wild flowers in the mud outside the front door of a crude, wooden dwelling. The picture was old and faded, but the warmth of the woman's smile was not. It dominated the frame. Her clothing was dark and tattered, but neatly arranged to look almost attractive. "Who is she?" Su Li asked.

"She was my wife. Her name was Jang So Ree. She was born in a tiny village in Cholla-do Province and taken from her home to Sakhalin by the Japanese in 1939, at age twelve. My beloved Jang died only two years ago."

The revelation shocked her, although she could think of no reason why a good man like Captain Subarov should not find love. "How did she die?"

"I'm afraid there's no simple answer to that. She was ill for seven years. Early on the local Soviet doctor told us she had a congenital heart defect. She would tire easily and sometimes had difficulty catching her breath. He said there was an operation that could repair the heart. She never had it. For the last two years of her life, Jang hardly got out of bed."

"Why didn't she get the operation?" Su Li asked.

His face tightened. "Because the Soviet bureaucracy refused to authorize it. Jang was a nonperson in the Soviet Union. Beyond that, she was the wife of a White Russian. The operation was expensive and only good Soviet citizens are deemed worthy of such an operation."

Su Li was nearly overcome with sympathy for this decent man. The photograph answered so many of her questions about him. "That's horrible, Captain-san, but how does it explain these letters and photographs?"

"That happened quite by accident, but it would never have happened at all without Jang."

"Please, tell me."

The knock on the captain's door announced the arrival of their tea. "Come in," he said. A crewman entered, handed them each a hot mug, ad left without a word.

Captain Subarov returned his attention to the old photograph. "We met after I was released from prison in 1947 and sent to work in the coal mines near what the Soviets named Novelsk in the southwest. Jang was one of the many Korean conscripts left behind in the Japanese exodus. Her job was to serve that horrible Soviet slop to the miners at midday. Most worked fourteen or sixteen hours. I lived each day only for that thirty-minute mealtime and craved it like a lily craves the sun. Even that nasty gruel tasted good in her presence."

She was hearing a love story. "What happened?"

"One day our gruel was served by some fat, Soviet pig down from Siberia and my Jang was gone, just like that."

"What did you do?"

The old captain smiled whistfully. "I quit the mines that very day, and found the hovel where she'd lived with her mother and two other families. I learned her mother had died. They told me Jang had moved to a village not far away on the south coast of Sakhalin. There was work cleaning fish. Russian fishermen had begun moving into the good Sakhalin harbors with big trawlers to be closer to the fishing grounds. They filled a void left by the Japanese. That's how I became a fisherman."

"So you found her?"

The captain laughed heartily. "And married her immediately, but none of this old history answers your question about the collection."

Su Li closed her eyes and imagined her Russian captain as a young man desperately in love. It was not so difficult. "I'm grateful you told me these things."

"You are a very dear person, Su Li, unburdened by the impatience of youth. As I say, it happened by accident. Jang was very special too, much like you. She had great empathy and that quality drew people to her. Some years ago she began to acquire these things."

It was all beginning to make sense. Knowing Captain Subarov, she might have expected a woman at the core of his story. "But how?"

"Because I was a sailor, people began to bring her old photographs and letters home detailing their experiences on that foreign soil. I was sometimes able to mail the letters from a foreign port, but only rarely. Jang became a kind of librarian or custodian of these records, I suppose. After a while the collection expanded into a sort of eyewitness record detailing the experience of the Koreans on that godforsaken island. The collection continued to grow long after I had to discontinue the mailing, although we had no idea how to use it."

Su Li heard another knock, and the first mate appeared without invitation. He handed the captain a torn sheet of paper and said something in Russian. The captain gave him the hand-drawn chart and the two men jabbered on for another minute. As the mate left the cabin, the captain returned his attention to Su Li. "We're coming in for some weather," he said. "Now we have two obstacles to avoid. You should finish your tea and go. We must be underway."

As he made for the door, Su Li stopped him. It occurred to her she might never get another chance to hear the story. "Please, Captain-san," she said, "the collection, finish your story."

The captain hesitated, then seemed to relent, although he did not sit. "All right, but only for a minute. When I became master of the *Irina* some years ago, my voyages often took me to the Port of Wakkanai. As master, I had much more freedom to move about. I saw a way to help the Sakhalin Koreans and, in so doing, honor my wife. I began taking Jang's letters in large numbers and mailing them to Korea on my stops in Wakkanai."

"How did you do it?"

"I set up a post box in Japan for return letters. For a while the letters were all answered by relatives in Korea. It gave the people great hope and started a flood of letters to Jang. She never told anyone how it was done."

"Then what happened with all the letters?"

"On one of my stops at Wakkanai I found the postal box empty. That was it. The replies just stopped cold. I knew someone was intercepting either the letters I posted or the replies from Korea. I couldn't figure who or why. I still don't know."

It could only have been the Japanese, Su Li thought, for the Korean government would have no reason to inhibit communications among these estranged families. "Then what did you do?" A sudden wave of nausea warned her of the rising seas and she knew their meeting was about to end.

"Well," said the captain, "people kept bringing things to Jang. She didn't want to turn them away. So we began to keep them all carefully. Before I knew it, Koreans started coming to her from all over the island with letters home detailing the tragedy of their lives. Some even had old, priceless photos they entrusted to her care."

"Some of these photographs are of very good quality. How did such poor people come to have them?"

"You haven't even seen the most graphic ones yet," he replied. "A Japanese photographer living on Sakhalin since the 1920s heard about Jang's collection and brought her dozens of old photographs. He took them during and after the Japanese withdrawal from the island. They show the terrible suffering. People looking like long-term residents of Auschwitz living in caves in the hillside or crude shelters made of scrap wood near the timber mills. Some have notes on the back with dates, even the names of the poor souls depicted."

"You had this plan in mind so many years back?"

"No, not at all. At first our intention was to give it all to the Americans, but we didn't know how. In retrospect it was a wise decision not to. Jang and I just decided to collect it and save it for the future, as a record of their suffering. Then my beloved Jang became ill and everything changed."

"Then after Jang's death the collection became your instrument of revenge against the Soviet Union," she suggested.

The captain paused. "That's how it was at first, but then I began to see what our efforts meant to the poor, wretched Koreans on the island. I began to see this work more as something good and meaningful than some dark, brooding act of revenge. I intend to complete this mission as a loving and lasting tribute to my beautiful Jang So Ree."

Captain Subarov touched her lightly on the cheek with that course hide she had now come to love. Su Li pressed his hand to her skin with all her strength, wanting to hold it there forever, warming it with her tears. She did not speak.

"She would have seen you as I see you, Su Li," the captain said, "as the beautiful daughter we never had. You must go now. Kim Tae Woo will take you to Hakodate on the south coast. You'll be there late tonight or early tomorrow. From there you can board the train to Wakkanai. You'll be back tomorrow night. Do you have money?"

"Yes," she replied. "I brought enough money with me."

"Very well. Consider your decisions carefully and exercise caution. I have faith in you. Remember, if all goes badly, stay with Kim Tae Woo. He is true as the North Star. I'll meet you in Wakkanai in three days. Safe journey."

5:30 a.m.
Wakkanai Municipal Airport
Statistically, Dan had a one-in-two chance of the Air America flight being canceled for bad weather, as his taxi arrived at the little terminal near Cape Soya Point battling a stiff wind from the north with

cloudy skies. It looked as though nature might give him the reprieve the OSI had not.

His latest conversation with Major Coughlin had caused Dan great distress. He'd been surprised by Coughlin's stoicism, considering the man's animated raving during their previous call. Then the major advised Dan that he'd been relieved of command and referred the call to his temporary replacement, a Major Bo Hickam. Dan saw no point in pursuing the extension with Hickam, since his maverick investigation had already cost Coughlin his job, hell, his goddamn commission.

It wasn't supposed to be like this. He'd never meant to jeopardize anyone's career. Emil Coughlin had chosen him carefully for this assignment, and had paid the price for his arrogance. It was clear now. All along the major had been consumed with his own advancement and had selfishly figured Dan for a drone soldier. Maybe he was right. Coughlin had wanted desperately to retire a Lieutenant Colonel, the Air Force colonel who never flew a plane, and be introduced at dinner parties as "Colonel and Mrs. Emil Coughlin." It wasn't much to ask from life, Dan thought, but it wasn't to be either. He should have felt anger toward Coughlin for using him, but all he could muster was pity. The same bureaucratic behemoth Coughlin had served with unflappable, blind loyalty for twenty years had stepped up and fucked him in the ass, just because it was horny.

Outside the terminal, facing the runway, he listened for the muffled, vibrating hiss of the twin C-47 engines that he prayed would never come. Standing there like a pillar in the freezing cold, it occurred to him that his betrayal of Coughlin, while entirely justified, had reaped no benefit to Reggie Kincaid or anyone else. He had abandoned them all to save himself.

He stared at the zippered courier pouch beneath his hand and noticed the cold sweat of his palm around the leather handle. Inside lay a single case file, a carefully typed, three-page report tucked just inside the cover. Thankfully, he would never see the damn thing again, not on paper anyway, but even now Dan couldn't drive the words from his head.

Based on witness interviews, inspection of physical evidence, and the subject's demonstrated lack of cooperation, it is this investigator's opinion that the cause and circumstances of the subject's injuries cannot be determined. Notwithstanding this, the subject's own statement to the first responding officer, in light of all the evidence, suggests the possibility of an inappropriate sexual relationship between the subject and an unknown male individual, first name Chuckie. It should be noted that the existence of this relationship cannot be confirmed at this time. Recommend access to classified material be terminated pending further review.

The distant whine of the C-47's engines drew his attention to the dead south, where the plane was heading into the wind on final approach. Dan's signature on that report would seal Reggie's fate. But what about the girl? Her quest to aid the Sakhalin Koreans, if true, ranked among the noblest and most hopelessly heroic endeavors in history. There was no point deluding himself; she was finished and so was this childish dream of hers.

The plane was taxiing now, only feet from the terminal, the added wind nearly fierce enough to tear the parka from his back. The door opened, and the lonely airport worker scurried forward with the rolling staircase. The other passengers were moving past him now, one, two…nine. What could a prosperous life in Hawaii ever come to if purchased with other peoples' happiness? Or his own honor? Loyalty is earned, never owed. Major Coughlin had been too weak to see the difference. Weakness was no crime, but strength a compass with which to steady a true course.

The plane was moving again, away this time, and Dan felt a tug on his arm. "Hey, Mista," said the taxi driver, "you clayzee? You miss prane. You wanna go back taxi?"

Dan lifted his duffel and smiled. "Sure. Take me to the train station. I think we still have time to make the Sapporo express."

EIGHTEEN

**All ain't what it appears to be,
but the truth will set you free.**

Thursday, 9:45 a.m.
Wakkanai

Chung Hok Kim, relaxing in the public bathhouse, stared with satisfaction at the already stale, but sensational headline on the front page of the Wakkanai daily paper: "Man found dead in hotel, American lover questioned." It had been nearly thirty-six hours since they'd found the body and the newspapers were just running the story. "You can be proud to be part of such an operation, Fu," he declared. "When this mission is complete, I'll see you are suitably rewarded." He turned away to conceal the coy smile.

Fu beamed. "I'm in your debt, sir. You were particularly brilliant in your use of the Japanese boy...unless—"

His apprentice's subtle arrogance never ceased to annoy Chung. It would inevitably keep young Fu from climbing to a higher position in the agency, even if Chung didn't. "Unless what, Fu?" he asked. "Tell me."

"Well, sir, I mean no disrespect, but have you considered the Americans might suspect our hand in the boy's death?"

Chung did not feel in the least disrespected. It was a question he had seriously pondered before deciding on a course of action. He flashed his most practiced look of satisfaction. "This was the central question I faced, and the answer is nothing less than delightful. Of course, they suspect our hand in the suicide note and the watch. Foster is aware of our displeasure at their handling of this Kincaid."

"Knowing the Americans," Fu said, "they won't stand by and do nothing while we flaunt their ground rules."

"Nothing is precisely what they will do," Chung countered. "The truth is they're pleased with the result of our insolence. They can deny any knowledge of or complicity in the plan; in fact, Foster won't even raise the question of our involvement. Believe me." Chung checked his watch. "We should go," he said, snapping his fingers for the female bath attendants. "There must be a dozen bathhouses in this city, Fu, and you drag me to the one staffed by these toothless mountain goats."

Chung turned south on foot outside the bathhouse and Fu said, "The car is parked in the other direction, sir,"

"We won't be using the car just yet," Chung replied. "We're only going a few blocks. I've decided to pay a visit to these Pachinko brothers the Japanese boy told us about. If they are as dumb as he said, we may be able to use them."

"Bu what of Su Li Young, sir? She might show up at any time, and she's sure to recognize us."

"I don't think so. With all that's gone on, she'll be desperate to contact Subarov. I'm sure that's why she's disappeared. There are others involved in this conspiracy. These people are very resourceful and might have any number of ways to arrange a rendezvous with Subarov." Chung figured he'd given his young agent enough food for thought to keep him quiet for the remainder of their short walk.

The pachinko parlor was not difficult to find. They never were. Chung marveled at the sheer number of white-shirted, office people wasting valuable time and money playing with those ridiculous little pinballs amidst the annoying racket of the unsightly machines. Surely they all had jobs. How could so many be here this early in the day? Chung found it difficult to believe these same people, not long ago, had seriously threatened to rule all of Asia.

He found one of the brothers almost immediately, patrolling the aisles of brain-dead players. The young man was extremely fit and well-developed for a Japanese, and Chung suspected proficiency in some form of the martial arts. "Hello," the man said.

Chung knew his command of Japanese wouldn't even fool an American and would fail completely in a complex conversation, so he decided to use Korean. "Yoshima?" he asked. "If you are Yoshima, I'd like to speak with you."

He saw the young man studying him with curious eyes. Chung was the only one in the place dressed in the homely garb of a fisherman. "Yes. I'm Yoshima Jiro."

"May we speak outside?" Chung asked. "I come on a mission for Su Li."

"Who are you? I don't know you."

"Please," said Chung, "outside."

A glint of fear invaded the man's expression. "All right. Wait outside then while I get my brother."

After a few minutes Yoshima walked out the front door with what looked like an identical twin. They even wore matching gray coats. "This is my brother, Yoshima Taro," said the man. "Who are you and what do you want?" They had obviously discussed the possibilities.

"I am Chung Cho Lee. I'm a fisherman and also a Korean, a friend of Captain Subarov and of Su Li Young. I've come to you on a mission for Su Li."

"Where is Su Li now?" one of the men asked.

He'd anticipated the question, of course. "She's in hiding. You've heard about Ishikawa's death, I suppose."

"Yes," replied the one on the left. "We heard about his abduction from Su Li and then read that bullshit in the paper. We know he was murdered and it was made to appear he had a homosexual affair with the American."

"It appears that way, all right. We're afraid these assholes may try to grab Su Li next. That's why she's in hiding. But there's more."

"What more?" asked the one on the right, no, maybe the left.

"Ishikawa knew the hiding places of some of the Sakhalin Koreans here on Hokkaido. Su Li fears the information is now in the hands of whoever hunts us. We must get to them quickly and move them somewhere where they'll be safe."

Chung thought he would need to give the performance of his life to pull this off, but these two were possibly the dumbest people he had ever met. "That would be a disaster," one of them said. "It's too late to go today. I'll go with you in the morning. Mei Ling knows the location of every single one."

"No," the brother said. "Both of us will go. Grandfather can handle the place for a day. If you have trouble you'll need us both. We're trained in the martial arts."

Thank God for me they are a pair of idiots, Chung thought. Still, it would be easier to handle one martial arts idiot than two. "If you don't mind the suggestion, I think it would be better if one of you stayed here in case something comes up."

"I'll go," said the one called Jiro.

"Very well, Brother," Taro replied.

"Do you have transportation?" Chung asked. "I have only a small car, not very reliable at that."

"Of course we have a car," said Jiro proudly.

Chung was already beginning to tell the difference by their tones of voice. Still, they had to be identical. No two people could be this stupid and come from separate eggs. "Won't we need something bigger than a car?" Chung suggested.

"You're right," Taro replied. "I don't think a car will do the job, Brother. Some of the roads you will travel are nearly impassable. The trip will require a heavy truck to negotiate the roads and to carry the people."

The Soviets would never knowingly send such dimwits to spy on South Korea, Chung thought. Still, morons such as these should never be allowed to reenter Korean society, regardless of their political allegiances.

1:10 p.m.
Sapporo, Hokkaido, Japan

Dan emerged from the train station to find an ample supply of taxis waiting at the curb. There was snow, of course, but the streets were clear to the pavement and the accumulation was nothing that would discourage a Chicago commuter; all in all, a far cry from Wakkanai. Three or four hours sleep on the six-hour run had left Dan feeling surprisingly refreshed, despite the spartan accommodations. He'd have an hour to grab a late lunch and easily make his 1500-hours appointment at the International Committee of The Red Cross. He figured the Red Cross was the only place he could get some real answers.

As he headed toward the first taxi in line, he heard an excited voice behind him. "Hey Joe, hey Joe," called the male voice. Dan turned to find a young Japanese man in a Yankees' baseball cap running toward him. "You no want that guy," said the man in broken English. "He no rike GI, and no speak Engrish anyway. I am Sato Ozuki at you sabisa, ichi-ban taxi driver for GI Come on, I take bag for you."

"Wait a minute," Dan said, overwhelmed by the man's attack. "What makes you think I'm a GI?"

The man grinned broadly, exposing crooked, brown teeth, and said, "Cheap croze, numba one. Tourist come for ski sropes, wear very expensive crozing. Come from north, numba two. Nothing up north but snow, Japanese peeparu and American Air Force-u."

Dan decided to surrender, handing over his small bag. "All right, Ozuki-san," he said, "you've got yourself a fare. I'm looking for the International Red Cross. The address is—"

"Don't worry," the man interrupted, "no need address. This prace is not far. I take you now." He took a firm hold of Dan's arm and whisked him toward the small, red taxi parked just beyond the station.

Ozuki turned back smiling from the driver's seat and pointed back to the two front visors. He said, "You rike my Poraroids?"

If Dan hadn't seen the snapshots clipped to the visors, it would have taken him a while to figure that one out. The crude photographs were all of Ozuki in or around his taxi with…It couldn't possibly be. He said, "Is that Andy Williams with you in those pictures?"

Ozuki shrugged as though Dan should have expected as much. "'Moon Riba,' of course-u," he replied. "Andy-san is my passona friend-o. He ski at Sapporo before. I am his driba."

"Small world," was all Dan could think to say. "Ozuki-san, I have three hours before my appointment. Do you know where I can get a good steak?"

"*Suteki*?" Ozuki said. "Of course, you must go to restaurant at Royer Hoteru. My friend-o, Andy Williams, eat every time at Royer. Very crose to your destination. You may walk. Good hoteru."

It sounded perfect and Dan settled back to enjoy the ride. It carried him through the heart of the city, and city it was, easily on the scale of Milwaukee or the Twin Cities. Dan was amazed at the myriad signs of prosperity. There was construction everywhere, not in the least deterred by the extreme weather conditions; not mom and pop style construction either. All over the place, big, modern towers were rising into the sky. The Winter Olympics of 1972 would soon bring the eyes of the world to this hidden gem of a city on Japan's most little-known island. Sapporo clearly intended to be ready.

On the drive, his mind returned to the dilemma at hand. Reggie's story about the Koreans was the most incredible tale he'd ever heard, but a part of him believed it already. The other part, the detective, could never accept such a fanciful tale without evidence, especially from the mouth of a twenty-year-old alcoholic. As much as he liked Reggie, it was a generous characterization. If there were anything to his story about abducted Koreans still held against their wills on Sakhalin, the Red Cross had to know about it. Dan figured this meeting would be worth whatever it cost in time. The stakes could not be higher.

The driver stopped in front of a large, freestanding, Western-style hotel. The marquee read "Royal Hotel" in bold, block, red letters. Ozuki turned back to face Dan, smiling and said, "You rike this hoter-u. Very good *suteki*. Maybe sureep obanight."

"Thank you, Ozuki-san," Dan replied, counting out the hundred-yen notes. As he opened the door, Dan's eyes caught the unmistakable image of the Red, White, and Blue flying proudly from a white building at the end of the street. "Is that the American Consulate?"

"Yes," Ozuki replied. "Red Cross around corner. You walk easy."

Dan handed him the fair with a generous tip. "Thank you, Ozuki-san. I wish you good luck." The kid probably wouldn't need it.

Ozuki had been right, Dan thought, feeling stuffed as a Christmas goose in the hotel lobby. It was as good a steak as he'd had in Japan, but didn't come cheap. What the hell. He could afford it. Prison meals were free. He regretted not taking a week or two earlier to spend some time in this city. There appeared to be very few Americans.

He turned left from the hotel entrance and headed up the street, the American Consulate building looming in his path the entire way. It was a large, white, stucco building in the style of a very upscale residence, just a hint of Spanish influence—maybe. It looked out of place and reminded him of something, but he couldn't say what. The building was surrounded by a black wrought iron fence and set back about fifty feet from the road. There was no guard at the gate and no indication that access was restricted. No surprise there. I doubt they get much trouble or walk-in business way up here.

The Red Cross office was a simple storefront setup with a small bronze plaque on the door. Dan walked in and gave the receptionist his name. He didn't have to wait long. A tall, red-haired woman appeared from a rear office and headed directly for him. She was over forty, for sure, but the kind of middle-aged woman whose pale-skinned face cried vibrancy and energy. She would merit a second look, even sober. The woman smiled warmly and offered her hand. "Mr. Matthews?"

Dan was already on his feet. "Yes," he replied.

"Sinead McNally, regional director. You're welcome here. Please, step into my office."

The office was small, even by Air Force standards, but positively sinking in paper and books. Still, it looked orderly to the point of being impressive. He suspected he had come to the right place. "Thanks for seeing me on such short notice."

"'Tis all right, Mr. Matthews," she said, making no attempt to hide the distinct Irish brogue. "Please, have a seat. I confess I have plenty of work, what with the coming Olympics and the preparations. But to be sure, t'was the subject of your inquiry that opened the door. I'm a bit curious why an American would be asking after the Sakhalin Koreans, the poor, godforsaken devils."

If the woman didn't say another word, the trip had been justified. "Well, ma'am, as I said, I'm with the OSI. It's an agency—"

"Ah, Jesus, Mr. Matthews, I didn't just roll out of the rice paddy. An investigation, is it?"

"I'm sorry. Yes, it's in connection with an investigation."

"And what is it you'd like to know about them?"

She wasn't in the least unpleasant, but obviously a woman with no time for frivolity or small talk. He liked her instantly. "Everything you can tell me. I've heard some stories that just don't make sense. I know the Japanese took conscripts for forced labor during the war. That's no surprise to me. Hell, they put American prisoners to work as slaves in war factories. What I've heard about the Sakhalin Koreans is different. I'm told they're still being held prisoners by the Soviets after twenty-five years."

The woman's expression turned deadly serious. "May I ask you a question first?"

"Of course."

"Do your superiors know you're about making inquiries into the

Sakhalin Koreans?"

He couldn't see any reason to lie. What would be the point? "No, ma'am."

"I thought not." Her posture relaxed noticeably and a kind of melancholy seemed to overtake her. "To get to your question, they never were prisoners exactly, even when the Japanese controlled the south part of Sakhalin, although that is the Japanese point of view, not ours. Technically, they were paid a stipend for their labor services under the sham legislation that allowed their conscription, but most of them never saw any money. It was kept in government accounts on their behalf and used for food and shelter. That was the government version anyway."

"Well, what happened to them when the Soviets took over?"

"For the most part it was status quo," McNally replied. "They were simply captured assets. They continued to work in the mines and the mills for nearly nothing. We know many went right on living in the work camps built by the Japanese."

"Do you have any idea what their situation is now?"

"The truth is we only know bits and pieces about their lives today. I can tell you the Soviets would love to send them all somewhere quietly, but they can't do it in the open at this late date without looking like ogres. South Korea and the Soviet Union don't even have diplomatic relations, and the hatred of President Park Jung Hee and his government for the Russians doesn't help. It's a three-way deal as you might say, but getting them all to cooperate in this problem has proved impossible."

She rose from behind the desk and walked over to a small table against the wall. "Would you like a cup of tea?" she asked.

"No, thank you. I had coffee after lunch."

She smiled, pouring hot water into the cup. "We Irish like our tea as much as the English. For that reason we seldom brag about it. I love the Japanese people, Mr. Matthews, but I simply cannot abide what passes for tea in this country. My sister sends me tea from the old country. It comes in a bag, mind you, but 'tis a great improvement over the local variety." She settled in behind her desk again and said, "Now, where were we?"

"The Koreans," he prompted, "about their lives today. I can certainly understand why the Japanese don't want to push the issue, but why are the Koreans not screaming bloody murder?"

"That is really the key, Mr. Matthews, and I believe, privately of course, that will never happen while Park Jung Hee is in power."

It was clear he was about to receive a lesson in international politics. "Why?"

"Many believe President Park is nothing more than a gangster," she explained. "They believe he actually sees himself as Japanese and is nothing more than a puppet of the Japanese emperor he once volunteered to serve."

He considered this new information in the scheme of things. "To be honest, I've wondered why the Koreans have been so quick to forgive and forget. It's not much of a secret that the Japanese brutalized them during the war."

"'Tis not a question of forgive and forget." She turned toward a large map of the Far East, framed prominently on the west wall. "To see them like that, you'd think they were kissing cousins. But it's not the Korean people who've let bygones be bygones. 'Tis Park himself and it has very little to do with forgiveness. 'Tis a fact that during the occupation Park changed his name to Okamoto Minoru."

It was all too much too fast, and more complex than Dan could have imagined. "Is that what you believe? That he sees himself as Japanese?"

She unleashed a mischievous grin. "Let's just say close ties with Japan have thus far been his hallmark. There is a school of thought that believes the current economic prosperity of the Republic of Korea is nothing more than an illusion financed by an endless stream of Japanese yen in the form of loans and grants. As a result, the theory goes, Park Jung Hee simply does the emperor's bidding. Mind you, I'm not saying I believe that myself, Mr. Matthews, if you understand my meaning. The Red Cross is strictly neutral, remember."

"I think I understand you perfectly, Miss McNally." He liked her style too. "Tell me, do you know how many Koreans are still on Sakhalin?"

"We have no idea," she confessed. "We believe the Japanese abandoned about forty-three thousand of the poor souls on Sakhalin in 1945. We have many accounts of horrendous treatment and inhuman conditions continuing until recently. Thousands have died. We really have no idea how many are left."

The idea that an atrocity of such magnitude might linger unresolved, and spill over into the free world nearly thirty years later, repulsed him. In such a context, it was not difficult to understand Su Li's passion for the cause. But she couldn't possibly suspect the extent of Park Jung Hee's complicity in this human tragedy. If Sinead's assessment were accurate, Park would never welcome those poor souls home. Where would Su Li's cause be then? "How do you get your information?"

"We get reports from the occasional visitor and pay very close attention. We have learned that many of the Koreans, the survivors I mean, now have homes—well, decent shelters at least—and families. Still, we believe the majority live in misery and unthinkable conditions without hope. The truth is, Mr. Matthews, we know there are thousands still suffering, but we lack the kind of evidence required to fuel our effort at generating international pressure."

It was almost beyond belief. "What are the chances these people will ever go home?"

Sinead rested her cup on the desk. Dan could swear her shoulders drooped, ever so slightly. "'Tis a very complex problem, with no happy ending in sight, I'm afraid. As a matter of fact, 'tis a problem that also affects hundreds of thousands of ethnic Koreans living here in Japan. Our organization has worked tirelessly for twenty-five years to repatriate the Sakhalin Koreans. Sadly, we'll likely need another twenty-five and more."

Her answer was difficult to accept without explanation. "How is that possible? If you know about it, surely you can embarrass the governments into a humanitarian solution."

"You would think so," she admitted, "but the real world of international diplomacy doesn't work that way. The great powers control the agenda. There's no shortage of evil and injustice in the world to stoke the fires of righteous indignation. Oh, they allow us our causes, the ones that don't conflict with their self-perceived national interests, and the ones they allow us are often more than we are prepared to handle. Just read the papers. Idi Amin feeds his own people to crocodiles with impunity. In Africa, two or three entire nations may die of starvation by spring."

This was a perspective foreign to Dan Mattews. His life was occupied completely by small things: people, one after another, with names and problems, orders to be obeyed and rules to be followed. The big picture was something he'd never considered, never had any reason to consider. "And just how does that relate to those people on Sakhalin?"

"Very directly, I'm afraid. You see, there are grave injustices in the world that mankind simply chooses to suffer with a stoic calm because it might upset the political status quo to do otherwise. There's always another chicken to pluck."

He had an idea what she meant, but wanted to hear her spell it out. "I'm not sure I follow."

"I don't mean to insult you, Mr. Matthews, but I'll give you an example. You so-called Americans have nearly succeeded in exterminating the real ones over the last two hundred years. Tell me, who has lifted a finger to stop you? Certainly not the British. Far from it because at the same time they were after killing off the Irish and the poor, black Africans to steal their land. I could cite more examples if you like. They are not limited to the land of the free and the home of the brave."

It couldn't get any clearer than that. "No. I get your point."

"Please, forgive me," she said. "You made this long trip in good faith and it was rude of me to be so blunt. For the life of me, Mr. Matthews, I just get so frustrated when people have to suffer and die because of practical political realities. I hope you'll allow me the salty language, but it's a proper load of shite and those poor devils over there on Sakhalin are a living indictment against the entire fucking human race."

This was a very unusual woman, Dan concluded, and would likely be as comfortable in a rowdy pub as a diplomatic ball. But she'd shared a part of herself with him, a total stranger. "It's a load of shit, indeed, Miss McNally, and I don't take offense. On the contrary, I appreciate your candor and your valuable time." He rose and offered his hand.

She responded to his hand with two of her own. "I wish you luck, whatever it is you're after. And don't hesitate to call again if you think I might be in a position to help."

With so much on his mind, Dan decided to take advantage of the attractive accommodations at the Royal Hotel and head back up to Wakkanai some time tomorrow. He might even look around the city a bit after another good steak and a few very stiff drinks. After all, Leavenworth wasn't known for its five-star service or fine cuisine.

NINETEEN

**Better to find a snake in the grass
than wait until he's up your ass.**

Friday, 8:00 a.m.
Wakkanai

The taxi was waiting when the Korean agents emerged from the hotel. "We'd like to play pachinko," Chung said to the driver.

"I know just the place," he replied, pulling from the curb. "It's downtown, not far from here."

Chung was brimming with confidence. He turned to Fu and said in Korean, "I might just as well have had this Yoshima pick us up at the hotel and padded our expense accounts with the taxi fare. It would be easy to let our guard down dealing with such fools. Perhaps it's something in the Japanese diet that kills brain cells. These people are not Koreans. They're Japanese with Korean relatives."

"But aren't you concerned that someone may have warned the woman in Asahikawa of our arrival?" Fu asked.

No matter how many times Chung demonstrated his mental superiority, this young upstart never seemed to get the message. "Highly unlikely. Su Li Young disappeared a day or two ago. She could only have gone to meet Subarov, and he's most likely lurking somewhere on the Sea of Japan, well removed from Japanese home waters. It takes time to make such a voyage. Besides, what if someone has warned the woman? What can she do? They're on their own. I doubt she has more than one or two people helping her in Asahikawa. Even in a month, they couldn't relocate all those people."

Fu smiled and shook his head. "I see your point. They can't very well call the police either."

"Or the Americans," Chung added. "I've given this great thought, Fu. I believe this will all unfold according to plan. If need be, we'll make adjustments. There's a chance Subarov will make his move now. If that happens, either the Americans will pick up his trail or we will find him ourselves."

"Sir, what are we going to do when we get the locations of the refugees? Surely you're not going to kill them."

"Nothing so clumsy, Fu. I'm surprised you would even think such a thing. Can you imagine how difficult it would be to dispose of two hundred bodies?"

"What then?"

"Be patient and learn. Make sure your weapon is well concealed on the trip. I don't want any unnecessary mistakes. We're just a couple of simple fishermen in aid of our countrymen."

As the taxi neared the area of the pachinko parlor, Chung addressed the driver. "Let us off here, please." Then he turned to his young protégé. "Fishermen don't go running around in taxis. This is what I mean about not letting our guard down. We'll walk from here. It's not far."

As they turned the corner on foot, Fu said, "May I ask why we left the other Yoshima behind, knowing our destination?"

"All in good time, Fu. One day you will learn to play this as a chess match where strategy can change from minute to minute." More likely he would waste his life in a basement office somewhere.

"Do you believe these people are dangerous to Korea, sir?"

Chung thought the question irrelevant, even a touch rebellious. "I'm not sure I understand your question." Maybe he just hoped he didn't understand it.

"Well, I was just thinking about the mission. It's just that, does it ever seem to you like we're just doing the dirty work for the Japanese?"

Enough was enough. The last word had barely escaped Fu's mouth when Chung's gloved hand lashed out and engulfed the younger man's throat, right there in the street. Chung watched him gasp desperately for breath and allowed the redness to boil up slowly in Fu's face. When bulging eyes signaled his last moments of consciousness, Chung relinquished the death grip and whispered, "Do not question your orders again, my young friend. At the moment you have a bright future with the agency."

The young man's chest heaved violently, then sucked air like a vacuum, the color slowly returning to his face. He struggled for voice. "That's not what I meant. I was just trying to understand, not questioning my orders."

Chung reminded himself to focus on the mission. "I'm sorry. I don't question your loyalty, but forget about trying to understand. It's not your job."

The color rushed back into Fu's face as he fought to maintain his balance. "It's all right, sir. I was just thinking how the Japanese will benefit coincidentally from our mission. It seems a pity; that's all."

The rage had come and gone. He would need the young agent's unfailing loyalty to complete his mission. "It's true enough, Fu. You know how I feel about the Japanese and you know why. The thought that they'll benefit doesn't please me either, but you must be careful. You're not so well informed that you can set policy for the Republic of Korea. We don't have the right to decide which assignments to accept and which to reject, nor should we. We're soldiers. We simply follow the orders of our superiors and trust in their judgment. Never concern yourself with why."

"I understand, sir."

If young Fu fancied himself a policymaker, his career in the Korean CIA would be short-lived indeed. "Let me ask you a question, Fu. Would you rather be back in the Tiger Brigade in South Vietnam chasing dirty men in pajamas?"

"Of course not, sir."

"Then listen to me very carefully. Not so long ago ours was one of the poorest countries on earth. You were born in a village just like mine. You remember what it was like. Park Jung Hee has given South Korea power and status. You and I have very good lives. You have a wife and children in a good school, but it will last only so long as our loyalty lasts. You must trust that Park Jung Hee has a master plan to deal with the Japanese and that he has correctly marked these traitors. Do you understand?"

"Yes, sir."

In another minute the two men stood directly outside the pachinko parlor. Chung said, "Now, let's get in there and see which one of these idiots will be driving us."

Sightseeing was the last thing on Chung's mind during the bumpy road trip to Asahikawa, but it was impossible not to admire the paradoxical beauty of the central Hokkaido rural landscape. He never noticed it before, but had to focus on something to keep from dwelling on subversive thoughts or talking to the retard driving the truck. Yoshima—whichever the fuck one it was—seemed to have gotten the message after the first thirty miles or so and had pretty much backed off the small talk.

In every direction Chung's eyes beheld an endless, white carpet of pristine snow over rolling hills, pastures, and lush, pine forests, punctuated by the occasional farmhouse. Japan was among the most densely populated nations on earth, yet vast tracts of this surprisingly beautiful northern island seemed almost to cry out for people. He puzzled briefly over why the Japanese ever bothered to rape, conquer, and finally annex his homeland of Korea earlier in the century. Massive areas in Korea were too mountainous and inhospitable even for roads. The Japanese would never be satisfied with what they have, he thought. It is their nature and it will be their undoing.

What bothered Chung at the moment were the Americans. Foster was becoming increasingly agitated by Chung's evasiveness, and Washington might easily move to usurp his operation. Chung couldn't allow that to happen. It would be a black mark on the Korean CIA. More importantly, it would bring the curtain down on his rapidly rising star in the intelligence service. So long as he moved swiftly and decisively, he could keep the Americans at bay. Who knows? With a little luck he might end up as Deputy Director before his coming forty-fifth birthday.

Chung thought it might help to find out just how much this moron knew, although Subarov and Su Li were probably smart enough to keep him pretty much in the dark. He said, "Do you know just how many hideaways we're talking about?"

"I don't know," Yoshima replied. "It could be a large number."

"When we get the locations, we'll have to work out the order of the pick ups. A couple hundred will mean five trips at least."

Yoshima scratched his head. "It could take some time. I know Mei Ling has them spread out pretty thin. Many are in the city, I think, staying one or two to a host family. Some are helping out on a couple of farms in the areas, although I never met a Korean who owned a farm here."

It sounded like there had to be a roster somewhere. There would be too many hideouts to keep them all straight without writing it down.

Chung was stiff and hungry by the time the old truck began flirting with the outskirts of Asahikawa. The rice cakes had disappeared hours ago, but there would be no time for rest and relaxation until the job was done. "How far is the place from here?" he asked the young idiot.

"It's just up ahead. Mei Ling will be surprised to see us. She'll be angry I didn't call ahead."

"She'll understand," Chung said. "We'll explain to her how we couldn't risk using the phone. It will be all right."

"I'm sure it will," Yoshima added, easing the truck to a stop directly in front of a row of old, two-story storefronts. "Well, this is it. It's not much of a restaurant, but Mei Ling is a good cook and she specializes in Korean and Chinese food. Will we have time to eat?"

"Of course," Chung said, already stepping from the cab. "We'll grab something before we set out to collect the people." He could see up to half a dozen customers busily eating at the bar. The last thing they needed was a crowd. Chung chided himself for not considering the timing. He didn't need an audience for what he was about to do and held up his hand. "On second thought, let's go eat somewhere else and come back when the crowd thins out. Mei Ling won't want us raising suspicion among her customers."

"Fine," Yoshima said. "I know a nice place a few blocks from here where we can get a good Chinese meal and a beer. Just follow me."

"Very well."

"By the way," Yoshima said, looking directly at Fu, "where are we taking the Koreans?"

Chung had no intention of letting his young, inexperienced protégé improvise at this point and said, "Su Li has made arrangements for all of them to spend the last few nights in a heated barn not far from the city. It will take us the rest of the night, but we should be able to collect them all and get out of here by morning. Then I'll buy you a big, fat breakfast."

"All right," Yoshima said, already bounding ahead. "I like the idea."

Chung leaned over and whispered into Fu's ear. "Go around back and cut the phone line. I don't want to take a chance on her getting a call in the next hour. Then dump this truck and pick up a smaller one in a parking lot somewhere where it won't be missed for a while. I'll meet you back here."

10:00 a.m.
Hakodate, Hokkaido, Japan
The boat's old showerhead, rusted from disuse, had coughed and spat a burst of mud-colored brew. The steady trickle of warm, fresh water that followed had purged the salt from Su Li's hair and the chill from her bones. She felt ready for whatever lay ahead as Kim Tae Woo jumped from the skiff into the knee-high water and pulled the tiny boat onto the rocks. His strong arms lifted her and carried her over the soggy shore, up to the side of the road. Two old women watched curiously from a wooden bench.

"The train station is only a short distance up the road," Kim said. "I wish you well, Su Li." He kissed her lightly on the forehead and turned back for the skiff.

Su Li had never been to the port city of Hakodate, but her only interest this day would be to leave. It was midmorning, she figured, and the road into the city was alive with traffic.

The narrow highway turned inland only a few meters ahead and she followed up the gentle incline, lined with homes and storefront businesses on both sides. At the top of the modest hill she could see the railroad tracks below, curving down from the north. She followed them with her eyes through a small industrial area and into a huge, covered building that could only be the station. It would be less than a fifteen-minute walk. She could only hope there was a morning train up to Wakkanai, or at least as far as Sapporo.

Su Li could not believe her luck. With a ticket in hand and eight minutes to spare, she would have time to call her mother, and dropped her coins into the phone box at the end of Track Three.

"My God, Su Li," Yoon Hae cried, "are you all right?"

"I'm fine. I'm in Hakodate and will be back tonight. What news do you have?" The train whistle made it difficult to hear. Su Li had to cover her free ear. "Speak louder Mother."

"The worst possible news. They found Hiro's body in a hotel room. The police say he may have committed suicide over a spat with his lover—our Reggie. They even found a note. It's horrible. I can't even imagine the pain his family must be suffering."

It was Su Li's worst nightmare come true, but hardly a surprise. She braced herself and tried to focus her thoughts. "What of Reggie?" she asked, one eye on the train.

"I hear he's under investigation by the Japanese police. They haven't ruled out the possibility that, that—"

"That Reggie murdered him," Su Li completed the unthinkable sentence.

"I don't know, but the Americans have placed him under house arrest at the base during the investigation."

"It is all spinning out of control now, Mother. I don't even know what to do, but I have to go quickly or I'll miss my train."

"There is one more thing. Taro just came to see me. Last night the brothers had a visit from a fisherman. He claimed you sent him. His name was Chung something or other."

Su Li could see the conductor, down the track, boarding the last of the passengers, but this conversation might be the most important of her life. "I sent no one to the Pachinkos. Who was he? What happened?"

"He told the brothers you sent him to move the Sakhalin Koreans to new hiding places. He said Hiro probably gave up their locations before he died. He took Jiro with him. They left for Asahikawa this morning. I tried to warn Mei Ling, but she's not answering her phone."

"Oh, Mother, what have I done? He must be the one who murdered Hiro. I have to make it Asahikawa."

"That's the last place you can go. Have you lost your head? There's nothing more you can do, Su Li. The people are in grave danger. We can only hope this animal won't harm them."

The train doors had closed and she could see the conductor's head peering both ways from the window. Su Li's own head was spinning in a whirlwind of emotions and she wanted to run from this unbearable burden as she had run from the old woman in Mei Ling's restaurant. But who would be left to save these poor souls if she abandoned them now? "Mother, there's no one else to help us. What am I to do?"

"Agent Matthews came to me," her mother said. "I think you should talk to him. Reggie made a decision to trust him. Matthews knows everything and is a good man. He'll help you; I know it. He said he was going on a trip but would be back some time last night or today."

She was ready to try anything, but the train was moving now, slowly creeping forward. "Reggie probably had no choice but to tell him, but what could he do even if he is on the base and willing to help?"

"If he did nothing but keep you safe, I'd be in his debt forever," Yoon Hae declared. "I'll send word to him at the base. If he's there I know he'll come to the restaurant. Will you call back?"

"Yes." Yoon Hae seemed to take some comfort in the prospect that the American might help and Su Li didn't see any harm in humoring her. "Mother, ask Taro to stay with you until I return."

"I will, but please don't go to Asahikawa alone. I beg you."

"I'll be all right," she promised. "I only want to find out what they've done. I'll stay in touch. Try not to worry too much."

"Su Li, wait," her mother pleaded. "There's something else."

A part of her wanted to cover her ears. "What?"

"The fisherman, Chung, is Korean. I don't mean Japanese-Korean. I mean he's Korean like I'm Korean, and Jiro tells me he speaks very little Japanese."

The bad news just kept piling up. "Then the Korean who appeared twice at the restaurant the day after Hiro vanished—"

"Yes, Su Li, he may be South Korean CIA."

The train was picking up speed. It might be too late already. "Good bye, Mother," she said, "I'll call again when I can."

Su Li ran from the phone booth, the receiver still hanging, and barely managed to swing herself onto the high entrance step of the last car. As the conductor opened the door she stepped inside, nearly oblivious to his scolding rebuke.

The South Korean CIA's involvement was a revelation Su Li was not prepared to hear, and its significance terrified her even more that the thought of murder. It was hardly possible. Their own South Korean government was probably working against them. It meant the Korean CIA may have murdered her beloved Hiro.

They had always figured President Park would not take up their cause because of his hatred for the Soviets, but that's a much different thing, she thought, than murdering to keep his own people from coming home. They had figured it wrong all along. They'd all fooled themselves into thinking these people could go back to their own villages and live out their lives in peace.

There was no time to grieve for her dear friend, not yet. She knew their plan was now in real jeopardy and feared for the two hundred people secreted around Asahikawa. She would soon learn their fate, but the success of the plan now rested squarely on the shoulders of Nikolai Subarov.

TWENTY

Here we are together on a northbound trip.
I can't make you trust me, but ain't about to take your lip.

Friday, 12:40 p.m.
Sapporo

Dan boarded the northbound, Wakkanai train at Sapporo station. He appeared to have his choice of seats in the coach car, where only eight or nine were occupied. As he slowly strolled the aisle of the Spartan rail car, he was more convinced than ever that someone up the chain of command had made a calculated decision to conceal the existence of some high-level operation from him, even to actively mislead him. The reason for the cover-up was obvious. This was an insidious and inhuman conspiracy, assisted in part by no less than the self-proclaimed, international guardian of human rights and leader of the free world—the United States of America.

The real question in Dan's mind was why his country would be involved in the first place. The United States could have no direct interest in what happened to a few displaced Koreans, so his government's involvement in this sordid affair had to be in support of another power. That opened up an infinite and dark web of sinister possibilities Dan couldn't even begin to imagine. The Japanese government seemed the obvious candidate, but there was no evidence of its complicity. It couldn't be the Soviet Union because it would be shooting itself in the foot.

An unusually plump woman in a traditional kimono appeared from the other end of the car, two young children in tow. He stepped to the side as they passed, tiny clouds of white breath bellowing in the not-yet heated air. Dan knew he had taken his first step onto a very short plank, but harbored no death wish or compulsion for self-destruction. An innocent Japanese boy had been murdered and an equally innocent American one had been framed, degraded, and humiliated in preparation for his unceremonious expulsion from the U.S. military. It sickened Dan Matthews that his country could become involved in such unholy business, but it also buoyed him because the knowledge of his government's evil doings was the weapon that might stop this madness. If only he could figure out how to use it.

His coach car was old for sure, with straight-angled, wooden seats facing each other, but clean and well maintained. Thankfully, it was heated, or would be soon, obviating the need for him to spend another eighteen hundred yen for the first-class car. He spotted a window seat at the end of the car and figured he could use the extra leg room.

He almost didn't see her at all. In fact, the message from his eyes to his brain didn't even process until he had passed her by. It had only been a fleeting glimpse, barely even a profile at that, but the image in his brain was clear enough to tell him it was she; that soft, shimmering hair ebbing back and forth like the hint of a wave in perpetual motion. He didn't have to turn and look either, such was the impression the woman had made on his subconscious.

It was easy to admit to himself, now that he no longer feared some Mata Hari persona. Su Li Young was possibly the most beautiful woman he had ever seen. Her face betrayed only a trace of Caucasian features and belied the stories of her post-war, American father. If anything, the unusually high cheekbones hinted faintly of Native American ancestry. No wonder Kincaid fell in love with her, he thought. No wonder every GI on the base drooled over her. To top it all off, the girl was legit, a bona fide, selfless crusader on a mission of mercy.

If only she weren't involved with Reggie. Besides, she'd be at least fifty-five by the time he got released from Leavenworth. Would she visit him every weekend and be happy holding hands once a month for the next thirty years? Humor wouldn't be enough to get him through this. Hell, maybe nothing would.

Her eyes were closed as he quietly settled onto the bench seat beside her, placing his overnight bag carefully underneath. The heavily bundled, old woman across the way frowned with displeasure, a message that she had seen into his demented and sex-starved Western soul to discover its evil intent. He frowned back and the old woman turned her head, embarrassed, but positioned her right ear carefully to intercept any conversation.

"I suspect if you were following me, Su Li," he said, "you would have done a better job of concealing yourself."

She gave no hint of being startled; her eyes remained closed. "I am not following you, Agent Matthews," she replied in English. "I didn't expect to see you on this train. My mother is a very resourceful woman, but she can't perform miracles."

She had obviously seen him coming. "I'm sorry. I don't understand."

Her eyes opened, but she turned them toward the window. "It's not important. Has your Japanese improved since our last conversation?"

"No. I'm afraid you'll have to stumble along in English, but it sounds to me like you'll do just fine." Her cool demeanor was no surprise. "Can you tell me what you're doing in Sapporo?"

Finally, she turned to face him, expressionless as far as he could tell. "Always the policeman. Yes, Agent Matthews?"

"Look, Su Li, we need to talk, but would you please call me Dan?"

"I think not," she answered, casting a wicked glance at the old Japanese woman eagerly embracing every word, "but we do need to speak. Let's move over there to the empty section."

With the old snoop at a safe distance, they sat facing each other and Dan said, "I'm sorry about your friend, Ishikawa, and about Reggie. I know you and he are, well, I—"

"You know nothing," she snapped; then seemed to sink back into a posture of resignation and despair. Those smoldering green eyes reflected the exhaustion of a woman shouldering a terrible burden, maybe even a lost cause.

"I know all about what you're trying to do," he said. "I also know you're in big trouble. If I can help you, I will."

"I don't know how you could help." A chink in the armor, however slight.

It looked to Dan like the girl was wrestling with her own judgment.

"What are you doing way down here in Sapporo?" When she didn't answer he said, "When have you last eaten or slept?"

"I can't think of sleep now Dan-san, not until I know what they've done with Mei Ling and the two hundred."

The significance of the familiar greeting was not lost on him. "What who have done?"

"My fellow Koreans in the service of the great President Park Jung Hee," she declared sarcastically. "It's the Korean CIA that hunts and kills us. Two of their agents went early today to find the people we've hidden around Asahikawa. I'm going there now."

Her boldness seemed to defy logic. "Alone? To do what?"

"I don't know what can be done, at least not until I know their intentions. But they know how to find the people."

He didn't hesitate. "We'll go together and figure something out." Dan expected the green eyes to reveal shock. Instead he saw only relief. "May I ask you some questions about your friend, Ishikawa?"

"Yes, but he's beyond help now."

"How was his English?"

She looked puzzled. "He was always very good in English at school," she said. "In secondary school Hiro focused his studies around English. His father is a banker and insisted that his sons become very skilled in your language. His English helped him get the job at the newspaper."

"So he knew how to write English?"

"Reading, writing, and speaking. He was very good in all three."

Ishikawa's proficiency in English was no great revelation to Dan, as he already knew the suicide note had been faked, one way or the other. But surely Inspector Tanaka had asked these questions of the family. He'd had plenty of opportunity to share the information with Dan, but kept it to himself. Dan apparently wasn't the only one holding back information. "You must be exhausted," he said. "Get some rest now if you can. We have a lot of work ahead of us."

She touched his arm. "What are they going to do to Reggie?"

He remembered her stinging rebuke and was more confused than ever. "They'll probably ship him back to the States when the investigation is completed. Then they'll give him a less than honorable discharge from service. I don't think he'll be charged by the Japanese authorities, just humiliated and disgraced by ours."

She seemed not to understand, as though permanent dishonor were not sufficient punishment for perfectly innocent conduct. "That's all that will happen to him? The Air Force won't try to put him in prison?"

"Prison? Why would you think they'd put him in prison?"

"No reason," She smiled weakly and eased her head onto Dan's waiting shoulder. He could feel the tension drain from her tired body as she fell instantly asleep.

Prison?

Three hours later the train pulled into Asahikawa station. Dan's shoulder and arm were numb, but he didn't have the heart to wake up the sleeping angel beside him. She looked too serene, too natural there snuggled up against his body, and he wasn't in any hurry to break the contact.

The train slowed, its brakes screeching into the tiny, covered station. Su Li's eyes fluttered open. She looked around the car for a moment, trying to get her bearings, then bolted upright. "Why didn't you wake me?"

"You needed the rest," Dan said, smiling. "Do you feel better?"

She seemed oblivious to the question. "We must get to Mei Ling's quickly. Do you know the time?"

"It's about 1545 hours." She looked at him as if he had spoken in gibberish. "I'm sorry. I mean it's fifteen minutes before four."

She nearly leapt from the seat, bounding over him toward the door. Dan noticed her small overnight case on the floor and grabbed it. When the door opened he hurried along behind her, holding the two small cases. Thankfully, an ample supply of taxis was standing by directly in front of the small station. The car nearly drove away without him.

"Mei Ling's Sunrise Restaurant," she told the driver, "thirteen Akachi-cho."

Su Li was in no mood to be restrained, but one way or the other he had to get control of the situation or they could both be dead in a matter of minutes. More than anything else, Dan longed for the feel of a forty-five caliber automatic under his arm, but the treaty with Japan had long ago nixed the practice of carrying pistols in civilian clothing. He'd learned from this Kincaid affair that the treaty didn't mean much to anyone these days. Ironic that he should be the only one observing it. Dan promised himself that, if he lived until morning, he'd have a pistol within arms reach until this business was finished.

He gently took hold of her arm in an attempt to break her focus. If he couldn't get her to listen, it wouldn't matter what he said. "Su Li, please listen for a minute. I need your complete attention if I'm going to help you."

At first he thought she would launch some blistering, verbal assault or even throw him from the moving car. Then her eyes softened. "You're right, Dan-san. You are trained in such things."

He tried not to look surprised. "Good. Now who is Mei Ling? Reggie didn't get that far in our conversation."

"She's my mother's friend. Mei Ling is responsible for hiding the Sakhalin Koreans. She keeps the list detailing where each is hidden. There could be as many as thirty houses or farms around the area."

"All right, these guys will be after the list. We must assume they have guns and are willing to use them. There's no way to protect against being shot. Let's just try and lower the risk a little. Tell the driver to drop us off a couple of blocks from the restaurant. We'll walk in from there and watch the place for a while. Does it have a back door?"

"Yes. It won't be locked at this time of day unless someone else has locked it."

They watched the small, freestanding, two-story building carefully for a while and saw no sign of activity, although it wasn't much past dinnertime. A few people seemed to stop and look in the window, but nobody entered and nobody left.

Dan didn't care to broadcast his presence by strolling past the place in a GI parka, but he had to know if they were inside. He turned to Su Li and said, "We need to know what's going on inside. Take a walk right by the front. Don't stop. There's plenty of traffic, so they won't suspect. Just take a quick look, then come back on the other side of the street."

"Of course," she said, already headed in the direction of Mei Ling's.

She did exactly as instructed and was back within a few minutes. "There are two closed signs in the window," she explained, "one in Japanese and one in Korean. I saw nothing inside the restaurant: no customers, no Mei Ling, nothing. But there is a back kitchen and a room upstairs."

He didn't like it. "We'll have to take a chance. You'll do exactly as I tell you. Right?"

"Yes." He had his doubts.

They slipped around the side of the old, wood structure toward the rear. Dan stopped just before the corner of the building. He saw the phone line had been snipped and pointed it out to Su Li. He held his index finger to his mouth and hoped she'd gotten the message.

Crouching under the back window, Dan made his way to the rear door. He signaled Su Li to stay put. The door was unlocked. Whether or not it squeaked was another matter. With a silent prayer on his lips, Dan pushed at the door ever so slightly, half expecting to be staring up at a the muzzle of a Walther PPK at any second. When nothing happened he held his crouch, dead still, listening into an eerie silence.

It wasn't completely dark outside, but dark enough that the place should have lights on. He couldn't detect a single one. They might be expected. You could only do so much before leaping into the unknown and he'd done it all. Dan swallowed hard and crept, not quite as silently as he'd liked, through the opening in the rear door and into the small kitchen. It was empty and his breathing slowed a little. The curtain into the restaurant was open, not a soul on the first floor.

Dan felt a hand on his back, triggering a close encounter with cardiac arrest. He turned to find familiar, green eyes in the semi-darkness. He should have figured as much. Then a thump from above. Someone on the second floor. Arguing with her now could get them both killed. He waved his arm horizontally, palm away, indicating she should stay behind him. Most likely a fruitless gesture. She nodded and he began to ascend the narrow staircase, creaking, wood stairs tracking his position for would-be killers.

He motioned for Su Li to hug the wall and lashed out into the flimsy door with the sole of his shoe. No gunfire, only his heart beating like a jackhammer. Aching for the feel of a pistol, Dan crept cautiously into the darkened room, a silhouette target for his concealed assassin. In the far corner he saw the wriggling forms of two people, an old woman and a young man, hog-tied with their mouths taped shut. No assasin in wait. Su Li rushed past him toward the victims. While she tended the old woman, Dan began to remove the tape from the young man's mouth.

The man was on his feet in a heartbeat, spewing waves of gibberish. Dan had never heard anyone talk so fast. It could have been

Korean, Japanese, hell, even English for all he knew.

"Mei Ling," Su Li cried. A blizzard of Korean words leapt from her mouth, fast and choppy. At times she and the old woman were talking at the same time, but it didn't seem to inhibit communication. When the young man joined in the animated conversation, Dan figured he'd just wait it out. Eventually, Su Li would have to tell him what happened.

Dan and Su Li helped the old woman down the stairs into the kitchen, where Su Li quickly put a light under a kettle of water while the young man escorted the old one out of the room.

"She'll be all right, Dan-san. She went to lie down. I'll bring her tea and my friend, Jiro, will see to her needs."

"What happened to them?"

"They were surprised by two Korean agents just after lunchtime. As we suspected, they were after the list of hideaways."

"Did they get it?"

She killed the flame under the boiling water and pointed to the countertop. "Yes. Will you bring that tray over to the table?"

The cups looked expensive, probably hand-painted china. His task completed, Dan said, "Why Korean agents? That doesn't make sense."

Su Li began to pour. "The Korean government considers these people to be Soviet spies."

He wasn't about to accept her declaration at face value. "Reggie told me something like that when he was talking about how your people got stuck over there, but I just don't buy it. That's not a good enough reason to start murdering innocent people. If the Korean CIA is involved, there's a better reason than that, and we need to find out what it is."

"But perhaps now is not a good time," Su Li suggested. "Those Korean agents have had the list for nearly four hours."

She had a point. "We need to find out what they've done with those people. Maybe it's not too late to throw a monkey wrench in the works."

"What?"

He smiled. "Never mind. It would take longer than four hours to pick up two hundred people at thirty locations."

"I don't want to think what they might do to them,"

He had no clue, but one thing was crystal clear. "Don't worry. Whatever they do, it won't include killing. This is a covert operation.

They'd kill two or three of us without blinking an eye, but two hundred is out of the question. It's just too messy. That's why they didn't even kill Mei Ling and your friend, Jiro. They know you can't call the police on them. They'll kill only when necessary."

"Mei Ling has a car we can use. She has all the locations in her head. Some are very near to this place."

His first instinct was to put Mei Ling in the car, but it could prove a dangerous ride. "Good. Get her to write them all down now. We'll start checking them out right away. We should know what they're up to very soon."

"Hakodate," Su Li said.

"What?" He thought they were about to start talking more gibberish.

"You wanted to know where I was coming from. I was in Hakodate, on my way back to Wakkanai. All the trains go through Sapporo. I met with the captain at sea. He's going to land with his collection in two days time at Abashiri. I don't know what will happen then, but he expects me to wait for him in Wakkanai."

Seemed there was a great deal more to learn. "What collection?"

"I'll explain later. The captain's collection is what they want."

At least it was the beginning of a plan. "Then Wakkanai is where we'll be. Let's go find out what they did with those people."

6:10 p.m.

"Why don't we follow them, sir?" Fu asked, perched atop a wooden crate and peering out through the front windshield of the van.

"Because they'll be back within an hour," Chung replied, careful not to show himself as he watched Su Li and the American drive off in the old Toyota sedan. "We can warm up and find a place to spend the night. When they see the old Koreans are gone, they'll come back to make sure the old woman and the dim-witted, muscle-boy are safe. Then we'll stay with them like a tail on a dog. They'll lead us to Subarov. Besides, Fu, both of them were carrying overnight bags when they arrived. The bags are still inside the restaurant."

"What about the American?"

Chung had already come to a decision on that question. "They haven't been able to control that cowboy to this point, so we'll deal with him ourselves."

"Killing him could start real trouble with the Americans," Fu pointed out.

He didn't need a subordinate to point out the obvious. "I'm well aware of that, but this time the Americans may have to live with it. Their agent has gone over to the other side."

"Once the Japanese collect all the refugees, aren't you afraid they'll figure out what's going on? Some of the old people might remember the woman's name or the restaurant and must know at least something about Subarov's plan or they wouldn't be here."

Truly, there was almost no hope for his young protégé. "Some of those old fools don't even know their own names. I doubt any one of them knows Mei Ling's. Even these amateurs would never have been so careless. If they do trace them back to Mei Ling, the trail will end there. The old woman would never give up her friends. Remember, Fu, our Japanese cousins no longer employ persuasive interrogation techniques."

"So the Japanese will believe they've simply broken up a smuggling ring," Fu suggested.

"What else would they think? They'll be looking for some Yakuza boys making extra money by importing illegal aliens. It happens all over the free world. The people pay money to get over here where the good jobs are. Plenty of Sakhalin Koreans have been smuggled in over the years without any thought of repatriation or rebellion. We're just using the Japanese as our jailers for a little while. They'll never have a clue. It's funny, really. When you think about it, they're saving their own asses and will never know it."

"Won't they wonder who turned them in?" Fu asked.

"Let them wonder. They'll come up with some theory that serves their own interest. It always happens that way. The point is those two hundred old layabouts won't be of any further use to the girl and Subarov. We're closing the noose, Fu."

TWENTY-ONE

**I'll show you mine, if you'll show me yourn.
They might hear the music, but they won't find the horn.**

*Friday, 6:20 p.m.
Asahikawa*

"That should be it," Su Li said, looking across at the modest, frame house only a few blocks from Mei Ling's restaurant.

Dan looked at the list in his hand. "Han Lee Min," he said. There were no cars nearby and no sign of activity anywhere. He opted for the direct approach. "Let's just go up and knock on the door. Do you know these people?"

"I know a few people on the list, but not these."

"How much do these families know about your plan?"

"Almost nothing. They know they are helping Koreans in need. That's all."

"Good. We have no idea how much the Japanese authorities know, but at least they won't learn more from these families."

Su Li nodded. "We did that for their protection as well as our security. I was beginning to think the Japanese authorities were unaware of the Korean CIA operation, but now I don't know."

Dan wasn't so sure. "Well, don't trouble yourself about it. I know someone who might help us figure this whole thing out. This person is an expert in practical political reality."

"Where do we find this person?" Su Li asked.

"In Sapporo, but we have places to go and people to see before we get there. Are you ready to meet the Min family?"

She grabbed his arm. "Wait, Dan-san. I'll go alone. These people may be frightened already and might not talk if they see a foreigner."

"All right, but don't go inside. Don't even leave my line of sight."

He watched as Su Li approached the front door and waited. In a minute she appeared to be engaged in conversation with someone inside. Then, exactly as Dan expected, she disappeared into the small, single-family dwelling. Next time he'd just figure out what she should do and tell her the opposite. He waited anxiously for a long fifteen minutes, but then she reappeared at the front door, exchanging customary bows as she departed toward the waiting car.

"Well," he said, "I take it they cooperated."

"Yes, of course, and gave me a cup of hot tea. The Japanese police were here early this afternoon and took the two Sakhalin Koreans with them. The family is very frightened. The police took their registration cards and ordered them not to leave the city. They fear they will be punished by the authorities."

"What do you mean, registration cards?"

"All Koreans must register with the government and carry an identification card as proof of legal residence." She then produced a laminated card from the small handbag in her pocket. "This is mine."

It seemed a bit Orwellian. "But you were born in Japan."

"It doesn't matter; we are aliens all the same. This family is frightened because they do not have the rights of Japanese citizens, and the authorities could make things very difficult for them."

"You mean they could go to prison or be deported?"

Su Li laughed, and for the life of him, he couldn't understand why. "In many ways you are like a newborn baby, Dan-san. There is nowhere to deport them. They could be sent to prison, yes, but that will likely not happen. It costs money to maintain prisoners and these people are not dangerous. They may suffer in more subtle ways, like at the children's school or at the father's job."

"This is all new to me," he confessed, trying desperately to crack a smile.

"Not so new, I think," Su Li countered. It was as if she measured his every word for accuracy of content. "The Japanese have a word for black-skinned Americans. They call them *kokujin*. It's not a nice word, but I think nicer than some used by white-skinned Americans."

"I get your point, Su Li. When it comes to racial prejudice, Americans don't take a backseat to anybody. Well, my bet is they've rounded up your entire two hundred by now. Maybe we should try one of the farms outside the city."

"Yes. There's a small farm less than twenty minutes from here. Six people are hidden there. Turn left at the next main street."

Dan eased the small car into first gear and headed west. He figured this was a good opportunity to work on his long neglected communications skills. "Tell me, Su Li; have you given any thought to what happens to Su Li Young when this is all over?"

"I don't think about that."

"You don't think about it or you don't want to think about it? The way I see it, if a miracle happens and all the Sakhalin Koreans go home and live happily ever after, Su Li Young is still stuck here in Japan. You won't be very popular here, and I doubt Park Jung Hee will welcome you home to Korea with open arms."

It seemed he had prompted her first ever consideration of the subject. For the first time in their brief relationship she looked vulnerable, even afraid. It startled him.

"And if we fail?" she asked.

Dan wanted to take back the words that had so cleanly pierced her shell of invincibility. This was not some iron maiden seated beside him, although he had begun to see her in that way. His words had unwittingly forced her to confront her own hopeless destiny. She had obviously succeeded in holding it at bay in the service of a higher cause. What right did he have to open the floodgates, unleashing a torrent of long-suppressed emotions? He could see them all in those ever-telling green eyes: frailty, fear—loneliness most of all. Dan was ashamed, and now he had no answer for the question his cruel insensitivity had spawned. A pathetic "I'm sorry," was all he could muster.

"Turn right at the next intersection," she said.

The winding road carried them in silence through the snow-covered, rural countryside. Dan figured he'd said enough already. Finally, Su Li rescued him. "Tell me about where you are from, Dan-san."

This was his least favorite subject, and he was already thinking of a way to change it. "Well, I was born in Chicago and never left until I joined the Air Force after finishing high school. I've only been back a few times since."

"Oh, yes, Chicago is in Irinoi. I studied it in school on the map. What about your family? Do you have brothers and sisters?"

"No. My father was killed in WWII. I have no memories of him. The Air Force has been my life since 1963."

"What about your mother?"

He saw his opportunity and pointed to the crossroads ahead. "Is this where we turn?"

She feigned irritation, folding her arms like a cigar store Indian. "You don't like to talk about yourself. Maybe you're rich with three cars and a big house on a Chicago mountaintop."

It was his turn to laugh and he made good use of the opportunity. "That's very funny."

"Funny?"

"No mountains in Chicago and no mansions in my past or future, I'm afraid. After this is over, I'll probably go to the military prison at Fort Leavenworth for a good long stretch. There are those who would argue I'm dangerously close to committing treason."

Then she smiled a happy smile. Dan was glad to see it, but it seemed strangely out of context, considering his last remark. "Perhaps we are two peas in the same pot after all."

He didn't even think about correcting her. "Perhaps we are at that, but I'm not sure I get your meaning."

She squeezed his arm playfully. "Reggie has told me many things. You are afraid to let go. I am afraid to hang on. Yet it seems we've walked hand in hand to the edge of a very dangerous cliff."

She would be enough to keep any man on his toes. "May I ask you a personal question, one pea to another?"

He was hoping for another smile, but it didn't come. "I think I know the question," she said. "Am I in love with Reggie?"

The girl was as intuitive as she was bold, he thought. "Well, are you?"

"Do not look for simple answers," she cautioned, "for you will always find one, but rarely learn the truth."

"All right, I give up. Is that some kind of samurai teaching or something?"

She smiled weakly. "Nothing so noble, but your question is difficult to answer. I know what the men on the base say about me because I hear the whispers. Some don't even bother to whisper, but I don't hate all Americans any more than I love them all. I'm no less a foreigner here than each of you since my own father was American."

He understood this was all part of her answer, and if she thought it was important, he wanted to hear it. "Was an American?"

"My mother never heard from him after he went back to the States," she explained. "Like many others, he promised to send for his loved one and did not."

It was a story as old as war itself. "I'm surprised your mother doesn't hold it against all of us."

"Why surprised? I believe it's quite natural. You must remember my mother's background gives her a more balanced view of life than most. Yoon Hae is grateful for what little she has, and even more grateful that we have each other. She believes something wonderful grew from the pain of abandonment. Yoon Hae did not teach me to hate, Dan-san. She taught me to understand, to follow my heart and to strive for honesty in all things." Her smile warmed. "I don't hate my father any more than I hate myself."

As near as he could tell, Su Li had just articulated her philosophy of life, probably without even realizing it, childlike in its simplicity and impregnable in its logic. "Thank you for telling me that," he said, because he didn't know what else to say. He still wasn't sure he understood this woman, but he knew such personal revelations are not made lightly and must be cultivated in the soil of trust. She was unique, special in a way that he had never imagined possible. But he needed to know more. "You didn't answer my question."

"I made love with Reggie because he was like a fisherman lost alone at night on the sea of floating ice," she explained. "Reggie is a good and decent man, but deeply troubled. His pain may never be lifted completely, but it was within my power to ease it for a time and my action didn't cause harm or pain to another."

"I think I understand," he said, and this time he thought he was beginning to. This woman lived somewhere beyond a great cultural divide and he might never make the crossing, not completely. Perhaps it was Su Li who really didn't understand some of life's most common tools of survival, like treachery, deceit, manipulation, and jealousy. In her simplistic, homespun philosophy, he found value far surpassing even her great physical beauty. He wanted to stop the car and hold her in his arms. He wanted to be naked with her in a dark room for a week. The hell with food and water. All he could think of to say was, "I think

I understand."

The smile turned mischievous. "That is very un-American of you."

Dan had no clue what that meant, but she was definitely teasing him. Before he compounded his stupidity, Su Li rescued him. "We'll be able to see the house from just over that hill."

This time they spotted the operation in progress and pulled carefully to the side of the icy road to avoid detection. The van and car were from the local prefectural police and the three uniformed officers were already helping the Koreans into the van in front of a small farmhouse. "Well," Dan said, "it looks like they've done an efficient job of picking them all up. We'd better get back to Mei Ling's and figure out what happens next."

Su Li couldn't avert her eyes from the scene until it disappeared behind the hill. "At least we know they'll be safe for now. The police have no reason to mistreat them, but what will happen now?"

He rested his hand on top of hers and smiled. "You might have a say in that yet."

As they neared the restaurant, the absence of an effective weapon heightened Dan's sense of caution. He pulled to the side of the road, still well out of sight from Mei Ling's.

"Is something wrong?" Su Li asked.

"I don't think so, but let's play it safe. Come on."

They walked to the building at the end of the narrow street and Dan peered around the corner in the direction of the restaurant. "Take a look at the van parked across from Mei Ling's. Tell me what the writing on the side says."

She strained and squinted for a minute in the direction of the setting sun. "I'm sorry. It's too far, even if I could block the sun's glare."

"All right, then we'll get you a little closer. Jump in the car."

He drove around the area to the north and came in from the west, dangerously near the small van parked between them and Mei Ling's restaurant. "Listen carefully," he said. "This could be nothing at all, but that van was parked in the same spot when we arrived. When you reach the corner, be very careful. They'll be just across the street from you. If they're hostile they should be looking in the other direction. Just read the writing. That's all."

"I understand," she said, as the pair quietly exited their car. Su Li was gone and back in the space of a few seconds. "It's the vehicle of a medical supply company: oxygen, wheelchairs, and general medical supplies, I believe."

"And do you see any hospitals around here? Do you see any doctor's offices, ambulance companies, or medical supply companies?"

"Not so much as a pharmacy."

"Our two Korean friends are most likely in the back of that van watching Mei Ling's through the windshield. They knew we would be back after checking on the refugees' situation. Very clever. They plan to follow you to your captain."

Su Li gasped. "We can't leave Mei Ling and Jiro like this. What can we do?"

"That depends if we want to get shot. Personally, I'd rather not, so I'll have to think about it."

"Jiro is a master of martial arts," she offered.

"But Jiro is in the restaurant," Dan countered. "We are not. Besides, bullets will beat karate every time. All we have to do is keep them from following us for five minutes or so until we get away."

"What can you do with no weapon?"

It wasn't easy, but he was one step ahead of her. "Maybe I have a weapon," he said, walking to the rear of the small car. He opened the trunk and removed the lug wrench from its place along side the jack.

Su Li shook her head. "They'll kill you before you get close enough to use it. Don't try this."

"Thanks for your concern, Su Li, but I'm no Charles Bronson. I've had training in the use of this weapon and I intend to use it for its designed purpose only. Now, you must promise me something, and this time I want you to mean it."

"Yes, Dan-san, I promise."

His hands were shaking and he took pains to keep them from her view. "If this goes badly, I want you to get in this car and drive away as quickly as possible. Go straight to Wakkanai. I know Mei Ling and your friend are still here, but I don't think these guys will hurt them. They could have done it before."

Dan crossed the street in the darkness some fifty yards to the rear of the parked van and walked directly toward the rear cargo door, hoping to minimize the chance of being spotted through the rear view mirrors. He figured if he could make it into their blind spot he'd have a chance. Someone had once told him if you can't see the side mirrors the driver can't see you. He was about to test the theory.

Two feet from the rear bumper, he dropped quietly to his stomach and removed the lug wrench from inside his coat. He chose the curbside rear wheel and with great care began to pry the cheap wheel cover from position. So much as a squeak and the Koreans would be on him with pistols.

The fucking lug nut wouldn't budge. They were all factory tight. He assaulted the goddamn thing silently from the prone position, throwing all his weight into the effort and felt the van rock under his power as the nut gave way. Dan waited for disaster, but nothing happened.

He adjusted position to loosen the second lug nut and caught sight of the spectator. He was an old, bent, Japanese man, carrying a shopping bag and dressed in the traditional garb underneath his very Western goose-down coat. The old man was standing there silently, perched on his wooden sandals, watching.

In a near state of panic, Dan prayed the old fart was not a Good Samaritan. Purely out of frustration and utter helplessness, he did the only thing he could think of. He gave the old guy the finger, with a violent thrust and a nasty sneer for good measure, in case the gesture might not have been recognized as an insult. To Dan's relief, the old man huffed, then clopped away in silence.

The rest of the nuts were a breeze. He figured the wheel on the Koreans' van was good for four or five hundred rotations. After that it would rotate itself right off the axle. Dan backed away slowly into the Koreans' blind spot, wet and tired, but undetected.

After a good meal and a change of clothes, Dan and Su Li left the restaurant with their two passengers and headed west, toward the small coastal village of Rumoi, the white van ever present in the rearview mirror.

In the midst of a nervous silence, Mei Ling initiated a short conversation with Su Li, after which, Su Li offered a loose translation. "She thinks we should spend the night at her sister's in Rumoi, Dan-san, assuming we are fortunate enough to escape these murderers. Rumoi is on the way, but Wakkanai is over two hundred kilometers to the north along the coast road."

"What do you think?" Dan asked. "We have another day before the captain will arrive anyway. Maybe it's better if we're rested." He glanced quickly in the mirror to see the van's headlights, maintaining the distance.

"I agree, and I'd like to call my mother to let her know we're all right."

"We can do that from a public phone box in the morning, when we're sure we are all right. The NSA will be after us by this time, and they have more resources than you can imagine." Then he surrendered to curiosity. "What was the last part of that conversation? You know, the part that caused all three of you to laugh."

"I asked if her sister knows how to make hamburgers," Su Li said. "I told her you don't eat raw fish or squid."

Dan gave her a sarcastic nod and searched for Mei Ling's eyes in the rear view mirror. *"Domo arigato,"* he said. Su Li didn't offer to translate the old woman's reply, but it was sufficient to stir a second bout of laughter among his three Korean passengers.

Within a few more minutes, ceramic rooftops and gray, wooden buildings gave way to pure, white fields and lush, pine forests in the semi-darkness. Then Dan spotted the explosion of sparks in his rear view mirror. The van had already disappeared from view. He would have given a week's pay to see the faces of the two Koreans at the moment the wheel fell off.

He turned to face Su Li. She had obviously seen it as well. The warmth and genuineness of her smile fueled him for all that might yet come.

TWENTY-TWO

**I've crossed that line and I ain't looking back,
so it's full speed ahead on the northbound track.**

Saturday, 8:00 a.m.
Rumoi, Hokkaido

Standing on the high rocks behind the small, rural cottage, it occurred to Dan that he could live happily in such a place as this, were it not for mundane things like money, politics, and race. A bright, blue sea and cloudless, matching sky had conspired to overwhelm him. The water on the Sea of Japan glistened, still and inviting, as the rising sun warmed his back.

He had come a long way from a violent and uncertain childhood and the sweltering jungles of South Vietnam, to be caught in a lethal vice of his own making. He was a fugitive now and there was no walking away from it. Right or wrong, good or bad, other people's molded concepts of morality held no relevance for him.

Dan Matthews had embarked on a journey of conscience, and in a short while it would come to an end. He had not sought it out. It had found him, wayward and unguided, like the needle of a compass gone berserk, and given his life a sense of focus and purpose.

A few weeks ago he'd never heard of Sakhalin Island, or Karafuto, or kidnapped Koreans or Su Li Young either. Until yesterday he'd never even done anything that wasn't somehow calculated to his own survival or advancement. He'd known plenty of beautiful women in his life, but not like that, not like her. Her beauty was penetrating and eternal. It would only grow brighter and more magnificent with age, making each wrinkle, each gray hair a monument to the possibility of the human spirit.

He hadn't heard her approach. Her voice was tranquil. "Good morning," she said and sat down beside him on a flat rock.

"It's beautiful out here," he said, still staring on the horizon, "almost beyond description."

"Yes, but don't be fooled, Dan-san," she cautioned. "Tonight the Soya wind might come to destroy your image. Such beauty is fleeting. With driving snow and bitter wind, your vision may quickly become one of despair."

He turned to face her. "That's a strange thing to say. What does it mean? What does it really mean?"

"I'm afraid, not of the Korean CIA, but of what I'm doing to others. What will become of those two hundred souls? And what of poor Ishikawa Yoshihiro? Who else will my actions harm?"

He put his arm around her and the words came easily this time. "Nobody knows what tomorrow will bring, but I believe in what you're doing. There's no other way to say it. You, me, Reggie, and your Russian captain, we'll get it done somehow. I promise you. In my whole life I've never been a part of anything this important."

"But Reggie is about to be arrested for murder."

For just a second he thought he'd misunderstood. "No, he's not." But there would be time for explanations later. "We need to decide what happens next."

"We'll go to Wakkanai tomorrow and wait for the captain. I'm the only one who knows he's going to make land at Abashiri. He'll be safe enough."

Like a racehorse blind to all but the finish line, she just wasn't seeing the big picture. He rose from the big rock and turned to face her. "I mean what do we do about Inspector Tanaka? I see now he has no intention of arresting Reggie for murder, but I get a sense he's more in the dark than we are."

"How is he in the dark?"

He reached for a bare hand, pulled her up to his side and was suddenly awash in green eyes and the scent of her hair. He wanted to draw closer and find her lips, but the big picture blocked his way. "We don't really know who's pulling the strings. My own government must be involved at some very high level. Somebody is pushing very hard to get rid of Kincaid, and now me. But at least we know the Korean CIA is involved at the operational level. Tanaka doesn't even know that, but he knows Ishikawa was murdered—not by Reggie—and the killers made it look like suicide. I think he suspects a link between Reggie's stabbing and Ishikawa's murder."

Her focused expression gave no hint of confusion or frustration. She said, "It seems to me we're better off with Inspector Tanaka 'in the dark,' as you put it."

It might have been their first serious difference of opinion. "Maybe not. I think we should tell him what we know about the Koreans. Exposing them just might neutralize the threat. I think he's on the level. Even if he doesn't catch them, they'd fade away quietly rather than risk getting caught on a covert mission in Japan. You'd be safe."

"But that would also expose our plan for the Sakhalin Koreans. The Japanese would never allow it. This we cannot do, Dan-san."

Su Li Young was a tough sell; but no surprise there. "All right. I understand, but Tanaka has all the resources we need. Let's see if we can get him to help. Is there a telephone in the house?"

"There will be a box in the village, up the road," she replied. "It's better."

"Inspector Tanaka? This is Sergeant Matthews."

"Ah, Sergeant Matthews," he answered politely, "where are you calling from?"

It didn't take long for the Air Force to get the word out. Dan wasn't even tempted to answer. "Why? Have you been out looking for me?"

"No, but I have called the base. Your superiors would like very much to locate you."

Dan's superiors had no doubt been arming Tanaka with all kinds of useful information, like they were looking to put him behind bars. "Yes, I'm sure they would, Inspector. This will be a short phone call. Look, I'm hoping you can tell me something more about the scientific results in this case."

The silence was not promising. "Perhaps it is I who should ask the questions, Sergeant Matthews."

Dan looked over at Su Li and shrugged. There was no telling what would come next. "Let me recount some facts first," Tanaka said. "A young American man is stabbed by two Asians. A woman is involved. A Japanese boy goes missing and is found murdered in a hotel. The murderer would have us believe he died at his own hand over the loss of his homosexual lover. The lover happens also to be the stabbed American. Do you see a circle forming, Sergeant Matthews?"

More like a noose, Dan thought. "Go on, Inspector."

"A few night ago there is a brawl in a very disreputable bar near the port district. Russians are involved. And who do you think is seen in this bar in the company of an attractive young woman?"

Tanaka had resources, all right, and was using them up at breakneck speed. Dan said, "My guess would be Ishikawa."

"Yes, you are quite correct. Now all of this might still be coincidence, I believed, until this afternoon when I learn a large number of foreign nationals, all old people, were apprehended in Asahikawa. This also is a very unusual occurrence."

Tanaka had been doing his homework, but he still didn't have a link. "So what do you make of all that? What do you think is the connection?"

"Please, I am not finished. Today, just now in fact, I have received the autopsy results, including toxicology screen. A microscopic puncture wound was found on this body in a very unusual place, between toes exactly. Accordingly, a comprehensive toxicology screen was ordered."

"Can you tell me what the results showed?" He already had a pretty good idea.

"This Ishikawa was injected with Sodium Pentothal before his death."

Only a different answer would have surprised Dan. "Truth serum, eh? Then what's your take on who killed him?"

"I would like to ask you this question," Tanaka said, "as you have more experience in matters of espionage and the secret services."

It sounded patronizing, but part of him wanted to come clean. Tanaka seemed tenacious enough to give the Koreans a really bad time, and yet… Dan held his left hand firmly over the mouthpiece and whispered to Su Li, "He wants to know who killed Ishikawa."

She shook her head firmly in a resounding no. It was her show. "Honestly, Inspector, I have no idea."

Tanaka was not amused. "I see; then perhaps you might tell me the name of this woman who keeps turning up in these most unpleasant situations."

Dan felt he was on safe ground here. "I can't help you there either. Sorry."

"I have studied English carefully, Sergeant Matthews," he said. "I know very well the difference between can't and won't. Let me assist you. I met a very attractive woman several nights ago at the home of the unfortunate Ishikawa family. This was a Korean woman, the name being Su Li Young. Are you not interested?"

He turned again to Su Li. She was huddled around him in the cramped phone box, no doubt thinking only of others, intentionally oblivious to her own fate. Dan was not, but he figured it was Tanaka's turn to gloat. The Koreans knew who she was, so there probably wasn't much harm in Tanaka knowing as well, except that it put him that much closer to uncovering her little plan. "You've got my attention, Inspector."

"I think this all has something to do with Koreans on Sakhalin Island," he said, "but none of this tells me who killed Ishikawa or what is the nature of this conspiracy."

Well, Dan thought, Tanaka was pretty much up to speed, and he'd gotten there all by himself. "So what happens now, Inspector?"

"Now I want the girl."

9:15 a.m.
Wakkanai

Chung pulled up fifteen minutes late, as planned, and found Foster shivering, but still standing, beneath the Soya monument. He didn't see another soul on the point. The wind was particularly ferocious as he closed to within shouting distance. After his recent experience at the hands of the other American, heaping some abuse on this one might bring some satisfaction.

He had specifically requested the meeting out at Cape Soya Point just to aggravate the fat NSA agent. The food, the weather, the car, it didn't matter to Foster. Everything was better in America. Chung would enjoy standing him up in the wind for a while, watching the expensive dental work chatter.

"Mr. Foster, you look cold," he said. Teasing was something Chung had almost never engaged in. He'd picked it up from these Americans, a bad habit of which he would rid himself soon.

Foster dispensed with the greeting. "Well," he said, "how did it go in Asahikawa?"

"The entire pack of old vermin has been scooped up," Chung replied. "There isn't much left of their plan. It's more or less a matter of mopping them up now."

"It isn't over until you have Subarov and the girl," Foster reminded him.

"I'm aware of that. I would have the girl standing next to me now, if not for your meddling OSI agent."

Foster bristled. "I've been standing out here forever. The fucking taxi driver wouldn't wait. If you don't mind, I'd prefer we talk in your car."

"Of course," Chung said amiably, hardly able to conceal his amusement. Foster had already covered half the distance.

Inside the car, Foster asked, "Do you mean to tell me he's with the girl in Asahikawa?"

"I'm not sure where they are now, but they're together; I can tell you that."

"Then what happened? How did they get away?"

The American was becoming more obnoxious by the moment. "Your man is working for them now. He was very fortunate and managed to get away from us, but not until after we had seen to the old ones."

"I know all about it," Foster declared. "He's AWOL."

Having just been played for a fool by the wily American agent, Chung was in no mood to be trifled with by the simple-minded one. He figured it was high time to lay down the law. "Look, Mr. Foster," he said. "We used an entire roll of film and a zoom lens taking his picture with Su Li Young. My man and I sat in a freezing truck for most of the day, until he left with the girl. Would you like us to send the film for development or will you accept that I am capable of identifying a blue-eyed giant in the land of brown-eyed Munchkins?"

"Your command of American colloquialisms is quite impressive, Chung," Foster quipped. "I believe it was Matthews, but why didn't you just follow him?"

The question was almost more than Chung could tolerate. He grimaced silently, but managed to hold his temper once again. He would need the NSA assets now more than ever and forced a muted response. "Things don't always go according to plan in the field."

"Your point is well taken," Foster conceded.

Chung started the engine and began a U-turn. "I'll drop you near your hotel," he said, "although it's not good for us to be seen together."

Foster huffed. "Did you expect me to walk back? I can tell you we tend to put a bit more planning into our clandestine meetings."

Chung could resist no longer. "Somehow our agency has managed to survive and prosper without Americans at the helm, Mr. Foster."

"I really don't think you have much use for Americans," Foster said, "but that doesn't alter my directive. This Matthews is a rogue and he's crossed over the line. I'll see that he's arrested and charged."

"I doubt you'll be able to find him until this business is completed," Chung countered. "I don't think he's going back to Wakkanai just yet."

"We're one step ahead of you, Chung. Every American and Japanese policeman from here to Tokyo is looking for him. He may even face a treason charge."

"Wonderful," Chung said, "but what can you do to get rid of him now?"

"We don't have people in Asahikawa," Foster said. "You know that. Even if we did, they couldn't be involved."

"My point, exactly. There's nothing you can do about him now anyway, not without exposing our operation. This Matthews is my problem for the moment, and you need to understand what might happen if he continues to aid these Soviet agents." A long silence ensued. "Do we understand each other, Mr. Foster?"

"You need to understand something," Foster said. It was the first time Chung had heard him speak with a sense of authority. "Whatever happens, you did not just ask for authority to kill an American military man, and I did not give it to you. Are we clear on that?"

Of one thing Chung was very clear: This mission would not be complete until he had personally dispatched Agent Matthews to hell. "Very clear. You and I shall never discuss the subject again."

"Any idea on your end where Subarov's cargo will come ashore?"

"Not yet, but soon I believe. Have your ships reported contact with his vessel?"

"Not a sign of him," Foster replied. "We're monitoring everything in the Soya Strait and right around the western coastline. At the moment there's nothing on the water that isn't supposed to be there. I'm getting regular activity reports."

Chung only wanted Foster to find the damn Russian and stay the fuck out of his way. "I believe something will happen within twenty-four hours. I will continue to check in with you periodically."

"Fine," Foster replied, "you've pretty much taken the wind out of their sails by grabbing up the Sakhalin Koreans. But that bitch will never quit, and Matthews has crossed the line."

Chung pulled to the side of the road, a bit farther from the hotel than Foster would have liked. "Subarov will not stop either," he cautioned, "but we'll have them soon."

"All right," said Foster, battening down his parka, "it's time to stop fucking around. This Airman Kincaid knows everything those people are up to. It's time I went over there to the base myself and had a talk with him. Whatever he knows, he'll tell me. I guarantee you that."

"Good. You know how to reach me." As the American stepped from the car, Chung grabbed his arm. "One more thing. Will you find out if Matthews is carrying a pistol?"

Foster brushed the hand from his forearm and smiled. "That I'll let you find out for yourself."

TWENTY-THREE

**Sticks and stones can break my bones,
but you had to fuck with my head.**

Saturday, 9:30 a.m.
Wakkanai Air Station

"Kincaid, wake up, for Christ's sake," came the cruel voice from down the hall. "You have a phone call. Sounds official, like a court-martial, brewing." He was very much awake, but just hadn't felt like getting out of bed.

Reggie had always been good at avoiding guys like Rob Norton. The trick was not to give them any ammunition, but it was all just useless theory now. Reginald Kincaid was the laughing stock of the base. He hardly ever left his room any more except for the allotted two hours of sanctuary in the library. The walls were beginning to close in. He found no relief in the chow hall either. The snickers and giggles were far worse than Rob Norton's compulsive hatred. A part of him wished Inspector Tanaka had just arrested him and carted his ass off to jail.

Doherty had been kind enough to bring him a six-pack once in a while, but it didn't bring relief. Strange, he thought, but his own dire situation was easier to accept than the anxiety he felt over the fate of Su Li and her mission. His entire life was a hopeless tangle of failure and heartbreak, with the exception of his small role in Su Li Young's mission to help the Sakhalin Koreans. Now house arrest had knocked him completely out of the game and he might never know her fate.

The questions tormented him. Was she able to get his information to her captain? Did Reggie do the right thing by confiding in Sergeant Matthews? It was all beyond his control now. He'd been rendered a helpless observer, and a blind one at that.

Reggie pulled on a pair of fatigue pants and made his way down the hallway to the only barracks phone. He picked up the receiver lying next to the phone on the small stand. "Kincaid here." He decided to ignore the smug figure of Norton, arms folded, resting against the wall not three feet from the phone.

"Kincaid," came the authoritative voice of an officer, "this is Major Hickam from the OSI. Get into uniform and report to the Security Police HQ in fifteen minutes."

Reggie had been expecting this call, in one form or another. Now he might never again see the woman who had given his life meaning and a short reprieve after so many long years of emptiness. One way or another, it was all coming to an end for Reggie Kincaid, he thought. Oddly, he didn't much care what form of rebuke the military might visit upon him. He would gladly have settled for a little inner peace.

Reggie had no second thoughts. He was proud of what little he'd done to aid Su Li and her cause, but had come to believe nothing could change the past. There's no such thing as redemption. He tried, but couldn't remember how he'd even gotten hold of the ridiculous notion that shame could be absolved by good deeds.

As a practical matter, he considered at that moment if he preferred a court martial and twenty years hard labor for treason to the humiliation of a General Discharge and separation from service as a homosexual. It was a no-brainer. A discharge would mean going home, or the place he once called home, and that he could never do. He'd find more peace with a private cell and a barred window. "Yes, sir," he replied, and headed back toward the room to finish dressing.

"Hey, Kincaid," came the tiresome voice of ignorance, "make sure you wear the frilly panties." The hateful, little man might just as well have been whispering to the wall.

Reggie found two security policemen with side arms standing guard inside the ancient Quonset hut that housed the lightly staffed 324th Security Police Squadron HQ. He'd been there before. They looked uncomfortable, even nervous, Reggie noted. Obviously they had been left to speculate as to the nature of this highly unusual assignment.

A chiseled, gnarly major in a Class A uniform soon appeared from the opening in the big cubicle. "In here, Kincaid," he said, motioning.

Inside, Reggie found another American, this one a little older and a lot fatter, sporting casual, civilian attire with a sling supporting his left arm. The older one was seated behind the squadron commander's desk. Only a civilian or a higher-ranking officer would be so bold. Reggie figured him for CIA, maybe even NSA. He didn't know whether to snap to attention and couldn't have cared less. Protocol was the last thing on his mind.

The major made the decision moot, pointing to the single metal side chair opposite the desk. "Sit." Reggie sat, knowing full well he would not help himself by talking.

The fat major took a half-sitting position on top of the desk, giving him the high ground for psychological purposes. The civilian only glared silently at Reggie. He figured concealing the man's identity was part of their interrogation technique.

"This conversation is long overdue, Airman Kincaid," the major said. "I'm here to ask you some questions and suggest you answer them honestly. You'll be kept here under house arrest until the Japanese authorities have concluded their investigation. What happens to you then will depend in part on your level of cooperation. Do you understand?"

"Yes, sir." Now he'd find out what they were after.

"Good," said Hickam. "Do you know a woman named Su Li Young?"

They want to ask a few baseline questions to see if you'll cooperate. No harm there. "Yes." Matthews had warned him not to volunteer information to Tanaka and to avoid narrative answers. It seemed like a good time to follow the advice.

"What's your relationship with her?"

Some things they knew for sure. The key here was to keep the mix right. "I fucked her."

Hickam sneered. "How nice for you. What else did you do for her?"

"I don't know what you mean."

"I think you do. Have you ever heard of Operation Red Snapper?"

Hickam had given up no clues as to the fate of Su Li or Matthews and had jumped directly to the heart of the matter. Reggie had to address this dangerous line of questioning without a hint of what this major knew. It would be beyond credibility to deny knowledge of the operation to track Subarov's boat in the Soya Strait. He said, "I've seen the operation plotted on the board in the Op Center and they set up a temporary analysis center with that name on it, but I don't know anything about the specifics."

"When is the last time you saw Su Li Young?" Hickam asked.

Off the hook already? He's not much of an interrogator. Reggie thought he could do better from watching TV. Still, he had no clue how much they knew. "I can't remember exactly." He did remember Dan telling him to plead memory loss if Tanaka had him trapped.

"Do you know where she hangs out? You know, friends, bars, relatives. That kind of thing."

Su Li had given them the slip. He wanted to jump up and clap in their faces. She was on the loose and Reggie was supposed to help find her. Fat fucking chance. "Major, I had sex with her once. Even that was only because she was too drunk to think about it."

The civilian was doing his best to look menacing. He rose slowly from the chair and began to flank Reggie on the right, coming to rest somewhere behind his peripheral vision.

"Well," said Hickam, "that's interesting. Then you fuck girls and boys? Tell me, when you fuck boys, are you on the top or the bottom?"

Reggie didn't reply. The question didn't call for one.

"When is the last time you talked to Matthews, you cocksucker?" came the angry voice from behind his back.

It was the question Reggie had been hoping to hear. It meant Matthews had joined up to help Su Li. The knowledge that Su Li and Matthews were together and still free strengthened and emboldened him. In that instant it all came together for Reggie.

Ironic that Rob Norton would be the one to unlock the door. Rob had been shooting his mouth off around the barracks about his temporary, top-secret assignment. He'd been taken off his regular supply truck and assigned to drive some high-ranking civilian around town and back and forth between his hotel and the base. But what was the name of the hotel?

The man appeared from his left side, so close to his face that

Reggie could feel the warm spray as he spoke. "Are you even listening, Kincaid? We have reason to believe you committed an act of treason in connection with this affair. Do you know what that means? Take a minute to think about it before you answer."

He knew more than they imagined. The question meant Captain Subarov was still at sea, somewhere beyond the reach of the NSA. He had successfully evaded detection in Red Snapper and they wanted to know why and how. At the moment their accusation was an educated guess, but once they began the process of examining his work schedule and determining his proximity to the classified data, they wouldn't quit until they nailed him to the cross.

Reggie was beyond intimidation, beyond the power of threats and retaliation. It really didn't matter if this character was guessing or getting ready to close the book because Reggie no longer cared what lay in store for him. He had to remember the name of the hotel. Agent Matthews was out there somewhere with Su Li, being hunted by his own government based on some blasphemous interpretation of national security.

He was right about Matthews all along. He was a decent guy and there could be no turning back. He and Su Li were committed now and would either succeed or be destroyed and swallowed up in anonymity.

Then it came to him, not the name of the hotel, but something just as good. Tony Capello's *josan* had a small apartment near the hotel. Norton had given Tony a ride back to the base several times late at night after dropping this guy at the hotel. Tony would know the hotel.

This civilian, if he was a civilian, was the key to Su Li's success, and maybe to her very survival. Agent Matthews would need a way to find him. "Go fuck yourself, sir," he said to Hickam, "and I'd rather not answer any more questions until I get a lawyer."

10:45 a.m.
Near the mess hall, Reggie saw a small group of enlisted types heading for the main gate and filed in quietly at the rear. He had a clear understanding of how the air base worked. Like every other policy at a remote station well removed from a war zone, confinement to base was enforced by a set of strict guidelines and procedural requirements that almost nobody followed. Wakkanai Air Station, specifically, was

mission driven. So long as the harvest of electronic intelligence remained fruitful and accurate, the brass seemed to tolerate a limited erosion of traditional military discipline. It was one of the reasons Reggie had come to feel so comfortable in this remote corner of the world, despite the obvious limitations imposed by the military structure.

The shit list was a collection of photographs posted on a bulletin board located just inside the door of the main gate security shack. Some of the photos were there as a part of administrative punishment, and others depicted airmen under medical quarantine for various forms of venereal disease. Then there was Reggie. In theory, the security policeman on gate duty was required to check the face of each person leaving the base against the photos on the wall. In practice it almost never happened during the long winter months, not even on a gray, soupy morning such as this.

The simple wave of an outlaw hand over a faceless parka hood was generally sufficient for escape. It was even easier if you blended into a small group of parkas. After all, Reggie thought as he waved to the guard in unison with the small pack of strangers, nobody ever snuck off a military installation to spy or commit sabotage. Getting back onto the base, on the other hand, was a significant challenge that Reggie saw no need to address.

He felt surprisingly calm, all things considered, as he trudged along through the foot or so of freshly fallen snow. He had almost convinced himself to see this place as home, and had even kicked around the idea of coming back here one day, when and if this nightmare finally ended. But a part him had always recognized that view as unrealistic. He tried to picture himself here in ten years or so, just released from Ft. Leavenworth, a civilian and a foreigner to boot looking for work in the most homogeneous society on earth.

No, he thought, Wakkanai had provided him a rock to hide behind when he needed it most. More importantly, it had given him the opportunity to do something good with his life, to make a contribution that might one day ripen into something really significant. He felt happy and proud to have seized that opportunity head on, but Wakkanai would never be home. Reaching his destination, he remembered to bend low under the door frame.

It was unusual to see a Japanese customer in Mama Young's, although Reggie had never been there in the morning before. The one at the bar drinking tea was young and fit, somehow different looking, leading Reggie to conclude he might be Korean. It made perfect sense. Of course, he was one of the Pachinko brothers Su Li had spoken of. With so many people after Su Li, her mother might be in danger and would require protection. He didn't have the heart to tell her it was like pitching a tent in a hurricane.

"Reggie-san," she said, speaking Japanese. "They all told me you were under arrest. What are you doing here?"

"I'm under arrest, Mama, but they don't have a jail on the base. I guess you could say I escaped. They send a guard to check on me every two hours or so, so I don't have long before they know I'm gone. Tell me what's happening with Su Li and Sergeant Matthews."

"I don't know where they are now, but Su Li called last night. The Japanese police arrested all the Sakhalin people hiding around Asahikawa. Su Li believes the Korean CIA is behind the operation. She and Matthews barely escaped from two Korean agents with their lives. They have taken Mei Ling to a safe place and are headed to meet Captain Subarov. I don't know where."

"That means I can't talk to her," he said in English.

"What?"

He switched back to Japanese. "Never mind. Then the Korean CIA murdered Ishikawa?"

"Beyond a doubt," Mama Young confirmed.

"What will they do now? There's no way they can go ahead with their plan now that the people are in custody."

"I don't know the plan now, but they believe there may be hope if they can recover the collection."

Reggie placed his hands on the woman's shoulders for emphasis. "There are things they need to know, Mama. You must tell Agent Matthews. There's a man on the base, an American agent. I don't know his name, but he's staying at the International Hotel in the city. He's involved in this up to his ears. I think he was the third man in the alley and was driving the car for the men who stabbed me. He'll have the answers Agent Matthews needs."

"I'll tell him exactly. But what will you do now?"

It was a larger question than she could imagine. He chose a table this time, in lieu of the same old barstool "I'm going to have a Sapporo, with a glass, please. And I have a taste for *poku-katsu*."

"I think they're right," she said, shaking her head as she reached into the cooler for a cold beer. "You are one crazy GI You never drink beer from a glass."

"There's always a first time, Mama. I guess I just want to get the full taste this time."

Mama Young laughed heartily, covering her mouth, lest he see her teeth. "You've tasted more beer than any human being I know, but you shall have your glass."

His food was ready in no time and she placed the hot plate on the table before him. "You're drinking very slowly, Reggie-san. What's wrong with you?"

It was his turn to laugh. "I told you, Mama. I'm trying to get the full taste. It's funny, but I don't really like the taste that much. Bring me another one though, just to go with this fine meal."

When she brought the beer her mood became serious again. "What will happen to my Su Li?"

If only he could do something to help determine that. He'd done all he could. "I honestly don't know. There's nothing more I can do. I only hope Su Li finds peace and happiness. She is…" No, best to leave it alone, he thought.

Mama Young touched his hand with the gentility of a landing butterfly and the message was not lost on him. "I'm truly sorry, Reggie-san. You are a good boy. I know my daughter cares for you very much, but I believe she was born to serve this cause."

"I know."

"How will you get back onto the base?"

Yesterday he might have considered that a problem, but not today. He laughed again and surprised himself with his upbeat mood. "I'm already under arrest, Mama, so they can't arrest me. Don't worry. I promise it won't be an issue."

"What will they do to you?"

"Nothing they haven't already done," he declared, and he knew they wouldn't. Then Reggie reached into his pocket, retrieved the envelope and handed it to her. "Give this to Su Li when you see her."

"Of course I will. Are you afraid they'll be sending you back to the States soon?"

"Yes, Mama." There was no point in telling her more. "That's it. Say, do you still have that old skiff out back?"

"Sure I do. It's not in bad shape. We keep the canvas cover on all winter unless we take it out to fish on a calm day. Why?"

"Do you mind if I drag it down to the water and go for a spin?"

"You're welcome to it," she replied, "but why do you want to go for a boat ride in winter? I have never known you to fish."

Her statement might have been the final irony in this whole crazy business. I do like to fish, he wanted to say, at least he used to. It was just the water he didn't like. He wanted to tell her how he and his brother would fish whenever they could get someone to drive them. They could fish from morning until dusk without so much as a thought of food. There was just no point. "I don't want to fish. I just don't want to ride into the city on the bus. I have something to take care of."

"Well, there's a can of fuel under the boat. If you can get the outboard motor started, you can take it, but be careful. Stay very close to the shore and keep a sharp lookout for ice. You never know."

Reggie hadn't played with an outboard motor in years, but had no doubt he could get the thing running in short order. "Thanks, Mama. What do I owe you?"

She smiled and made a sweeping motion with her hand. "Go," she said in English, "before Mama kick you in pants."

"Thank you." He reached for his parka.

"Wait a minute," said Mama Young, switching back to Japanese again. "Su Li told me you've been afraid of water since you were very young."

Reggie knew he didn't want to leave it like this. He couldn't. "I was. I really was, but I think I'm over it now." He leaned down and kissed her on the cheek. "I may not see you again, with them sending me back to the States and everything, but I'll never forget you. And I have to tell you something about Su Li."

"Yes, Reggie-san, I'm listening."

"In my entire life I have never known a person as beautiful as your daughter, not by any standard of measurement I can think of."

TWENTY-FOUR

**The Ice Man cometh, so you better lie low.
With luck he'll be a legend soon in Kyongsang-do.**

*Saturday, 3:30 p.m.
Abashiri, Hokkaido, Japan*

Chung felt vindicated as the car neared the coastal city of Abashiri. He could smell the ocean, just beyond the hills, even hear the distant sounds of waves and ice crashing against the rocky cliffs. His patience with the bumbling fat man from NSA had not been in vain. Their technology truly was magnificent, he thought. The American NSA had located Subarov, God only knows how, like a needle in a haystack. Now he was Chung's for the taking and nothing could stop him.

"Have you ever been to this place before?" asked Fu from the driver's seat.

"I was bouncing around places like this when you were still begging chocolate from American soldiers," Chung replied. "Abashiri is a city only in a relative sense. Anywhere else they would call it a coastal fishing village. Were it not for the fish, this place wouldn't exist."

The car came over a hill on the main road into town, giving them a midday, panoramic view of the Sea of Okhotsk below. From their perch on the high ground, the vast expanse of ocean seemed to threaten the small, frozen city like a menacing tidal wave, with gigantic blocks of drifting, white ice clear to the northwest horizon. "Shit," Fu said. "Where did it all come from?"

"It came down from the north through the Sea of Okhotsk," Chung explained. "Abashiri is the world's lowest latitude for drifting ice flows. The funny thing is, most of it is broken up and melted only a few kilometers from here."

"But Wakkanai is only a couple of hours away," Fu said. "There isn't a sign of it there."

Fu was bright, to be sure, but still ignorant in so many ways. "The water there is warmed by the Sea of Japan, but sometimes one of these great blocks of ice will survive to reach Wakkanai and collide with an unsuspecting fishing boat."

As the ice-packed road descended into the city they passed a park on the left. There were huge blocks of ice, well over a dozen in geometrically perfect squares, each resting on a reinforced wooden pallet. "What are those for?" Fu asked.

Chung allowed himself a laugh. "Aside from fish, ice is all they have to sell in this fucking place," he said. "They're preparing for the Drift Ice Festival. I think it begins in a couple of weeks. Each February they carve massive ice sculptures and put them on display with a powerful array of nocturnal lights and fireworks. It seems like a waste of time and effort to me, but I suppose it's better than sitting in your cold house all winter with a bottle of sake and a fat wife."

"How did the Americans find him?" Fu asked, getting back to the subject at hand. "It looks too dangerous for shipping out there."

"The Americans are great technical warriors," Chung explained. "They are attached to their technology and much prefer it to manned combat. They no longer have the stomach to fight real battles, but don't underestimate their technical abilities. That's what my friend, Captain Subarov, did and it will now cost him his life."

"How did he underestimate them?"

Chung never tired of being superior. "Subarov thought he could escape detection by sailing north along the east coast. Small ships rarely brave those waters in the winter months. He was right, of course, but he just didn't appreciate the capability of the electronic intercept station at Wakkanai. They have the ability to simultaneously intercept every radio transmission on this part of the globe in any weather, regardless of the strength of the signal. He used his radio to keep track of the ice. He had to."

"But he couldn't have been foolish enough to identify himself," Fu suggested.

"He didn't have to," Chung countered. "He used a false call sign. The Americans were not fooled. No trawler would be headed on that course for the purpose of fishing."

"But if he makes it he could come ashore anywhere."

Chung seriously considered that his young protégé might already be functioning beyond his level of competence. Experience can be acquired with time and hard work, he thought, but without an analytical mind, no agent could perform efficiently. "Not anywhere," he said. "I told you the ice breaks up not far from here to the south. There's a small peninsula. It's clear and protected on the south end. That's where he'll come ashore and that's where we'll wait. I have his exact position. He's circling just outside the three-mile limit waiting for nightfall. We need to stop and get some cold weather gear and supplies. He might slip in early, and I don't want to take the chance of missing him."

From their position on the low cliff atop the coast road, Chung spotted a tiny natural inlet with a clear channel through the rocks. The place offered some protection from rough seas and easy access to the road. He figured Subarov would surely have ventured close enough to find the place before retreating to the safety of international waters.

Just to the south, above the inlet, Chung could see a high bluff with a commanding view of both the shoreline and the coast road. "There, Fu," he said, pointing. "That bluff is where we'll wait. This road should wind around a bit and take us right there."

"I see it, sir," Fu answered, the car already moving up the road. "It looks like the perfect place. I'd say our longest rifle shot will be one hundred eighty meters or so."

Good. Fu was already thinking about the kill. Chung knew his own skill with the modified M-1 sniper rifle was negligible compared with that of his deadly, sniper-trained, young protégé. Now he needed to establish the ground rules. "Understand one thing," he said. "Subarov is mine. I don't care if the shot is one meter or one centimeter. It will be my bullet that fells the Russian. Are you clear about that?"

"Perfectly, sir."

As the car's engine strained to climb the last incline, Chung himself began to feel the anticipation. This, after all, was the climactic moment of his profession: a snapshot in time when all of the training, tracking, investigating and deception would come to deadly fruition. Chung Hok Kim was much more than an assassin, but was not ashamed to share Fu's reaction; for there was nothing to match the exhilaration of the kill.

"Stop here," Chung said. They appeared to be just below the high cliff that would support their ambush. He checked his watch and saw they had nearly two hours until nightfall. Chung needed time to consider the terrain and choose the most advantageous shooting position.

They left the car out of sight and walked up in the deep snow until reaching the edge of the high bluff. The coastline looked to be a generally inhospitable place for a small launch or dinghy, with jagged rock formations sprouting from the water in all directions. "You were right, sir. This is the perfect place. There's no other place to land from a small boat."

Chung looked down on the rocky inlet and smiled. "Yes, my young friend, I believe the Russian is ours."

"Should we dig in, sir?"

"Yes. Let's get the shovels and equipment. We'll dig a shelter and have something to eat."

Fu was already turning toward the down slope. "I'll bring the rifles as well."

Crouching low in the makeshift shelter under the warm, wool blanket, Chung struggled with his unsettling emotions, as Fu scouted the moonlit horizon with powerful binoculars for signs of their prey. In all his years as an agent, he had never before allowed personal feelings to invade his planning or execution of a mission. It was as if, by his own choosing, the entire legacy of Chung Hok Kim now rested on the outcome of the Nikolai Subarov affair. Chung struggled to understand why Subarov's utter destruction had become a prerequisite to his own survival.

Chung carefully removed his precision weapon, now fully assembled and loaded, from its waterproof case. Methodically, he checked the bolt action and firing mechanism for the umpteenth time. Darkness had settled onto the horizon and the air grew colder by the minute. "Anything yet?" he asked.

"Not a thing, sir."

The disdain he felt for the Russian defied Chung's highly developed professional ability to analyze, evaluate, and draw logical conclusions. To his core, he wanted to kill them all today: Subarov, Su Li Young, and the meddling American investigator. He wanted to erase them from his memory, along with the pathetic old Koreans from Sakhalin. He wanted to return to the mundane, but satisfying work of assassinating double agents and orchestrating high-level defections from North Korea. But, thanks to this dissident Russian and a handful of geriatric, Korean weaklings, Chung might never again view his career or even his life in the same satisfying terms. He hoped Subarov would die slowly.

"Look," Fu said. "He's coming in. I see the boat."

Chung scrambled to his feet and peered over the top of the embankment. He saw two men in the small craft. At three hundred meters he could make out the frame of a bicycle or motorbike of some kind partially hanging off the side. They waited and watched. No words were spoken between Chung and Fu, even as the little boat's hull scraped the rocky shore and the smaller man jumped out, pulling the craft and its contents up onto the smooth, rocky bed. Subarov, wearing a wool stocking cap, stepped onto the shore, then lifted a small, wooden trunk from the boat and carried it safely to higher ground.

The smaller man, probably the ill-tempered Nivkhi who'd split Fu's head with a bottle, followed close behind with a small motor scooter. Chung could feel the dampness in his palms. The two stopped briefly for conversation, then headed up the sloping, snow-covered ground toward the road, the powerful Nivkhi carrying the scooter over his head. Subarov stopped for a breather halfway up the fifty-meter trek.

"Don't shoot until we see what the other one does," Chung whispered. "If he heads back down to the water, let him go."

"Right."

Chung watched as the two men secured the box to the back of the scooter. Subarov swung his leg over the bike and prepared to kick start the motor as the Nivkhi watched. "We'll have to take them both. I'll take Subarov. You take the other one. Line up your shot and fire when

I do. Are we clear?"

"Perfectly," Fu replied. Fu was not one of the brighter young agents in the service, but when the fighting started there was none better. The Nivkhi would never know what hit him.

Chung heard the scooter's anemic, underpowered motor whine to life and steadied his rifle. He would have preferred a full torso shot, especially in the moonlight, but at least it was a stationary target. Then Subarov turned ever so slightly to the right, as he prepared to jump down on the starter pedal, offering up a portion of his chest to the sight scope.

Chung was ready and squeezed gently on the trigger, shattering the stillness of the coastal hills. Fu's shot followed so closely to his own that Chung never heard it. He saw both men drop like stones to the icy road, Subarov still straddling the scooter, but now in a horizontal pose.

Instinctively, Chung began his descent from the hill with his rifle in the ready position. He saw Fu on his left with a precautionary interval in between. This would be the most dangerous time to underestimate Subarov, and Chung remained focused and alert, as though preparing to finish off a wounded bear.

At fifty meters he could see Subarov's right arm moving from under the bike, beside the lifeless corpse of the Nivkhi. Chung stayed low as the hill settled into a flat shoulder beside the road. He circled to move in from Subarov's rear, reducing the chances of a lucky shot from a hidden pistol. The old captain had struggled onto his right elbow and kicked off the bike with his left leg. As his right arm disappeared beneath the coat, Chung lunged forward, smashing the butt of the heavy M-1 squarely into Subarov's chest. The Russian went momentarily limp, his head smashing into the icy road.

Chung reached into his coat and removed the German Luger from the old man's belt, casting it off into the deep snow. Subarov was stirring again. Chung was grateful for the opportunity to make him suffer.

Chung could see the powerful round had torn a gaping hole in Subarov's left shoulder. "Do you want me to finish him off?" came Fu's voice from his left.

"No," Chung said, holding up his palm to emphasize the importance of the command. The man would bleed to death in a matter of minutes, but protocol called for a swift bullet to the head at close range and a prompt departure from the area. Well, fuck protocol this time, he thought. Chung couldn't resist a confrontation. "You never had a chance, Nikolai," he said in Russian.

The Russian smiled. It was a taunting, triumphant smile and Chung found it deeply disturbing. He had a sick feeling in his gut, like when you know you've forgotten something, but just can't put your finger on it. "Song Hee Choi," Subarov said, "my old friend and shipmate. I can't say I'm happy to see you, but I have been expecting it."

"So you figured out I was the one who upended your little scheme?"

"Almost immediately, but, until recently, I couldn't decide exactly which freedom-loving peoples you work for."

It was not the answer Chung had been hoping for. This Russian was a crafty devil. Seized by an overwhelming sense of panic, he turned to the box, still half secured to the back of the bike. "Keep an eye on him, Fu," he instructed, and began to untie the ropes from around the trunk. He dragged the small trunk clear of Subarov, shattered the lock with a single blow from the butt of the M-1, and tore open the top. As he feared, the trunk was empty. "You fucking old shit. You set this whole thing up. You wanted the Americans to find you heading straight into the drifting ice."

The old man strained to force another smile, blood escaping from the corner of his mouth. "Aside from being a treacherous lout, Song, you're a clever fellow and a worthy seaman. You would not have believed anything less dangerous. I needed you to believe it."

Chung was upon him in an instant, driving the old man's head into the packed ice again and again. "You old fuck, where did you hide the contents of the box?"

It looked like Subarov was doing his best to smile again, but all he could manage was a bloody cough. He said, "What will you do if I refuse to talk? Kill me? My greatest satisfaction in this affair is the look in your eyes now that you know your mission has failed. I'm told Park Jung Hee does not suffer fools well."

"I swear to you, Subarov, if you don't tell me where those documents are, I'll torture that girl for a month before I let her die."

"I don't think you will, Song," Subarov managed to whisper, "because she is smarter than you. You are nothing more than a contemptuous bureaucrat. You would ignore the cry of your own innocent countrymen, even murder them without ever asking why. I take great joy in your failure, Song, enough to sustain me on my journey to heaven or hell because I know what it will bring you."

In a state of cold rage, Chung leveled the rifle at the old captain's face and took careful aim. Subarov didn't flinch or even blink. The bullet parted the bridge of his nose cleanly and turned the ice red beneath his head. "I will finish with you in hell one day, old man." He hoped killing the others would bring more satisfaction.

TWENTY-FIVE

**Maybe there are no brave men,
just frightened ones who swallow hard and jump.**

*Sunday, 3:45 p.m.
On the road to Wakkanai*

The day was unusually bright and the fierce Soya wind dormant, as if luring them up the freshly cleared road to Wakkanai. The benign weather had shortened their trip and Su Li's spirits were still buoyed by recent events. She felt almost happy, her head resting on Dan's shoulder, as the tranquil sea to her left sparkled in the falling sun. In those quiet moments, it was as if she and Dan were driving to the relatives for a holiday meal. Dan seemed to sense her contentment and did not shatter the moment with words.

Spending an entire day resting in Rumoi had seemed to restore their energy, if not improve their chances. By tomorrow, the Korean CIA would have no further interest in Mei Ling, and her mother's friend would be safe enough in Rumoi, especially with Yoshima Jiro looking after her. Now she could think only of her mother. With Korean spies on the loose and the American military fully engaged in the hunt, Su Li needed to know Yoon Hae was safe and well.

Dan was right, of course, in suggesting a phone call to Yoon Hae from Rumoi last night might prove a disaster. If the Americans were capable of intercepting foreign language radio communications from great distances, why should they have difficulty listening to a single phone conversation across the road from their Wakkanai base?

She recognized the coastal village of Shosambetsu, roughly halfway between Rumoi and Wakkanai City. Dan pulled up near a phone booth in the village proper. "I think it's all right to call your mother from here," he said. "Just be careful what you say."

Yoon Hae answered on the second ring. "Mother, are you all right?"

"I'm fine, Su Li," her mother said. "Taro is still with me and there has been no trouble, but Reggie was in here earlier. He gave me very important information for Matthews."

The news surprised Su Li. "Reggie is under arrest at the base, so how did he get to the restaurant?"

"I believe he escaped, for a while at least. I think the Air Force will send him back to the States very soon. He gave me a letter for you."

Su Li didn't like the sound of it, but thought it best not to continue the conversation. "Mother, listen carefully. I'll give you the number to this phone box. Go to a public phone and call me back: two-six-four-five-two-two. Don't say anything else. Do you understand?"

"Perfectly," Yoon Hae said just before the line went dead.

The brief conversation with her mother troubled Su Li. Why would Reggie need to give her mother a letter, unless he didn't expect to talk to her again? Surely he knew Su Li would be returning to Wakkanai shortly. If it were true, and they were sending him back to the States, they could find a way to see each other, or at least talk on the phone. She thought it best to keep focused on the mission. "My mother will call back in a minute," she said to Dan, slipping back into the passenger seat. "I think you should talk to her. Reggie came to see her and gave her a message for you. He believes it is very important." She saw no need to mention the letter.

Su Li heard the phone ring and turned to Dan. He was already out of the car and nearing the phone booth. She waited anxiously for what seemed like an eternity as Dan and her mother spoke. He was barely into the car again when Su Li pounced on him. "Well, what was it?"

"It seems Reggie escaped house arrest to give her this information. I think it's lucky for us he did. He told me where to find the American who's running the NSA operation against us. He's working hand in hand with the Korean CIA. I think I'm going to pay him a visit when we get back to Wakkanai. I'll have to be very careful and keep a low profile because I'm a wanted man. For sure they've listed me as AWOL."

"What's that?"

"Absent Without Official Leave. It's kind of the first step toward desertion."

She had a good idea what kind of trouble she had dumped on Dan Matthews, but this wasn't the time or place to talk about it. She figured he could take care of himself. Reggie, on the other hand, was another story. "What did she say about Reggie?"

"Well, she said something strange. I'm not sure what to make of it."

"What?"

"He borrowed the little boat she keeps out back. He said he had something to take care of and he didn't want to ride the bus into the city. He took her boat. That seems odd, doesn't it?"

That was it. Her worst fears were confirmed. She sighed deeply as the last reserve of hope rushed from her soul and puddled onto the floor beneath her feet. She wanted to tell Dan Matthews everything she knew about Reggie, but couldn't bear to violate Reggie's trust. In time she would confide in Dan, but not now.

Su Li rolled down the window to feel the cold breeze on her face. The branches swayed and the snow swirled as the wind once again gathered strength, but she could no longer feel. She said his name, "Reggie," for the last time, and watched the word float slowly from her lips into the cold and flutter off to another place on the bitter Cape Soya wind.

"What's wrong?" he asked. She did not answer and he did not press. Dan Matthews seemed to have a sense for such things.

She wrapped her hands firmly around his arm and cradled it with her head as the car resumed its journey up the coast road. The arm was lean and strong. She could feel it, even beneath the parka, but it was only flesh and blood, like every other arm. It could not reshape her past or mold her future; yet, she drew comfort and strength from the contact and wanted never to let go.

Dan broke the silence. "I'll drop you at the pachinko parlor when we get to Wakkanai. There's some business I need to take care of."

* * *

Sunday, 8:20 p.m.
Wakkanai

Perched on a small chair behind the door of the tiny, darkened hotel room, Dan tried to will the Arctic chill from his bones. Turning on the electric space heater was not an option. It might be enough to sound the alarm for this character, whatever his name and agency. He knew they all carry guns, with exception of the OSI, of course.

It didn't help to think about Hawaii either. In fact, he labored to drive the images of coconut trees and warm, blue water from his mind. Dan figured he should have been out buying tropical, civilian clothes. But the thoughts were only torment now, snapshots of what could never be, and no good would come from them. Still, he couldn't block the picture of himself in a bathing suit on the deck of a boat, sucking on a big Mai Tai. Instead, he was marching headlong, of his own free will, to a kind of very personal Waterloo.

In another week, his friend Grant in Hawaii would wonder why he hadn't shown up or called. A simple phone call to Tachikawa Air Base would close the door forever. But you make your own bed and then you sleep in it. He'd make the same choices again for the same reasons and wasn't about to throw in the towel, not just yet.

He was half dozing, but his mind sprang to full alert as he heard the sound of key in lock. Dan seriously wondered if the cold had rendered his muscles stiff and temporarily useless. He had no idea of the man's size or proficiency in hand-to-hand combat. Dan had two weapons: the element of surprise and a longneck blackjack he'd picked up at an open market in Bangkok. He intended to use both to his best advantage.

The door opened. Dan could see the man's shadow dissect the narrow room as he crossed the threshold from the lighted hallway. What if he wasn't alone? It was too late to worry about that now. Dan's right arm whirled from the shoulder and the lead-packed tip of the leather blackjack whipped with spring-loaded ferocity and hammered into the back of the stranger's head. The man's knees buckled, dropping him to the floor in a helpless daze.

Dan was on him, nearly in rhythm with the fall, patting him down with the skill of a street thug. The automatic weapon protruding from under the man's arm in a shoulder holster was an obvious starting pointing. Dan tucked the powerful weapon into his own belt and completed the operation in silence, finding only a wad of cash and a thick wallet in the agent's trousers.

With his target subdued and grimacing from the pain in his head, Dan turned his attention to the space heater and switched the starter knob to high. He grabbed one of the armless, wooden chairs from the small table and placed it near the heater, across from the shell-shocked American agent. Dan straddled the chair and breathed deeply. "All right," he said, opening the wallet, "let's see who we have here."

"You've really crossed the line this time, Matthews," the man said. "You must have a fucking death wish or something."

Dan ignored the remark and removed the identification card from inside the wallet. "Lance Foster of the National Security Agency." Stevie Wonder could see the I.D. was for real, so Dan was most likely dealing with a liaison officer of some kind, definitely not a secret agent. "We nearly met once before, in Major Coughlin's office I believe."

Foster was in obvious pain from the growing lump on the back of his head, but tried to take command of the situation. "I don't think you know just how serious your situation is, Matthews. You've just added another ten years onto what your already facing, but I'm willing to give you the benefit of the doubt and help you out of this situation."

It wouldn't hurt to listen. Dan had all night. "Go ahead."

"I think you've been duped. I think the girl has sold you a bill of goods and you felt sorry for Kincaid. You started to work this case in good faith and the facts led you to some disturbing conclusions. Am I right so far?"

It was far too late in the game to start second-guessing hard won conclusions. "Keep talking."

Foster grimaced, rising partially from the floor to rest his back against the bed. "The problem is you didn't have all the facts, but that wasn't your fault. You couldn't have known everything because even that idiot Coughlin didn't know everything."

"Just how much did he know. I'm curious."

"He thought this whole thing was about stopping the infiltration of spies and saboteurs from North Korea. So everything you've done up to now can be explained. That makes sense to you. Doesn't it?"

"Then Coughlin knew all along Kincaid was innocent."

"Can I get up?"

"Just answer my fucking question."

"Yeah, he knew all right. I told him this was a counterespionage operation with high-level National Security concerns."

Dan shook his head. "And that was enough for Coughlin to serve up a perfectly innocent airman."

Foster shifted on the floor, grimacing in pain. "Come on, Matthews. Do you think we're playing Boys Scouts here? Coughlin was more than willing to serve you up too, the minute you started deviating from the program. Anything to save his own ass."

"What happened to him?"

"He's finished; already put in his retirement papers. Coughlin's a fool. All he had to do was come down here and handle this himself. He misjudged you, Matthews. You have character. That's what did him in, and it's ironic."

"Why so ironic?"

The NSA man forced a smile right through his pain. "Because now it's going to do you in."

Dan waved the pistol in a vertical motion. "Get on the bed."

Dizziness apparently cut the man's effort short. "You got me good."

If he was looking for sympathy, it was in the wrong place. "What about Ishikawa Yoshihiro?"

"What's that?"

Foster's prior answers had provoked only disgust, this one rage. Dan snarled. "Not what," he said, "who. He was the young Japanese man they murdered—you murdered. What are the facts that justify that?"

Foster sighed, lifting himself successfully toward the mattress on wobbly legs. "Let's be clear about this. We didn't kill anyone. The Koreans did that, and they would have killed you too if I hadn't stopped them."

Dan needed to know the exact nature of his country's involvement. He wanted to hear that South Korea had misled the United States into aiding this operation, just like Coughlin had misled Dan. "Does our government know that Su Li Young and Subarov are trying to help innocent Koreans held on Sakhalin Island?"

Using his hand, Foster checked for blood beneath the lump. "You can't possibly know they're innocent."

The canned, emotionless response told Dan he was on the right track and stoked the flame of his anger. "Don't give me that bullshit, Foster. I've seen those people with my own eyes. I know Su Li Young and I know Kincaid. More importantly, I know the truth. The question is whether you know it too."

Gingerly, the NSA man leaned back against the headboard. "You only know the truth from their perspective," he reasoned. It was an admission, but Dan could almost predict the rest of it. "You're not in a position to know the whole picture. You're a goddamn staff sergeant. There are serious issues of national security at stake here."

Dan laughed. He had his answer, and now he wanted more. "You're beat to shit and facing the business end of a forty-five. Are you going to tell me my security clearance isn't high enough to hear the truth? The truth is the only thing that will get you out of this room alive, Foster. After all, what more do I have to lose? And don't tell me some bullshit about not wanting to embarrass the Soviet Union."

"All right, I'll tell you the truth. It won't matter because you'll be in prison in a few days, or dead. The truth is this entire Security Service installation at Wakkanai is a joke. It's a ruse, designed to distract the Soviets' attention from the real intelligence gathering. Oh, it was useful once, but that was a long time ago."

"What the hell does that mean?"

"It means the tens of millions our government spends on this base every year is just an investment to protect the real source of intelligence."

A bulb flashed in Dan's head. "Of course. The Korean CIA."

"They have Sakhalin and the entire Soviet Far East covered tighter than a blanket with agents—real agents—the kind that take pictures and tap phone lines and turn Soviets against their own. It's something we can't do, and everything they get comes to us."

"So you really don't care why the Koreans are doing this to their own people," Dan suggested. "The question doesn't interest you. You're only purpose here is to protect your source of intelligence."

"I know it sounds cold, but that's exactly right, and it's our source of intelligence."

It was all more than Dan could digest in one swallow. "But why are the Koreans doing this? And don't give me some crap about not wanting to repatriate Soviet agents. That's hogwash."

"The truth is I don't know why they're doing it, but I confess I've thought about it. I honestly believe our government doesn't know either."

Dan had to fight the overwhelming urge to pummel this man into a bleeding corpse. "And that's it? You just write off the deaths of innocent people and thousands of shattered lives as the cost of intelligence?"

Foster flashed a kind of gotcha smile. "What was the Hiroshima bomb, Matthews? How many innocent people died in that? Have you ever complained about it? Does it keep you up nights? Somehow, I doubt it. Did your father fight in the war? It might have saved his life." This time Foster laughed openly. "Are you starting to see what you've done? What you're about to do?"

He was. He did, and Foster might be right. His logic was impeccable, but the man's little patriotic speech just didn't carry the weight it once might have. Foster probably saw him as a weak-kneed, spineless traitor under the spell of a beautiful woman. But Foster couldn't see with Dan's new eyes. It really wasn't about Su Li at all, any more than it was about the innocents of Hiroshima and Nagasaki. It was about who you are, what you are, and what's really important.

"There's still time to make this right," Foster reasoned. "You could get your discharge and put this all behind you. Don't betray your country like Kincaid did. They'll lock you up for twenty years without anyone ever knowing what happened here. When you get out, you'll end up a lonely suicide victim like Kincaid."

"What did you say?"

"I thought you knew. They found his body floating near the port this morning. It was half eaten by fish. It looks like he took a small boat out into the strait and went for a cold swim. He was still wearing his parka."

Poor Reggie, Dan thought. It was headed in that direction all along. How could he not have seen it? The Koreans would have murdered Reggie, given a chance, but it hadn't been necessary. Su Li had known from the moment he told her about Reggie borrowing Yoon Hae's boat. But how did she know? "How did he betray his country? Tell me."

"Before he lost his access to classified material, he was privy to details of an operation to track Captain Subarov's vessel to the coast of Hokkaido. We believe he gave the details of that operation to Subarov, but you probably know all about that now."

If Reggie had done that, he hadn't told Dan. Why would he? He thought he was protecting Dan by keeping it quiet, giving him deniability. "I don't doubt Reggie Kincaid killed himself, but his blood is on your hands, Foster, you and every stinking bureaucrat and government official you work for."

"And just how do you figure that?"

Foster truly had no clue, the quintessential government man. "You made him out a liar when you knew he was telling the truth. You tormented him with allegations of homosexuality. Finally, you called him a traitor for following his conscience. Let me explain something. I don't know exactly how I feel about Hiroshima, but at least we didn't knowingly drop the bomb on Americans."

Foster's expression turned stone cold. "You'll rot in hell, Matthews. It's almost over for you anyway. The police have your Sakhalin Koreans and Subarov is fish food somewhere on the Sea of Okhotsk."

Then why was Foster in such a panic for him to back off? If they had Subarov and the collection, Su Li was beaten, unless… "Thanks for the information. I'll call the hotel in an hour and have them come up and untie you. Now turn over on your stomach and grab your ass."

TWENTY-SIX

**There are wounds not even a doctor can mend.
They don't show; they don't bleed, but they're worse in the end.**

Sunday, 9:15 p.m.

Dan arrived at the pachinko parlor to collect Su Li, and Taro greeted him before he even reached the door. He looked excited, even upset. He was yapping something in Korean, but it may as well have been sign language. Dan caught the name, "…Yoon Hae," in the animated monologue and understood immediately.

"Did she go to Mama Young's?"

A vertical nod told him Su Li had once again ignored his warning and placed herself in grave danger. Somebody, anybody, might be watching for her to return there. He was out the door in a flash.

He rapped softly on the back door and Su Li answered. "Dan-san, I'm sorry. I had to talk to my mother, but I was very careful. There are no spies and nobody seems to be watching the place."

It was hard to stay angry with her. Spies? "You might have made a living at this in another life, but a very short one. Now please, get away from the window and let me inside."

"My mother is in the restaurant," she explained. "I haven't shown my face in there."

He didn't bother removing his parka. They wouldn't be staying long. "You already knew about Reggie. Didn't you?"

"Yes," Su Li replied, glancing over at the small kitchen table. "I knew he was gone."

Dan spotted a white envelope lying almost ceremoniously in the center of the table, alone, apart and unwanted, like a wartime telegram from The Defense Department. "Are you going to open it?"

"Yes. I think we can open it together."

Dan shed his boots as Su Li went to a small drawer beside the sink, returning with an intricately engraved letter opener. It looked like sterling silver. "We don't have much use for this. Mother brought it from Korea. It belonged to my grandmother and was a treasure easily concealed in her clothing. It's the only thing she has from Korea. Mother and I have never gotten mail of any importance, until now."

They sat opposite each other as Su Li carefully unsealed the flap and removed the contents. She lay the twenty-five, crisp, one-thousand yen notes on the table, unfolded the letter and read aloud:

"My dear Su Li,

I am very sorry about Yoon Hae's boat. I know the fish you catch with it are important to your livelihood. I believe this money will be enough to replace both the boat and motor. If the boat gets back to shore intact, please use the money to help in your cause. It's not much, but I think the Sakhalin Koreans are no longer only your cause. You have made them mine as well and the endeavor has sustained me. I leave you with the hope that my effort has aided in our just cause and that you will prevail. Circumstances do not permit me to stay longer. I do not regret my actions, any of them, but rather believe I have been a part of something good and noble, now leaving on a high note. I choose not to live with the obstacles in my path, and I am very tired. I would like to see my brother again.

Su Li, please do not be sad. Whatever joy and satisfaction I have known in my life have come from you. Trust Agent Matthews. He is a good man and will help you finish what we have started. I will never forget you.

Love, Reggie"

Dan removed his wet parka and let it rest over the chair back. A long silence ensued. Curiously, Su Li did not cry. As the hot tea cooled, she continued to stare at the letter, as if she were seeing the words for the first time. Dan finally broke the silence. "His brother's name was Chuckie, wasn't it?"

"Yes," she replied, her eyes still locked on the letter. "Reggie was fifteen years old, younger by two years. The two were fishing together on a small lake, a family holiday. The boat capsized and the brothers couldn't swim. Reggie held tightly to the boat and tried to reach his brother as the older boy struggled on the surface."

"I think I understand," Dan said. "He watched his brother go under and couldn't bring himself to let go of the boat. He's been living with that memory all these years."

She turned her eyes away from the letter. "This time he let go of the boat," she said. "I think he needed to know he could. It was something that was going to happen one day anyway. Better to happen like this. He was a brave man. In a strange way, I think he came to understand that. It just wasn't enough to save him."

There was no time to grieve—for either of them. "The NSA agent told me Reggie used his access to classified material and gave Subarov a way around the island. You knew about it, didn't you?"

"Yes. I knew. I would have told you, Dan-san—later."

"It's all right. I understand. You did tell me, in a way, when you talked about treason."

"Yes."

Dan reached across the table, resting his palm on her hand. "Hell, it wasn't treason. Reggie was a decent person who tried to do the right thing. He was afraid his whole life; everybody is. Reggie knew he was walking off a cliff by helping you, but he just swallowed hard and jumped. Maybe that's all bravery is."

At that moment Yoon Hae brushed past the curtain dividing the living quarters from the restaurant, whispering excitedly in Korean. Dan had more bad news to dispense, but it would have to wait.

"Come," said Su Li. "We must go now. Taro spotted three Air Force policemen with sidearms. They just left the base and are headed this way. We must leave now out the back."

"Damn. I guess I didn't tie the rope tight enough. What about your mother?"

"She and Taro will be fine for now. There will be customers here until late tonight. They wouldn't try anything in front of Americans, especially across from the base. She'll go with Taro tonight."

Scurrying up the rocky shoreline left them exposed to the road for long stretches at a time. Even under cover of darkness, two silhouettes against the silvery gray horizon could be easily spotted from a passing vehicle. They stayed low where necessary and took periodic rest behind the hull of the occasional wooden kelp boat. As the lights of Wakkanai city closed in, they stopped briefly to rest inside an abandoned drying shack.

"Where are we going?" Su Li asked. "We can't leave Wakkanai now. The captain will probably arrive tonight."

There was no other choice. It had to be now. "No," Dan whispered, "He won't. That was the rest of the bad news."

"He's dead," she said, as though she had been naive not to expect it. Her eyes were stoic and emotionless. "It is good you told me now, for I'm drained of grief today."

"It appears he is. The NSA guy made reference to it. I think it's true because he knew the captain was to the east, in the Sea of Okhotsk. I don't know any of the details, but I get the impression Subarov had the last laugh."

"What do you mean?"

"I'm fairly certain they don't have the collection."

"What makes you believe that?"

"Think about it. If they had the captain and his collection, this thing would be over. They'd have won. But it's not over by a long shot. They want us more now than ever."

Without warning, a powerful beam of light invaded the darkness thru the empty window frame, rendering them blind. "Halt," came the voice on the dark end of the beam. "Both y'all raise your hands slowly and walk through this doorway. I have orders to shoot both y'all if you resist."

Dan recognized the voice and struggled to put a name to it. "Do as he says," he told Su Li. "They're operating under special orders. He won't hesitate to shoot."

Dan heard the powerful whistle in the man's mouth signal their position to the other Security Police in the area. Bozman…Bozwell… What the hell was this guy's name? Rockwell. That was it. "Airman

Rockwell, you know who I am?"

"I know who I thought you was," the young man replied. "Now they want you for questioning in an espionage investigation."

"You don't believe that shit, do you?" Dan pleaded. "I treated you right, Rockwell. Now, you know as well as I do how the military can fuck somebody over when they have a mind to. That's what they're doing to me right now. For Christ's sake, I need your help."

A long silence. Then Dan heard gathering footsteps of the other policemen fighting their way through the snow down to the rocky shore. "I can't help you, Agent Matthews," Rockwell replied. "There just ain't nothin' I can do. If you run, I'll have to shoot." Then he hesitated. "But, hell, my aim is really bad at night."

He didn't need to spell it out. Dan grabbed Su Li's arm and was away into the darkness in a heartbeat. Three shots followed closely, the bullets no doubt launching harmlessly out over the water. "They're running," Rockwell shouted, "back up the road, over to your left."

As the noise of their pursuers faded, Dan and Su Li stayed low on the slippery rocks between the water and the snow, emerging into the crowded port bar district less than a mile up the road.

With a decent supply of yen and a loaded pistol, Dan figured he needed only a good night's sleep before taking on the world, which was almost precisely his task. "We have to find a place to spend the night while we figure out our next move," he said, "somewhere they won't find us."

Su Li flashed a look that might have passed for a smile on this sad day. "We should go to Kim Tae Woo's house," she said. "It's less than three kilometers from here."

No doubt another player in Su Li's deadly game, Dan thought. "Why there? Who is Kim Tae Woo?"

"He is a friend, a very good friend."

Su Li had never approached Kim's house on foot from the park below. A stranger might easily pass this magnificent park at night, camouflaged in white, and never suspect its presence, but for the illuminated, stone pillars, reaching out for the heavens. She pointed up to the monument from the road below. "This is Wakkanai Park," she said. "Kim's house is on top of the hill."

"Looks like just a bunch of snow to me. I don't see a house on the hill. Is there an elevator or something? I'm dog tired."

Su Li wondered if she would ever understand his sense of humor. "You'll see it soon enough," she said, "and you'll get there on foot. In spring, this park is alive with color. There are perhaps four thousand wild Cherry trees in the park. Kim and his wife are very fortunate to live here. One can see all of this from his small garden. On a clear day, even Sakhalin appears clearly in the distance."

As they began the uphill trek, he said, "When this is all over, I don't ever want to see the coast of Sakhalin again, or Wakkanai either. Hell, if I don't ever see ice or snow again, it will be too soon."

Su Li couldn't be certain of the message, but it wounded her nonetheless. Maybe it was only a harmless expression of frustration. It wasn't like she had any great love for this frozen piece of rock herself. Still, everything Dan wanted so desperately to forget was everything Su Li had ever known. This had been the worst day of her life, and Su Li had never felt more alone. She should never have allowed herself to think of him in that way. They were too different, Dan Matthews and she.

As they plodded up the icy, winding road, their walk became a noticeable climb. "Are you sorry for helping us, Dan-san?" she asked. "No good has come to anyone from this business."

He wrapped his strong arm around her shoulders and they began to walk as one. "I'm not sorry. I'm afraid, afraid because I don't see the way out of this, for either of us. I want to find a way, at least for you. Everything I did I'd do again, and I'm willing to face the consequences. I'm in love with you, Su Li. Don't you know that yet?"

Su Li was ready and willing to face her complicity in the death of a poor, tormented American boy who wanted nothing more from life than a little peace of mind. She still bled for Hiro and had not even begun to grieve for the old Russian whom she would have chosen to be her own father. It wasn't fair for Dan to do this to her now, not now. Real love and the things that go with it were not in her future. She had long ago banished such childish notions from her mind, choosing instead to devote her life to something larger and more important.

"Did you hear me, Su Li?"

"No," she said, unable to meet his gaze. "I didn't hear you. Sometimes the English words just float together and are lost on my ears."

"I see." He loosened his grip around her shoulders and their pace fell out of rhythm. Su Li felt a chill. "Well, we have to decide what to do with the box, in the event we get our hands on it. This thing is a lot more now than the two of us can handle."

"We can proceed with the plan," she said. "Without Hiro it will be more difficult to attract the international press, but we can go to the news bureaus ourselves."

"But the plan just won't have enough teeth to do the job," he countered, "not without the survivors standing right there to testify."

Dan Matthews was right again and she knew it. "What then?" she asked, for she could think of nothing else.

"I don't know. It's clear we still have leverage. They must be very familiar with the contents of that box, because they're still willing and eager to kill us for it. I say we take it to Sapporo. I have a friend there who might be able to help us. This person has more than a passing interest in the Sakhalin Koreans."

They turned again and began the final climb to the hilltop house. Su Li pulled the chime chord at the front door and Kim's wife answered almost immediately. "Ah, Su Li, you are welcome. Come in, come in." The woman spotted Dan in the shadow. "Who is this?"

"It's all right," Su Li said. "He's an American, Dan Matthews. He's been of great help to our cause. We have come to see Kim Tae Woo." Su Li turned to Dan. "Dan-san, this is Son Yee, the wife of Kim Tae Woo."

Son Yee returned Dan's bow. "My husband is at sea, fishing, but he put in yesterday and brought me something to give you."

They stowed boots and parkas in the small outer foyer and Son Yee escorted them to the round table, dominating the main sitting room of the house. A boy of eleven or twelve was lying on his stomach in the middle of the room, focused on the blaring television. The woman quickly chased him away and switched off the TV.

He could be a grandson, Su Li concluded. From the pictures around the house, it was clear they had only daughters, and much older. Kim and his wife must be raising the boy. She wondered if this family had endured other tragedies.

"You must be freezing," the woman said, "and exhausted as well. Rest now and I will make tea and something to eat."

"I'll help," Su Li said, already rising from her knees.

"Nonsense," the woman countered, and Su Li settled back to rest, wishing slumber could rise up and save her from all these burdensome thoughts.

Son Yee returned to them carrying a tray of refreshments. Placing the tray on the table, she removed two keys from beside a cup and handed them to Su Li. One looked like a car key and the other a numbered key for a locker of some kind. She said, "What you came for is in a locker at the train station. My husband said to take his car. Rest here tonight, have a hot bath and leave in the morning. You'll find fresh linens on the shelf."

"We won't put you out of your house," Su Li said.

"Don't worry. My husband instructed me to take the boy and go to my mother's down the road when you showed up. He thinks it will be safer for the boy and me."

Su Li nodded. The boy? "Kim is right. My American friend and I are not popular at the moment."

Son Yee leaned over and touched her shoulder "I must go now. Please be safe, Su Li-san."

10:35 p.m.

Foster answered the hotel door while holding a wet cloth to the back of his head. His gate was unsteady, Chung noted, as the American seated himself on the bed. "Well, he has my gun now. He was at Su Li's restaurant just a little while ago. The SPs almost nabbed him, but he and the bitch got away on foot. They're somewhere in the city as we speak."

Chung honestly wondered how the Americans ever got to the moon. "We can be certain they now have the things Subarov was protecting. A single pistol will hardly deter us from our task."

"They must be headed to Sapporo," Foster reasoned. "We know their plan calls for something dramatic. It has to. Otherwise, why waste all the risk and effort smuggling in two hundred people from Sakhalin? Sapporo is where the major news bureaus are. They're going to stage some kind of big show there."

Foster reached for his coat on the nearby chair, and Chung said, "Please, you stay here and rest for awhile. If anything turns up, I'll know where to find you."

Foster flashed him a suspicious look, but did not reply.

"Don't worry," Chung assured him. "We know they're still in the city tonight. I'll call you the moment we learn something."

Foster seemed relieved. He draped his coat back over the chair. "I suppose I could use the rest. Thanks. But do you agree with me about Sapporo?"

"I agree that was their plan originally, but without the Koreans, the show would not be entertaining or persuasive. I believe they'll take their treasure directly to the international press and seek support there."

Foster nodded. "Yes. I think you're right. After all, the two hundred Sakhalin Koreans haven't quite vanished. The press would follow their trail in custody and have a field day with this. There is no way to cover up the arrest and detention of those people. It could become a huge international human rights story. I can promise you, the Japanese would not be pleased about being drawn into the quagmire. I'm certain they don't ever want to hear the words Sakhalin and Koreans in the same sentence."

Chung had tried to drive the notion from his consciousness, but he knew Foster was right. Getting the Japanese police involved, even unknowingly, had been a major gamble, and possibly a big mistake. Chung's orders were specific. *Your mission shall be conducted and completed in such a way as not to alert our friend and ally, Japan, of your presence on their soil or the nature and extent of the threat you seek to address.*

Chung knew very well what the flowery language of his section head had meant: We don't want the fucking Japanese to know about Subarov's plot or our role in stopping it. Chung had long ago learned not to question or even contemplate foreign policy questions, but the contradiction nagged him like a surly wife. He was doing the Japanese a huge favor in wiping out this threat to expose one of their many wartime atrocities. Still, if the world's major newspapers got onto the story, the arrest of the Sakhalin Koreans would make it seem the Japanese themselves were behind it. That could be decidedly bad for Chung's career, even his health.

"I'll be going then," Chung said, reaching for the door. "You'll hear from me."

Foster stretched out horizontally on the bed. "Good. And Chung, the OSI has issued an alert for their arrest. It's gone out to every U.S. military installation in Japan and, more importantly, to the Japanese authorities nationwide. Matthews is wanted on suspicion of espionage now and considered armed and dangerous. That Korean woman is wanted as an accessory. The two of them together should stick out like a sore thumb."

Chung feared just such an announcement. If the Japanese got their hands on Su Li Young, he would be exposed. He had to find Matthews and the girl himself, and quickly, or find himself in some very hot water.

TWENTY-SEVEN

**He's left us a gift: three small bags filled with hope.
Now this may get much worse, but we'll just have to cope.**

Monday, dawn

Su Li awoke in the quiet of first light. Sheer exhaustion had rescued her from a sleepless night of torment and grief. She felt surprisingly rested and relaxed. Her eyes fell upon the sleeping form of Dan Matthews only an arm's length away. She studied his expressionless face, there in the semi-darkness of the room.

It was not the face of Charles Bronson, chiseled and hard. The eyebrows looked a bit thin for an American, and the jaw was perhaps not so well-defined as the one in her dreams so many years ago. But it was a pleasant face, a good face, even with the deep-set, steel blue eyes concealed in slumber. She wondered what he would look like without the closely cropped GI haircut. The conjured image of Dan Matthews on a surfboard with brown hair in his eyes made her giggle.

Behind the face, she knew, dwelled a human soul in turmoil. Where Reggie had embraced her cause as a pathway to his own redemption, Dan Matthews had taken it up as a kind of inherited burden, like a family debt of honor. Where Reggie believed he had nothing to lose, Dan Matthews would see his life's work go for naught as his dreams of Hawaii faded into a bitter remembrance of Su Li Young and the havoc she wreaked upon his life long ago on the frozen wasteland of northern Hokkaido.

How could he possibly be in love with her? Su Li knew better than to play with such words, but she could not deny the change in herself. Charles Bronson or not, she felt safe in his presence. She trusted him in a way she had never trusted; not the kind of blind, innocent trust born of naiveté, like the kind she had placed in Paul Greenberg, or even the kind of benevolent trust she had placed in her beloved Reggie. This was an unguarded embrace of Dan's strength, an instinctive reliance on his judgment and wisdom when her own fell short.

His eyes opened unexpectedly and captured her stare. The look ripened into a smile. "Good morning," he whispered.

Su Li returned the smile. "Tell me about Chicago."

"What's to tell? I was an only child and my father was killed in the war when I was very young."

"We don't have to talk about it, you know."

"No, I don't mind. It's just that it wasn't a happy time for me. I kicked around the streets a lot, got bounced out of three high schools before I finally finished, barely."

"And your mother?"

The left corner of his mouth turned upward, but it wasn't a smile. "My mother, yes. Well, she had her own problems you might say. She tried her best, I suppose, but she wasn't a strong person. Losing my father pretty much finished her."

Su Li could feel the pain in his words and decided to push no farther. "Do you have snow in Chicago?" she asked, and his face told her she should have known the answer.

"I used to think so. In fact, many Americans consider Chicago to be a cold, snowbound frontier land. But having seen winter in Wakkanai, I would say it snows only a little there."

"Why did you join the Air Force?" she asked.

"My, aren't we inquisitive this morning?"

She pulled the covers over her head in a mock gesture of embarrassment. She did not pull them down, but they seemed to come down slowly on their own, revealing the full form of her nakedness to the budding dawn and the steel blue eyes of Dan Matthews.

The sudden cold brought goose bumps clear to her toes. Dan seemed to notice them and smiled, sliding his warm, lean body beside her on the narrow futon. He pulled the covers up, until only their heads were protruding, and turned his eyes to hers. "I could stay like this for a hundred years," he whispered. She did not want to cry and fought to hold back the tears. It had never been like this. This man did not need her, nor did she feel a need to save him or help him or reward him.

This was no boy or father figure, no loud-mouthed GI in heat. Dan Matthews was a man, with the smell and feel of a man. She had looked deep into his soul over these last days and would cherish the view for the rest of her life. Su Li wanted him to please her like she had never been pleased and make her cry for joy beneath him. "I want to make love with you," she said. It was as close as she could bring herself to saying the words she most feared.

Dan kissed her gently, and her mouth opened to receive him. They explored each other in silence for a minute, an hour. Su Li did not know or care. He covered her face and neck and breasts in a tingling, sensual assault of moist lips as she wrapped her leg around his powerful thigh. Su Li could feel him growing against her, even as her breast leapt to his gentle caress. There was no quiver in his touch. She was delirious with pleasure, and when he finally filled her, she wanted him to stay forever.

8:00 a.m.
On the drive to the train station, Su Li realized her life had changed forever in the few short hours since dawn, but she needed to vanquish selfish thoughts and focus on her mission. They were two now, acting as one, and she believed Dan's experience in such matters would surely improve the odds of success.

What had the captain left at the train station? It could be some written instruction regarding a change in plans. The captain had last seen her and Kim together at sea. Why would he not simply tell her himself? Thankfully, her answer lay only a short drive away.

As the station came into view, Dan eased Kim's car into a small, snow-cleared spot beside the road. He pulled the hood up over his head and said, "I'll take a look first, just to make sure there's no surprise waiting for us."

Su Li laughed and said, "That's my job. Wearing that GI parka, you may as well have an American flag on your back."

He nodded his head. "Right, but be careful and come straight back here."

She tried to walk as though she had somewhere to go, all the while checking the area around the station for suspicious vehicles. The few she could see were nearly all invisible beneath an overnight covering of snow. The one that wasn't looked like a small delivery truck with an empty cab.

As she had expected, the train station itself was nearly deserted on this Monday morning. Inside the small, unheated station she saw several elderly people, including one couple, and the usual handful of workers. To the far wall was a bank of three ticket windows, only one of which was manned.

The lockers, a solid wall of nine or ten across and perhaps eight high, were placed opposite the ticket windows. Most of the lockers were still fitted with the red-tipped keys, indicating availability. If there was danger in the station, Su Li couldn't see it.

Feeling confident, she approached the lockers and removed the red-tipped key from her pocket. The key numbered sixty-four and she found herself standing directly facing the matching locker. She saw no need to waste the time or effort involved in going back for Dan when she could just open the locker and bring the contents to the car. Besides, curiosity wouldn't let her leave without solving the mystery.

The lock opened easily, and she peered inside before reaching. The small locker was stuffed to capacity with paper bags. She removed them one by one, shopping bags, three of them, like the ones she carried from the market almost daily.

She reached inside the largest of the three and removed a handful of stuffed envelopes and neatly tied bundles of letters. Her heart nearly stopped. It was the captain's precious collection, the very one she had seen on his boat.

Her pulse raced, palms damp with sweat despite the cold. Now the small building looked more like a tiny closet. Every face in the place seemed to be staring at her, strategically positioned to block her escape. Maybe they were all working together. Why hadn't she just listened to Dan?

She scooped up the bags and headed toward the door, fully expecting chaos at any moment; no one moved or even acknowledged her presence. She was clear of the building and heading for the car. She picked up her pace and saw the familiar GI parka moving up to meet her. "Dan-san," she said, "I have the captain's records. He didn't bring them to Abashiri. Kim had them all along."

"You shouldn't have opened that locker," Dan scolded. "Anyone might have been watching. You should be more careful, Su Li. Let's get them to the car and get the hell out of here." The street was nearly deserted, but they were still a fair distance from the car.

"I'm sorry," she said. "I couldn't resist."

Even with the precious records in her possession, Su L's thoughts turned to the gathering winter storm from the northwest. She had suspected as much from the darkness of the morning. "We dare not take the train to Sapporo," she cautioned. "It will make us easy to find, but driving will be very difficult now on the Wakkanai peninsula. We should go quickly. Even if we can make it safely, the trip will be at least seven hours by car."

"Let's get to it then," Dan replied, fumbling for the car key as they walked briskly in the snow.

"Kim must have rendezvoused with the captain again after he dropped me in Hakodate, or maybe they just transferred the box while I was still asleep. Yes, that's it. He gave Kim the box with instructions, then continued up the east coast."

"He must have known the NSA would track him right up to Abashiri," Dan reasoned. "That allowed Kim to slip into Wakkanai unnoticed."

She couldn't understand why Captain Subarov would not trust her with the knowledge. Dan seemed to sense her disappointment. "It had nothing to do with you," he said. "Subarov knew the Korean CIA and God knows who else are after you. He knew you might be taken alive, and he couldn't take the chance of you giving up the collection. Those letters and photos are irreplaceable historical records. They could go a long way to keep something like this from happening again. He had to keep you in the dark, but I don't think it pleased him."

"What can your acquaintance in Sapporo do for us?"

"Maybe nothing, but that's the only option I can think of at the moment."

The trunk opened easily, and they began to arrange the precious cargo inside so as not to spill out in a chaotic mess. "If everything else fails," Su Li said, "we can go to the New York Times and the major news bureaus with the collection. I know it won't be the same, but it may help those two hundred people in some way, and it might raise some attention for the Koreans on Sakhalin."

"I know you're right, Su Li, but I'm on really dangerous ground here."

"What do you mean, Dan-san?"

"Look, we both know my government is involved in this. What it's really about is protecting American intelligence sources on Sakhalin and the rest of the Far East."

She was beginning to see the picture. "I think I understand. Those sources are all South Korean. Is that it?"

"That's it in a nutshell," he confirmed, slamming the trunk lid closed. "Protecting you from the clutches of those bloodthirsty Koreans is one thing, but anything else might be, well—"

She completed his sentence. "Treason."

"Yes, treason."

"I'm familiar with this word," she said softly. "It's caused me much distress recently."

"I know, and there are some things I just can't do. Come on. Let's get in the car and get the hell out of here."

She touched his arm and he stopped to face her, still standing at the back of the car. "These things are questions of conscience," she said. "Together we'll find common ground. I've placed you in a terrible position, but don't worry."

"What do you mean?"

"There will be no way out of this for me now, whatever happens. I'm prepared for what comes, and will accept my fate happily if we can help my people with these documents. But I can't bear the thought of destroying the life of another friend."

He smiled and asked, "Is that what I am?"

She punched his arm playfully, forgetting for a moment the seriousness of her message. "You know what I mean. I'm afraid you will share my fate, if not my prison cell. If your friend in Sapporo can't help us, I'm going to finish this alone."

"I wish it could be different, Su Li," he said. "The future doesn't look bright for either of us right now, but don't give up hope. We have something these governments want very badly. Let's not jump the gun. We'll talk to my friend. She understands how to play this game by their rules."

"They'll be looking for us everywhere now," she said.

"Yes, and I'm sure they've already figured out we're going to Sapporo. Hell, there's nowhere else to go on this island if your goal is to make a splash. We'll need to be very careful. Traveling together, we won't be difficult to spot." He moved around to the driver's door and said, "Maybe we should travel separately."

"I won't split from you," she said defiantly, facing him across the roof of the car.

He opened the door. "And what about when this is all over?"

"We'll see what tomorrow brings," she said, knowing all such questions are answered in time. As she reached for the door handle, Su Li heard the high-pitched sound of screeching tires from behind. From the corner of her eye, she saw Dan launch the car keys off into the deep snow. By the time she turned, the white delivery van was upon them, the blurred figure of a man already springing from the rear door only inches from where she stood. Before she could react, his arms snatched her up like a rag doll and pitched her head long into the slowly moving van.

The man landed squarely on top of her in a crushing blow that deflated her like a blown tire. He rolled and sprang to his feet with the guile and quickness of a cat. Before Su Li could make a move Dan launched through the door, hitting her kidnapper's midsection.

Gasping for breath, Su Li rolled to the side of the van, assaulted by a searing pain in her left shoulder. The two men crashed to the bare metal floor. She could hear the van's engine struggle and whine for acceleration in the unplowed side street as the Korean managed to free the pistol from beneath his coat.

Dan's powerful hand ensnared the Korean's wrist as the pistol flailed wildly in Su Li's direction. "Jump, Su Li," Dan shouted. As Su Li struggled to gain her footing, the close combat intensified, with the cargo doors swinging wildly only inches from Dan's head. The Korean was straddling Dan's midsection and dangerously close to breaking the death grip on his pistol hand. Despite the dizzying pain in her shoulder, Su Li's legs did not fail her. She rose and threw herself at the Korean, head down, like a missile in flight.

She caught him unawares and squarely with her good shoulder, knocking him hard into the sidewall of the van. She landed only inches from Dan and saw him, already struggling to his knees. The gun. In attacking the Korean she had inadvertently freed the pistol to finish what the dark-haired man had started.

The Korean, lying prone on the floor, was already taking aim. Instinctively, Su Li braced her booted foot against Dan's ribcage and pushed with all the strength at her command, sending Dan flying through the open door onto the snow-covered street.

Before the van could turn back onto the main road, she saw the shrinking figure in the American parka, face down in the snow. Then she saw him move. She was sure of it, and felt the strength already returning to her battered frame.

TWENTY-EIGHT

**Lie to me once, even twice if you like,
but I won't be taking a called third strike.**

Monday, 9:25 am

In the bathroom mirror, Dan's wounds appeared mainly superficial, but included a number of assorted aches and pains that would no doubt leave some ugly bruising. His worries were another story entirely. Discarding the bloodsoaked paper towels, he reached for a few coins and headed out into the train station in search of a public phone.

"*Hai, moshi-moshi,*" said the familiar voice over the receiver.

"Inspector Tanaka? This is Sergeant Matthews."

"Sergeant Matthews," Tanaka said, obviously surprised to hear Dan's voice. "Where are you?"

"That's not important, Inspector," he replied, "but the girl you're interested in, Su Li Young, has been kidnapped."

"Kidnapped? Please tell me; who has kidnapped this girl?"

He had business with Tanaka, all right, but strictly the face-to-face kind. "I'm not certain, Inspector, but I'd like to give you all the information I have. I think it will help solve your murder."

"Yes, of course, Sergeant Matthews. How long will it take for you to get to the Prefectural Police Headquarters?"

Could the man really think sergeants were that stupid? "Inspector, I'm not going there. You're no doubt aware that my employers are looking for me."

"Yes, this is true, although our meeting shall remain a completely private thing."

Dan had learned that this Japanese code of honor thing had all sorts of convenient exceptions. He had no doubt Tanaka would rat him out, but was betting the inspector wanted his information first. "It's not that I don't trust you, but they have people out looking for me all over Wakkanai. Your office is a bad idea. How about we meet at the train station in fifteen minutes?"

"Could we make this meeting in one hour? I cannot leave my office just yet."

That's about how long it would take NSA to mobilize a security police detail. "Fifteen minutes."

With some rice and hot tea in his stomach, Dan felt prepared for whatever happened next. He settled onto a cold bench inside the station, one with a good view of the door. He saw the fedora appear from the Toyota parked directly in front of the building and decided to let Tanaka come to him. The inspector arrived empty-handed. He walked directly to Dan's bench and took a seat.

"I was very surprised to hear from you," Tanaka said, dispensing with formalities. "From our last meeting, it was my opinion you did not wish to help with that investigation."

"Oh, no, Inspector, your opinion was quite wrong. You were correct about Su Li Young. She was very much involved in this business, although I believe she's done nothing criminal."

"And this woman, of course, is what brings you here," Tanaka suggested.

Dan found his remark curious. "I just told you she was kidnapped, and I'd like to help you find her. Doesn't that interest you? You were plenty interested in her the other day."

"Of course I am interested, but the investigation has changed since the other day."

A bad smell had just settled over the station. "How has it changed? Do you still want to solve the murder?"

Tanaka removed the trademark fedora and began to play with the brim. "Sergeant Matthews, there is no need for mistrust. Tell me what information you have."

Something about Tanaka had changed too, and Dan needed to know what before giving away the farm. "I'd like something from you first. Tell me about the crime lab results, as much as you know."

"Well," Tanaka said, "I say this investigation has been closed."

"What? What does that mean? You caught the killers?"

It looked like the inspector was counting tiles on the floor. "There are no killers," he said in a halting voice, as though speaking to no one in particular. "Our investigation has concluded that this boy died from a suicide."

He wasn't hearing this. "That's impossible. You know that. The boy was murdered. What about the puncture marks? The toxicology screen? You have solid proof he was murdered."

Tanaka placed the hat back on his head, then sighed. "This was a tragic mistake, I am afraid. The autopsy findings were in error. This puncture mark was really a small injury and was not made by a needle."

A bee sting maybe? "The results can be checked. Do another autopsy."

"That also is impossible. This body has been cremated."

Back in the neighborhood, Dan remembered, the urban raccoons never attacked the garbage on cold nights. The cold deadened their sense of smell. It had taken Dan a while in the cold, but now he was close enough to the garbage to smell the aroma clearly. He smiled and said, "Of course, I should have guessed. On the phone I told you I had information about the murder. You had a chance to give me the news then. Why didn't you?"

"I thought it better to speak in person."

Fortunately, Dan hadn't come to this meeting to put all of their lives into Tanaka's hands blindly. Like loyalty, trust is earned, and Tanaka had simply not paid the price. Dan said, "Let me ask you a question. What's the reason you wanted to delay this meeting for an hour? Your station house is only a short distance away. You could have walked in ten minutes."

Tanaka squirmed uncomfortably on the bench. "I was very busy today. There is nothing else."

But not too busy for a little double-dealing. "And who did you call after you hung up with me?"

"I called no one, I assure you."

Dan's pulse raced, his left palm clammy around the cold steel of the Colt. He had to suppress the urge to turn and look out onto the street. "You're lying. Somebody warned you off this case. Somebody very high up told you to put the clamps on it. Who was it?"

Tanaka looked toward the door and started to rise, but Dan grabbed his arm in a vice-grip and held him to the seat. "Don't move, Inspector. I have a pistol bigger than your dick. It's pointed at your gut. Just settle down and relax. Now, the Air Force has people out there waiting to arrest me, don't they?"

"Yes," he admitted, small beads of sweat forming under the brim of the fedora, "but you should understand, this is a matter of national security and—"

"Save it, Tanaka. I've heard that bullshit before. Now listen carefully. You and I are going to walk over to the refreshment stand, then slowly around the corner into the bathroom. Do you understand?"

Tanaka's eyes were fixed on the bulge in Dan's left pocket. "Yes."

He kept his captive at arm's length as they walked, staying half a step behind. Dan's right hand maintained its lock on Tanaka's upper arm, as much to keep the big man at bay as to hold him in check. With Tanaka positioned between himself and the door, Dan was able to scan the outside perimeter as they walked the length of the station.

They were out there somewhere, the dark blue Air Force cars, but he found no sign of them. Even the CIA couldn't coordinate a proper operation like this in twenty minutes. Whoever was in charge, they'd have to rely on GI-issue Security Police and their blue Fords. They were most likely hiding nearby, he figured, with one or two radio surveillance guys in windows somewhere close.

Around the corner of the deserted refreshment stand, he pushed Tanaka through the swinging bathroom door. A small window provided enough light for his purpose. "On your knees, now!" he ordered. When Tanaka stalled, Dan lashed out with his right foot, catching the man flush behind the right knee. Tanaka collapsed onto the tile floor.

"You will regret this action, Sergeant," he said. "I have done only my duty in this matter."

He knew Tanaka was right, or at least that's how the Japanese detective saw the game board. "Right, Inspector. I know the whole speech. You're a team player. You live to serve the group. You defer to society's judgment over your own. Another guy gave me a similar speech recently, but it was about killing a hundred thousand people. Save it. I'm not interested. I live by my own rules for the moment."

"What will you do? They have many armed policemen outside. You have no chance to escape."

Dan laughed. "What do you think I should do? Surrender? The Japanese didn't respect soldiers who surrendered. The last thing I want is to lose your respect, Inspector. Take off the fedora slowly and flick it back here. Don't turn around."

Tanaka did as instructed. "If you go out with me now, you will not face charges for what happened now in this station."

Dan reached for the fedora. "I don't think I like that deal. You've lost your credibility, to say the least. Now the nice, tailored overcoat, take it off slowly. Unbutton it with your left hand and toss it back."

"You are acting dishonorably," Tanaka said, working on the second button.

The guy was hung up on honor, but hadn't a clue what it means. "Want to talk about honor? Where's the honor in letting that family believe their boy killed himself over his male lover? Where's the honor in that?"

Tanaka bristled, even from his knees, as he threw the coat to the ground. "The honor of Japan is at stake in this matter. This Ishikawa family has a duty as well. This family must bear its burden for the nation."

That kind of thinking had gotten the Japanese into more trouble than they could handle. "It's hard to argue with someone like you, Tanaka. There's a certain point where duty ends and conscience begins. Duty is a convenient thing, I guess. It keeps you from having to think. Well, to be fair, we have a lot of guys like you too. You know, I'll bet whoever scared you off didn't even tell you what this is all about; did he?"

Tanaka did not reply. Dan said, "I was right, wasn't I? He didn't have to tell you. He just needed to say it was patriotic. Well, don't feel bad because he probably didn't know anyway. The guy who called him gave him the same bullshit. Now your boot laces, one at a time."

The laces were leather, and strong. Dan used one to tie Tanaka's hands firmly around the steel water pipe beneath the sink. With the other he bound the inspector's feet tightly together, and used his own scarf as a gag.

Placing the fedora on his head, Dan faced the mirror and tipped the hat forward, ever so slightly. "You go for the Lee Marvin look, I noticed," he said without looking at Tanaka. "I like the show, *M-Squad* I mean, but I prefer the hat lower on the eyes and to the right, more Sinatra."

The overcoat might have been tailored to fit Dan. Just a hair long in the sleeves. He took the Colt from his coat pocket and showed it to the helpless inspector. "You don't really have to show your hand when the other guy folds, but it might make you feel better."

The overcoat pockets were narrow and shallow, so he had to stuff the big pistol in his belt. "Oh," he said, "I almost forgot. The keys?"

"In the right pocket of the coat."

Dan checked. He also found a package of cigarettes and a Zippo lighter. "Sure enough. They should be in here to get you in a few minutes if all goes well. Sayonara, Fuki-san."

Dan pulled the wool collar up around his neck and made straight for the front door, as if he hadn't a care in the world. Once outside, he stopped lazily and lit up a smoke. His hands shook so badly he nearly couldn't put the flame on the butt. He walked directly to the waiting Toyota, aware his performance was being critiqued by unfriendly eyes.

The Toyota started up on the first try, and the new, improved version of Inspector Tanaka pulled away, leaving the train station in his rear view mirror. He might have turned out of sight, but couldn't resist waiting until the tiny, blue Fords in the distance began descending on the station from all directions.

It occurred to Dan that he had nowhere to go. He was running out of money and had used the last clean shirt in his small overnight bag. Too exhausted to think straight, he'd need to reenergize or have no chance at all to help Su Li. Yoon Hae's place was not an option, so he headed for the only safe house left, Kim Tae Woo's.

He turned the Toyota toward Wakkanai Park and considered his options. He still had one big ace to play. Even with the captain dead and Su Li in their grasp, the Korean agents wanted what was in those shopping bags. They probably wouldn't harm her until they got their paws on the captain's collection, and Dan had it stashed away safe and sound.

Without the emotional impact of the collection and the two hundred survivors, Su Li's plan would be finished and she would no longer pose a threat. Surely the Korean agents understood that, and might let her go free if they could secure Subarov's treasure. After all, they were professional operatives, not psychotic killers.

Yes, he thought, it might still be possible to save her. He could trade the collection, an even swap. The Koreans wouldn't be hard to find. They'd probably be in the market for a deal and Foster was the perfect go-between. But getting his hands on Foster again might prove difficult.

Then he thought of Yoon Hae Young. She had a right to know her daughter's situation. He'd have to have a talk with her before he made a move.

TWENTY-NINE

**You're damned if you don't, and damned if you do;
so just draw your cards, and play the hand through.**

Monday, 8:50 p.m.

Dan awoke in Kim Tae Woo's sitting room to find Yoon Hae kneeling beside him quietly. There was no telling how long she'd been there. The woman wore her terrified suspicions openly in her tired eyes, but her composure held rock steady. "I'm happy to see you well, Dan-san," she said. "Son Yee has told me you ate two bowls of rice and raw fish before going to sleep."

He tried to smile. "I must have been really hungry." He pulled himself up on the futon, resting both arms on his knees. It would be best to come right to the point, he thought. "I'd much prefer that your daughter be sitting here with you, Yoon Hae. She's been taken by the Korean CIA. I couldn't protect her."

The woman showed no emotion, as if she had been preparing for the news. No surprise there, for tragedy had become her inevitable companion, a familiar, dark shadow casting its pall across her life at will. "Is she dead?"

"I'm sure she isn't." In truth, he could only pray. "There was a struggle, and when they escaped with her she was shaken up, but alive and well. I'm certain they'll use her to try and get their hands on Subarov's letters and photographs from Sakhalin. They'll want to make a trade. Those things are what they've been after all along. Believe me, they have no reason to kill Su Li."

"Not at this moment," she added.

Since their first encounter, Dan had suspected the old woman's wisdom surpassed his own. He'd been right, and anything less than complete candor would do her an injustice. "You're right."

A look of determination settled on the old woman's face and she spoke in a slow, deliberate voice. "Do you have the things they want?"

"Yes. I have everything."

"What will you do?"

It seemed like a no-brainer. "Whatever's necessary to get your daughter back."

"Then you're prepared to give them what they want?"

Why wouldn't he be? "Of course I am. If it means giving those things to the Koreans, then so be it. Some photographs and letters aren't worth Su Li's life. I'm in love with your daughter, Yoon Hae. I want her to be my wife."

He could not detect a reaction. "And do you speak now of what is good for Su Li, or what is good for Dan Matthews?"

The woman had never betrayed such a sophisticated command of English. Her question startled him in both its delivery and its content. He did not comprehend her meaning and said, "I'm only thinking of your daughter." Why was he defending himself for trying to prevent her death? "Those things could buy her life."

It occurred to Dan that she had not moved a muscle during the entire conversation. Her intensity was a sign, he thought, reflecting the importance of her message. He waited for Yoon Hae's words to free him. "Maybe," she said, "but Su Li would rather die than have those things lost forever."

He wasn't hearing this. How could the old woman spew such nonsense? But she wasn't even finished yet. "Su Li values this cause beyond her own life and would gladly die to save it. Americans, above all, surely understand this idea, Dan-san."

He thought of his father, whom he barely remembered, and the great World War II. Yoon Hae was right, of course. Still, he would rather have Su Li alive and hating him for fifty years than let her be tortured and killed by these godless animals. "Can you say you would hate me if I used those things to save your daughter?"

As Dan watched the tears slowly gather in the wells of her eyes, he began to see that the persona of Su Li Young was no accidental blessing of nature or God. She was her mother and her mother was she.

Finally, Yoon Hae moved, settling back on her heels with bowed head. "No," she whispered. "Do what you believe is right. If you truly love my beautiful Su Li, you will do what is best."

11:00 a.m.
Dan made the call from a public phone box in the heart of the city. As expected, Foster had been waiting by his hotel phone and answered on the first ring. "Matthews?"

"That's right, Foster. Now shut up and listen. I'm sure you know your Korean fuck buddies have kidnapped Su Li, and I have what they want, what all you patriotic, defenders of freedom want. I want you to contact them and give them this message. A bunch of old photographs and letters don't mean shit to me, but the girl does. I admit that. I propose a simple, straight up trade: the girl for Subarov's collection."

"I'll pass that message on," Foster said, "but there's nothing I can do for you. On top of disobeying a shitload of orders and assaulting a Japanese policeman with a pistol, you helped Airman Kincaid betray his country."

That was a mouthful and Dan took a second to digest it. "I what?"

"I suppose you'd like me to believe you know nothing about it," Foster said.

"Foster, I don't give a fuck what you believe. Tell me what you're talking about."

"Okay, I'll bite. It's possible you really don't know, but you'll have to ask your girlfriend. She knows. She put him up to it."

Dan could only pray he'd have the chance. Foster said, "Why don't you be smart, Matthews? Let's wrap this up together. It's still not too late for you. Bring me the collection and I'll do everything I can to help your girlfriend."

"Nice try, Foster, but no cigar."

"Fine, be the Lone Ranger, but think about the rest of your life. When you get finished with your twenty in Leavenworth, there's that little matter of humiliating Tanaka and stealing his car. You really pissed him off, and you're number one on his hit parade right now."

It hadn't exactly slipped his mind. "Before you can do anything to me, you have to catch me."

"That's precisely the wrong thing to say, Matthews."

Dan knew he still needed Foster to accomplish his task, and forced his temper into submission. He backed off a bit. "I'll give them the fucking collection, but I want the girl alive. How much control do you really have over the Koreans?" He couldn't believe anything out of the NSA man's mouth, but he wanted to hear him talk about these Koreans. Foster might let something slip, something that could help Su Li.

"I know what you're asking," Foster answered. "Can I keep them from killing the girl? The answer is yes."

"Like you kept them from killing the Japanese kid? Or were you part of that all along?"

"We had nothing to do with that. These are rough boys, all right, but their mission is that collection you have. If you give it up, they'll let the girl go. They've already assured me of that. Bring it to my hotel tomorrow at nine in the morning to make the exchange. Don't bring anyone else. Just come to the hotel and wait outside the front door."

Dan didn't have the luxury of a plan, so he had to play it by ear and trust his instincts. Sinead was his insurance policy, so he needed her close by, but not too close, when the party got rocking. Wakkanai was getting too hot to stick around. Dan had enemies everywhere in the city, on base and off. It might be smarter to take this fight to more neutral ground. He said, "It's not gonna work that way, Foster. Tell the Koreans to bring her to Sapporo and wait. I'll call you and leave a message with the details. Check for messages every three hours."

"Hold on. That won't work. They won't bring her to Sapporo and sit around just because you say so."

"How about because you say so?" Dan said. "You're the one who controls them. Right? They won't kill Su Li because you'll tell them not to. So what's the problem? You tell them that's the way it is."

Foster stammered, but nothing intelligible came over the receiver. Dan had his answer, but it wasn't the one he'd wanted. "You're a fucking liar, Foster. You don't have any more control over these animals than I do. All I care about is the girl. If she dies, I'll kill you. I swear you'll wake up one morning with your dick in your back pocket. That's something for you to think about."

"I think we understand each other," Foster said.

"I think we do. Tell them to go to Sapporo with Su Li unharmed and they'll get what they came for." He hung up the receiver before Foster could reply.

12:35 p.m.
Chung fiddled through his coat for the car keys and called to Fu. "I'm going out to call Foster and get some food. I'll return soon. Keep a close eye on her. She's a shifty bitch."

Until now, he had not used the safehouse on the outskirts of Wakkanai. No place is safe when you have something to hide, he thought. The less you use it, the better. It had been rented and prepared for his possible use surreptitiously by staff from the ROK Consulate in Sapporo. They had prepared another one in Sapporo, just in case.

The small, inconspicuous house was close enough to the bustling city to provide the anonymity he required, but far enough removed from potentially nosy neighbors to provide some measure of security. The Consulate had done well.

The woman, tied and seated on the matted floor, had not spoken since her capture nearly three hours before. It was always best to give them a while to exercise a little imagination. With the girl in his hands, Chung figured it was only a matter of time before he scooped up the contents of Subarov's box. Matthews would surely come to him now, obviating the need to squeeze the girl for information.

What a pity. He would so enjoy torturing this woman to a slow death, but Chung was a disciplined, government operative, not a sociopathic killer. The woman would die, of course, but she might escape Chung's preferred method of execution in favor of a single bullet to the temple.

Foster answered on the first ring. "Chung, it's about time. But then I guess you're keeping pretty busy with all the kidnappings and murders." The comment amused Chung and served only to reinforce old conclusions. "Matthews has what you want. He's willing to trade it for the girl."

"Good," said Chung. "We are getting somewhere at last."

"Matthews said he'll call me tomorrow with the details of the exchange. You should go to Sapporo and wait."

The last part stunned him, and Chung longed for the feel of his hand around Foster's throat. "And you presumed to agree?"

"It's not like I had a choice."

Chung reminded himself to focus on the mission. "Why Sapporo? He has something up his sleeve."

"He only wants the girl released safely," Foster explained. "It's just a more neutral, public place. That's all."

"You allowed him to believe he could dictate the details of the exchange?" Chung asked. "Did you demand a way to contact him?"

"Look, Chung, my job is to assist you. You wanted me to act as your messenger boy. I did that. Do you think he gave me his phone number, or the address of where he's staying?"

Chung recognized the sarcasm, but forced himself to ignore it. "Why Sapporo?" he asked again. "I don't like it."

"Think about it. What can Matthews do with all that stuff on his own? Hell, he doesn't even know anything about the Sakhalin Koreans, except what the girl told him over the last couple of days. In his hands, those old papers are only good for starting a fire. I think he's only interested in the pussy."

"Your Matthews is more intelligent than you believe," Chung countered. "In fact, Mr. Foster, I think he should have your job. He is not finished yet, and I know who can tell me what he might be up to."

"That's another thing we need to talk about," said Foster. "What have you done to the girl?"

Foster was acting less like a liason and more an operational commander all the time. Still, Chung managed to at least control his resentment. "We need the girl. You are not dealing with fools. She is alive and well."

"I figured that. I'm more concerned about after or during the exchange. There's been enough killing. You know how my employers feel about that. I believe its been discussed with your superiors."

Foster's last revelation was nearly enough to push Chung over the edge. How dare they go behind his back? "Listen carefully, Mr. Foster. Do not presume to tell me how to complete my mission. I have listened to your demands and catered to them without question. I understand your concern for your own countrymen, but your right to object ends with them."

"It has nothing to do with humanitarian concerns. The girl can't hurt you once you have the collection. Subarov is gone. Hell, even the old Koreans will vanish in a few more days. The girl will just fade away. Killing her will only increase our risk of exposure."

There was no point in arguing with this buffoon. He was powerless to alter Chung's plan. "Of course," he said. He wanted to be sure the message wasn't lost on Foster. "We will take all necessary care to minimize the risk of more fatalities."

Chung only wished Foster could see his smile through the wire.

With two piping hot orders of miso ramen under his arm and enough sushi for himself and Fu, Chung headed back for the car. He was still in no mood to pamper the girl, but the trip for food had given him time to gain control of his emotions and work through this building sense of impatience.

He hated the girl as much as he'd hated Subarov—no, more. The fact that she provoked such emotional upheaval in him only made it worse. She was a high-minded cunt, arrogant and flush with an air of superiority and self-righteousness. She had never known hunger, poverty or even real cold. The girl had no concept of what it meant to be Korean, had never even been to Korea; and yet, she would proclaim herself the Messiah of this ragged, malcontented band of old mountain goats. He hoped he could kill her in a very painful way, so as to wipe out her stink and every memory of her existence.

Despite his hatred, Chung could not deny a grudging respect for the bitch. Su Li Young had proven a worthy opponent, and would easily outmatch most of the North Korean and Chinese professional operatives he had encountered in his long intelligence career. She might easily detect any small loss of control and use it to her advantage. But why did he hate her so much? Perhaps her bravery and devotion to such a hopeless cause unjustifiably shamed him and made him question his own identity as a Korean.

He entered through the front door of the house and found the miso ramen was cold, but Chung was in complete control again. "Warm this up on the stove, Fu. We will eat and then give this bitch the scraps."

When he could eat no more, Chung placed the bowl of scraps beside Su Li on the floor. "Here you are my dear," he said, "a bowl of scraps for you. You'll have to bend over and eat it like the good bitch you are."

To his disappointment, he drew no reaction from the girl. She sat stone-faced, eyes defiantly forward, not down. After a few minutes he spoke again. "Maybe you don't like the miso ramen, bitch. Is that it? Or do Chinese noodles not agree with you? Oh, I understand. The mix is not seasoned to your liking." He unzipped his trousers and promptly pissed into the bowl, the unspeakable mixture splattering Su Li's clothing and face as it fell.

Chung was enjoying himself. "Try it now," he bellowed. "I think it's much sweeter."

The woman smiled and turned her eyes to meet his own. "You will never get him, and you'll never see the collection," she said in perfect Korean.

"Really?" Chung asked. "Well, you may be happy to learn your brave American is begging to trade those old pictures and letters in exchange for your life."

There was no mistaking it. He saw her face twitch, ever so slightly but without a doubt. He had struck the cord of his pleasure. "Why, Su Li," he said, "you're fucking this one too, aren't you? Are you in love with him? Do you have some simple-minded notion that he shares your devotion to this misguided cause?"

"You will see," she replied coldly.

"Oh, yes," he said, "I will see his face as the bullet rips through that nasty, disease-ridden brain of yours. Now I think it's time you and I talked a bit. Does that sound like fun?"

Her stoic silence was no surprise. He said, "I know you and Matthews picked up Subarov's little gift at the train station. Where were you taking it? What was your plan? Were you taking it to one of the newspapers?"

Chung didn't expect her to break down and cooperate at the drop of a hat. He had to lay the groundwork and define the subject and limits of the interrogation. Beating the information from her was out of the question. The woman was simply too willing to die for her cause. Besides, he needed her in reasonably good shape, face intact, in case he needed to feign some kind of exchange with Matthews.

It was really no secret where the pair had been headed. Sapporo was the only logical destination. Beyond that, even Su Li might not know what Matthews would do next. In a sense, Su Li's interrogation was of little value. Whatever their plan, Matthews would surely change it now. The most he could hope for from Su Li was to learn the details of the original plan with Subarov. It wouldn't help him find

Subarov's letters and pictures, but it would look good on his final report.

Perhaps he could rile her a bit. He stood tall over her slumped form and smiled. "I took great pleasure in killing your beloved Captain Subarov. I admit he was brave, much as you are, but in the end that's not much protection from a bullet."

"He died as he wanted to die," she said.

Chung smiled. "You didn't know he and I were friends, did you?"

"I doubt that very much," she replied. She was talking, and that was a start.

"Of course," he added, "he knew me by a different name. It was Song Hee Choi. The captain and I were shipmates and quite good friends."

He watched her eyes narrow as small furrows invaded the smooth, blemish-free skin on her forehead. "You were never his friend," she said, "even when he thought you were a simple Korean fisherman. He never trusted you with important information."

"He is dead and I am alive," Chung said in victory.

She spat on the floor in a contemptuous display. "You are scum, worse than a traitor. You take some demented pride in earning your living on the corpses of your helpless countrymen. Dan Matthews will kill you, or I will kill you myself."

"You are bold," Chung said, "but very foolish. I'll make you a promise, Su Li. I won't kill you until I have the collection. Together, we'll watch the old pictures and letters burn to ashes. Then you will slowly learn the price of your folly." If there were a way to safely keep this cunt alive to the end, he would find it. She did not deserve a quick bullet in the head. "Pack our things and check the equipment, Fu," he said.

"Where are we going, sir?"

"To Sapporo, to get what we came for. We leave in an hour."

THIRTY

**He'll only give you one chance, so keep your eye on the prize.
You once called him brother, now cut him down to size.**

Monday, 9:40 p.m.
Sapporo

Finding the car keys in five feet of snow was no easy task, but Dan managed to dig them out and retrieve Kim's car with its precious cargo.

He rolled into Sapporo well after dark. The place was alive and throbbing with excitement in anticipation of the coming Snow Festival. It was scheduled to begin tomorrow, he knew, but looked to be in full swing already.

His route to the Royal Hotel took him right past the famous Odori Park in the heart of the city. The narrow, mile-long park was literally packed with a geometrically arranged series of massive white and crystal-like sculptures of ice and snow. From the car window he saw giant statues of animals, fantasy scenes, even one he swore was a replica of the White House. Each was awash in a dazzling, multi-colored blanket of lights. Hoards of camera-toting tourists besieged the downtown streets around him, mingling easily with the many festival workers and curious locals.

"I *ras chai mas*, Mista Stephens," said the slightly too eager hotel clerk. "This mean, Welcome to Royaru Hoteru. I am Kato. Preeze, you may caru if you require anything." Kato smiled. "Anysing at aru." The man glanced curiously at the information card. "You businessman from Chicago, I see. This you first time in Sapporo?"

"Yes," Dan replied, counting out thousand-yen notes on the counter. The clerk didn't look familiar. But even if the man recognized him from his last trip, he'd never put a name with the face. The hotel was packed to the gills with Westerners, by the look of the crowded lobby. "Just call me Earl. I'm with American Elevator Systems."

With a hot shower under his belt and three priceless shopping bags under his bed, Dan expected to be asleep before his head hit the pillow, but the weight of his many troubles denied him even that most basic and temporary escape. He figured a drink in the hotel bar might help him unwind and reached for his trousers. He'd seen a sign in the lobby for the Sky Bar on the top floor of the hotel.

It was a short—and warm—elevator ride up to the Sky Bar. On another night, in another life, he might have enjoyed the place. The walls were clear glass and pitched out at the top, like they were falling to the ground. He had the uncomfortable feeling of sitting perilously atop a flagpole, but the feeling soon passed. The place was nearly empty. He made his way to a small table at the edge and waited for the server.

Sapporo on a clear, winter night was something to behold from above, an endless sea of decorative lights in every direction, stretching far beyond the confines of Odori Park. Everything was lit: windows, buildings, streets, even a huge, circular park in the distance, where tiny, anonymous forms labored into the night to ready more great ice sculptures and floats for the coming festival.

Dan had barely touched his Suntory and water when he heard the sweet, confident voice in only slightly broken English. "May I sit and talk with you?" the voice purred.

His eyes turned from the distant park and fell upon the attractive figure in the tight, blue dress. She was no more than twenty-five, probably closer to twenty, impeccably dressed to look mature and smartly coifed in a short style with exactly the right touch of makeup. She carried a fur coat around her arm, and prominently. "Of course," he replied, but even as he said it, wished he hadn't.

There had been many other nights in many other places, when a woman like this had helped him drive away a lonely fog in a foreign land, but not tonight, not in this place. "My date stood me up," she said. It was about what he'd expected. The way she said "stood me up," told him other Americans had heard this story. "My name is Mitsuko," she announced. "Are you a businessman?"

He didn't know or care what her angle was, whether she was a hooker or just looking to latch onto an American with money for a while. Maybe she was a hundred percent legit. No matter. "Nothing so glamorous," he answered, "or lucrative. I'm just a plain old GI My name is Dan."

The girl looked disappointed, but showed no sign of being deterred. "May I have a drink, Dan-san?" she asked.

There was no harm in a little conversation. The waitress had obviously been expecting it and was already making her way to the table. "Are you from Sapporo, Akiko?" he asked.

"No. I am from a small village in the north of Honshu. I work in Sapporo. There is many opportunity in Sapporo now with Olympics coming."

After her second drink and his third, Dan found that small talk with this beautiful stranger couldn't free him from incessant thoughts of Su Li Young. Looking at the girl's slender figure in the short dress, he tried to picture Su Li in such a dress and wondered if she would ever get the chance to indulge in such banal triviality. He bristled silently at the unfairness of it all. "Tell me something, Akiko," he said. "Is there anything you'd die for?"

Dan had surprised himself with the question, because he asked it without any consideration of its effect on his unsuspecting young companion. Cruelty was not his intent, for Dan had never felt the need to judge others. This girl no doubt had her own story of woe, probably a good one at that, and yet he somehow resented the seemingly frivolous and uncomplicated nature of her existence.

She looked at him like he'd just grown another head. "I do not understand," she said.

He was relieved the girl had not taken offense, and reconsidered his uncharacteristic rush to judgment. Maybe it wasn't resentment he was feeling at all, but simple jealousy. That was it, all right. This girl, whoever she was, unencumbered by some self-imposed, all-consuming devotion to a higher cause, was free to do exactly what young people are supposed to do. She could fall in love on a whim, trek off to some tropical island for a week, or elope with a perfect stranger. She could be happy or sad or frustrated or any goddamn thing she wanted without any catastrophic consequences to someone else. He wanted options like that, for himself and for Su Li. Why couldn't he and Su Li Young have met under such circumstances? "How old are you? Twenty?"

"I am nearly twenty-two," she replied.

Dan's first question was still pending, but now he really wanted to know the answer. Maybe it would help him understand. "Well, is there anything or anyone you love so much that you'd give up your life rather than see it destroyed?" She was trying to force a smile, no doubt weighing the evidence. Was this GI out of his mind or just having a little fun with her? He knew it wasn't fair to use the girl like this. "Never mind. I'm not trying to scare you. I have a friend about your age. I'm just trying to figure out some things. You're a very beautiful girl."

The last comment seemed to settle her. "I can show you the nightlife in Sapporo, Dan-san. It is still early."

Not so long ago he would have jumped on the invitation. He drained the last of his drink and plunked the empty glass on the table in a gesture of finality. "Thank you, Akiko," he said. "I've enjoyed your company, but I must be up and out early in the morning and I have a very important phone call to make. Good night." He smiled, turned, and walked out of the bar.

10:50 p.m.

Chung stepped into the street and inhaled the cold, night air. He found it a welcome relief from the stuffy, second floor apartment. The lack of wind and clear Sapporo sky, he noticed, were in stark contrast to the harsh environs of Wakkanai. The music from the bar directly below the safe house had been grating on his nerves, not to mention the effect of being cooped up with Fu and the girl. He would stretch his five-minute walk to the phone box into ten, and organize his thoughts in preparation for the scheduled check-in with his section head in Seoul, Lee Hyun Min.

Lee had never been a field agent, but as Section Chief, held the fast track position to Assistant Director. His primary qualification for the job was his marriage to Park Jung Hee's favorite first cousin.

Chung and Lee had once been fast friends, having graduated from the same American CIA training class at The Farm, not far from Washington D.C. Soon afterward their career paths parted onto separate tracks, Lee's having proved much the faster of the two.

Chung could see the lights of the big festival in the distance as he moved closer to the town center. He had always considered himself brighter than Lee, with far superior analytical skills, and harbored deep resentment over his friend's meteoric rise through the ranks. But Lee had remained loyal enough to his old friend by keeping him inside the section, rewarding him with promotions and dropping the most high profile assignments into his lap. All in all, Chung figured, he didn't have much to complain about, but would be ever vigilant for his chance to trump the opportunistic Lee.

The streets were teeming with people this close to the park, but he found the phone box empty. It took several minutes for the proper code checks before Lee's voice came onto the line. "This is Saki," he said in bad Japanese. "It's good to talk to you." Saki was the section chief's code name in the operation.

"Yes, this is Suki," said Chung. "I report that our vacation is proceeding very well. We have identified our cousin and she's with us now in the big city."

"That's good, Suki-san, but what is your intention?"

It seemed an odd question. "We'll secure the gift you want most, but we might need to trade something for it."

"Suki-san, listen very carefully. You will make very certain that no harm comes to our cousin. Do you understand me?"

Chung seethed so badly that he could not force himself to reply. His agency routinely deferred to the Americans like servants. The real insult for Chung was that Lee felt it necessary to conceal the phone call from his masters on the other side of the Pacific.

"Did you understand me? Confirm that you understand me."

Chung had no choice. Direct insubordination was out of the question. But there were other ways. "I understand, Saki-san, but may I ask why? Our cousin may become very dangerous to us."

"We don't want our neighbor's family to become aware of our plans. This is most important to us. If you discipline our cousin in any way, many questions will be raised. This will be very bad for our family. Our cousin is no longer important if we have the gift in our pos-

session. She must go home safely. Do you understand me?"
Chung knew precisely how to handle this. "Yes. I understand."
"Good. Then report on your next schedule when you have the gift."

The walk back to the safe house had taken only five minutes, he noted, and was not nearly so peaceful. He decided to keep moving until his temper subsided. The conversation with Lee Hyun Min had left him feeling decidedly disturbed and suspicious. The boss had seemed almost disinterested in his progress report, focusing instead on Chung's plans for the troublemaking whore tied up in the safe house. Lee Hyun's cryptic, but unambiguous order not to harm the girl under any circumstances was an ominous signal.

He carefully examined Lee Hyun's logic that another dead or missing person in connection with this affair would unnecessarily increase the risk of exposure, and found it flawed. Lee's reasoning was merely a prepared attempt to justify a questionable directive, and Chung found the device insulting. The girl's life was now irrelevant to the mission, he knew. Its success or failure was entirely collateral to her fate.

He turned off the quiet street onto a narrow, winding lane of seedy bars and neon lights, nearly void of pedestrian traffic. In truth, Chung reasoned, the disappearance of this Su Li Young, an unwelcome spawn of Japan, would hardly raise a ripple on the ocean. On the contrary, killing her was the logical thing to do. True, she was now powerless to interfere with the completion of Chung's mission, but her continued existence presented an undeniable long-term threat. Whatever his government's reasons for suppressing the status of the Sakhalin Koreans, this girl would never stop fighting against it for as long as she lived. That much was clear. If Chung did not seize the opportunity to shut her up now, his government would regret it later.

Across the street, he saw two decidedly underdressed bar girls trudging determinedly through the snow in high heels and around a building, as if being late for such work mattered.

Surely Lee Hyun Min and the higher ups at the Korean CIA knew these things about Su Li Young, Chung thought. Then why would they give a shit whether or not he disposed of the girl? He knew the answer to that question was the cause of his uneasiness. In the world of espionage and counter-espionage, he had come to know, only a very few at the top were privy to the whole picture.

He turned right again. The lights dimmed and Chung found himself nearly back where he had started. The street of small shops and apartments would lead right to the safe house.

Lee Hyun Min, he figured, might have even believed that bullshit about risking exposure. After all, Chung's boss was a professional desk jockey, whereas Chung's battle-tested instincts warned him to beware, for there might be another game afoot.

Of one thing Chung was certain, as he neared the bar beneath the safe house for his rendezvous with Foster: He had to get his hands on Subarov's collection. That was still the key, even if his own government had betrayed him by taking out an insurance policy against his failure.

With those documents actually in his possession, any reason, however clandestine, for keeping the girl alive, would evaporate. Any number of things could go wrong during an exchange, resulting in an unfortunate death, and who could blame him for an accident?

For Chung, possession of the collection was now the key to his survival, but somehow, it was no longer enough. Despite the overwhelming logic of his position, killing the girl was something Chung needed to do—for himself.

He entered the bar and spotted the overstuffed American, on a stool, facing the door, nursing a beer. Chung was prepared to deal with Foster, but the drunken car salesman at the microphone, belting out an intolerably offensive rendition of "Moon River," was more than anyone should have to bear.

THIRTY-ONE

**She's a little old for me, but I sure like her style.
Maybe she can keep us alive for a while.**

Tuesday, 9:00 a.m.

Dan put down the phone and looked at his watch. The call from Sinead McNally in the lobby had come precisely at nine a.m. as agreed. He opened the door and waited for her to step off the elevator. She appeared in a snappy, blue business suit, her hair up and the long coat draped neatly over her arm. Her slightly worn, blue eyes were still bright and eager, giving him the overall impression of someone arriving for a job interview. It pleased and reassured him.

He greeted her with a hug and a kiss on the cheek, both of which she returned warmly. He had only met with her once, but had come away feeling she was a person of peculiar knowledge and ability—and someone he could trust. "Thank you for coming, Miss McNally," he said. "I know my request was a bit unusual. Come in."

She laughed. "Everything about you is a bit unusual, Mr. Matthews. You may drop the 'Miss McNally' and call me Sinead, and I confess you left me with a curious itch after our last conversation. I knew to my soul you were mixed up in something about the Sakhalin Koreans, but for the life of me, I couldn't imagine what. Have you now come to enlighten me?"

"I have, indeed, Sinead," he replied, falling momentarily into her rhythmic style of speech. He went to the bed and retrieved the three shopping bags, placing them one by one on top of the rumpled bed covers. "I'm going to tell you a story and it will take a while. Have you had breakfast?"

"Not yet, I'm afraid."

He was near starved himself. "Good. We'll order room service, and by the way, you can call me Dan."

"Very well, Dan, and breakfast will be courtesy of the Red Cross petty cash fund," she added, smiling.

Dan looked at his watch and realized Sinead had listened to his rambling for nearly an hour, never once interrupting him with a question. "So what do you think?" he asked.

She looked up from the small table and said, "May I see the things?"

"Of course," he replied. "They're all right here. Help yourself. Do you read Korean?"

"Quite well," she answered, settling onto the edge of the bed. She reached gingerly into the first bag, as though extracting some uniquely valuable archeological find.

Dan moved back to the chair and watched as Sinead examined the contents of the many envelopes and packets there on the bed, slowly and methodically, carefully returning each batch to its package as if it had never been disturbed. He could read the impact of the old things in her face, like a slide show of reactions, each letter or old picture triggering a fresh display of raw human emotion. Such was the power of this terrible bundle entrusted to him.

Through Sinead's face, he struggled to understand the real value of these old things to Su Li and her people, for keeping them would likely be a death sentence to Su Li Young. He might second-guess that choice to his last breath, but that was clearly her choice. He could endure the consequences if he could just understand why she would prefer a lonely, unnecessary death to a long, happy life with him.

If he chose to make the trade, he might yet save her life, thereby leaving her cherished cause unattained and beyond reach, maybe forever. But she might survive, still young and altruistic enough to embrace the old cause in a new way. If she died, then the best hope of the Sakhalin Koreans died with her.

Whatever his decision, Dan had banished his own selfish concerns from the equation. Either way, Su Li Young, this most precious and beautiful of human souls, would be lost to Dan Matthews forever, because she would either be dead or would never forgive him for trading away her dream and the sum of her life's work.

Finally, Sinead turned to him. "What is it you want from me then?"

"I honestly don't know," he said. "I guess if I can't help Su Li, I still might give her dream a happy ending, if that's possible. I have these things and Su Li wants someone to use them to help those people on Sakhalin."

"And you think I might find a way to use them to help the Koreans on Sakhalin?"

"Yes. That's it, assuming I can't get her back."

Sinead walked over to the chair and touched his shoulder gently. "I see your dilemma clearly, Daniel. You love the girl. 'Tis as plain as the nose on your face."

"More than I ever thought possible," he answered. "The thing is, if we make those things public now, she'll die for certain."

Sinead eased onto the chair across from him, bringing the two eye to eye. "Sure I have no experience in such matters, Daniel, and I don't want to add to your burdens, but have you considered these fellows will likely kill her even if you attempt a trade?"

She'd gone directly to the heart of it. Part of him had known it all along, but the bigger part couldn't face it. He could never give up hope of saving her, but maybe the only sure way to save any part of her was to put those old letters and pictures to good use. That Korean would never let her go alive so long as he had the choice. "Of course I have. If I thought trading them would save her for sure, I'd gift wrap the fucking things for the Koreans. But if she dies, we can't lose this collection. It's all that's left of her."

"I think you've made your choice then."

"That's the point, Sinead. The choice isn't mine to make. It's hers and she's already made it, but I just can't live with it. I'll play it by ear and do what I have to to save her, but I promise you I won't lose Su Li and her collection. If this goes badly I want you to find a way to use these things as she would have. The only thing I could do is take them directly to one of the major news organizations and hope for the best.

There must be a better way."

"If it comes to that, I'll try with all the resources at my command," she assured him. "I hope we won't need to go directly to the papers. I doubt you could get near any of the major news bureaus anyway. Even if you did, those things wouldn't have the same impact coming from you, an American with some half-baked story about a Russian fisherman and his private network of spies. If by some miracle someone believed you, they'd play it as a big, explosive headline and the story would die in a week. "

He'd already figured that out, but was short of options. "It may come to that anyway."

The near corner of her mouth formed a mischievous twist. "I have an idea."

"Let's hear it. I'm light on ideas right now."

"Stall them a couple of days if you're able. Let me try to arrange something now with the things, something in the way of a backup plan."

Dan had no clue where this was going, and she wasn't about to tell him, but he shuddered at the thought of where he'd be now without this woman's help. "That's interesting. Is it actually possible you could make some kind of deal with the people behind this mess?"

She shrugged. "I'm willing to try. What they want is to keep this entire nasty secret under wraps, just as it's been for fifty years. I might be able to make your trade at the diplomatic level and save some bloodshed, maybe even yours and Su Li's."

"I like it."

"And possibly even help those two hundred old people sitting in Japanese jails."

"That would mean a lot to Su Li," he said, "even if she never talks to me again. Can you do it?"

"If there's a way, we'll find one. It's better to make a deal while we're holding the cards, as the Americans say, rather than to just release the collection in our own home-styled, public relations campaign."

Dan felt himself slump in the chair. "If it comes to that, Su Li will already be dead."

"I'm afraid so, and the governments involved would all go into damage control mode. They'd claim the entire collection is a pile of forgeries. You wouldn't find a trace of the two hundred they arrested.

The Japanese would probably send them quietly back to Korea, but it wouldn't be the repatriation Su Li hoped for. Their lives would be even more miserable than before."

It was all too difficult to accept. "But if the world press grabbed hold of the story—"

"I told you, the world press wouldn't give a piss about the story because they'd have been scooped by the New York Times, or whoever."

If he was going to trust her, there was no reason to hold back. "All right then. Let's do it your way, Sinead."

Sinead reached across the table and touched his arm gently. "This is still a longshot, Daniel, and I may not be able to help Su Li, not in the way you want, but whatever happens, I'll do my damnedest to give her dream a happy ending."

He liked the way she called him Daniel. There was a message in it, he thought. He wasn't sure how it translated, but it came with a deep commitment. He said, "Then I'll stall and hope for the best. Tell me: Why are they all so afraid of a bunch of old photographs and letters? I know they're important evidence, but they're only letters and pictures, not worth killing for."

"I think I can explain. Have you heard of Anne Frank?"

"Sure. Every kid learns about *The Diary of Anne Frank* in school."

"Well, imagine a thousand Anne Franks, each with a diary. Then imagine a few of them might still be alive, each able to read her own diary to the world and answer the questions of a hungry world press. Can you see the impact of such evidence on world opinion? I'm not just talking about the Sakhalin Koreans. I'm talking about every oppressed and persecuted race and ethnic group in the entire world."

This was all a part of Dan's education. "When you put it that way, yes. That would make sense if it were the Japanese, or even the Soviets, trying so desperately to obtain these things, but it's not. It's the South Koreans, and that doesn't make any sense."

"It makes more sense than you know," Sinead countered. "As a representative of the Red Cross, I'm not supposed to express political opinions, but I hold some very strong ones. Do you remember when I explained how some people believe Park Jung Hee is a puppet of the Japanese?"

"Of course."

"Well, it's not just some people who believe it. I believe it myself very strongly."

The inference was nearly too fantastic to even consider. "You're not suggesting this has been a Japanese operation all along, are you?"

Sinead rose from the chair and walked over to the window, as if considering whether to answer. With her back turned to him and her eyes upon the white city, she said, "That's exactly what I'm suggesting. I have believed for years that the Japanese government has been using the Korean CIA as its proxy agency to carry out politically sensitive and controversial operations to cover up wartime atrocities. The comfort women are a perfect example."

Dan wheeled in the chair. There was so much about these people he'd never know. "What are the comfort women?"

She turned back to face him, though he could see only her outline before the bright, morning sun. "'Tis a group of Korean women I've been working with. They call themselves that. There were several hundred of them at one time. They were kidnapped by Japanese authorities during the war and placed forcibly in government-run brothels. The brothels were intended to raise the morale of Japanese troops."

"Jesus Christ," Dan said, "why haven't I heard about that?"

"The same reason you haven't heard about the Sakhalin Koreans before now. The South Korean government refuses to press their claim with the Japanese. As a matter of fact, South Korea has actively suppressed the voices of these women and threatened them with reprisal if they persist."

"A few weeks ago, I would have dismissed a story like that as horse shit," he said, "but now it just sounds like business as usual."

"Money will buy almost anything."

True enough. For it would take the wealth of nations to insure Su Li's safety. "So, you're saying the Japanese use the Korean CIA as a kind of private contractor to do their dirty work?"

"Exactly, but only a very senior group of high government officials. One will never find written evidence of such matters. They will go to any length to protect the so-called honor of Japan."

He was becoming better educated every minute. "That would explain Tanaka."

"The Japanese policeman you spoke of?"

"Yes. I was right on target about him. He was warned off this case. I don't think he had a clue why. Somebody told him to be a good soldier and bury the whole thing."

"Does that surprise you?" she asked.

"You mean does it surprise me he just followed that order blindly?"

"Yes."

The ringing startled him. He stared at the phone on the nightstand, but didn't move. "Nobody knows I'm here." The phone rang…three…four times.

"Maybe it's the front desk," Sinead said.

Dan frowned. "Maybe." Then the ringing began again. "You answer it."

Sinead reached for the receiver. "Hello?" Five seconds passed. "Hello?" Slowly, she replaced the receiver onto the phone as if it were filled with nitro. "The line was open. Someone was there but wouldn't answer."

"Great," said Dan, reaching for the three shopping bags. "There are only two ways out—the elevator and the staircase. It doesn't look good, but we'll have to face the music."

"They might not know you're here," she reasoned, reaching for her coat. "Whoever it is might be calling all the rooms occupied by young Western men. My voice might have thrown them off."

"Or tipped them off," he countered. "Let's get out of here."

They hurried down the eighth-floor hallway toward the elevator. As they passed the bank of three doors, Dan said, "Keep moving. We'll take the stairs."

They ducked through the door marked "Emergency Exit" in English and headed down the dimly lit stairwell. Dan grabbed Sinead's arm. "Walk slowly and quietly. Listen for other people in the stairwell. We may have to duck onto another floor and play a little cat and mouse."

"Who do you think it is?" she whispered.

"I wouldn't venture to guess. My own government has been involved in all kinds of shady business over the years, but it's difficult to imagine something like this. Whatever your political views, even you would have trouble believing President Nixon would ever do something so patently immoral."

The staircase was still deadly quiet as they reached the fifth floor. "So the Koreans themselves have no real national policy, misguided or not, against the repatriation of the Sakhalin Koreans?" he asked.

"When you talk about South Korea, you are talking about Park

Jung Hee," Sinead explained, "and he couldn't care less what happens to the Sakhalin Koreans either way."

"I don't understand that. Those are his own people. They were essentially kidnapped by an invading power. Doesn't he understand that?"

"That fact is irrelevant to him, as are the people. Park Jung Hee has always wanted to be Japanese anyway. He would have the world believe the group has been contaminated with thousands of Soviet spies, but that's only a cover story to explain why he's never spoken up for those poor souls. In truth, he's been under orders from his Japanese masters for years to oppose their repatriation and keep them quietly on Sakhalin."

They reached the third floor landing and still not a sound, save the echo of their own whispered conversation. "Then the Japanese know everything that's been going on," he suggested.

"Oh, probably not. That's the beauty of it. They don't want to know. These agreements are made only in personal conversations at the very highest levels. I'm certain even the Prefectural Police who arrested those two hundred Sakhalin Koreans still have no idea what's going on. They think they have some ordinary, illegal immigrants."

"If what you're saying is true," Dan said, "I'm surprised our Korean CIA adversary made that move. He risked directly involving the Japanese, thereby exposing their complicity."

"You're quite correct, but keep in mind he has no idea about the true arrangement. He thinks he's keeping Soviet spies out of South Korea."

"It's all pretty disgusting," he said. "Three good people died to bring this story to light, and Su Li's chances are looking pretty slim. We have to make their deaths mean something."

She stopped, turning to face him on the second floor landing. "We have a shot. At least we know the players, and I believe I've learned something about the game over these last twenty years."

He smiled. "Is that what you called practical political reality?"

"You are a very quick study, Daniel. I'll need a few days to make some unofficial high-level contacts, but I can't promise anything."

"I can't give you three. I can give you two. Look, I'm no diplomat, but how would you get four governments to solve a thirty-year-old problem in two days anyway?"

As they reached the first floor exit, she smiled. "The rules, Daniel.

Will you trust me with these things for the next two days?"

"That's why I came here," he answered, handing her the three precious bags. "I have to trust somebody and you're it."

As he reached for the doorknob, she held her palm against the door. "We don't know what's on the other side of that door," she said, "but there's one thing you need to be clear about."

"What?"

"If I can find a way, and you decide to use the documents to help the Sakhalin Koreans, Su Li's safe return may not come with the package. On that score, you may be left to your own devices."

"If that's the way it plays out," he replied, "I'll go it on my own. But Su Li's captors must believe I still have the collection with me. As long as they believe that, they'll keep Su Li alive. I don't even know if we'll make it out of this hotel, but remember that, Sinead. Whatever deal you can make, the governments must understand that, for the moment at least, the collection is still in my control."

"Don't worry," she said. "As far as the governments will know, I have only a few samples, with the possibility of obtaining the entire lot before you release it to the media."

"Good," he said. "If we get away, I'll call you in forty-eight hours. If you don't hear from me by then, I want you to use these things in the best way you can to help those people."

"Of course I will."

"And Sinead," he added, "On the chance I actually have to trade the collection, I need to know you'll be ready and able to give it back to me on a moment's notice."

Sinead removed her hand from the door and stepped aside. "You have my word."

THIRTY-TWO

**Some guys can shrug and get over a slight,
but others can't shake it until there's a fight.**

Tuesday, 9:45 a.m.

Dan cracked the door barely enough for the light to pass, but sufficiently to dampen his hopes. He thought he should have hung that fedora out to dry on a fish rack somewhere rather than leave it in the backseat of the unmarked, police Toyota. Tanaka had gotten the overcoat back as well and was obviously out to avenge his humiliation and the theft of his prized possessions.

Gently, he closed the door and turned back to Sinead. "It's the Japanese cop from Wakkanai." You'd never find a Detroit cop looking for you on a Chicago street, but here it was different. The police were national, so a detective from Wakkanai might pop up anywhere on Hokkaido working his case. This time Tanaka wasn't working the Ishikawa case. This time it was personal, he figured, and the man had Dan Matthews directly in the crosshairs.

Tanaka was across from the stairwell, maybe as close as forty feet, talking to the desk clerk, a photograph in hand. He could only have gotten Dan's picture from the Air Force. The clerk on duty hadn't seen Dan's face, so it was a fair bet Tanaka was just checking out a group of suspects with Western names, probably men traveling alone.

"What's he doing?" Sinead asked.

"He's asking questions about me, right over there at the front desk."

"Jesus, Mary, and Joseph," she said, "how did he find you here?"

"I have no idea. Maybe he's just a good detective, or I made a stupid choice. What better place to look for an American in Sapporo than a Western hotel?"

Dan peeled back the door again, almost imperceptibly. "Oh, shit," he said, "he's coming this way."

Tanaka was walking directly toward the staircase, on a straight path between Dan and the front door. He was trapped. His best chance, it appeared, was to catch Tanaka by surprise, but it seemed a slim one. He was already within the detective's line of sight, and he'd be dead meat the second Tanaka opened the door.

Then he heard Sinead whisper, "You'll need to carry all three shopping bags, Daniel. Wait for me in front of the American Consulate. Do you remember where it is?"

"Sure," he replied, "but—"

"Just shut up now and watch for your opportunity. 'Tis the last place they'll expect you to be loitering."

He was about to ask what she was thinking, when she brushed him aside and opened the door. She was already in the lobby and running berserk across Tanaka's path and to his right, hysterically screaming something in Japanese, while pointing down the hallway past the elevators. Everyone in the parlor-sized lobby began to run or move for cover. Tanaka reached across and grabbed her by the arm as she streaked by. He was trying to calm her down.

She fought to escape Tanaka's grasp, all the while pointing and yelling. Dan could see she was pointing to the women's bathroom down the hall. He sensed his moment.

Tanaka released his grip and bolted past the elevators without so much as a glance and down the hall, followed closely by a couple of burly hotel security men. Scooping up the three bags, Dan shuffled quickly toward the exit, head low. He dared not look for Sinead, but caught a glimpse of her engaging two well-dressed hotel types beyond the desk.

He hit the street wishing it were ten p.m. instead of ten a.m. A little darkness would have come in handy. Sinead's performance had done the trick, for now at least. But Tanaka would likely not be dissuaded. He'd get suspicious eventually and would intensify his efforts. Within an hour he'd find the right clerk, show him the photo and be hot on Dan's trail again.

Tanaka's hard-on for Dan was a big break for Foster and the Korean, he figured. In his unswerving devotion to the Rising Sun, not to mention his own bruised ego, Tanaka would do their dirty work and be none the wiser for the experience. Pulling this off would be near impossible anyway. Doing it while dodging the Japanese police —well, he didn't want to think about it now.

As he head up whatever the hell street it was, three shopping bags in hand, Dan considered the significance of this latest development. With Tanaka breathing up his ass, he couldn't give Sinead forty-eight hours. It would all have to play out tonight without Sinead's help, the old-fashioned way.

He looked up through the seven-foot, wrought iron fence and thought, yes, the place reminded him of The Alamo, not so much the likeness of the two structures as the images they cast.

He'd seen The Alamo in San Antonio, not in Davy Crockett's day, of course, but during boot camp seven or eight years ago. He'd been struck by the way the façade of the ancient relic stood face-to-face against the concrete, urban landscape, almost like a barrier set down in the main street, daring the Twentieth Century to beach its walls. It was a stubborn reminder of San Antonio's past, good and bad, and in a way America's.

This building, although architecturally distinct, projected its own twist on the message. It hinted of Spanish colonial influence. Like The Alamo, it sat perpendicular to the main street at a T-junction, staring down the throat of the new Sapporo, but strangely out of place. It was pure white stucco and in considerable disrepair, with two tall columns standing guard at the front entrance beyond the high, black fence. To the eagle-eyed observer, the American flag atop the rounded roof might be visible for miles. The message it conveyed, Dan thought, couldn't possibly engender affection from Japanese passersby. Ironically, the entire picture seemed to fit his situation like a glove.

He spotted Sinead behind the wheel of a white car as it came to a stop beside him. To his surprise, she was smiling, although her hair and clothing gave no indication of a pleasant experience. "Get in,

Daniel," she said, motioning to the passenger's seat.

Her smile proved infectious, and that too surprised him. "I can't believe I'm smiling," he said. "Was there anything funny about what just happened?"

She pulled away before he'd even closed the door. "I suppose 'tis a question of perspective. I've read all the James Bond novels, you know. As a child in Ireland I always wanted to be a spy like Humphrey Bogart in *The Maltese Falcon*." Dan didn't have the heart or the energy to correct her. "Ah, but sure we have no spies in Ireland, not since England won the war against Germany anyway."

"I think you'd make a wonderful spy, Sinead," he said. "Now will you tell me what just happened?"

"I told them there was a fellow in the ladies' loo waving his pecker at the girls. T'was the only thing I could think of at the time."

Humor aside, Dan knew it was a badly needed stroke of luck when he'd stumbled blindly into the International Red Cross office that day looking for information. "All right," he said, "so now what? This Tanaka is like a bloodhound. I can't stall this for two days. It has to be now or never."

Sinead turned her eyes from the road, startled. "But Daniel, I can't help you if you do that. I don't even have time to copy these records. What will you do?"

"I have to think, but first I need a place to operate from. I can't very well go back to the Royal." They were heading west, he noticed, toward the outskirts of the city. "Hey, where are we going anyway?"

She smiled. "You'll see in a minute. I think I know the perfect place. Rest your eyes now."

She drove through the honeycomb-like streets of Sapporo, all teeming with people about the business of living, until she came to a whitewashed, cinder block wall in the middle of a densely packed, low-rise, residential street. "This is where I live," she said.

He didn't see a house. "Where?"

She laughed. "It suits my shy personality. You can't see it from this side of the wall. Come."

She parked along the wall and they entered the property through a narrow, iron gate. Inside, he saw a small, single-story house, dwarfed and nearly obscured by a breathtakingly beautiful garden under a glass ceiling. Inside the hidden greenhouse, they crossed a hand-laid, stone bridge over a pond. Richly colored vegetation surrounded them amidst the soothing sound of falling water against rock. The humidity and lush smell of vegetation made Dan think immediately of Vietnam. "Wow," he said, "you've become quite at home here, I'd say."

She laughed again, but this time he detected a note of irony in it, maybe even something else. "The garden was here when I rented the old house," she explained. "But it was a complete disaster back then. I've made it my hobby, you might say."

"More than that by the looks of it."

"'Tis all I have to occupy my mind these days. I do have a husband, but he's abroad in the diplomatic service. We don't see each other very often now."

Dan thought it best not to pursue the subject. "Well, your garden is beautiful."

Sinead stopped on the front porch, before the solid-wood front door and turned to face him. The blue eyes seemed to grow heavy with sadness. "Thank you. I take great pride in it. It's become a part of me, I suppose. But there was a time in my life I'd hoped for other things, the things you and Su Li might yet enjoy."

The comment had caught him flat-footed. Sinead had just opened a window into herself and allowed him a quick glimpse of the interior. He was unaccustomed to such acts of unselfishness, but not ungrateful. "Thank you, Sinead," was all he could manage.

"Well," she said, leading him through the doorway into the foyer, "that's it then. You'll stay here. You may use the telephone. By the time Tanaka makes the link between us this affair will be long ended."

They both removed their boots and arranged them carefully outside the interior, sliding door. "This will work, Sinead," he said, surveying the comfortable space. "This will work just fine. I'll call Su Li's mother right away and tell her what's going on. She may need a way to contact me."

She was gone ahead of him now, into the main part of the house. "Now Daniel," he heard her say, "whatever will you do about the collection?"

He couldn't see her, but by the sound of dishes and clanging pots, she was in the kitchen, probably making tea. He saw the plush leather chair, out of place amidst the oriental motif, and dropped his tired body into its folds. "Well," he replied, "They're not going to let her go when they get their hands on it. I'm convinced they plan to kill her anyway, so I was hoping to find a way to get her out without giving up the collection. I'd like to have a backup plan in place for the collection in case it goes badly."

"And?"

"I was going to leave you somewhere safely out of sight with the collection. That way, if Su Li doesn't make it, this wouldn't have all been in vain. You could use those things to finish her work. We don't know if that's even a possibility, and the collection might help save her life. I'll have to take it with me. It's all or nothing."

She reappeared and sat on the mat beside him. "Then you'll let it go to the Koreans, if that's what it takes?"

"If that's what it takes. Now I have to call Foster's hotel and leave a message. We'll do it tonight."

"Where?"

Dan smiled. "I found a place that just might give us a chance."

3:40 p.m.

Chung was developing an intense distain for this bar, but it seemed almost tolerable in the afternoon. He chose a strategically located stool. "Beer," he said to the bartender, and turned to see Foster's ample frame in the doorway.

The American took the stool beside him. Chung was tiring of small talk and banter with this ignorant NSA man. "May I assume Matthews has contacted you?"

"Yes," Foster replied. The American had stashed his sarcasm and bravado, replacing it with a subtle aura of hostility. "I'm to meet him at Odori Park at ten o'clock tonight. When he has proof the girl is alive and well, he'll retrieve the collection. It won't be far away. We'll do the exchange right there in the park."

"Good. He's in a hurry and might be panicky. That could work to our advantage."

The bartender strolled into view and stood directly in front of Foster, wearing an unmistakable frown. He spoke in Japanese. "This isn't the public library. Order a drink or hit the road."

Foster looked at Chung and said, "What's his problem? He doesn't sound very friendly. Do you know what he said?"

Chung fought to suppress the laughter. "I think this man may have had a cousin at Hiroshima in 1945. Perhaps we should finish our conversation outside."

As they reached the door, Foster said, "I should tell you, I've made sure the Japanese detective gets periodic updates of information. He's very tenacious and determined to close the door on our Agent Matthews."

Chung was irate at the disclosure. "What? The Japanese are to have no knowledge of this operation."

Foster motioned like he was going to pat Chung on the back, but stopped short of contact. Fortunate for him. "Relax, Chung. Tanaka has no clue and couldn't care less. He's a company man; would have made a great kamikaze during the war. We're just putting his personal vendetta against Matthews to good use; in fact, we almost got lucky. He damn near grabbed Matthews at the Royal Hotel this morning."

It was a brilliant tactical adjustment, Chung thought, and this American fool had no doubt stumbled upon it blindly. "Good," he said. "We've pushed up his timetable and knocked him off balance."

"Exactly," Foster said. "It should be a simple matter now."

Chung didn't even try to suppress the condescending smile.

THIRTY-THREE

You'll kill me or I'll kill you,
then have that cake and eat it too.

Tuesday, 9:50 p.m.

Dan arrived at the meeting place with ten minutes to spare. The park was crowded by any standard, with tourists from all over the globe lazily gawking at the myriad snow and ice sculptures while enjoying the local cuisine from the open-air food stands. Despite his dire situation, Dan couldn't help but marvel at the intricate detail of the illuminated, crystalline White House, right there in Odori Park, not fifty feet away from his seat on the stone bench.

He judged this White House to be one-quarter scale, although he had never actually seen the real thing up close. Such was the power and artisanship of this magnificent illusion that he could almost envision President Nixon sitting behind his desk in the Oval Office, just beyond the three frosted windows on the second floor.

What would a psychologist make about his choice of locations? he wondered. It was as good as any other public place, but he couldn't deny the added sense of irony. A few weeks ago he'd have seen this mock White House as rich in symbolism, maybe even sacred ground. Now it was just a white house made of water, a reminder of how complex and uncaring the world had become. Only the presence of the full-scale Japanese flag, flying opposite the Stars and Stripes and flanking the great pillars like an oversized left bookend, pulled him back from the illusion to the grim business at hand.

Dan leaned against the iron fence in the cold to await commencement of the festivities. He knew going to the newspapers with the collection wasn't an option. He'd given a lot of thought to that over the last two days. His country might be justified in calling him a traitor if he did anything to expose the South Korean agents on Sakhalin. Even if he left out the part about the Korean CIA, reporters might find a way to piece it all together. Some lines can never be crossed, he thought. He'd have to trade the collection for Su Li's freedom, or accept her death and let Sinead implement the compromise solution.

There was never really any decision to make. A part of him had known that since they snatched Su Li at the train station. He could never let her die if it was within his power to save her. He loved her more than he had ever loved. There was no denying it. But his decision to give up the collection fostered no guilt because there was another reason she couldn't die.

He spotted a man in a long, brown overcoat studying the exhibit from the opposite side. Or was he studying Dan? There was simply no way to know at this point. He'd keep an eye on him.

Whether Su Li understood it or not, her single-minded devotion to their cause was worth more to the Sakhalin Koreans than ten barrels full of evidence. She might never see it that way, but Dan believed it and the people she helped believed it too. Those poor souls would suffer a far greater loss with the death of Su Li Young than with the loss of Subarov's collection.

Despite the high stakes and desperate odds, Dan had never felt more alert and exhilarated. This was a game far beyond the scope of his experience. Still, he seemed to have a kind of knack for it, like a kid who just sits down at a piano one day and starts playing Bach. He noticed that the man in the brown overcoat had moved off.

He wondered if Sinead McNally's involvement in this business had filtered down to Foster. Once Tanaka started making inquiries, the cat would be out of the bag, and NSA had ears everywhere. He and Su Li had chosen this path, but Sinead might become an unwitting casualty.

Try as he might, Dan still had no idea what Foster really thought about all this or how far he was prepared to go to help the Korean CIA.

Was he prepared to kill? It would be easier reading a Japanese comic book, but he had to find out.

Foster's primary mission was protecting the flow of human intelligence from Sakhalin Island and the Soviet Far East. Dan understood his own government couldn't care less about the Sakhalin Koreans, one way or the other. Were they prepared to turn a blind eye while the Koreans continued their killing spree on Japanese soil?

Whatever else, Foster was a professional with no ax to grind beyond a little lump on the head. The NSA man knew enough about this business to see clearly that Dan and Su Li were innocents caught in a web of politics. He hoped that knowledge might reduce the odds a bit for him in the event things got really nasty. Foster wasn't about to be his buddy, but there was no reason why the guy should go out of his way to help these two Koreans kill him or Su Li. Dan liked his odds better if he could somehow neutralize Foster as an adversary. He also knew he might just be reaching for rainbows.

The NSA man was a minute late, too soon to start worrying. It should come as no surprise, Dan thought, but the Americans were using the Korean CIA in exactly the same way the Japanese did. The quid pro quo could encompass a long list, indeed, when one considered the degree to which the ROK depended upon the United States for its security. It might be anything from fighter jets to cold cash.

By all appearances, Park Jung Hee operated his CIA like a private, clandestine army for hire, not only to the Japanese, but to any Western government willing to pay the price. As a private army, the Korean CIA was a perfect vehicle. There was probably no line it would not cross in terms of illegal operations, like assassinations and high-level blackmail. Like the Japanese, the arrangement gave the Americans credible deniability.

He spotted Foster heading deliberately in his direction from the north end of the park. Among the festively clad tourists, Foster stood out, looking exactly like an overweight secret agent on his way to a clandestine rendezvous. The NSA man was hatless in the cold, with the collar of his long, gray, coat turned up around the back of his neck.

Foster sat down on the bench behind and Dan did not acknowledge his presence in any way. "I like it better when I can see you from a ways off," Foster said. "Finding you hiding behind doors is a bit too painful for my taste."

Dan walked slowly over to the bench and sat. "Let's get it done.

Where's the girl?"

"Not so fast," Foster cautioned. "You didn't really think you were going to call all the shots. Did you?"

He didn't, but he intended to call as many as possible. "I did, actually, Foster, but I'm a realist. Who calls what shots depends on who wants what the most. Doesn't it?"

"My Korean friend is here," Foster said. "He's watching us now. I'm afraid he won't bring the girl here until you bring the collection, and he's convinced it's the genuine article."

"Let's not kid ourselves. Whoever he is, he's out of control, and he's counting on the fact that I have no experience in these matters."

Foster chuckled. "Well, he does have a point there, I'm afraid."

"So where do you stand, Foster? How far will you go? Will you help him murder the girl, even if he gets his fucking prize?"

Foster smiled. "You surprise me. I stand squarely on the side of liberty, as always." Then the smirk disappeared from the man's face and Dan was looking at the face of a government agent, a real one, on a mission. "Look, you've stirred up a real hornet's nest, but you know very well what I care about. I care about the Soviets learning what you know about certain operations on Sakhalin."

"I'm not a traitor."

"Not yet, but you're closer than you know. It's incredible that you still have a way out of this, but you do. I don't give a fuck if you cut this Korean's balls off and feed them to the sea gulls. I can't stand the guy. For that matter, I don't care if you do it to each other. I just need to know this thing won't spin out of control; so let's try and get this exchange done without anyone getting hurt. Nobody wants you going off half-cocked with those items you have."

This was the opening Dan had been waiting for. "And what if I've changed my mind about making the exchange?"

"What is that supposed to mean?"

It was time for Dan to try a little character assessment. "It can't surprise you to learn the girl doesn't want me to exchange the collection for her life."

"Don't think you're going to hang around here and just waltz away with the girl and the collection unscathed. You're way out of your league, here, Matthews. This Korean is ruthless. He'll cut you to ribbons and have a good time doing it."

On that score Foster was probably right, but it was precisely what

Dan intended. Now see which way he'll break when the shooting starts. "Look, I'm perfectly willing to give up those things if it'll save her. Just tell me if I'm pissing up a rope."

Foster hesitated. It was a good sign. "I don't know. What the hell. I'll tell you this much. If the trade goes bad, you'll kill him or he'll kill you. Considering the lump on my head, I don't give a fuck either way. If I had to make a bet, I'd say I don't like your chances. The Korean has a young protégé with him, very tough. The second you give those things to the Korean, or to me, my job is done."

It was the answer Dan needed. "That's all I can ask for."

"You know, Matthews, you have a real talent for this cloak and dagger stuff. I prefer a desk myself, but I wasn't born yesterday. I said I wish you well, but don't confuse that with warm and fuzzy feelings. I just have a problem with helping to kill my own countrymen, no matter who they are. Just keep in mind they didn't send me here to help you either. Are you ready to meet our allies?"

"Sure. Signal your Korean to come over here. We'll set the ground rules."

"I told you, that's not the way it works. They won't come over here until I verify you have the collection. I want to see it, wherever it is, and it better be there, all of it."

Dan shook his head. "I need to know where your buddies are first, and Su Li too. I want to see all three of them—now."

"Fair enough. I assume you have the collection somewhere nearby."

"Near enough that I can get to it, but far enough that he can't."

Foster turned completely around and waved his right hand twice in a wide semi-circle. "Look directly down the walkway, at the far end of the park. Do you see the Ferris wheel?"

"Yes." The whole damn park was lit up like County Stadium on game night, and he could see the massive wheel looming high over the proceedings in the distance.

"Now, keep watching as the benches come over the top."

One, two, three passenger benches came swinging slowly over the top, the occupants only tiny blurs with arms and legs. "It's impossible to see that far," Dan said.

Foster produced a pair of binoculars. "Here. Use these."

Frantically, Dan focused the binoculars on the distant wheel and began searching the faces of the revelers, belted into the gently swinging bench seats in twos and threes. Bench by bench, the faces appeared in agonizingly slow motion over the top of the turning wheel to face the scrutiny of his lens. Then he saw her, dressed in the familiar blue parka and seated between two nasty looking Asians, one of them waving in his direction. Her eyes were closed, her face emotionless and blank, but she looked to be alive and unharmed. Dan growled. "Bring her here."

"The collection first. I want to see it."

"Wait here." Dan walked slowly around the corner to the left and stopped about fifty feet from Foster, in front of the small, snack vendor's cart. Dan walked behind the cart and retrieved the two briefcases lying near the wheel. He handed the old vendor two one thousand yen notes, the second half of his baby-sitting fee. "*Domo arigato.*"

Foster hadn't moved a muscle. Dan stood between him and the Ferris wheel, and placed the two thick cases on the ground. "Help yourself," he said, "but stay between me and the Ferris wheel. I'm not wild about the thought of a bullet in the brain as I'm standing here."

Foster opened the case on Dan's left and removed a stack of envelopes and folders. He made a cursory examination of the contents, returning them to the case. "It's insane. All this fuss over a few Polaroids and some homesick letters. You know I didn't know what these things were until today, and it's just as well."

"Why? Because three people have died for them?"

Foster's only reply was a cold stare. He performed the same abbreviated ritual on the second case, then backed away slowly. "All right, I'm satisfied. Now let's get the party started. He waved again, in exactly the same manner, this time with his back to the Ferris wheel. "They'll be here in a minute. Remember, there are two of them. I wouldn't do anything foolish. Give them the cases. I'll do what I can to get the girl away safely. I'm not into killing women or American soldiers."

Or saving them either, Dan wanted to say. "Is that your friend?" he asked, spotting the lone, rugged figure in a stocking cap slowly closing the distance. He could see the other Korean, Junior, trailing by perhaps a hundred yards, Su Li in tow. She was wobbly, eyes half closed, obviously drugged up to keep her cooperative.

"That's your boy."

The cold, black eyes were already narrowed and trained on Dan as they came into his view. The short man stopped directly in front of

Dan, close enough to make his point, but far enough that he didn't need to look up. Both hands were no doubt intentionally buried in the pockets of his button-up, short, wool coat. Dan's own hand nervously caressed the butt of the automatic handgun in his coat pocket. If the man had blinked even once, Dan didn't see it. Ignoring Dan, he said to Foster in English, with no hint of emotion, "Does he have it?"

"Right there in those cases. No doubt about it."

The Korean turned his gaze toward Dan. "You are either very brave or very stupid to come here alone, Agent Matthews. Either way, you are not in command. You will move away from the collection now. Nothing will happen until I have the things in my possession."

Dan had no intention of letting the Koreans control the game. "Listen carefully," he said, loud enough for the one in charge to hear, "I don't give a fuck about the collection, but I do care about the girl. There's no point in denying it. Those things aren't worth her life. I'm perfectly willing to give you the entire collection, but you won't ever get your hands on it if you harm her. So don't try to have your cake and eat it too. You won't touch it until I know she's safe and out of your reach."

"Walk away from the box slowly," the older Korean said. "When I get to the box I'll free her and you'll both be on your way."

Dan removed the set of keys from his pocket and hurled them toward his primary adversary. They landed only inches from the man's feet. "Those are keys to a blue Toyota," he said, "parked on the street directly to the north of the park. You can see it from here. It's the third car east of the intersection, facing west. Put Su Li in the car and bring the keys back here. Do it yourself. Your bunk-buddy behind you is going to stand quietly like a good boy. I want to see her wave to me from the front seat. When you give me back the keys, the same keys, I'll back away slowly and leave the box."

The one in charge smiled and motioned for his stooge to join him with Su Li. When the three stood roughly abreast of one another, he took hold of Su Li's free arm. She looked as though she might collapse if the two men let go. He smiled and said, "You cannot kill me before I kill the girl."

It didn't take much imagination to envision the barrel of his pistol jammed into the small of Su Li's back through the Korean's pocket. Slowly, the black-eyed man began to close the distance between himself and Dan, using the barely conscious Su Li like a human shield as he tightened the noose on Dan. The Koreans had no intention of making an exchange. They wanted it all: Dan, Su Li, the box, everything.

The handgun in Dan's pocket was cocked, with a round in the chamber. His hand felt warm and steady around the cold steel. He might only get one shot. There was no doubt of the first target. At twenty feet Dan could make out the arrogant smirk and gloating, black eyes from behind Su Li's head. In two, maybe three seconds, people would start dying. If he couldn't save Su Li, he'd send both these godless fucks to hell.

The Korean hesitated and Su Li's eyes opened wide. From the corner of his eye, Dan spotted the two blue uniforms and the familiar fedora closing slowly on the left. The cops were unarmed. They were looking straight at Dan. Tanaka pointed.

Before he could shout, Dan heard a blood curdling voice screaming bloody murder. You didn't need to be a linguist to know Su Li was yelling for help. She'd been lulling this goon to sleep, all the while fighting off the effects of the drug to regain her wits and her strength for this single chance.

Su Li's captor hurled her violently into the wrought iron fence. She slumped to the snow as the uniformed cops charged to her rescue. Tanaka seemed torn between saving Su Li and taking his vengeance on Dan, but happily made the right choice. The Korean was prepared for their onslaught and whirled on Tanaka first, catching him squarely on the chin with a devastating heel kick.

Dan saw Junior's punch coming in time to avoid its full impact. He lunged to the right as the fist glanced off his cheekbone, opening a gash on the side of his face and sending him flying head first into an iron fencepost. More cops had joined the fray, but not nearly enough.

Groggy and struggling to ignore the searing pain, Dan saw that two uniformed cops had descended upon his assailant, the younger Korean. Tanaka and one of the other policemen were lying harmlessly in the snow like cop-skin rugs, felled easily by the older agent's martial artistry, but the black-eyed Korean was nowhere to be seen.

Dan struggled to his feet. He wanted to grab Su Li in the confusion and run like hell, but she had disappeared from the scene. His eyes were now bloody, his vision blurred. He strained to wipe away the blood with a cold, wet sleeve. He had to get the cases before this guy finished off the cops.

Pushing his way half blind with the cases through the gathering crowd of onlookers, Dan headed in the direction of the blue Toyota. He had to get Su Li. Within a few seconds, his vision cleared enough for him to see the black-eyed Korean in the distance, stuffing the listless form of Su Li into the backseat before easing the Toyota into the late night traffic of downtown Sapporo.

By all indications, she was still alive, but the thought held little consolation for Dan. If this Korean had his way, she would soon be dead. The whole fiasco had ended in failure for all involved. The Korean agents had failed to secure the collection and Dan had failed miserably in his only chance to save Su Li.

Walking toward Sinead's house, Dan took great care in not being followed. A part of him hoped Su Li was dead already. It would spare her the inevitable price of the Koreans' defeat. The sadistic, black-eyed piece of shit would no doubt seek to ease the pain of his own humiliation and vent his anger at Dan by inflicting great suffering upon Su Li. Dan had never felt so utterly helpless.

Despite the odds against saving her now, he couldn't quit trying as long as she might be alive. Foster was now his only link to the Korean agents and the man seemed to have vanished into thin air.

Though committed to continue the quest, Dan tried to prepare himself for the worst. He was wrong about it being a failure for everyone. This didn't have to mean failure for Su Li or her dream. She would see it as a victory, as difficult as that was for him to accept. This was not the time to quit on her or let down his guard. There might come a time to grieve for Su Li Young, but only after he had helped make her dream live. When he'd delivered the collection safely, the rest would be up to Sinead McNally.

THIRTY-FOUR

**They say the good die young, and maybe that's true;
but believe me, asshole, they're not talking to you.**

Tuesday, 11:15 p.m.

Back in the poorly lit, unfurnished apartment, the old pain in Su Li's shoulder had returned, and the new one in her lower back had taken hold. Chung's sedative, whatever it was, had pretty much worn off, replaced by a splitting headache. She longed for another shot of the drug, but Chung no doubt had other plans for her. She knew they wouldn't include pain relief.

Chung was over near the sink, tending to his cuts and bruises. The Korean's smoldering anger and nervousness told her Chung was as much in the dark as she. They were both impatiently waiting for his protégé to walk through the door. Chung wanted him to be carrying a box, Su Li praying to see the man enter empty-handed or not at all. For the moment, she had no idea if Dan Matthews was even alive.

What a hypocrite she was. In the tension of the standoff only minutes before, she would have embraced her freedom, even at the cost of the Captain's collection. Su Li Young had learned something about herself in those gut-wrenching few minutes; more than anything else, she wanted desperately to go on living.

It wasn't that she feared death. She didn't, at least not in the way she feared pain. Whatever happened, she knew, this Korean would redefine her understanding of pain in horrible ways she could only imagine. The very prospect of what lay in store chilled her to the bone and was almost more than she could bear. Thank God it was all out of her control now, for she would surely betray her own mother to stop the pain.

But pain was nothing compared to the thought of oblivion. She mourned the inevitability of her impending death more than she could ever fear pain. Su Li had long ago acknowledged her stubborn nature, and in her stubbornness, would cling to the pain as a sign of life until death dragged her kicking from its clutches. She wanted to live.

She wanted to know the things other people know: marriage and children and stupid problems that don't matter at all. She wanted a chance to dress up and go out, to dance the night away and sing karaoke until dawn.

More than anything, she wanted a chance to be with Dan Matthews again, to tell him… Surely he knew already. He was wise, honest and true, with a selfless, single-minded determination to save her. And he wasn't a phony like she. He would have done anything to save her, even trade the collection, and nearly succeeded. He made no bones about it. And why not? She would be grateful now if he had. How could anyone render a harsh judgment of such a man?

She refused to feel guilt or remorse over her internal surrender. The fate of the Sakhalin Koreans was no longer in her hands. She had done all she could. She would suffer and die, regardless of their fate, regardless of Dan's fate. There was nothing Su Li could do about it any more. Good. Thank God she no longer held the power to betray.

Then Su Li heard footsteps on the stairway. Fu appeared in the doorway, beaten and bloody but without the box. "Where is it?" Chung asked.

"The American got away with it," Fu replied. "One of the policemen was a good fighter. By the time I finished with him, the American was gone. I had to leave before more police arrived."

Thank God.

Chung turned slowly to face Su Li, his eyes wild with rage. He removed the automatic pistol from its shoulder holster and extended it in Fu's direction, butt end first, his eyes maintaining their deadly fix on a terrified Su Li. "Hold this," he said. "I wouldn't want it to drop into her hands accidentally if I should be carried away in the moment."

Fu took the pistol and backed away slowly as Chung advanced. Crawling like a caterpillar on her bound hands and feet, Su Li scrambled to evade her attacker, but there was no escape. She propped herself into a corner in a sitting position to await her fate, but not meekly. There was strength left in her legs and she would not waste it.

When he was over her she could see the maniacal, twisted smile. There was no point letting him control the action. Falling to her good shoulder, Su Li lashed out toward his groin, driving her legs at the target with the power of a jackhammer. Chung sidestepped the blow easily and returned it with an unrestrained grin. "This will be more fun than I ever imagined," he said.

With one able fist, he lifted her into the air and pinned her against the wall, ramming the fist ever tighter under her chin until she gasped for air. His face was so close she could literally feel his stench. Then she saw the blade, only inches from her face. "Don't worry, little one," he said, "it's not time for serious play yet. We'll just get to know each other a bit first."

Su Li felt the blood charging back into her hands as Chung's blade slid easily through the ropes. She embraced the rush of air to her lungs as she dropped like a stone to the floor. "I am a man of honor," he said. "I want this to be a fair fight."

His backhand was a blur, but she saw it coming from the left. Su Li might have avoided it, were she not still disoriented from lack of air. It caught her flush on the cheek and propelled her head into the matted floor. She lay dead still, the thin stream of warm blood flowing into the corner of her mouth. She felt no pain, her senses blocked by the incessant, accelerated rhythm of her own heartbeat drumming in her ears.

"I want our time together to be special," Chung said, as if talking to a young daughter. "I promise we will make the most of it."

Su Li was resolved not to go quietly. Spitting the blood from her mouth, she launched the only counter-assault left in her arsenal —words. She forced an exaggerated, unmistakable smile. "Do you think they will write songs about you in South Korea?" she asked.

She was determined to manufacture a laugh, and surprised when it came so easily from her battered frame. "You are a killer of women," she said. "You are a pitiful, spineless weakling, outmatched by a simple waitress and an American sergeant. I will spit in your face with my last breath, if you have the courage to come close enough."

Although she wanted to live, Su Li knew her words might serve to shorten her suffering. For a fleeting moment, it looked as if Chung might succumb to a massive stroke, then and there, such was his visible reaction to her verbal assault.

"In a minute you will hold your bowels in your hand," he said. "Then we will finish our conversation over a cup of tea."

Su Li could not see past the knife. It kept growing bigger, so she closed her eyes. She might not have heard anything less deafening; the explosion punctuated the deadly tension with a violent exclamation.

Perhaps she was shot, but where? Surely she'd be able to feel a gunshot wound. It would be painful, but maybe not. Beyond her throbbing head and aching bones, her brain might not even detect a small bullet hole. Shot or not, she was alive and her pain was no worse than before. She opened her eyes. Chung was facing her, only an arm's length away. The knife was gone from his hand now, lying harmlessly on the floor. His lips moved, forming words, but the ringing in her ears blocked the sound.

He began to wobble, teetering forward, finally collapsing into a dead fall. His head glanced off the thin wall as his muscular torso landed in a heap across Su Li's lap. A large pool of blood gathered around her skirt. Su Li could feel the sticky mess on her leg as she struggled to breathe beneath the full weight of this most-deserving corpse.

Even amidst this barrage of chaos, Su Li soon realized precisely what had occurred. She could not contemplate why Fu had killed his superior, but wondered only if she would be next. Fu pushed at the limp carcass with his booted foot, and Chung's body rolled onto its back, the lifeless, black eyes still open, but the rage replaced by a benign stare.

Fu picked up the knife and freed her legs. "Can you walk?" he asked.

"You tell me," Su Li said. "What will happen when I do?"

"You're free to go," Fu said. "I have no reason to harm you further."

She had at least a dozen questions on the tip of her tongue. Why did he do it? Did his employers order him to? Has he turned against his government? She decided not to tempt fate. Fu was not shy. The man's last encounter with Chung had told her that. If he thought she needed information, he would give it to her.

Su Li struggled with her parka as Fu towered silently over the body of his unsuspecting victim. "You should know," he said, without looking in her direction, "I would have killed you myself had it been necessary."

"I'm grateful my death was unnecessary then," was all she could think to say. "What will you do now?" Had the man turned on his own government and become a rogue? If so, why?

"I'll go home to my family," he replied. "Then I'll go back to work. Everything we do is not shameful. You wouldn't understand."

Su Li didn't care to understand. She understood what she needed to. The man had either killed Chung because he was ordered to or because he refused to allow the torture and murder of another human being. She wouldn't be dolling out hugs and kisses, but this man had saved her life and she would never forget it.

Fu's back was still turned as she hobbled painfully toward the door. She slipped out quietly, greeted a moment later by the frigid, night wind from the northeast. It seemed to clear her head a bit and ease the pain.

Su Li had no clue where to go, and began to walk in the direction of life, farther into the city. She wondered if Fu himself had precipitated the decertification of Chung as an agent in good standing, or was he just blindly following orders? Maybe he just killed Chung on his own because he'd had enough of his lunacy. None of this mattered to Su Li or to her cause, but she couldn't drive the thoughts from her mind as she continued her painful walk to freedom.

She would never know for certain, but would rather believe Fu was a good person inside. She wanted to believe he was a man of conscience, with self-imposed limits, and would never have let her be tortured. Was Chung's murder strictly administrative punishment for a failed agent gone off the deep end or the act of a decent man drawing a line in the sand? Su Li would have to have to extract that answer from Fu's soul and she didn't care to ever know him that well. After all, though he had never mistreated her in any way, this Fu had at least passively participated in the murder of her dear friend, Ishikawa.

There was no point in delving further into the question, because it no longer mattered. She had to get to a phone and call her mother. Yoon Hae would be worried to death. Besides, her mother might know where to find Dan Matthews.

11:40 p.m.

"I can only imagine how you feel," said Sinead, swabbing his cheek wound gently with alcohol. "The bleeding has stopped for now, but you'll need stitches soon."

"Jesus Christ, Sinead," he said, leaning forward in her leather chair, "do you think I give a shit about a scar on my cheek?"

"I'm sorry, Daniel. I—"

"No," he said, "I'm sorry. If not for you, this whole thing would have turned out even worse. I didn't mean to offend you."

"Lie back now," she instructed. "I'm not quite so thin-skinned. I know very well what's on your mind, but it will do no good to dwell on it. Su Li has always been prepared to pay this price to help her people. I swear to you, we'll find a way to help them."

"That's not enough for me, Sinead," he protested. "It was enough for her, but not for me."

She paused for a moment, then said, "Nevertheless, that's the task facing us, and we'll find a way to complete it."

"You're right, but I'm not ready to write her off yet. You're talking like she's dead already." The cheek wound throbbed with pain. The salt in tears burns just like alcohol, he thought. A momentary sense of resignation seized him. "I did everything I could to trade those goddamn letters and photographs for her life. I was so close, Sinead. I just can't let it go. If I only knew where the Korean took her…"

"Wouldn't this Foster know?" Sinead asked, handing a cold compress. "Here, hold this on the wound."

"You would think so." The compress felt cool and soothing on his scalp. "The two of them being so close, but my suspicion is he doesn't have a clue. He as much as told me the senior Korean agent is out of control and would never let Su Li go alive. It's like he's washed his hands of the whole mess, as if he could. Anyway, he's vanished into thin air. I won't find him unless he wants to be found."

Sinead sat down on the floor, beside the precious shopping bags. "Do you think Foster told the Japanese police you'd be at the park?"

In all the chaos and the whirlwind of emotion, he hadn't even considered the question. "I don't know," he replied. "It's certainly possible, but I don't know why he would. Tanaka's presence is what blew their chance to get the collection. Why would Foster do that, subvert his own mission? On the other hand, Tanaka is a smart cookie. It might have been just good detective work. There's really no way to tell."

"I suppose it doesn't matter," she said. "The end result is the same."

"I got the impression Foster wanted us both to get out of there alive. The Korean CIA had other plans, and I think Foster knew that."

"So he might have called the police to help you," Sinead said.

"It's possible. I'd like to think it was to create enough confusion for me to get Su Li out of there alive. Maybe he thought he could get away with the collection in the confusion. I guess I'll never know, but all this speculation isn't helping Su Li. There must be something we can do. I can't just sit here and let them murder her."

"I've made all the calls I can think of," she said, "the same backdoor diplomatic channels I've been using all along."

Dan stared at the large briefcase beside the chair. "What's that?"

"I brought it to put the things in," she replied, touching one of the rapidly deteriorating reinforced paper bags.

"Good thinking. Do you think there's a chance you can get the South Korean government to lean on these guys in time?" Dan knew it was more a plea than a question. Even if he didn't already know the answer, he could read it in her eyes. They were strained, like they wanted to look anywhere but at him.

"No, Daniel," she answered. "It would be wrong of me to give you false hope."

It wasn't beyond the realm of possibility that the Koreans might want to try another trade. Nothing had changed, really. They still wanted the collection and Dan still had it. He figured he and Sinead had to buy some time.

He rose from the chair to test his equilibrium. Aside from a raging headache and a split skull, he seemed fully functional with not a trace of dizziness. "We should eat and pack enough things for a few days. We have to leave. Tanaka's no fool and it won't take him long to show up here."

"I have a friend from the IRC," Sinead said, "a Japanese woman, but completely trustworthy. I'll call her. She can hide you for a few days."

"Good. Then we'll wait and see if the Koreans want to play another game of *Let's Make a Deal*."

THIRTY-FIVE

**As my ship sails off onto the ominous sea,
the shore now a memory, I think of thee.**

Wednesday, 12:40 a.m.

The ringing door chime ended their departure preparations and sparked a churning sickness in Dan's gut. They'd waited too long, he thought. Tanaka was like a bronc rider who just refused to be thrown. "Is there a back door?" he whispered, carefully placing his fork down on the still untouched scrambled eggs.

"Yes," Sinead replied, "but we still need to use the front gate to leave the property."

"What about over the wall?" he asked. "It's only five feet or so. I can lift you."

"We can try, but the wall is ancient. They were all built with shards of glass embedded in the concrete along the top. It's very dangerous."

He hesitated, wondering if they should just grab the cases and run like hell. Whoever was on the other side of the door knew they were there and had been given plenty of time to prevent their escape. "Ask who it is," he said.

Sinead spoke through the closed door, Dan beside her, Colt in hand. "Who is it?" she asked in Japanese.

The reply came in accented English from a sweet, heavenly voice back from the dead, "I'm looking for Dan Matthews. Is he here?"

Su Li needed medical attention, for sure, but she was in one piece and seemed generally healthy and in good spirit. Her first question didn't surprise him at all. "Do you have the collection, Dan-san?"

He smiled. "Of course I do," as if he'd never been willing to part with it. There would be plenty of time later for confessions. "How did you know to find us here? Have you talked to Yoon Hae?"

"Yes," she replied. "My mother told me where you would be." She smiled and tugged gently on his sleeve. "I am happy you still have the captain's things. We may yet do something good with them."

Dan turned to Sinead. "That's where my friend comes in. Su Li,. this is Sinead McNally. She's an executive with the International Red Cross, stationed here in Sapporo. She has a lifetime of insight into international politics and diplomacy. Better than that, she's been trying to help your people on Sakhalin for many years."

Su Li bowed and said, "Dan has spoken of you often, Miss McNally. It's my great pleasure to meet you. Will you help us?"

"I'm prepared to try, Su Li," Sinead replied. "Now come in and eat something, my dear. I can't imagine what you've been through."

"We thought you were Inspector Tanaka," Dan said, helping her to the leather chair, "come to drag me off in handcuffs." Only then did it occur to him to ask, "How in God's name did you get away? I saw the Korean stuff you into the car and drive away."

"It seems there was an unspoken disagreement between my two captors," she explained. "The leader is dead at the hand of his companion. If he hadn't killed the one called Chung, I would be dead as well."

"That doesn't figure," Dan said, kneeling beside her. "Why did he do it? Did they have an argument?"

"I do not know," Su Li said. "I only know Chung is dead and the other one, Fu, allowed me to leave alive."

Sinead reentered and handed her a mug of hot milk. "Drink this now. It will have to do because we can't stay here. I'll bring along some bread and fruit."

Dan had no idea what to make of Su Li's story, one Korean agent murdering the other to set her free, but something about it didn't ring true. He needed desperately to question her in greater detail, but first she needed to regain her strength. "We'll find a safe place for you to rest. We can talk about this later."

Su Li was adamant. "No, Dan-san, I need first to know what Miss McNally can do," she said, touching his arm. "I'll be all right. Believe me."

Sinead took the cue. "Well, what I have in mind is a bit of diplomatic blackmail, I suppose. The International Red Cross enjoys a well-deserved reputation for neutrality among the nations of the world, even the great powers. That's really the only thing that might make it work."

"Make what work?" Su Li asked.

Sinead sat beside her in the traditional style. "I'll try to explain. The Japanese government is quietly calling the shots at the highest level, pulling the puppet strings of the Korean CIA. That's the easiest way to explain the dynamics involved."

"But those were Koreans chasing us, not Japanese," Su Li said. "Koreans killed Ishikawa."

Sinead held up her hand. "I can explain that. The South Korean CIA under Park Jung Hee is a comprehensive, well-oiled mechanism for concealing the extent of Japan's crimes against other Asian peoples during the war."

"I'm not sure I understand," Su Li said.

Dan said, "The Korean CIA secretly works for Japan. Japan pays Park vast sums of money."

Su Li's eyes narrowed. "That's quite a lot to accept. So dealing with the Japanese is the key?"

As the two women talked, Dan opened the briefcase and carefully began to transfer the small bundles from the shopping bags. They were running out of time.

"In a sense you're right, Su Li," Sinead said, "although it might be more accurate to say motivating Japan to action is the key. At the risk of oversimplifying the problem of the Sakhalin Koreans, it's always been fair to say Japan is the key factor. They'll be repatriated and reintegrated into Korean society only when Japan removes the many obstacles it has in place."

"And what about the Americans?" Su Li asked.

Dan reached for his parka and said, "Su Li, we really have to get out of here. We can talk on the way." He turned to Sinead. "Grab what you need and let's move."

Su Li was out of the chair and steady on her feet. Her strength seemed to have no limits. She finished the last of the milk. "I'm ready."

Sinead appeared from the bathroom with a large handbag. "We're off then," she said.

"What about the Americans?" Su Li said, not to be deterred.

"The Americans' interest here is in maintaining the careful balance of international stability and protecting their intelligence assets on Sakhalin," Sinead explained. "There is a potential here to seriously upset that balance and create increased tensions between the Soviets and the West. The Americans will do what it takes to preserve the status quo."

"Do you have everything you need?" Dan asked.

"Yes," Sinead replied.

Su Li said, "Then just how do you propose to deal with these governments, and how will the collection help?"

Dan peeled back the curtain and stared into the darkness. The damn wall around the property gave him fits. He could see the lighted, attached greenhouse clearly enough, but the other side of the wall may as well have been Kansas. He had no idea what lay on the other side. They'd just have to risk it.

"As I said, diplomatic blackmail," Sinead answered. "All the governments know about your collection and fear its dissemination, especially the Japanese. So long as I have the collection, I might be able to use it as an axe over the head of Japan and the others to gain concessions for your people on Sakhalin. The Koreans are only an afterthought and will do whatever the Japanese decide."

"What kind of concessions?" Su Li asked.

"Not everything you want," Sinead said, "not right away, and not as your original plan might have done."

"All right," Dan said, heading for the door. "Let's go. We'll head straight for the car."

"What then?" Su Li asked, as they stepped out into the glass garden heading for the yard. "What concessions?"

"Whatever I can get, and keep you and your friends safe as well."

Su Li seemed to ponder Sinead's frank assessment as they moved swiftly from the house into the cold night. "Good," she said. "Then we'll have to complete this task one step at a time, however long it might take. Now I'd like to see the collection."

They were moving quickly through the garden now. "Oh yes," said Sinead, "I almost forgot." She produced a small bundle of pictures from her pocket. "This one has your name on it, along with a note. I took the liberty of removing it from the collection." Su Li took the packet and said nothing as they slipped through the gate into the dark.

Dan had parked Sinead's car nearly a half mile away, to be safe, and now wished he hadn't. The three kept moving along the deserted streets as Dan pondered their next move. He and Su Li would have to keep out of sight for a few days while Sinead weaved her way through her diplomatic maze toward some kind of solution.

With Ishikawa gone and the two hundred refugees in Japanese custody, there was only so much they could achieve with Subarov's collection. The way out for Su Li now had as much to do with Sinead's diplomatic skills as all the rest combined.

He spotted the small sedan where he'd left it, on a quiet, residential street among a dozen or so similarly anonymous vehicles. They piled into the car and the engine finally turned over on the third try. Dan breathed a sigh of relief. "All right," he said, "we'll warm up the engine for a minute, then head to your friend's house, Sinead."

In the backseat, Su Li began to untie her gift from Captain Subarov. "Dan-san," she said, "will you turn on the dome light for just a minute?"

In the light she read aloud, translating the Japanese characters as she went:

> "My Dear Su Li...This is my family...I pray my son, Sergei, will forgive me one day for leaving him in a foreign land. I could not keep him safe on Sakhalin after his mother died... Please explain everything to him, as only you have a true understanding of these things...There are no other pictures, and I fear I will not return from this voyage. Please give them to my son. With love, Nikolai Subarov."

She leafed through the photos with Sinead, one by one, giving each to Dan in turn. The first picture was of the captain's wife, Jang, the same one he had shown her aboard the *Irina*. There were less than two dozen snapshots, all black and white, but each a treasure: mother and son, father and son, all three together at the wheel of the *Irina*.

"You didn't mention Subarov had a son," Dan said.

Su Li smiled. "I didn't know until now," she said. "Do you remember the boy in Kim's house?"

"Sure," Dan replied. "I wondered about him. They seemed a little old to be his parents."

"They're not," she declared. "The boy is Captain Subarov's son, Sergei."

Dan smiled. "Well, I'll be damned. I think you'll have a lot to tell him about his father."

Su Li turned to Sinead. "Will you keep these for me? We don't know what may happen in the coming hours."

"Of course."

Suddenly Dan saw the plus-sized silhouette moving slowly out of the darkness, directly into the car's path. He switched on the headlights and the beams engulfed their subject in an explosion of brilliance. Foster squinted but held his ground, now less than ten feet from the hood. Frantically, Dan threw the gear in drive, cut the wheel, and pressed on the gas pedal. The car barely moved. The engine raced but the wheels refused to turn. Block. Foster's radiated smirk told him the game was up. He rolled down the driver's window and waited.

"It's no use," Foster said. "You're car won't be going anywhere." Then he laughed. "But you and your girlfriend will, minus your cargo."

Dan saw a pair of headlights in his rearview mirror, then a pair from each side, until his eyes were useless to aid escape. "They're all around us," he said.

"Who is it?" Sinead asked. "The Japanese police?"

"No," Dan replied, "this looks like an all NSA show."

"Not quite," Su Li said. "Look behind you."

Dan turned to see Junior, the young Korean who'd slashed his face and saved Su Li's life, approaching the car cautiously from the rear.

"I want to see your hands, all six of them," Foster shouted. "Now!"

"What can we do, Dan-san?" Su Li cried.

"Nothing," he replied. "Just do what they tell you. They can't hold Sinead. It would cause too big a stink."

"He's right, girl," Sinead added. "You'll be all right. I'll make certain of it. I know the right buttons to push."

"But the captain's collection," she said, "they'll destroy it. Then we are beaten?"

"It would appear so," answered Dan, clasping his hands behind his head.

"Now," Foster said, "out of the car, one at a time. You first, Matthews."

"Do as they say," said Dan, slowly opening the driver's door. Su Li and Sinead followed suit. Foster approached Dan from behind and removed the Colt from his pocket. "Hopefully," he said, "you won't mind returning this. I trust you took good care of it for me. I still owe you a bump on the head too. I won't forget that."

Then Foster turned to the young Korean agent. "All right," he said, pointing the gun into the passenger compartment, "get your briefcase and be on your way. I'd say our little collaboration is finished."

The Korean looked a bit confused at first. Foster's sign language helped convey the message. The man scrambled into the back and came out with the case. Still staring down at the hood, Dan said, "Foster, did you have the Korean agent killed just so you could follow Su Li?"

Dan could hear the Korean going through the case. "Maybe I was wrong about you, Matthews," Foster said. "You might not have the aptitude required for this kind of work."

He was beginning to think the man was right, but he'd hardly classify that in the category of character deficiency. He said, "Humor my inferior intellect then. Did you have anything to do with Chung's death?"

Foster moved around to the front of the car, into Dan's field of view. He said, "Let's just say Chung's death was an internal thing, some administrative cleanup within the Korean CIA. The man got out of control and made some inexcusable mistakes, I'm told. There is little room for tolerance in the Korean CIA; but it did present us with an opportunity."

"An opportunity to steal Subarov's collection?"

"It all depends on your perspective, I guess," Foster replied. "I preferred to see it as an opportunity to save your girlfriend's life. Have you forgotten about that already?"

Dan doubted Foster's sincerity plenty, but the man's logic was flawless. Su Li was alive only because these two men had saved her, regardless of their motives. He hadn't forgotten. "Point taken," he said. "Still, you're here to steal the collection, right?"

"We don't see it as stealing," Foster said, "but it's probably better for all involved if the things in those cases disappear forever. Our Korean friend will see to that."

Dan heard a car engine roar as one set of headlights disappeared. It would be the Korean, no doubt on his way to the airport. "I see," he said. "So what happens now?"

"To you or your girlfriend?" Foster asked.

"Why don't you just give me a general wrap-up?"

"Sure. You're going to jail, Matthews. What happens to you after that isn't up to me. I can envision quite a lengthy list of charges. Then there's that little matter of Inspector Tanaka."

"And what will happen to Su Li?"

"You mean your troublesome little cherry blossom there with the great ass? That's not up to me either. As far as I'm concerned, she's free to go right now with the IRC lady. It's a good bet Inspector Tanaka will want to talk to her. She's been right in the middle of a number of deaths and some very deep shit."

"Do you not have the courage to speak to me directly?" Su Li asked.

Apparently he didn't. "That woman is truly amazing," Foster replied. "She led you all around by your dicks like some kind of Pied Piper. You're the only one who survived, Matthews. I guess that makes you the lucky one. You can think about that one at your court-martial. Now put your hands back on top of your head."

One of the plainclothes officers, probably OSI, slapped the cuffs on Dan's wrists and escorted him to the waiting blue Ford. As the car pulled away into the sleeping city he turned to see her one last time. She was still standing with Sinead near the car. It was the first time he had seen her cry, really cry, but it didn't surprise him. The tears weren't for herself. She wasn't the kind to face fear or personal tragedy with tears. She had been born to a single, noble purpose and had nearly seen it realized. Now she would continue to live as an outcast, alone and isolated, that sense of purpose undiminished but forever beyond her grasp.

THIRTY-SIX

**Believe none of what you hear and half of what you see.
You're going through some changes, boy, and it's all because of me.**

One week later
Yokota Air Force Base, Tokyo, Japan

The dingy, gray visiting room seemed perfectly appropriate to the occasion. "Sergeant Matthews," said Brad Duncan, the baby-faced, JAG officer in impeccably tailored dress blues. "I'm not sure what to say. Yours is the most incredible story I've ever encountered."

Ever encountered? This kid couldn't have finished law school more than a year ago. "Let me guess, Lieutenant Duncan. There was no NSA operation in Japan, right?"

"That's right."

"And there is no such person as Foster?"

"Exactly," the young lawyer replied, "and I've spoken to Inspector Tanaka from the Prefectural Police."

"Well, this should be interesting. I can't wait to hear what he says."

"To be honest, he was dumfounded by my questions," Duncan said. "He claims he spoke to you at the scene of a suicide in Wakkanai. Apparently the death had something to do with this Kincaid you were investigating. He claims he's never seen or heard of you since." Dan might have written the whole thing as a screenplay—a black comedy.

Life in the guardhouse was pretty much as expected. He had twelve or thirteen hours every day to sit around on a cot and relive every minute of this entire fiasco. Funny, he thought, but the only thing he actually regretted was the way he'd treated Reggie.

He'd come to believe over the last week that he might have saved Reggie's life, had he just taken that leap of faith a few days earlier. The rest of it he'd do again—and again and again. He and Su Li had come pretty goddamn close to making a real difference.

So now this high school kid with bars was questioning his entire story. Well, in truth it was almost more than Dan himself could believe. In a couple of weeks he'd managed to become an outlaw renegade to the Air Force, fall in love, play cops and robbers all over Hokkaido, and wind up in the slammer facing enough charges to... Come to think of it, he still didn't know the charges. He said, "Say, Lieutenant Duncan, what did they decide to charge me with anyway? Will I ever become a burden on the Social Security system?"

"Well," the young man said, "that's the thing that really gives me pause."

"How's that?"

Duncan kind of leaned back in the chair and scratched his head. "When they brought you in here, it was all kind of hush-hush, you know, classified, limited access, all that. It was a pretty big deal."

"And now?"

Duncan shrugged his shoulders. "I've just been advised that you'll be given the option of accepting administrative punishment under Article Fifteen. That's why I'm here."

"That doesn't make much sense," Dan said. "Administrative punishment is for minor offenses. I've got people, agencies, hell, whole fucking governments waiting for a crack at my ass."

"Apparently not," Duncan replied. "Under the government's offer, you would admit to insubordination, disobeying a direct order and being away without official leave."

"And what would the government offer me in return? Execution?"

"Reduction in rank to Airman Second Class, forfeiture of thirty days pay and immediate discharge."

There had to be a catch. "What kind of discharge?"

"Honorable."

It was beyond comprehension and Dan wondered at first if it might still be a part of the game. "Is this some kind of sick joke?" he asked, seeing no particular reason why his own lawyer might not be involved in this dirty business. "What the hell is going on here? Yesterday I was some lecherous traitor under twenty-four guard and today I'm a harmless prankster?"

"Look," said the young officer, "I don't understand it myself. It's highly unusual, and frankly, it makes me think there's something to your story. But that's not my job here. I don't need to go into all that. The fact is they want you out of their hair, pure and simple. Will you accept the Article Fifteen?"

"Does Major Hickam know about this?" Dan asked.

"I suppose he does, since it's your commanding officer who will administer the punishment. Why should it matter? He's a major. There were much higher forces at work here. Now, will you accept the punishment?"

Dan smiled and said, "I suppose so."

"Good," Duncan said, closing his briefcase. "I'll inform Major Hickam of your decision. You should be released and transported over to Tachikawa Air Base within a few hours. Oh, you have two visitors waiting, two women, I believe. Would you like to see them?"

She was wearing a pleated, navy jumper and sky-blue blouse, open at the neck. Her eyes were clear and rested, with the polished glint of emeralds. His memory snapped a still picture for old age. There was an easiness about her that made him think she knew of his good fortune, and maybe something more.

The tall airman in starched fatigues and empty holster broke the hallowed silence. "There's a no-touching rule for visitors," he said. "Visitors on their side of the table, prisoner on his." Then he smiled, and in a more relaxed voice said, "But since you'll be released as soon as the paperwork is finished, I guess the rules don't apply."

He just wanted to hold her at first, to look at her and inhale her presence. Neither of them spoke a word and Sinead finally interrupted the reunion. "If you young people would care to get out of jail, we have some things to discuss. There will be time enough for the other nonsense."

They all took seats around the gray, metal table. He said, "I suppose you've heard I'm getting out of the service with a slap on the wrist."

"Indeed we have," Sinead said. "Indeed we have."

"There's more, Dan-san," Su Li said, squeezing his hand, "so much more."

"Well, I've got an hour or so," he said. "Until then I'm a captive audience."

Sinead said, "Have you wondered why they decided not to bring serious charges?"

"I've only known about it for five minutes, but I assume it's got something to do with keeping a lid on this whole affair."

"Very much so," Sinead added. "A public court martial would have proven an embarrassment for the United States and absolutely infuriated the Japanese government."

"I don't understand. According to my lawyer, the whole government apparatus went into denial mode. He would never have gotten access to NSA records or classified information. Hell, even the Japanese police went into hibernation. I would have been the only witness. Nobody would have paid attention to a crazy story like that without corroboration."

Su Li smiled and said, "You would not have been the only witness."

It was instantly clear what she meant. He looked at Sinead. She said, "I let it be known to the Air Force and the NSA that I was privy to their entire menu of reprehensible conduct."

"So you threatened to testify on my behalf?" he asked. "You threatened the United States government?"

"Precisely. I was about to notify your young lawyer of that fact when we all reached a satisfactory agreement. The diplomatic grapevine has been quite busy over the last week, Daniel."

"I owe you a lot then," he said, leaning back in the chair. Then he remembered Su Li's collection and how its destruction had ended her dream. He turned to her. "I'm sorry about your collection. I wish it had turned out differently."

Her answer rocked him. "I was very pleased with how it turned out."

"I don't understand," he said.

Sinead said, "The rest came as quite a shock to me, Daniel, although in retrospect it makes perfect sense."

"What makes perfect sense?" he asked. "You're both hiding something from me."

Sinead spread the English language *Tokyo Gazette* before him on the table, bearing yesterday's date. Near the bottom of page one he saw the article entitled "Foreign Ministry issues invitations for multilateral talks on future of Sakhalin Koreans."

He read silently as Sinead capsulized the article for him. "There will be four-way talks in Seoul at the vice-ministerial level. Representatives of Japan, South Korea, the Soviet Union and the United States will participate. This is a real breakthrough, Daniel."

"This is perfect," Dan said. "This way nobody is embarrassed or loses face. But what about the two hundred people already in Japanese jails?"

"It will all begin with the quiet repatriation of your two hundred here in Japan as a show of good faith. They'll be returned quietly to their own villages in South Korea or placed in decent government housing in Seoul, whichever they choose. The IRC will establish and administer a trust fund, insuring medical care and enough money to live on. I suspect the Americans came up with the money from one of their clandestine budget items. The IRC will continuously monitor their status to ensure good treatment. In the meantime, high-level talk will commence among all the governments."

"How do you know the commission will do the job?" Dan asked.

"Because the time is right and the incentives are powerful," Sinead answered. "The United States has secretly pledged funds for the long-term repatriation and reintegration costs. They'll ensure the people are well cared for. It's an opportunity for all the nations to resolve a festering problem none of them wants."

"It won't be an easy job," Dan said.

"Indeed it will not. There will be many difficult issues to address, like health care, housing, and compensation; but this is a good beginning."

It was too much, too fast; none of it made sense. "Hold on," he said. "The collection was lost. Subarov is dead. You had nothing to negotiate with. How the hell could this happen?"

"It was nearly a complete surprise to me, actually," Sinead said. "I had very little to do with it. In a way, Su Li made it happen, with a lot of help from you, Reggie Kincaid, Ishikawa, and many others."

"And you, Sinead-san," Su Li said.

"You've completely lost me, Sinead," said Dan.

She laughed. "It's quite logical, Daniel. And what are the Japanese if not logical? The Sakhalin Koreans were out of the closet and onto the table. They weren't going away, not ever again. At least three people died to bring this issue to the world stage and many more were ready to do so. Just look at the length the Japanese had to go to get rid of those old photos and letters. They couldn't suppress what's happened over the last two weeks. It was far too big."

"I think I'm beginning to understand," he said. "In the end it wasn't Subarov's collection they were afraid of."

Sinead smiled. "I think you do understand, Daniel."

Su Li said, "Then what were they so afraid of that they would allow the world to learn of this injustice?"

"It was you, Su Li," Dan said. "They were afraid of you. You started an avalanche that would gain speed and power until it reached its objective. Nothing could stop it."

She looked genuinely surprised. "It's true," Sinead added. "They were afraid of you and all those like you who would never let this cause die. They were afraid of Subarov, Ishikawa, Reggie, all of them and all the others who would surely follow."

"It's quite a victory, Su Li," Dan said. "You know how hard my own government worked to prevent it."

"Don't be so certain of that, Daniel," Sinead cautioned.

"Why not?" Dan asked. "Foster did his part."

"He may have done more than you know," Sinead countered. "You've been quite impressed with Tanaka's skills as a detective, but to turn up at that spot in Odori Park at precisely ten p.m. the man would have to be psychic or—"

"Tipped off. I thought about that. The coincidence sure seemed strange at the time. And the only ones who knew the location of the exchange were me and Foster."

"There was no other way Tanaka could have known," Sinead said.

The connection still seemed implausible. "But why?" Foster had done everything he could to foil Su Li's plan. He'd helped drive Reggie to suicide. "He hates me and he's got a lump on his head to remind him. Still, if Tanaka hadn't shown up, Su Li and I would probably be dead."

"Maybe that's your answer." Sinead suggested. "It might be he'd just had enough of the senseless deaths."

The door opened and the guard stepped back into the room. "You ladies will have to leave now," he said.

Sinead held up her hand to him and said, "Just one moment, please."

Dan took the theory a step further. "Then Foster might also have been behind Chung's killing."

"Wouldn't that be the ultimate irony?" Sinead added. "What if he were killed by his own agency because the Americans wanted him out of the way?"

"I see it," Su Li said. "He was sacrificed for money and power in the same way the Sakhalin Koreans were."

"Of course," Sinead said, "it's all pure speculation, mind yee."

"Sure," Dan said, as they all rose from the chairs, "pure speculation. That's all."

Su Li smiled broadly, almost making the facial cuts and bruises disappear in the glow. "I think it'll work," she declared. "We'll never be able to thank you for your help, Sinead-san."

"Not at all, my dear," Sinead said, blushing. "In fact, 'twas the most fun I've ever had with my britches on."

They all laughed.

"Then it's over," said Su Li.

Dan smiled and embraced her warmly. Her green eyes had recovered their full sparkle. "Yes," he said, "It's over. It means you've won. It means the world will learn the story of the Sakhalin Koreans, and soon the comfort women, and God knows who else. It means that, over time, your people can go home to grow old in their own villages or in decent housing in Seoul with their needs cared for. It means, you've won, Su Li. You have fulfilled your dream for others and now you're free to think about yourself for once. It means you can think about where you will go—and with whom. You can think about us."

"I don't have much practice thinking about myself," she said, "but be careful; I might easily learn."

He smiled again, and this time the smile seemed to stretch the length of the room. "On second thought, you won't have to. I can think about you enough for both of us. Tell me, have you seen enough snow in your life?"

She laughed, a genuine and carefree laugh that warmed his heart. "I've seen enough snow for many lifetimes."

"Good," he said, "but I'll bet you've never seen a palm tree or a black sand beach. The minute I get back to Tachikawa I have to call a man about a boat."

EPILOGUE

March, 2000
Ansan, Republic of South Korea

It was the happiest and the saddest day of Su Li Matthews existence. Despite the richness of her life, Su Li felt completely alone in that moment, standing before the full-length mirror in her posh, Ansan Hilton Hotel room. The new, blue suit with matching shoes and white, lace blouse may as well have been a housecoat and slippers, for all she cared.

It was a mistake to come here, she thought. Su Li Young was unworthy of personal accolades. She had finally come to the land of her mother's birth, not as a stateless refugee, but as a respected, foreign dignitary, to cut a ribbon and dispense a few patronizing remarks to some of the old Sakhalin Koreans and gathered politicians.

It wasn't that she objected to a five-hundred-unit apartment complex for the Sakhalin Koreans. On the contrary, Su Li had never completely stopped working for the cause, even from her home in Hawaii, and she considered Japan's large financial contribution to the project another step in the right direction.

But a part of her couldn't help feel shame over the hypocrisy of the staged event. She worried that her participation might be seen as an endorsement of the painfully slow progress of repatriation and compensation.

"Mother," came the voice of her beloved daughter, "what's wrong with you? Why won't you answer me?"

"I'm sorry, Reggie," Su Li replied, "I guess I'm just nervous about all the hoopla, and finally being here after all these years brings back so many memories."

Reggie pulled Su Li gently away from the mirror and smothered her in a warm embrace, unleashing a flood of emotion. "Oh, my dear," Su Li said, "you just don't know all the pain it dredges up. I wish your father were here with me now." She immediately regretted saying it. Although her daughter was a grown woman with a son of her own, Su Li was still the mother, and needed to act like it. Now Reggie was crying too.

"I'm proud of you, Mother," Reggie said, "and Dad was proud of you too. I know what he'd say if he were here. He'd say you're being too hard on yourself. He wasn't the only one who understands you. I know you think you could have done more for those people somehow, but it's not true."

Su Li wiped the tears from her eyes. Two deep breaths later she was back in control, for the most part. "And what could you possibly know about that, my dear Reggie?"

"I know you," Reggie answered.

Su Li turned to face her daughter head on. "Did my makeup run?"

Reggie smiled. "No. In fact, I've never seen you look more beautiful."

"Really? Well, there was a time I didn't think about such mundane things as makeup. I don't think your father would have cared if I'd never started wearing it."

"I miss him too," Reggie said. "You were very lucky to find each other."

"I was the lucky one, Reggie. Your father believed from the time we met that he would never be the most important thing to me, that he would always take a backseat to this obsession of mine."

"That's all right. He was okay with that."

"I know he was," Su Li replied. "The thing is, it wasn't true. Once, many years ago, when I thought I was about to die, I realized I would give up everything, even my commitment to the Sakhalin Koreans, just to see him and hold him one more time. I never told him that, and I don't know why."

"Then let's do this for him," Reggie said.

There was a knock at the door. Reggie opened it and in walked the mayor's aide followed by an old and dear friend. Su Li made no attempt to conceal her glee. "Sinead," she cried, rushing to greet her friend with a hug. Sinead would be close to eighty by now, but still sharply dressed, blue eyes alert as ever. "It's so good to see you, my friend. I'm only sorry Dan couldn't be here as well."

"I was so sorry to hear of his passing," Sinead said. "He was still such a young man. My own husband died of cancer as well. It's nearly ten years now. My, but just look at you, girl. You can't be eight stone, no bigger than the day I last saw you in Sapporo thirty years ago."

"You've never looked better yourself," Su Li said.

"Tell me, did you keep the farm after Daniel passed away?"

"I couldn't bear to part with it. It was never a proper farm anyway, just a good piece of land with a view of the bay. After Dan retired from the police force, he took a real interest in his little Kona coffee and Macadamia crops. I lease the land now, but I love the house and will never sell it."

Sinead turned toward Reggie and gasped. "Jesus, Mary, and Joseph," she said, "as I live and breathe, if she isn't the incarnation of Daniel Matthews."

"Sinead," Su Li said, "this is my daughter—our daughter—Regina Matthews. She has a son, Nick. He's back in Orlando with his father."

"My God almighty, Regina," Sinead said, "but you have the bluest eyes I've seen since your dear father's, the Lord have mercy on his soul."

"Thank you," said Reggie, "I've heard so many wonderful stories about you while I was growing up. I'm very proud to know you."

"I think we should go now," the mayor's aide said in English. For the life of her, Su Li couldn't remember his name from this morning. "It's nearly two and the car is waiting."

Passing through the streets of Ansan, Su Li was stunned by freshness of everything. All the buildings appeared new or recently renovated. The houses were all modern, many as big and expensive as those in

Hawaii. "It's not at all as I pictured it from my mother's descriptions," Su Li said. "It could easily be a city in the United States."

Sinead laughed. "You'll have a few days to relax when this is over. There's plenty left of the old country your mother knew. I'm sorry she never got to see it again."

"I'd like to see it for her," Su Li said.

"We'll take a trip to the south, to Kyongsang-do. You will see beautiful rural countryside, lush mountains and countless, tiny fishing villages. Ansan has none of these things, but it was carefully chosen for this project. It's a planned city of some five hundred thousand people, a wonderful example of modern South Korea. Your people will do well here."

As their car neared the construction site in the bustling urban district, Su Li spotted a group of elderly people holding up a dozen or so identical placards and a crude cloth banner. Su Li's attention was drawn to them, even as the mayor's aide ushered them toward the waiting dignitaries near the entrance to the complex.

She tried to make out the Korean writing on the cardboard signs, but both her eyes and her memory of the Korean symbols had been failing miserably over the years. She turned to Sinead. "Look at the group of old ones over there. Can you make out the signs they're waving? It looks like they have my name on them."

Sinead took one look in their direction and stopped dead in her tracks. "It's quite astonishing, Su Li," she said. "Most of them say the same thing: 'I am one of Su Li's two hundred'."

"What about the banner?" Su Li asked, somewhat embarrassed at her lack of proficiency in the language.

Sinead stared a moment at the crude banner, her eyes swelling with tears. She turned to Su Li and hesitated. Then she said, "Well, I suppose a rough, cross-cultural translation would be, 'Welcome home Su Li Young, The Soul of Kyongsang-do.'"

For a brief moment, Su Li was completely overcome with emotion, and Reggie had to steady her. She walked slowly toward the group, ignoring the protest of the mayor's obviously agitated assistant.

As Su Li drew nearer the group, a great cheer began to swell within it, far more imposing than the mere sum of the collective voices, and carried her away to another time in another place. A second crowd, larger in number and younger, stood directly behind the old ones. The families. There were perhaps a thousand people gathered all together.

Su Li held fast to Reggie and waded into the enthusiastic crowd, feeding ravenously on this banquet of affection. She couldn't recognize a single one personally, yet she loved them all beyond description, for they had become her single most important contribution to her fellow man.

Su Li graciously accepted the warm embraces of the old ones, their relatives and friends, as the mayor's frustrated aide simply abandoned his efforts to keep the schedule. Then, as Su Li prepared finally to join the other dignitaries for the ceremony, she felt an eerily familiar touch on the back of her hand. She looked down to see a woman, old and bent, but still steady on her feet. The woman was very short, and even Su Li could see only the top of her head.

"I'm grateful I lived long enough to see you again, Su Li," the woman said in Korean without raising her head. Su Li at once recognized the haunting voice from her past, the voice she had confronted so many times in her dreams. "You and Mei Ling once helped me and my dear sister, Song Yen."

Su Li bent and embraced the old woman lovingly. "I have never forgotten you," she said, "or your sister, Song Yen."

"When I came home to my village in Kyongsang-do so many years ago," the woman said, "my mother was still alive. I was able to be with her in her final years and tell her many things about Song Yen and our years on Sakhalin. Of course I have no children, but I still have my brother and many nieces and nephews. You have given me all these things, Su Li."

For a moment Su Li could not speak through her tears. "I was unable to talk to you that day," she said. "I've been ashamed all my life."

The old woman smiled and brushed Su Li's cheek softly with her course, brittle fingers. This time Su Li did not cower from the touch, but rather inhaled of its intimacy. "What are words?" the old woman asked. "I saw the goodness in your heart. There was nothing more."

Su Li Young felt as though she had come full circle. She kissed the old woman affectionately on the cheek and looked deep into her eyes, as though she were taking a snapshot to last a thousand years. She cried again.

Some tears were for her beloved Reggie, some for the noble Captain Subarov who gave birth to her dream. Others were for her dear friend, Ishikawa Yoshihiro, and even a few for her husband, Dan Matthews, the one true love of her life. The rest were tears of joy from a life filled with love, and blessed with the opportunity to serve others.

"I'm coming to Kyongsang-do for a few days," she told the old woman. "I'd like to sit and talk with you, about Song Yen and many other things. I'd like to meet your family and drink tea. Tell me, what is your name?"